MAY 2022

LADY RACHEL'S
DANGEROUS DUKE

Christine Merrill

MILLS & BOON

First Published in Great Britain 2022
by Mills & Boon, an imprint of HarperCollins*Publishers* Ltd,
1 London Bridge Street, London, SE1 9GF

www.harpercollins.co.uk

HarperCollins*Publishers*
1st Floor, Watermarque Building,
Ringsend Road, Dublin 4, Ireland

Lady Rachel's Dangerous Duke © 2022 Christine Merrill

ISBN: 978-0-263-30170-0

05/22

MIX
Paper from
responsible sources
FSC™ C007454

This book is produced from independently certified FSC™ paper
to ensure responsible forest management.
For more information visit www.harpercollins.co.uk/green.

Printed and Bound in Spain using 100% Renewable Electricity
at CPI Black Print, Barcelona

To Havoc:
who was with me through more books than I can count.
Good boy.

Chapter One

'No.'

When it came to proposals, Rachel Graham had said the word a dozen times to a dozen different men and felt no desire to change her answer. It was not that there was anything wrong with Lord Perriman, who knelt before her, the perfect image of what a supplicating suitor should be. It was simply that she had no intention of marrying anyone, now or ever.

'You are practically on the shelf,' he reminded her, unconvinced by her refusal. He had lured her away from the Duke of Belston's ball to a remote sitting room to make this proposal in private. Now he was giving her a look that had nothing to do with the sort of love and devotion Rachel expected to see in a candidate for her hand. 'I do not think you have the time to be particular when it comes to marriage.'

'And I do not think a true gentleman would remind me of the fact,' she said, moving back on the settee to put distance between them.

'I have your father's permission,' he added, as if this would make a difference.

'You should marry him, if he is so fond of you,' she said, annoyed. After three years of her being in the marriage mart, her father was more than willing to give her to any man that asked. He did not understand that this casual attitude towards her future happiness made it even less likely that she would say yes to a man of his choosing.

Lord Perriman rose, brushing off the knees of his breeches as if he was shaking off her rejection. 'I doubt you will get a better offer.'

'I will take my chances,' she said, rising from the settee and walking towards the closed door. She stopped by it and pointed a finger at it as if she had the power to command him from a room that was not hers.

He gave her a speculative look. 'If we are found here unchaperoned you will have to marry me, you know.'

The thought was an alarming one. She

liked the idea of a forced marriage to him even less than the politely arranged one he had been suggesting. 'We will not be found,' she said firmly.

'If there was a commotion, we might,' he said, still considering. 'If you should cry out, for example.' His arms were reaching for her as he stepped between her and the door.

'I have no intention of crying out,' she retorted, glancing round her for a weapon but finding none.

'Then you will be a willing participant in what happens next. That is, in my opinion, far better.'

'Or you could leave the poor girl alone. She has said no, and a true gentleman would accept her answer.' It was a voice that she had not heard in two years, yet it was as familiar as the beating of her heart. But Rachel doubted that Perriman was as well acquainted as she with the man who they had not noticed sitting in a darkened corner of the room. Thus, he did not share her desire to sink through the ground in mortification.

There was a flare of light as a candle was lit from the banked ashes in the fireplace. The Duke of Scofield stepped out of the shadows, his tall form even more menacing than usual in the half-light.

He had not been a duke when she'd known him, only Hugh Bethune. Nor had he been the talk of London, a man widely known as a cold-blooded killer.

'Really?' He directed the single word to Rachel in a tone of obvious disappointment. From his height of over six feet, he squinted down at her companion as if he were examining some lesser animal that had wandered into the house by mistake. 'Perriman, is it?'

The other man gave a moan of acknowledgement.

'You should make sure the room is empty before you start to make romantic overtures. And doubly sure if you mean to make threats.'

'I did not mean—' Perriman said hurriedly.

'How strange,' the Duke interrupted, his movements as slow as those of a cat stalking a mouse. 'You sounded quite sincere to me. Perhaps, if the lady wishes to leave us alone, we can discuss the importance of honesty— or, for that matter, honour—when speaking to the fairer sex.'

'That will not be necessary,' Rachel assured him hurriedly. Considering Hugh's reputation, she doubted that the unfortunate Lord Perriman wished to be anywhere near him, much less abandoned to face him alone. 'I believe my friend is aware of his mistake and wishes to go back to the ball.'

'That would be best,' Perriman said, grabbing for the door handle.

'Go, then. And if I hear that you have said a word about what happened here…' The Duke shrugged. 'That would be most unfortunate.'

'Of course, Your Grace,' Perriman said in a faint voice, then disappeared and left the two of them alone.

Rachel made to go after him. But before she could leave the Duke reached over her and leaned a hand against the door, shutting it. 'It is better that you wait here a few minutes and arrive back at the ballroom alone,' he reminded her. His voice had lost its menacing edge, but it was still different from the lover's tone she remembered.

It annoyed her.

But most of all it bothered her that, after all this time, her heart still beat faster at the sight of him. Without meaning to, she was searching his face for differences from the man she had loved two years ago.

It seemed that, for him at least, far more time had passed. She thought she saw a few strands of silver shining amongst the gold, and his eyes no longer lit with mischief as he smiled at her. Instead, he looked tired and a little sad.

'The last time I spoke with you, you did not care for me or my future,' she reminded him. She had accosted him in the street to offer condolences on the death of his father. She had expected some sign that they would meet in private to discuss it. Instead, he had given her the same look he'd just used on Perriman and dismissed her as if they had no history at all.

Was it a flicker of the candlelight, or did she see him flinch at the memory? 'What I did in the past was for your own good.'

'For weeks you told me that you loved me,' she said. 'And then, when you should have needed me most, you pretended not to know me.' Of course, the words of love had been said in private. In public, it had been a different matter entirely.

'I did not think you would wish to be associated with a murderer,' he said with a bitter smile, and she saw the lines forming at the corners of his sea-green eyes, making him look much older than his twenty-nine years.

'We both know that the rumours are not true,' she snapped. 'I was with you in your room the night your father died, and I saw your face when you learned of his murder. You knew nothing about the crime. I'd have told the Bow Street Runners the truth if you'd asked me to.'

'And ruined your reputation in the process,' he said with a shake of his head. 'You should not have been in the house at all, much less alone with me.'

'We were doing nothing wrong,' she insisted. He had promised marriage and all the pleasures that came with it. She still dreamed of his passionate kisses, the feel of his hand sliding up her thigh and the whispers of what they would do together as soon as he could secure an advance on his portion of the estate. 'I would not have been ruined had you wed me as you promised.'

And now he said nothing, just as she feared he would. Despite what he had claimed during their clandestine meetings, it seemed it had never been his plan to marry her. Apparently, time had taught her nothing for here she was again, alone with him and hoping for something that would never be. 'What happens if I am caught here with you tonight?' she asked.

If she had hoped for some assurance that he would make things right this time, she was disappointed again. He reached for the door and shot the bolt. 'This will prevent any surprise interruptions.'

Her heart jumped and she took a deep breath to steady it again. She willed herself not to look at him, for she was afraid of what she might do now that he was close enough to touch. 'You have done more than enough to protect my reputation, Your Grace. Too much, in my opinion.' And yet, not the one thing she wished above all others. 'If you would be so kind as to unlock the door and check the passageway for people, I will be going now.'

'A moment longer,' he said, a wistful note creeping into the deep, silky voice. His hand circled her wrist, the gentlest of manacles preventing her exit as effectively as the lock. 'Two at most.'

'We have nothing more to say to each

other,' she replied, but her own voice was hoarse, as if rejecting the lie.

'You know that is not true. I, at least, have something to say.'

'Then say it,' she snapped, wondering if there were words that would make any difference after all this time.

'It is only that I am sorry,' he said, his voice low and urgent. 'I never meant to hurt you. I never meant to leave you. But there was no other way.' Then he turned her wrist in his hand, unbuttoned her glove and pressed a kiss onto the bare flesh where her pulse was beating.

Before she could respond, he unlocked the door and pushed her out into the hallway, shutting the door behind her.

That had been a mistake.

Hugh walked across the room and sank back into the chair that he'd occupied when he'd been interrupted by Rachel and her suitor, trying to regain control of his feelings. It had been over two years, but the memories of the kisses they'd shared were never far from his mind. The brief taste of her flesh just now had been like opium, heady and addictive, bringing the old senses flooding back until he'd wanted to fall to his knees and beg for her hand as Perriman had done.

She was every bit as lovely as he remembered. Her long black hair was piled on top of her head in a tangle of braids and curls. Her eyes were still the same clear blue as a country sky in spring. And her body…

He closed his eyes, remembering how much he had seen of what was hidden tonight beneath a demure white gown. He would give a year of his life for another glimpse of those breasts.

When he'd realised she was in attendance tonight, he had come to this room to escape a meeting. He rarely received invitations to public gatherings and had grown good at accepting only those where there would be no chance that he and Rachel might meet.

But tonight his instinct had played him false, and fate had been cruel. He had been forced to sit mute while another man had proposed to his beloved. The relief when she'd refused marriage had been as strong as it had been unreasonable. He had no right to care about her future. She was free to marry whom she liked.

He could not help but notice that in two seasons she had not married anyone. And she had refused Perriman just now. It raised the unattainable dream that somehow they could still be together.

But he was not free. He had his sisters to think of, and the family's tainted blood. His father's murder, and the unspeakable things that had happened afterwards, had convinced him that the world would be better off if none of the Bethunes reproduced. Margaret had escaped him for marriage and a home of her own. Even if Olivia magically disappeared from his house and care, there was his own black reputation to consider before seeking a wife.

Title-hunting mothers might forgive a little drinking and whoring, and claim that reformed rakes made devoted husbands. But none of them were likely to tell their daughters that a murderer fell into the same category. Instead, they frightened the girls with cautionary tales of the Duke of Scofield and the fate of anyone who crossed him.

Only one woman knew the truth, or as much of it as he was able to tell. But just now she had given no indication that she wished to renew their acquaintance, even though she was free to do so. Perhaps it was time to stop torturing himself, dreaming of the one woman in London who he wanted but could never have.

Chapter Two

The next morning, Rachel sat with her parents at the breakfast table, her mind still on the meeting of the night before.

'Scofield was at the Belston ball last night. Can you believe the nerve of the man? Mixing with polite society as though he has any right to.' Her mother was buttering a muffin with short jerks of her knife, as if punishing it for the Duke's presumption.

'He is a peer,' Rachel's father pointed out in a reasonable voice. 'As such, he has the right to go almost anywhere. If Belston did not turn him out, there was little that the rest of us could do other than quietly disapprove. I expect we will see more of him before the season is through. They are scheming on some bill in the House of Lords, and it requires that

Scofield at least appear to his equals to be a reasonable man.'

'They should snub him,' her mother suggested. 'He is, when all is said and done, a murderer.'

'Accused murderer,' her father replied. From his lower-ranked position of an earl there was little he could do about the behaviour of a duke other than to keep his opinions to himself. But when he was at home he spoke freely. 'Of course, in the two years since his father's stabbing, there has never been another suspect, nor was there any sign that the murderer came from anywhere other than inside the house.'

'It was right next door and we saw and heard nothing,' her mother recalled. 'The Bethune dog did not bark at all.'

In Rachel's too informed opinion, this meant very little. She had sneaked out of her own house and past Caesar the pug often enough to know that he could be bribed to silence with a soup bone.

'But still, he has not been convicted of a crime,' her father replied. 'A title goes a long way in protecting a man who made no bones about his dislike for the old duke. And, according to the servants, he threatened his father's life at the dinner table that very night.'

'Suppose he is innocent?' Rachel said, trying to drop the suggestion into the conversation without drawing attention to herself.

'Then he is a damned fool for not saying so. He should be shouting from the rooftops that he is unjustly accused. Instead, he seems to go out of his way to appear guilty. He makes a joke of his reputation and casually talks of ending the lives of those who cross him.' Her father shook his head. 'And then, there is the matter of Richard Sterling, who was found stabbed and dumped in the Thames after arguing with Scofield. Two murders in his past are more than a coincidence.'

'It shows a kind heart to think well of him, my dear,' her mother said, turning to her. 'But you do not know him as the rest of us do.'

'Of course not,' Rachel agreed, starring down into her chocolate and losing herself in memory.

She had been but a child the first time she had seen Hugh Bethune from her bedroom window, walking in the garden with his little sisters. And even then she had not been blind to what a handsome young man he was—tall and blond, with broad shoulders and the features of a prince in a fairy tale. She had thought that some day this was the sort of man she would want to marry.

She had not confessed the idea to her friends or his sisters, knowing that they'd have teased her unmercifully if they'd known the truth. Instead, she had kept her feelings for Hugh a cherished secret, dreaming of the day she might be old enough and pretty enough to catch his attention.

Years had passed before he had noticed her watching him from her window. Long enough for her fleeting thoughts to have developed into a full-scale infatuation. Once he had smiled and waved in her direction, and the greeting had been the only topic in her diary for weeks to come.

When she had finally grown old enough for a season, she had hoped above all else that he would notice her again. He had, only to explain politely that, though he might have liked to pursue her, he could not afford a wife. His father, Old Scofield, had been notoriously tight-fisted in money and affection, refusing his son a courtesy title and keeping his allowance to the bare minimum. Until the old man changed his mind—or, God forbid, died— there would have been no marriage for Hugh Bethune.

She had smiled and reminded him that it cost nothing to talk with a neighbour over the garden wall.

And so it had begun. Covert conversations from their respective gardens had led to a few all too brief dances at balls and long chats at routs.

And then she had suggested that she visit him in his room. He had argued that it was improper but had been impressed by her daring. And in no time his objections had given way to an invitation.

The house had been dark, for Hugh's father had skimped on candles as much as he did on any other household expense. It had made it easier for her to remain anonymous, the hood of her cloak pulled low over her face as she'd knocked on the kitchen door which had been opened by the housekeeper, bribed and sworn to secrecy by Hugh.

Without a word, she led Rachel to the servants' stairs, pointed up then turned away with the slightest sniff of disapproval.

Rachel had climbed alone and had been met at the top by Hugh, who'd wrapped her in his arms and escorted her to his room. And then, when the door was closed…

'Rachel!'

She started out of her reverie and looked at her father.

'Once you are done with your breakfast, I wish to see you in my study.'

'Of course,' she agreed, her mouth suddenly dry.

When they were alone a short time later, her father did not bother with preamble. 'Perriman says you refused him last night. In fact, you frightened him away. He was in a mad rush this morning to withdraw his offer.'

'He was not for me,' she said, purposely omitting the details that had soured him for her.

'The man had fifteen thousand a year and an excellent family,' her father snapped. 'And you refused him.'

'Because I did not love him,' she replied,

praying that this would be enough of an explanation.

'Love,' her father said with a huff. 'That is a thing for the lower classes. You need to have more sense.'

'I am sure there is another man who would suit me better,' she said with an embarrassed shrug.

'Then name him and I will arrange a match,' he replied.

For a moment, Rachel considered telling him the truth. But, judging by the conversation at breakfast, there was no way they considered Hugh as a suitable husband for her, so she held her tongue.

Her father noted her silence and shook his head in disappointment. 'I did not want to discuss this matter in front of your mother, because talk of what is to come only upsets her. But you, my dear, must understand that the estate is entailed to my cousin, and you and your mother will have very little when I die. Unless you are sensible and marry well.'

'Surely the situation is not that dire?' she asked. 'Your health is good.'

He laughed. 'You cannot see as far into the future as the tip of your nose. My health is fine, but I cannot afford to be short-sighted. None of us know our allotted span on this earth and our lives can change without warning. I want to see you settled, and soon, for your own good and that of your mother.'

'But not to Perriman,' she said, trying not to shudder as she thought of how eager he'd been to dishonour her to secure her hand.

'Then who?' he asked. 'Do you have someone in mind?'

'No,' she replied hurriedly, closing her hand over her wrist which still felt the heat of a kiss. 'I have met no one as of yet.'

'Then I suggest you take the next man I find for you. You talk of love, but that is a girlish fancy. Once you are married, you will find that security is even better than emotion, and not nearly as fleeting. The process of making a good match need not be as complicated as you are making it. I will find you a kind man who will make you a good and caring husband. In return, you will be a good wife to him.'

'I will try,' she said, unwilling to give him a definite yes without knowing the man he might choose. She had hoped that the final decision would be left to her and she might be allowed to keep her broken heart to herself and remain a spinster.

But that was before Hugh had kissed her.

Though it had hardly been a kiss, if she was honest. She had been courted by men who'd been far more forward than that. But none of their kisses had moved her as Hugh could with a single touch of his lips. It was clear that he still cared for her. But it seemed that, now that he had the money to do it, he was no more eager to marry than she was.

It was probably because most eligible girls were too frightened of the supposed murderer to allow him to court them. His dire reputation was unearned. She knew that better than any other person in England. If her family was worried about it, after the initial shock wore off, she was sure her father would be satisfied with a rich peer for a son-in-law.

The question was, how to make Hugh act on his attraction to her? It was rare to see him out in public, and last night was the first time in ages that she could remember having been at an event he'd attended. Even then, he had made no effort to imply that there would be anything more between them than that kiss of apology.

But he was wrong. She loved him then, she loved him still. If she had to marry, there would never be another man for her than Hugh Bethune.

'Hugh!'

The Duke of Scofield started, nearly dropping the brandy glass he had been holding. When it caught him unawares, the sound of his own name still cut through his heart like a knife slash, for it made him remember *her*.

He set the glass on the corner of his desk, wondering if Olivia would smell the liquor on his breath and question his drinking so early in the day. She had only herself to blame for that. In this, the second year of their mutual captivity, he was no closer to deciding what to do about her than he had been on the day that their father had died.

His younger sister, Margaret, had solved one problem for him by eloping. He was still not positive who had committed the murders, but he had not wanted it to be dear, sweet Margaret. Thus far, Peg's husband, the newspaper reporter who had stolen away with her, was annoyingly alive, as were all of their acquaintances.

If Peg had been the mad one, and she'd not been able to help herself from committing mayhem, then he should have seen some sign of it swirling about her now that she had ample freedom to act.

Olivia, however, had lost a suitor in the Thames. When it had happened, society had been quick to blame Hugh for the death of Richard Sterling. He knew his own mind and was sure of his innocence.

But Olivia's state of mind and innocence were other matters entirely. After their father's death, Hugh had done his best to contain both girls from leaving the house unescorted, fearing that the guilty one might attack again. But Olivia still got away from him on occasion. If he were a betting man, the money would be on her. She had always been the shrewder of the two girls, and the one over whom men were eager to sympathise about her evil brother and his cruel restrictions on her socialising.

She was calling him again but he ignored it and stood, stepped to the window and touched the glass, spreading his fingers until his palm was flat to the surface, reaching towards the house on the other side of the garden wall and the woman who was never out of his heart or mind.

Rachel had not yet married. He wished she would, for it would save him the torture of wondering if she still thought of him, and if any of those thoughts were kind. Last night, she had seemed more angry than pleased, for he was quite sure he'd broken her heart with the way he had treated her after his father's death.

She'd had every right to think he was going to make her a duchess. He had promised marriage often enough in those days, and the pledge of a future together had convinced her that it would not be too sinful to sneak next door and into his room for some early lessons in the art of love.

Perhaps it was the prolonged excitement and denial of climax, but no woman before or since had heated his blood in the way his sweet Rachel had. He had rushed to her that night, barely noticing one of his sisters darting down a darkened hallway and laughing as she entered their father's study. His mind had had room for nothing but Rachel.

They had been together for only a few minutes when the screaming had begun downstairs and the servants had come to summon him. His father was dead. Murdered.

He had rushed Rachel from the house moments before the Runners had arrived, away from the chaos that ensued. Then he had cut her on the street when she'd tried to reach out to help him. There was no help. Not for him and not for his sisters.

He had broken what was left of his own heart on that day, but it hardly mattered. His heart, his mind and his life were no longer his own.

'Hugh!'

He shook his head to clear it and answered, 'Here, Olivia.'

His sister stuck her head round the door of the study and stared at him, obviously annoyed. 'I have been calling for you all over the house and you did not answer.'

'Well, you have found me now,' he said in the mildest tone he could manage. 'What do you wish of me?'

'The same thing I always wish of you. I would like to go to the same places you do without a phalanx of your hired guards escorting me.'

'You wish to go to Parliament or my club?' he said, being deliberately obtuse.

'You went to a ball last night,' she reminded him. 'At the Duke of Belston's townhouse. Why would you not take me along?'

'I would not have gone myself, except I need his support for a bill I am putting forth. If not for politics…' He shrugged. 'And last night you were too inebriated to leave the house.'

'It is unfair of you to remind me of that,' she said with a wince. 'I would not have drunk so much ratafia if…' She stopped, unwilling to admit the difficulty that had caused her to resort to consoling herself with spirits. The man he had hired to watch her had caught her attempting to elope with her current beau, Alister Clement. Clement had been left in a ditch on the road out of London and she had been brought home in disgrace.

'I admit I was indisposed last night,' she allowed. 'But I am fine now. Let me accept one of the other invitations you receive,' she said with a longing tone that might have influenced him had she been a normal girl. 'There is no need to keep me locked in this house, nor to have me watched.'

He could not help a bitter laugh. 'It would be easier to believe that if you had not helped Margaret to elope a few months ago.'

'I did not help her. She did what she did on her own. It had nothing to do with me.' He was sure it was a lie, for the denial came too quickly, as if it had been rehearsed.

'You did nothing to stop her,' he reminded her. 'And now, you wish to go about without even your sister for chaperone.' She was looking for an excuse to meet with Clement. Hugh had forbidden the fellow from courting Olivia more than once, and yet he did not leave. Nor, it seemed, did he have the brains to plan a successful elopement. After his last attempt, Olivia had retreated to her room with a decanter of ratafia to sulk and drink herself silly.

It was fortunate for Clement that she had turned her anger inward instead of against him. He might have ended up as dead as Sterling, the last poor sod that had not managed to spirit her away.

This morning, she was sober again, though as she smiled encouragingly at him she squinted at the sunlight as if it hurt her eyes. 'Peg may be gone, but you can trust me.' Her voice was plaintive, but it did not hide the lie. He had lost the ability to trust either of his sisters on the day their father had died.

'My rule stands,' he said. 'You will not go about town unaccompanied by a servant and you have no reason to go to social gatherings in the evening while you are still in mourning.'

'We have been out of mourning for over a year,' she snapped, gesturing to her gown, which was a light blue.

'But that does not mean that you need to rush back to socialising. If you need fresh air, you may go to Bond Street, as long as Mr Solomon is there to watch over you.'

'I would rather stay home than go anywhere with your watchdog,' she said with an unladylike grimace. For some reason, she had taken a particular dislike to her latest guard.

Perhaps it was because the fellow was doing his job. Yesterday had been Liv's and Clement's second run for Gretna, and Michael Solomon had stopped them both times.

'If you do not want to go out with the man I have hired to protect you, then stay home and stop complaining,' he said. His stand taken, he stared down at his desk, searching for a distraction to end the conversation. He grabbed a pile of papers and shuffled them, hoping that she would take the hint and leave.

'You cannot keep me here for ever,' she said.

'We will see about that,' he replied, and felt the door slam as she left his study. The thought of a lifetime trapped in this house with his sister was a nightmare. All the evidence pointed to the fact that she was both mad and dangerous. After what he had done to protect her from prosecution, maybe he was mad as well. But, if it kept her from the hangman's noose, he would lock the doors against the world and they would stay here, together and alone.

Chapter Three

It was one thing for Rachel to decide that she would marry the most notorious man in London and another to get him to agree to it.

She brooded all night and most of the next morning, trying to think of a way to orchestrate another meeting with Hugh. Even though he lived next door to her, she had not seen him for two years before last night. It would take an astronomical amount of luck to run into him again in a day or two.

As a distraction, she took her maid and set off for Bond Street and a day of shopping. But not even a new bonnet was enough to take her mind off the problem.

At last, they settled for refreshments at Gunter's. Rachel stared down into a plate of delicate lemon biscuits, still unsatisfied.

'Tilly,' she said to her maid, 'What is one to do when one knows the man one wants to marry, but he is so reclusive that it is a trial to even meet him?'

The maid gave her a curious look. 'Is this a man that your parents would approve of?'

'He is purely hypothetical,' she said quickly, afraid to give away the truth, since she was sure that Hugh was exactly the opposite to what her father was hoping she would agree.

'Well, if Mr Hypothetical won't come to you, then you must go to him,' the maid said with a grin.

It was a simple answer. But perhaps this was a simple problem that she was making unnecessarily complicated. He was right next door. If she manufactured a reason to visit his sister, she might see him as well.

But there was a rumour about that Lady Olivia was still in mourning and not at home to visitors. The *ton* had given up attempting to gain entry. Surely that did not include neighbours? It had been years since Rachel had been close to Olivia, but that did not mean that she could not renew the childhood friendship they had shared. After all the time spent in seclusion, she would probably welcome anyone willing to see her. And, once the door was opened by the sister, the brother could not avoid her for ever.

Then, to her surprise, Lady Olivia walked into Gunter's escorted by a gentleman. But when Rachel looked closer she realised that he was not a gentleman at all. He was the man she had seen standing guard in the back garden of the Scofield townhouse. Hugh must have hired him to see to the security of the household.

Her new plan to befriend Olivia was abandoned as quickly as it had been hatched, for something about the posture of the two convinced Rachel that they had no desire for her company. Instead, she turned away from them and stared at their reflection in a mirror on the wall so she might study them without being observed. It was not that unusual to see a young lady escorted by a servant, but that was not how this looked at all. Liv seemed to be enjoying the man's company, chatting easily with him, smiling and leaning in to hang on his words as they gossiped over their food. As Rachel watched, Olivia leaned even closer, staring intently at the man who accompanied her.

This was an interesting development. She wondered if Hugh knew of it. More importantly, she wondered if he might want to hear of it. If it was true that Olivia was not allowed to mix with society and the gentlemen who might court her, it appeared that she had found a way round the restrictions. She was smiling at the man she was with, laughing at something he'd said. Her eyes sparkled as she looked at him. Then she tugged on a curl in a way that drew his attention to the shining gold of her hair.

He stared at it, and Rachel saw a flash of hunger in his eyes before he moderated his emotions and looked at her as a gentleman should, as if her words were more important to him then her looks.

Rachel's resolve wavered. It was spiteful of her to want to deny them their happiness. Perhaps she could make it up to them later. But for now, this sighting was something she could use to her own benefit. Tattling on his sister would give her an excuse to talk to

Hugh again. But she had to get to him before he learned of it himself.

She emptied her teacup and told Tilly to gather their packages. Then, without acknowledging her neighbour, they summoned the carriage and returned home. When they arrived, Rachel announced that she was still in mood for a walk, and assured her maid that her company was not needed as she did not mean to go farther than down the street to stretch her legs.

Once out of sight of the girl, she hurried next door, knocked and requested an audience with the Duke.

As Hugh finished his third brandy of the day, a footman appeared in the doorway of the study and presented him with a calling card.

'Lady Rachel Graham?' he asked and felt the world tipping violently around him in a way that could not be blamed on the liquor.

'She insists that you will want to see her, once you hear what she has to say,' the footman replied, before Hugh could tell the servant to deny her entry.

'Show her to the green salon. I will be there shortly.'

The servant retreated and Hugh allowed himself a moment of panic, wishing that at least he had a mirror to see if he was presentable enough to receive visitors. Then he reminded himself that he was not required to dress for uninvited guests and, much as he wished to spend time with Rachel, he owed her nothing, nor was there anything she could do to help him. The sooner the visit was over, the better it would be for both of them.

He strode down the hall to the green salon and greeted her with a frosty, 'Lady Rachel?' trying to ignore how delightful she looked in a deep-blue walking dress.

'Since we are in private, is it necessary to be so formal?' she responded with a smile that made his loins ache.

'Since you are unchaperoned and uninvited, I would prefer formality,' he said, unsmiling.

'Well, the least you could do is sit down in my presence,' she said. 'You are making me nervous.'

Then they were both uncomfortable. He doubted sitting would make him feel any better, but he also doubted that it would make things much worse. He took a seat in the chair opposite to the settee she occupied and folded his arms. 'Very well. What brings you here today?'

'I am here because I have news that I think would interest you,' she said, then added, 'It is about your sister.'

'Which one?' he asked.

'Olivia,' she replied. 'I just saw her at Gunter's, having sorbet with a handsome man.'

His brow furrowed. 'Was he a gentleman with dark hair, sharp-featured with a slight build?' If Solomon had permitted a meeting with Alister Clement, Hugh would sack him without references.

'No,' she said with a sly smile. 'He was the man I sometimes see sitting in your back garden.'

'Solomon!' he exclaimed, relieved. 'The man is an employee and is doing his job as escort.'

'He did not look like an employee,' she said, sounding uncommonly smug. 'They looked quite cosy.'

'Really.' Apparently, the animosity Olivia had displayed towards him was all for show.

She had taken it into her head to charm Solomon and the fellow, who had been on the job for less than a month, was already succumbing.

'And now, I suppose you are going to threaten to end him?' she enquired with a sigh.

If Solomon touched his sister, this time it would be more than a threat. 'If you did not want me to act, why did you bother to tell me?'

'I do not care if you act,' she said. 'But I hope you will spare me the false threats that you scatter about London like breadcrumbs for birds. I know you too well to believe them.'

He did not think that she would be fooled, but that did not mean he owed her the whole truth. 'I am not the man you remember,' he said, rubbing his temples to dissipate the headache gathering there.

'You are more,' she said without hesitation.

'I have a title,' he said. 'And the money, of course.'

'And I am sure you manage both with wisdom and skill.' She was smiling at him, as if admiring an honour he had done nothing to earn.

'Next, you will be telling me that my father would be proud,' he said with a bark of laughter. 'We both know that he hated me and would have lived for ever, if he could have, just to deny me the succession.'

'But that does not mean you wanted him dead or were capable of doing what everyone thinks of you,' she returned. 'I ask you again, why do you make no effort to clear your name?'

He wanted to speak, but the words would not come. It would be such a relief to talk about what had happened after she had left him that night. But, other than a brief respite from the pain, it would change nothing. At last, he said, 'Because sometimes it is better for people to believe a lie than to know the truth.' Then, he stood and gestured towards the door. 'Thank you for the concern you have shown my family. And now, the footman will show you out.'

'Wait,' she said, ignoring the servant and holding her seat. 'When will I see you again?'

'You will not,' he replied. This renewed contact with her was almost more than he could stand. Each moment she sat here, he could feel his resolve weakening and the growing urge to live selfishly, do what he most wanted and let the devil take the rest of the world. 'These recent meetings were aberrations, and they will not continue.'

'After what I have told you today, you owe me at least a dance,' she said, smiling again.

He shook his head. 'Perhaps your feelings are not as strong as they once were, or perhaps you do not understand how difficult these encounters are for me. But, I can assure you, we cannot and will not be together now or in the future as anything more than casual acquaintances. What we once had is over. I suggest from now on you make an effort to avoid me as studiously as I have been avoiding you. Good day, Rachel.' Then, as she showed no sign of leaving, he exited the room and went back to his study, slamming the door behind him.

That had not gone at all to plan.

Rachel had probably been naïve to hope that he would be grateful enough to welcome her information. But she had been positively stupid to think that he would reward her by agreeing to see her again.

At the door to the receiving room, a footman shifted from foot to foot, probably trying to decide the best way to put her out.

She smiled at him, making a great show of composing herself in preparation for leaving, while struggling to find a way to salvage the situation. He had called these meetings painful. And he had said it with what sounded like disguised longing in his voice. Despite what he might say aloud, he wanted her still. He loved her still.

If love was not dead, then she could not abandon him, no matter what he might claim to want from her.

She rose and followed the footman down the hall, pausing again as she passed a console table on which the morning's outgoing post was stacked. Casually, she brushed against the letters, knocking them to the floor.

The footman rushed to grab them, but she was faster, scooping them up with an apology and placing them back on the table where they had been.

But not before taking note of the directions on several of the notes. Her mother had a similar stack of responses to dinners and balls leaving the house that very morning. If she wanted to see Hugh again, she knew exactly where to look.

Chapter Four

Two nights later, Rachel prepared for a ball at the Earl of Canfeld's home, taking pains to hide the nervousness she felt at the thought of the evening ahead. After years of avoiding and being avoided by Hugh, it felt odd to stalk him in this way, and to dress in a way that she hoped would please him above all others.

She chose a gown of green silk that would stand out from the crowd of virginal white that made up the usual wardrobe of unmarried females. With it, she paired the same gloves that she had been wearing the night he had kissed her wrist. She wondered if he would remember them.

When they arrived, she did her best to separate herself from the ever-watchful eyes of her mother and looked around her nervously as her dance card began to fill without any sign of Hugh's arrival.

When he did appear, she was on the floor and unable to go to him without slighting her partner and walking away in the middle of a dance. Instead of focusing on the steps, she watched over her shoulder as Hugh worked his way through the receiving line, made nice to his hostess and prepared to leave the room again, probably for the card room and the company of gentlemen.

She could not let him escape so easily. They were almost at the bottom of the set. Once there, she excused herself from her partner, claiming fatigue, and rushed down the hall that led to both the ladies' retiring room and the card room. She caught Hugh before he could disappear behind the door, calling, 'Your Grace, a moment of your time.'

He turned back to her with a look so dark that, for a moment, she had no trouble believing his evil reputation. 'How may I help you, Rachel?'

'I was wondering if you planned to dance this evening.'

Now, he simply looked annoyed. There was also nothing in his face to reveal that he knew her in any but the most remote of ways.

'No.' He did not bother to embellish the word with a reason.

'I wonder if you might reconsider,' she said. 'There are many of us who must go unpartnered for the lack of interest of the gentlemen here tonight.'

He was about to say no again. She could see it in his eyes. So she reached to the wrist of her glove and gave a deliberate flick, opening the button that he had undone when they had been alone at the last ball.

Exposing a single inch of skin was surprisingly effective. His eyes were riveted to the spot. He wet his lips, as if he was eager to taste, totally undoing his previous frosty greeting.

For a few seconds at most they were alone in the hall, out of range of hearing of the other guests. But people were heading down the corridor towards them, so she pressed her advantage. 'If you say no, it will appear that you have cut me. It will cause far more attention to our relationship than a simple yes will do.'

The look he gave her now smouldered with anger. 'We have no relationship. Not any longer.'

It was a lie. She was sure of it. So she refused to move on, letting the other guests grow close enough to hear the silence stretching between them.

When the strangers were almost upon them, he surrendered. 'Perhaps one dance would not be so unusual.'

'Of course not,' she said, offering her dance card to him. He had not chosen a waltz, but a simple country dance that required a minimal amount of physical contact. It was not as romantic as she'd hoped, but it would have to do to start with. She smiled up at him, unable to disguise her feelings. 'That was not so hard, now, was it?'

'More difficult than you can imagine,' he said, turning back to the card room and away from her.

As she went back to the ballroom, her mother caught her at the doorway and touched her shoulder. 'Your father said that you and Lord Perriman did not suit.'

'Do not worry,' Rachel said quickly. 'I am sure there will be other offers.'

'I have counted the guests tonight and cannot find a single one that you have not already rejected,' her mother said with a shake of her head.

'Not a single one?' Rachel resisted the urge to smile and correct her.

'No one acceptable,' her mother allowed. 'There are several who are so near to spoken for that it is not worth bothering.'

'Every night does not have to be a husband hunt,' Rachel reminded her. 'Perhaps tonight I will have to content myself with refreshments and dancing.'

'You are far too easily contented,' her mother said with a huff.

'It is better than being difficult to please,' Rachel shot back, fanning herself vigorously. 'And now, if you will excuse me, Mother, the music is beginning and I must go and find my next partner. I have no intention of being rude, even if nothing is to come of it.' And, even better, she must be ready for the moment when something did.

When the time to dance arrived, Hugh was surprisingly nervous. It was nothing, he told himself. He was a grown man, not a school-boy, and had partaken freely in pleasures of the flesh far greater than a turn around the floor with an innocent young lady.

But was she innocent? He had not taken her maidenhead, but he had done far more than he should have with a woman who'd not been betrothed to him. They had been so sure that marriage was only weeks away that she had allowed him liberties and he had accepted eagerly.

And then, everything had changed.

He had not even expected to see her tonight, since he normally avoided the ballroom at such gatherings. But she had found him, and he had succumbed far too easily to her plans. And there had been a plan, he was sure. She had sought him out twice now, and there was no sign she would stop. He must find a way to put an end to this before she became convinced that she was making progress in reuniting with him.

He approached her at the beginning of the chosen dance and wordlessly bowed over her hand, trying not to look too closely at the broad expanse of flesh displayed above the bodice of her gown. Then the music began and they moved in silence. But he could feel the eyes of the crowd following their every move.

'People are staring,' he muttered as they passed in the patterns of the dance.

'I should think you would be used to it by now,' she replied. 'From what I understand, people often stare at you.'

'But they do not stare at you,' he reminded her. 'In dancing with me, you have made yourself notorious.'

She smiled, unperturbed. 'I think I should rather like being notorious. It sounds much more interesting than being a wallflower, which I very nearly am.'

'You would not have to be, if you just accepted one of the offers you have got,' he reminded her.

'Like Perriman?' she asked and made a face. 'You were quick enough to save me from him when you had the chance. If you wanted me married, you could simply have remained quiet.'

'That was different,' he insisted. 'He was attempting to take advantage.'

'As you would have, if you wanted a lady enough,' she pointed out, giving no quarter.

'We are not talking about me,' he said through clenched teeth. 'We are talking about you.'

'And my need to marry,' she said with a sigh. 'You remind me of my father.'

'That is not what any man wants to hear from a beautiful young lady,' he said, then snapped his mouth shut to prevent any more inanities from escaping.

She laughed. 'Your Grace, did you just flirt with me?'

He hadn't meant to. And yet, when he was with Rachel, it was hard to do anything else. 'Do not put too much into it,' he retorted gruffly. 'I am well known as incorrigible.'

'And now you are joking,' she said with a smile that lit up the room. 'Given time, who knows what you might be capable of?'

The statement shocked him back to earth, for that was exactly what he feared. When one had already done unspeakable things, what else might lie in the future?

'I am not going to allow another dance, if that is what you are thinking,' he replied in a firm tone to caution himself as well as her.

'Everyone here will tell you this one was a mistake.'

'And I will not listen to them,' she said, still smiling. 'There is no harm in dancing.'

'If that is all you expect,' he replied.

'What else could I possibly want?' She blinked innocently, calling attention to her sable lashes and bright eyes.

'More than I am willing to give,' he shot back with a warning shake of his head. 'Do not try this trick again or, so help me, I will leave you standing in the hallway like the wallflower you pretend to be.'

And then, to his relief, the dance was over before she could think of anything to say in response. She dropped a curtsy, as if nothing unusual had happened, but there was a brittleness to her smile. As she turned to walk to the edge of the dance floor, he noticed a tightness in her shoulders, as if she were recovering from a blow.

And, God help him, it was all he could do to keep from running after her with an apology. To be with her set him free, and freedom was weakness. These meetings could not keep happening or he would shatter like glass, blurting his secrets to Rachel and anyone else who would listen. If he did not want to see his sister in the madhouse, he must be strong and stay away from Rachel Graham.

'Rachel!' Her mother rushed to her side as soon as she was free of Hugh and whispered, 'Whatever did you think you were doing, accepting a dance from that man?'

'It was only a dance, Mother,' Rachel replied, experimenting with a defiant roll of her eyes. 'We are neighbours and have known each other for years. And he is a duke. I could not exactly refuse him.'

'You most certainly could,' her mother said, pulling Rachel by the arm towards the door. 'If you did not notice, he did not bother dancing with any of the other young ladies here, probably because they all had the sense to say no.'

'He didn't ask anyone else,' she argued. Of course, he hadn't asked her either. She had bullied him into it and made him angry. They had not parted well. But there had been a moment—during the middle of the dance—when he had been his old self.

'I have no idea what reason he would have

for singling you out,' her mother said. 'But we must be sure it does not happen again. For now, we are going home before you cause any more trouble.'

As she was rushed from the room, she caught the eye of the dangerous Duke of Scofield, who gave her a look that could only be described as, *I told you so.*

Rachel spent the night puzzling over the best way to proceed. It was clear after her parents' reaction that she could not treat Hugh as she would any other gentleman, dancing and flirting in the open. She did not mind the staring so much as her parents' response to it. She would never have a chance to weaken Hugh's resolve if she was rushed out of the room and home each time they danced together.

Nor did she think Hugh would come if she invited him to meet in private. He was far too conscious of his reputation and hers. But at the Belston ball he had jumped to her defence the minute he'd thought she was in danger.

She smiled as a plan occurred to her. It was a risk, of course, but she must focus on the reward.

* * *

The following night, Hugh made plans to be much more cautious when it came to socialising. Rachel had not precisely tricked him into dancing. More likely, he had tricked himself, responding to the slightest pressure and giving her what she'd asked for.

It seemed years of avoiding temptation had made him weak when it had finally been presented to him. Now that he could no longer avoid her, he must be careful not to encourage her desire to rekindle what they'd once had.

If she was present tonight, he would know better. Since he was going to a rout, there would be no dancing, which would make it impossible to repeat the mistake of last night.

There would be little of anything, if truth were told. The crowd was shoulder to shoulder, circulating through rooms cleared of furniture. The noise and heat of bodies pressed tight together was oppressive and made him wonder who had ever thought that this was a pleasant way to spend an evening.

He supposed it was too much to hope that she would not be there. In the past, she had been so angry with him that if their paths had crossed she had studiously ignored him and he had done the same to her. But, now that he had revealed some tiny bit of his feelings, she would not leave him alone.

He moved through the crowd, following the eddies and flows of the mass of people packed into the room and having a few short conversations with the men brave enough to approach him. Surprisingly, a few young ladies were foolish enough to meet his eye. It seemed that the single dance on the previous evening had make him a nine days' wonder amongst the debutante set, who were now daring each other to talk to him.

He had Rachel to thank for that, he supposed. When he saw her again, he would tell her not to help him any more.

If. If he talked to her, which he had no intention of doing. It was strange how easily his mind was swayed to do exactly what she wanted him to do. The woman was a witch.

And suddenly, there she was before him, bumping against him as the crowd pushed in on them from all sides. Her gown was the same blue as her eyes, and she smelled of violets and spring time, reviving his spirit, so it was possible to ignore the throng of people around them. 'Your Grace,' she said, stooping to get the fan that had been knocked from her hand by the press of the crowd.

'Allow me,' he said automatically, grabbing it from the floor before she could dip to give him a view of her cleavage. As he picked it up, a piece of paper fluttered out from under it. He grabbed it out of the air and turned it over to read the scrawled note.

Meet me in the library at ten.

When he met her eyes again, she looked properly guilty, as one should when caught setting up an assignation.

He looked at her with narrowed eyes. 'What are you up to now?'

'Nothing,' she said, then added, 'Nothing that concerns you, at least.'

'After last night, you are already meeting another man?'

'Last night?' she said with a laugh. 'Last night was just one dance out of many, Your Grace. And, as I remember, you gave it to me most unwillingly.'

It had seemed like so much more to him. But a sip of water might seem like a torrent to a man in a desert. 'You still should not be meeting alone with men,' he said, feeling as old and starchy as he probably sounded.

She laughed again. 'I will take your opinion under advisement,' she said. 'Although, you are the last person in the world who should caution me on such a thing, given our past history.'

He looked around to make sure that no one had heard, and she laughed again. 'Do not worry about me, Your Grace. Perhaps I am simply doing what my father wishes of me and finding a suitable man to marry.' Then, she snatched back the fan from him and disappeared into the crowd.

The nerve of the woman. She had cornered him on the previous evening, hunting him down like a stag. Tonight, she was willing to throw him away in favour of a stranger. If he had taken the time to watch who else she had danced with on the previous evening, he might have had some idea who she was meeting. But, for now, he was aflame with curiosity.

Or perhaps it was simply jealousy. He was standing silently in the crowd, glaring at anyone who might come near him, unwilling to move forward or back. He checked his watch. It was a quarter to ten.

Unable to help himself, he went in search of the library.

When he arrived, the room was dark and he was alone. Whoever was coming, he had got there ahead of them. The question was, what did he mean to do now? Did he skulk in the corner, as he had during the Perriman incident, and only declare himself at the last minute?

Of course, last time he had not intended to reveal himself at all. He had sat in his chair, quietly horrified, convinced that he was going to be forced to listen to the loss of his love. Instead, Perriman had been an ass and he'd had reason to intervene.

This time, he could not exactly hide himself and wait to see if he was needed. If he witnessed an indiscretion, she would be forced to marry whoever she was with to avoid dishonour. It was better that he make his presence known immediately and put a stop to things before they progressed.

Whoever this suitor was, he would not want to go forward once he knew he was not alone, and it was quite possible that both Rachel and the gentleman would flee back to the main rooms and give up their plan entirely.

He waited in silence as the clock drew closer to ten and, as it struck, the door opened and Rachel entered, closing it quickly behind her. Then, she turned to him and smiled. 'You were early.'

'I only came to keep you from doing something foolish,' he said, suddenly suspicious.

'And what did you think I was doing?' she asked, still smiling.

'Meeting a man unchaperoned.' He stated the obvious.

'Well, I do not see how you could have put a stop to it,' she said, giving him a significant look. 'Here we are.'

'But the message…' he said, confused.

'Was for you,' she finished. 'And you responded, just as I knew you would.'

For a moment, he did not know how to feel. He was irate, of course. Who would not be, when trapped into a liaison by a duplicitous girl? But there was also a strong and annoying sense of relief that there was no other man she was interested in. 'I should go,' he said, stepping towards the door.

'Surely you can wait for a moment,' she

said. 'We have to be careful not to be seen leaving together, as you said the last time we were alone.'

'Have you learned nothing from your time with me?' he asked with a sigh. 'I would think the near disaster of the night my father died would have been enough to teach you the dangers of meeting unchaperoned with men.'

'It taught me the pleasures as well,' she said with a smile that shot through his body like Cupid's arrow. Then, she took a step closer to him, the firelight making her pale skin glow like opal.

'What you remember is a thing of the past,' he said, trying not to think about it. 'We are very different people than we were.'

'Do not tell me I have grown old,' she returned with a moue of displeasure. 'It was not so long ago that you called me the most beautiful girl in London.'

'You are no less lovely than I remember,' he said, and immediately regretted the acknowledgement. It would do him no good to feed the attraction between them. Instead, he must find a way to nip it in the bud. 'I am not blind,' he continued. 'You are one of many pretty girls here tonight. But I am no longer as easily swayed by such things as I was.'

And now he felt guilty for the hurt look in her eye. 'Is there someone else you would prefer to be here with?' she asked, her voice tart. 'If so, tell me now and I will leave you alone.'

He should have lied. Pulled a name from the air and deflated her hopes. Instead, he hesitated, which earned him a smile of triumph from her.

'You are being ridiculous,' he snapped. 'Did you orchestrate this meeting between us so that I might reveal my feelings for someone else? If so, it is unworthy of you. And if you tricked me into coming here so that I might be forced to flatter you...'

'I am not trying to force you to do anything,' she said hurriedly. 'I just wish that you would do what you want to do.'

'And what is that, since you are such an authority on my moods and whims?' he asked.

'You want to be with me,' she insisted. 'You know you do.'

'It is not a matter of wanting,' he said, frustrated. 'We are not children any more and cannot act on each fleeting desire that crosses our minds.'

'Fleeting desire!' she said indignantly. 'Was that all I ever was to you?'

He should declare her correct and storm from the room. A short, brutal lie was the only thing that would close the door to her for ever. But he'd told too many lies in his life already and none, so far, to Rachel. He had no desire to start now.

'You know that is not true,' he said at last, with a sigh. 'You meant everything to me, and it has been hell on earth to give you up, to search *The Times* each day, expecting to see the announcement that you have married. Though by doing so, you will put an end to the torture.'

And this was what honesty accomplished. Now, she was smiling at him as if his misery was a gift to be savoured. 'That is all I wanted to hear,' she said, beaming at him. Then she crossed the few steps that separated them and launched herself into his arms.

He thought he remembered the feel of her lips, sweet and innocent, on his. But this was different, like being kissed by a stranger. She had been an eager pupil when they had been together last. But today she was the aggressor, pressing her body to his in a way intended to arouse.

He grabbed her arms, intending to push her away. But his grip gentled as his fingers sunk into the soft flesh, and he heard her moan of delight mingling with his own. Her mouth tasted like raspberry, tart and sweet at the same time, her kisses like champagne, going straight to his head and taking him back to a night when the whole world had seemed to wait on the moment she would say yes.

There was no dancing at this party, yet he felt music deep in his bones, light under his skin, singing in his soul and making him sway against her in the most intimate of waltzes. He wanted her, she wanted him and life was simple again.

And then he remembered what awaited him at home, and the need to be tightly controlled at all times, lest the truth come bursting out. The reality crashed back into him, leaving him panting and angry.

But she felt none of the turmoil he was experiencing. Though the kiss had ended, she was still smiling, rubbing her lips with a fingertip. 'That was even better than I remember.'

'You should not know about such things.' He growled. Who had taught her to kiss like that? Surely not him, for he remembered being able to control himself when he'd been near her.

She shrugged and smiled, and he remembered that she had been the very devil as a girl, totally unaware of what madness she could drive him to. In fact, she had been the one to suggest they meet in private, and he the one unable to resist. She, above all others, had the ability to undo his plans with a flash of skin and a wink.

'It is time for you to go back to the party,' he said, clasping his hands behind his back.

'Perhaps,' she agreed. 'Once you tell me when we can meet again.'

'We cannot,' he replied, trying to bring order to the chaos in his head. 'It is far too dangerous.'

She walked towards the door and, without meaning to, he felt his arms reaching to draw her back. He forced them to his sides before she could turn and see.

As he expected, she spun around and stared at him, as if expecting to catch the truth in his expression. 'It is just as dangerous to stay apart,' she said, giving him a curious look. 'My father is eager for me to marry and might be arranging a match even as we speak.'

'That is as it should be,' Hugh replied, trying to ignore the jealousy that the suggestion of her marrying raised in him. 'You must marry eventually.'

'If you think so,' she said with a curious look, 'You had best do something about it to secure the desired result for both of us.' Then she listened at the door for a moment before opening it and darting out into the empty hall, leaving him alone.

Chapter Five

The next morning, Rachel woke with a smile after a night of pleasant dreams, all of them about Hugh.

He had been angry with her, of course. But he had responded like a jealous lover when she had given him the slightest provocation. And he had rewarded her with the best kiss since the last one he had given her. Now, the question was how to get another from him.

After breakfast, Rachel's father called her to his study. He was smiling at her in approval, and she wondered at the reason for it. If he had known what she'd been about last night, she was sure he'd have greeted her in a far different manner. Instead, he gestured to the chair in front of his desk and steepled his fingers, looking over them as if he were about to present a gift with his next words. 'There is a new suitor for you. A serious candidate, who meets all the specifications you might raise.' He finished with a nod of satisfaction, as if acknowledging a difficult job well done.

'Who now?' she enquired, running her mind down a column of remembered and rejected names, trying to marshal her features into something other than an apprehensive frown.

'He is five years older than you, good-humoured and sensible,' her father said, ticking off the fine qualities on his fingers. 'And proclaimed by your mother to be quite the handsomest fellow I have talked to. He also has a modest fortune of his own and will inherit enough beyond that to keep you in a manner slightly better than you are used to.'

'Does he have a name?' Rachel asked with a sigh. She supposed the suspense was meant to raise her hopes. But, as with all the other times they had had this discussion, she felt nothing more than prolonged dread. If the man was not Hugh Bethune, then she did not want to hear of him.

'Edward Graham,' her father said with a triumphant wave of his hand.

'Cousin Eddy,' she murmured with a grimace.

'Do not make such a face. There is nothing wrong with the fellow.'

'He used to pull my hair,' she said, covering her curls with a hand.

'That was nearly twenty years ago when you were both children. He has changed much since then, as have you.'

'But that does not mean that we would want to marry,' she said, alarmed.

'He, at least, is willing to consider it. When I die, you will be in his care anyway, if you do not marry first. He is my heir, after all.'

'Stop talking of death,' she pleaded, covering her ears. 'You are not any nearer to that than you were the last time I spoke to you.'

'Actually, I am, if only fractionally. But my current good health does not change the fact that my money and this house will go to him. You owe him respect as the future head of the household. And if you suit, as I think you shall, a marriage will be a damned efficient way to see to your comfort and that of your mother.'

'Efficient,' she echoed with a shudder.

'Do not let your mind be overrun with excuses before you have even talked to the fellow,' her father said with a huff. 'There is no reason that a sensible choice might not also be a happy one. If you allow yourself to think that true romance must be better if it is hopeless, you will never find the happiness that is right under your nose.'

'Thank you,' she replied, her mind racing. She rose from the chair and glanced towards the door. 'And now, if you will excuse me, I must go and prepare…' For something. She was not sure what. But she could not stand to be in this room another minute, listening to reason. And, in one thing at least, her father was right. There would never be a man more 'under her nose' than Hugh, living right next door.

She left the study and went upstairs to her maid. 'Tilly?' she called as the girl put the finishing press on her gown for the evening. 'Do you know anyone in service at the Duke of Scofield's house?'

'Several,' the girl admitted. 'There is Lady Olivia's lady's maid, of course. We share our half days and—'

'What has she told you of the schedule of the house and its master?'

'Only that His Grace is very strict with his sister. She is never allowed out of the house without an escort and there are guards in the yard to prevent her from leaving.'

It confirmed the identity of the gentleman sitting under the tree in the back garden. But it did nothing to help her learn Hugh's plans for the day.

'Does her brother keep regular hours as well?' she asked hopefully.

'He is generally out of the house in the morning to exercise his horse and has his duties in Parliament during the season. But beyond that his nights are a mystery to the household.'

'But he is on Rotten Row in the morning?' she said eagerly.

'I believe so.'

'Then prepare my habit,' she said with a grin. 'Today, I fancy a ride.'

Rachel arrived at Hyde Park a short while later on a fine mare with a spirited temperament, a footman following behind on a pony as chaperone. The poor fellow was an uneasy horseman, so she left him at the gate, assuring him that she would be perfectly fine travelling the Row without his company.

It was quite likely that he would be able to see her most of the way without following. She was wearing a crimson velvet habit with a high hat trimmed with plumes and rode a horse that was almost blindingly white. She had come here to be noticed and had spared no effort.

Now, she just had to track down her quarry. She brought the mare to an easy trot, slowing to chat with friends as she worked her way down the path until she could see a man on a black horse, riding alone. Although the other riders tended to crowd each other and ride in clusters, there was a ring of empty space around Hugh, as if the rest of the *ton* feared that he had some contagious disease.

She watched him from behind as she worked her way through the trail of carriages and horses, slowly gaining and preparing to make her move. She doubted that he would say anything if she pulled abreast of him. He would be stubborn, she was sure, refusing to acknowledge her, hoping to make her give up and go away.

But he would never fail to help a woman in danger. So she waited until she was clear of other riders, then spurred on her horse and deliberately lost control of the reins. She shot past the Duke at an uneasy gallop, feigning incompetence. In truth, she could have gained control whenever she wanted, for she was an excellent horsewoman. But this was a time when it was better to be helpless than self-sufficient.

She had guessed correctly. She had gone only a few yards when she heard galloping hoof beats gaining on her from behind. A moment later, a strong male hand reached out and grabbed her horse's harness, slowing it to a walk.

'Thank you,' she said, adjusting her hat and raising her eyes to find…

Not Hugh. This man was dark-haired, blue-eyed and vaguely familiar. He smiled at her in a way that was clearly intended to charm. 'If you are afraid that I am going to pull your hair again, you needn't worry. I have not done such a disreputable thing to a girl in at least a year.'

'Cousin Edward,' she said, forcing a smile.

'None other.' He tipped his hat, beaming at her. 'I certainly did not expect to meet you again under such alarming circumstances.'

'Nor did I,' she said, then added a smile and a 'Thank you so much,' after remembering that gratitude for the rescue was necessary.

'You are most welcome. I am very happy to have been of assistance. Allow me,' he said, gathering her reins and handing them back to her. 'Unless you would prefer that I lead your horse for you? I know how upsetting something like this can be.'

'I am…' She bit back the announcement that she was quite capable of handling her own mount, and that the supposed mad gallop had been less than twenty yards in a public park. 'I am all right. But thank you for the offer.'

'At least allow me to ride with you back towards the front of the park. I will accept nothing less.'

So she found herself with an escort after all. And one that would leave her father with the idea that she was in full cooperation with his plans for her. To make matters worse, as they passed Hugh his eyes met hers for only a moment and held a look that implied he knew exactly what she had been about and was more annoyed then impressed.

She smiled back at him, doing her best to pretend that her day had not just gone horribly wrong.

That night, Hugh had promised to attend a ball at the Duke of Haughleigh's townhouse, but he cried off, fearing another interruption of the evening by Rachel. After this morning's appearance in Hyde Park, it was clear that she had learned his schedule and meant to track him through London until he surrendered, which he had no intention of doing.

He could not risk another lapse of judgement like the incident in the library. That had only emboldened her to make that dramatic attempt to attract him this morning. He'd have been worried for her if he had not known that she was an excellent rider, totally capable of regaining control of her own mare.

Another gentleman, not so well-informed,

had rushed to her rescue instead. It served her right if she ended up engaged to someone who treated her like the fool she pretended to be. She would be miserable, and he would be…

Not the least bit satisfied by her unavailability. But it was in his nature to be unhappy, so he had best get used to it, and so had she. He stalked to the writing desk and put pen to paper, addressed a missive to the house next door and dropped it in the outgoing post. Then he went back to his room, alone.

The Duke of Haughleigh's ball was an unmitigated failure. The food was excellent, of course, and the music exquisite. Rachel could not imagine a more perfect evening except for one thing—there was no sign of Hugh. She had imagined another brief meeting, and perhaps another kiss.

Instead, she had to pretend to be happy for hours while feeling utterly alone. It was surprising how quickly she had grown used to seeing Hugh and how empty she felt when he was not nearby.

And, though she did not think it possible,

when she got home things got worse. She found a letter addressed to her, clearly delivered in the last post of the day. She immediately recognised Hugh's bold hand and rushed with it to her room, imagining that the words inside would make everything all right again.

Instead, she found a brief, scribbled note.

Rachel,

I know what you were trying to do this morning and I have no intention of letting you make another attempt. Do not look for me again, as I am suspending all social outings until further notice. In the end, you will see that this is for the best.

He had not bothered to sign it—not offered so much as a 'sincerely', much less a declaration of love. Nor had he bothered to begin by calling her his dear.

She crumpled the paper and tossed it into the fire without regret. There was nothing on it that was worth saving to read again. She had been dismissed coldly, brutally, and without reason to hope.

Once the last of the paper had turned to

ash, she crept down the stairs and went out of the door to the back garden, wrapping herself in a cloak that hung on a peg by the kitchen door. She could see his window from a place by the back gate, dark as one would expect at nearly three in the morning.

Where was he? Had he stayed home, as his note had implied, or had he gone somewhere that she did not want to know about? Did he have a mistress, as so many men did? Or had he been alone all this time, brooding on the past? He might be up in that room right at that moment, tossing and turning in his bed and thinking of her.

She stooped to the ground and picked up a pebble, switching it from hand to hand and gauging the distance to the glass.

Then she dropped it again. With her luck, she would break the pane instead of drawing him to the window. He might be up in that room, sound asleep and not thinking of her at all. And she might be the biggest fool in all of London for chasing after a man who did not really want her. Though everything about it seemed wrong, maybe she would be better off listening to her father and settling for someone decent but attainable.

Then she heard a sound from the street outside, the irregular step of boots on the cobbles. When she turned to look, it was the man who had been with Lady Olivia at Gunter's. He was staring up at the house, just as she had been, focusing on a window a few doors down from the one that fixated Rachel.

She felt a rush of kinship for the stranger, who thought he was unobserved and showed none of the reserve she was used to seeing in gentlemen, even those who claimed to be in love. She murmured a prayer of apology, for it was unfair to see such naked emotion that she was sure he would have hidden had he known he was observed.

If he was the man Hugh had set to watch his sister, it was pointless of him to pine for her. A duke would never allow an employee to marry into the family. Even worse, she might be in love with another and know nothing of the contents of this fellow's heart, which would likely be broken by her inevitable betrayal.

In this, they had something in common.

She crept to the gate and slipped through it, walking silently down the street to stand at his side.

'Stay away from her.'

He started when he noticed her, turning away from the woman silhouetted in the window above them. 'I beg your pardon?'

'Stay away,' Rachel repeated. 'There is nothing but unhappiness for you if you involve yourself with her, or anyone else in the house. Leave before it is too late.'

Then she followed her own advice and hurried down the walk. When she was almost out of sight of him in the darkness, she darted behind the nearest tree, waiting for him to pass. Instead, she heard his footsteps fading in the night as he walked away in the direction from which they had both come, allowing her to creep back to her own garden and home.

It had been foolish to accost him in that way, and with such a dire warning. But for a moment they had been partners in misery and, if she had dared, she would have thanked him for that. She did not see that unhappiness changing for either of them any time soon.

Chapter Six

The next morning, Rachel came down to breakfast exhausted from a sleepless night, only to find her parents wide awake and smiling at her with approval. 'We heard what you did yesterday and are pleased that you decided to take my wishes to heart with such alacrity,' her father said, nodding as he sipped his coffee.

'Your methods are unorthodox, of course,' her mother said, her voice tinged with concern. 'But I was young once, and understand the desire for a grand passion instead of the sterile way these things can sometimes go…'

'What have I done?' Rachel asked, trying not to sound as tired as she felt.

'You have reintroduced yourself to Edward, of course,' her mother said, much more happily. 'You allowed him to rescue you yesterday morning on Rotten Row.'

'He mentioned it to me last night,' her father added. 'He spoke admirably of your spirit.'

'I am sure you were in no real danger,' her mother observed. 'But it was a rather outlandish way to catch his eye and I am glad that you did not tell us of your plans beforehand.'

'Oh,' Rachel replied, unsure of what more to say. It appeared that her actions had been utterly transparent and yet completely misconstrued. 'I will not do anything like that again,' she promised. Especially as it had been so unsuccessful.

'I believe an offer is forthcoming, and when it arrives—' her father began.

She cut him off. 'I would still prefer to be courted in the usual manner. I do not want to marry a stranger, after all.'

'He is not a stranger,' her father began. 'He is—'

'Perfectly willing to wait, I am sure,' her mother interrupted, much to Rachel's surprise. She smiled sympathetically at her daughter. 'If we speak to him again, we will remind him that it is never a good idea to take a lady for granted. He will woo you as you wish. Won't he?' At this last, she gave her husband a significant look and waited for his assent.

'There is no rush, I suppose,' her father said with a sigh. 'As long as the matter is settled in the next few days.'

'Days?' she said with a gasp.

'Weeks, surely,' her mother said with a calming wave of her hand. 'Let her have the remainder of the season to enjoy. A marriage then will be just as satisfying as one rushed into now.'

Her father sighed again. 'Weeks, then. But do not think you will be allowed to dangle after the man and then cry off. You will be married—if not to him, then someone else. I will not go through another season of waffling.'

It was not actually waffling to refuse proposals if one intended to remain unmarried. But it appeared that would not be an option, nor had she figured out how to convince Hugh to marry her. She would have to work much harder if she did not want to end up wed to Edward.

'And perhaps we shall see Edward at Vauxhall Gardens tonight,' her mother said. 'I wonder if there is a way to inform him of our plans that does not seem too forward?'

'I am sure that is not necessary,' Rachel assured her hurriedly.

'Nonsense. I will send a note, inviting him to accompany us, and we will bring your maid to act as chaperone, should the two of you want to go off alone.'

'Yes, Mother,' she said, wanting to do no such thing. But, if she had the misfortune of meeting her cousin, it would be much better to have Tilly there to prevent intimacy.

'And, above all, you are to stay away from the dark walks,' her mother reminded her.

'What are they?' Rachel said with an innocent blink, then worried that she had feigned too much naivety to be taken seriously, because her mother gave a huff of disapproval.

'Make sure you come home as ignorant as you left, or you will never be allowed outside of this house again.'

That night, as it always did, Vauxhall Gardens dazzled Rachel with its many twinkling lanterns and its novel attractions. But she did not want to admit that the thing that pleased her even more than acrobats who had come all the way from India was the fact that Edward was otherwise engaged and unable to accompany them. She needed a diversion from the prospect of his impending proposal and was ready to lose herself in the night's entertainments.

She was applauding politely, as a pair of boys walked on their hands, when she noticed a familiar face moving through the crowd on the opposite side of the circle. Hugh was there, walking with purpose towards the dark walks at the back of the park. In that space, the lanterns were few and far between, and the entertainments took place between young men and women who had managed to slip away from chaperones and dally on the benches and follies shielded by shrubbery.

Rachel grabbed her maid's hand and yanked her towards the edge of the crowd, calling to her mother that she was indisposed and would be back soon.

When they were out of sight of her parents, she wasted no time in reaching into her purse and producing a gold sovereign, which was more money than Tilly would see in several months. 'I need you to give me some time alone,' she said, holding the coin just out of reach.

'If your father finds out…' the maid said with a worried frown.

'Then he had better not,' Rachel said with a nod. 'And no one need know it is me.' She glanced to her side, where a vendor was selling decorated masks, and reached in her pocket for more coins, purchasing one. 'I promise I will not remove this until I am back.'

'Perhaps, if I turn my head for a moment, you might be lost in the crowd,' her maid said, staring back towards the acrobats.

Rachel dropped the coin into her hand and said, 'Let me borrow your cloak.' Tilly handed it over and she pulled it on, shrouding her body in the plain woollen cape. Then she put on her mask and walked into a swirl of revellers, letting them sweep her down the path towards the dark walks.

Vauxhall Gardens was as it always was, loud and crowded, garish and annoying. But it was the least romantic place Hugh could think of in which to meet Martine Devereaux, which would help to avoid reminding her of old times. He was sure that most men would tell him that a renewed relationship with his former mistress was exactly what he needed to clear his mind of the desire for Rachel. One woman was very like another, when the lights were out.

But that thought was abhorrent to him. Now that he had kissed Rachel again, his mind was too full of her to think of other women. The only thing possible was to suffer the effects in private, as one did with an ague, waiting for the mad recklessness to pass and for life to return to normal.

Martine was walking towards him from across the promenade, an inviting sway in her hips and a smile of invitation on her face. She was beautiful, of course. But tonight he could not remember what had attracted him to her in the first place, other than the assumption that a man of his station would and should have a mistress and that he should try for once to be normal.

When Richard Sterling had taken her away from him, he had gone through the motions of playing the jilted lover, but had been secretly relieved to have rid himself of her so cheaply.

Now, he smiled back at her to prove that

there were no hard feelings and kissed her lightly on the cheek.

She gave a coquettish laugh and replied in kind. 'It has been a long time, Scofield.'

'It has indeed,' he agreed. 'Almost a year since you left me. And, from what I hear, you have fared well since our parting.'

'I miss Richard, of course. But my new friend has been generous,' she admitted with another coy smile and a flourish of her hand to showcase the stunning emerald bracelet she was wearing.

'It is good to hear,' Hugh replied. 'For I was wondering if you could do a favour for a generous old friend as well.'

She gave him a sidelong look. 'It would depend on the favour, and the friend.'

'A trifle, really,' he assured her. 'I need a note written in a feminine hand.'

'That is all?'

'A certain young lady of my acquaintance is fixated on an inappropriate suitor. I wish her to believe that the man she is mooning over has another, more persistent female of whom he has not told her. A jealous wife, perhaps.' He shrugged. 'I will leave the details to you. But it should be something that would put her off the fellow, or at least make her suspicious of his motives.'

The courtesan's eyes sparkled with excitement. 'How duplicitous of you. And is this young lady a favourite of yours?'

'She is my sister,' he said, embarrassed. 'She will not listen to me, of course. She is falling for the fellow whom I hired to watch her. Anything I might say will make her more set on him than ever. I learned that much from the elopement of my other sister. But I thought if another woman told her that this Solomon can't be trusted…'

'An anonymous note to terrify her away?'

'Or at least to make her ask difficult questions of the man,' Hugh said with another shrug.

'Say no more. You shall have your note for a kiss and a packet of the biscuits that fellow is selling over there.' She pointed an elegant finger in the direction of the nearest vendor.

'As always, you are a queen amongst women,' Hugh said, raising her hand to his lips and kissing the fingertips in admiration.

Behind him, he heard a strange, sighing sound and turned to see Rachel watching him, in shock. She was wearing a simple cloak over her gown and one of the garish masks that was popular with the throng this evening. It was as if she was there in disguise, although he had no idea who she might be hiding from.

'What are you doing here?' he demanded, feeling as shocked as she looked.

'I was here with my parents and I saw you in the crowd,' she admitted, then looked in horror at Martine, who was still standing at his side.

The courtesan stared back at the girl with interest, and then shot a quick glance at Hugh, giving him a knowing nod. 'If our business is finished, I must be going to write that letter. I will have it delivered to your home. Fare thee well, Scofield.'

'And you, Martine,' he said, then turned back to Rachel. 'Now what is the meaning of following me about London?' he asked, trying to be stern.

'I am not following you,' she said, her eyes darting away as if she feared he would see the truth in them. 'Not all about London, anyway. I did not expect to see you here.'

'Then you will be walking away now,' he said, raising his eyebrow and waiting.

'Who was that woman?' she asked, craning her neck to watch his retreating former mistress.

'That is none of your business,' he replied. 'And where is your chaperone?'

'We decided that we would both have more fun if we separated,' she said with a grin. 'And am I not correctly attired for a night on my own? In this costume, no one will recognise me.'

And yet, he had, without a second glance. 'I think you should go back to your maid,' he said cautiously.

'Not until you tell me who that woman was,' she replied stubbornly.

'An old friend who is doing me a favour,' he said, wondering if she would believe the truth. Then he pulled her down to sit on a bench at the beginning of the dark walk. 'You must stop pursuing me in this way. I cannot give you what you want.'

'Then the least you can do is explain why,' she said, touching his hand.

'I cannot do that either,' he said. 'Just know that things have changed since we were together and what we had is gone.'

'Do you mean that you do not love me? That there is someone else?'

Here again was a moment in which he should lie. All he had to do was tell her that he no longer loved her, and it would hurt her so much that she would go away. He wet his lips and prepared the words.

'Swear on your honour that you do not love me,' she said. 'Then perhaps I will believe you.'

He shut his mouth again.

She gave him a hopeful smile. 'As long as you do not deny me, I cannot help but hope.'

'And as long as I live, I cannot marry you,' he said in return. 'And on that I can swear. There is no point in hoping. All hope was lost two years ago.'

'Then what can you offer, other than marriage?' she enquired.

'Nothing honourable. Nothing proper.'

'And suppose I do not care if what happens is proper?' she asked.

He should not be surprised. She never had before, when they had loved each other freely and hoped for the future.

Her hand slipped into his, squeezing encouragingly. 'Suppose there is only tonight?

The darkness is only a few feet away and will hide all. Suppose I have less than an hour before anyone notices that I am gone? What can you offer me then?'

It was an invitation that he was too weak to resist. The feel of her fingers moving against his, warm and soft, made him imagine how the skin of her throat would feel if he pressed his lips against it. What harm could it do to have one last kiss? He rose and took her by the hand, walking towards the dark walks and intimacy.

Then he froze, the prospect of romance forgotten. His sister was coming out on the same path, led by Michael Solomon. 'What the devil? Olivia? You are not allowed to be out of the house.'

'She should not have got this far. I am to blame for that. But there was no sign of whomever she intended to meet,' Solomon said hurriedly.

It was complete fustian, of course. The man's cravat was undone and there was a flush on his cheek that hinted at mischief.

Olivia had the nerve to lie as well. 'I was not meeting anyone. I came here for my own pleasure.'

'If I were to believe that, it would be even worse,' Hugh snapped, glaring at her. 'That would mean that you have been wandering about London at night with no chaperone at all. We will discuss what you have or have not done tomorrow, when we are both home.'

'And just what are you doing here?' Olivia asked, taking the offensive to draw attention away from her own sins. 'And who is your friend? I do not believe you mentioned where you were going when you left tonight, or where you might be. You only said that you did not mean to come home.'

Behind him, he heard a gasp of alarm from Rachel.

He'd meant nothing by the statement when he'd told the servants not to expect him. Certainly, he'd had no intention of spending the night with Martine. He had thought to make a late night here and then go on to his private apartments to keep from disturbing the household. But neither had he expected to come upon Rachel or to have Olivia questioning his motives.

He glared at Solomon, trying to gain control of the situation again. 'Take her home immediately and see that she does not stray again.' Then he turned and rushed up the path to find Rachel and explain. But it was too late. She was already lost in the crowd.

Chapter Seven

Rachel pounded her pillow for what seemed like the hundredth time and rolled, with a moan. The sun was rising and the night had been sleepless, filled with self-recrimination.

Hugh had probably slept well in the arms of the exotic woman he had been meeting, who had not worn a mask out of fear of tarnishing her reputation. She probably revelled in the reputation she already had.

Just as bad, she had been near to dragging Hugh into the dark to make love to her. And then he had seen Olivia and she'd been totally forgotten. It was his responsibility to care for his sister until she married, and she doubted he would take a wife until Olivia was safely wed. But how could they ever be together if he refused to allow Olivia to marry?

If she insisted on pursuing him, she should face the fact that she would never be the full focus of Hugh's attention. It was one proof that, as he kept telling her, he was very unlike the man she remembered from years before.

And yet, when he dropped his guard and looked at her, the old hunger was still there. No matter what he said, he still wanted her.

That night, to her relief, Hugh was not at the ball she was invited to. She was still unsure of what she thought about the lady he had been visiting in Vauxhall, if she could indeed be called a lady.

If he had a mistress, or a woman he preferred, it was Rachel's own fault for discovering the fact. He had not asked her to follow him that night, nor had he promised fidelity. In fact, he had been quite insistent that there was no future for them.

Why was it so hard for her to accept?

And now, Edward had arrived, looking every bit the dashing suitor that she did not want to see tonight. He was speaking with her father and bowing deeply over her mother's hand. Then, the three of them turned to look in her direction and her mother was escorting him to her to make sure that the courtship progressed as it should.

'You remember your cousin Edward,' her mother said with a smile large enough to be called a grin. 'Of course, introductions are hardly necessary. I believe you met last in Hyde Park.'

'Of course,' Rachel said, smiling politely and dropping a curtsy. Then she offered her dance card, as was expected.

When her mother was out of earshot, Edward said in a soft voice, 'I am aware that your father has great expectations for a match. But, I must assure you, I am more interested in what you have to say than what he wants. Although I understand it is the practical choice, I am sure we both hope for something more when marrying. Do not feel you have to rush to a decision. I am willing to wait.'

'Thank you for your understanding,' Rachel said, surprised. It was exactly what she had hoped to hear from suitors who had come before him. Thus far, she had been disappointed.

Later, she discovered he danced divinely. He joked with her, and she laughed. When he offered to get her a glass of champagne, she accepted, and allowed him to take her out onto the veranda to look at the stars.

He was polite, pleasant and handsome. He made her laugh. It almost disappointed her that she felt nothing more than friendship when she looked at him. If she was not in love with another, she might have agreed with her father that fondness was a good enough reason to accept an offer.

It was almost reason enough, but not quite. Hugh was not as good a dancer, and it had been years since they'd laughed together. But she could not stop thinking of him. They had been friends once. She simply had to remind him of the fact. Then, he would see that building a life together would help with whatever problems kept him apart from her now.

But at the moment none of that mattered. On the ride home, her parents would demand to know what she thought of Edward and she could not think of anything to say other than the truth. He was an unobjectionable young man. She would happily recommend him to any of her friends. But she did not want to manufacture the passion necessary to marry him, or to lie with him as a wife should.

She was not even supposed to know about the marital act, much less form opinions on men based on her taste for it. And she certainly could not admit to knowledge or preferences pertaining to it when answering her parents.

As expected, when they got into the carriage she was quizzed on how the night had gone. She was evasive. What did one say about a man that had nothing particularly wrong with him? If she did not come up with something when he offered, she would have no excuse at all.

In the end, she announced that they had had a very nice talk but that no promises had been made on either side. She looked forward to seeing him again and to getting to know him better. It was an evasion that would buy her time as she tried to decide what to do about her love for Hugh.

The trip to Vauxhall had been a disaster from start to finish. Hugh had thought that an evening away from Rachel would clear his head and allow him time to settle the growing problem of his sister and her watchdog.

Instead, he had managed to stumble into a place where both matters became worse.

Either Martine had meant to hurt him or had totally mistaken what he had asked for when they'd been together. Instead of a letter with a gentle warning from woman to woman that Solomon was already married, she had sent an anonymous threat in red ink that had terrified Olivia's maid and left his sister suspicious but unmoved.

Olivia refused to admit to her feelings for Solomon, so he could not tell whether they were genuine or merely a desperate grasp for any hand that would bear her out of the house. But he could not imagine that she was serious. Had she learned nothing from Margaret's hasty marriage and ban from the premises?

He had lost one sister, and now it seemed he would lose both if he did not lock the doors and guard them himself, like the mad tyrant everyone thought he was.

And, after seeing him with another woman, Rachel was convinced that he had an *inamorata*. It was probably for the best. She was avoiding him again, as she had before. It was simpler that way. If he had no intention of marrying, a future between them was impossible. His love for her had done nothing to change his opinion that his whole family was blighted and it would be better if the line died with him.

And now, after only a day apart, there were rumours that she would be engaged to another very soon. It seemed that the brief flair of eagerness for his company had burned out, and she had sought another the first moment he'd disappointed her. It should be reason enough for his own feelings to cool as well.

And yet, it was not. The fact that he had succeeded by hurting her made his own pain greater. At least, before, he'd known he had one true friend in the world, even though he could not be with her. Now he had betrayed her, he was left with no one.

His desk was littered with crumpled paper, notes begun and discarded to explain that what she had witnessed was nothing of import. That he had meant to spend the evening at his club after a late night so as not to disturb the household. That anything between the courtesan and him had cooled almost as quickly as it had begun and was long over.

But to write to her would only raise false hopes in them both. It was better that they parted in anger than drifted on in false hope with no chance of a future.

His resolve to stay out of her way and mind his family lasted almost a week. Then he returned to the house after a night at his club to discover that his sister was gone again.

This time, according to the servants, she had got a head start on Solomon, who had taken off in pursuit when he had arrived this morning.

He quizzed the staff until he had a good idea of her destination, then considered. In the past, he had trusted Solomon to bring her back safely. But the way the two of them had looked at Vauxhall left no room for innocence. So Hugh packed a bag and called for his carriage. If he did not act now, he would be tracking the two of them all the way to Scotland before the day was out.

The coachmen took him as far north as they could before stopping for the night. Then they continued in the morning, stopping at each inn on the road until they arrived at the Silver Hare and heard a report of a couple meeting illicitly and sharing a room.

Hugh waited in the coffee room until Solomon and Olivia appeared, looking far too happy to be honest. If Hugh was truly the sort of man given to solving his problems with violence, he'd have called Solomon out, or at least taken him to the coach yard and thrashed him soundly.

But to act in such a way would spread the rumours about Olivia faster than making a discreet exit. So, he sacked Solomon and hauled his sister home in disgrace.

It was time to give up the idea that he could hire a guard for her that she could not outwit or corrupt. Olivia was exhibiting a growing defiance to his wishes and sometimes he wondered if there was any point in trying to control her any more. He was exhausted with worrying what she might do next, and increasingly unable to stop her in her attempts to escape the house. And now he had to worry about the possibility of a bastard.

Should she be with child, he would rush her to the country for her confinement and refuse to bring her back to London next season. It would mean leaving his seat in Parliament empty. And, more difficult still, it would mean no more visits, however brief, with Rachel.

In the short time they had been together again, he had grown used to seeing her. It was a dangerous habit to get into, this taste for forbidden fruit. Maybe it was for the best that he took his sister, retired to his estate and left the city and its many temptations behind.

Almost three weeks had passed since Vauxhall, and when Rachel came down to breakfast both her parents were remarking over an announcement in *The Times*.

'The oldest Bethune girl has married,' her mother said with a smile. 'Her sister has put the announcement in the paper and describes it as a "Scottish wedding".'

'Elopement,' her father said on a grunt. 'There is no hiding the truth.'

'Who is the husband?' Rachel asked, holding her breath.

'A Mr Solomon,' her mother replied, brows knitting. 'I do not know of a Solomon family. Perhaps they are foreign.'

'Don't be ridiculous,' her father said with another huff. 'Scofield would never allow her to associate with foreigners, or anyone else for that matter. This Solomon is probably some common tradesman and she has left the house under a cloud. Scofield would never let her meet a proper gentleman.'

'I am sure they are very happy,' Rachel said, smiling in relief. It seemed that the poor gentleman mooning at the window had succeeded after all.

'Happy to be away from Scofield, more like,' her father said.

'It does not matter, now that she is out of the house,' Rachel said, trying to resist the urge to stand and cheer. Hugh no longer had the excuse that he must for care for his sister and postpone his own marriage. He was free.

There was still the problem of his reputation, of course. But it did not matter to her, as she knew the things said about him were not true. Once they were married, she was sure that society would consider the stabilising influence of a wife as having changed him for the better. Slowly, the past would be forgotten, and she would have the man and the life that she had always dreamed of.

Later, Rachel looked out of her bedroom window, surprised to see Hugh sitting under the tree in the garden where his watchman had often sat. He had a bottle of brandy beside him and, as she watched, he took a long pull on it, tipping his head up and letting the liquor slide down his throat.

Then, as if he truly could feel no pain, he pounded his head on the trunk of the tree behind him.

Unable to help herself, Rachel hurried down the stairs and through the kitchen, out into her garden, then out the back gate and down the path to the Scofield gate, wiggling the loose bolt and letting herself inside so she could rush to sit beside him.

'What is wrong?' she asked, taking the bottle from his hand.

Hugh snatched it back and took another drink. 'Does something have to be wrong for a gentleman to wish a drink in the privacy of his own garden?'

'If that gentleman is you, then, yes,' she replied. 'I have not seen you out here in more than a year, nor do I expect you to be drinking your breakfast.'

'The seat is supposed to be occupied by a guard,' he said with a huff. 'Someone to keep Olivia from running wild. But a fat lot of good it did me to hire Solomon.' He pointed a finger and poked her in the middle of the chest. 'You know as much as I do about how that turned out. You saw them together and warned me. But I allowed myself to become distracted.' He gave her an arch look, as if blaming her for the lapse in attention.

'Your sister married him,' she said, trying not to smile. 'We saw the announcement in *The Times*. And they took the dogs?' she added, noticing the quiet of the empty kennel.

'Gone,' Hugh confirmed with a sweep of his hands. 'All gone. And it is just as well. Those damned pugs hated me even more than my sister did.'

'I am sure she did not hate you,' Rachel assured him, trying to forget the fear in Olivia's eyes the night she had been caught in Vauxhall.

'I gave her no reason to love me,' he said, taking another pull on the brandy bottle. 'But I swear, what I did was for the best. I tried to watch over them both, to keep them safe from the world, and to keep the world safe from them. But it was not enough. They have got away from me, and Lord knows what will happen now.'

Rachel could not stop the laugh that escaped, even though the situation was obviously serious to him. 'You make it sound as if they were dangerous prisoners.'

The silence that greeted this comment made her wonder at the truth of it.

She chose her next words with caution, unsure of what had happened. 'We noticed that Margaret has already married.'

'Eloped,' Hugh corrected. 'With a newspaper reporter who wanted to investigate me.'

'How interesting,' she said, watching for his reaction.

'She lives in a cottage,' he said, shaking his head. 'And claims to be happy. I saw her there yesterday. Olivia was there as well.' The bottle sloshed in his hand as he made an expansive gesture. 'They flaunted the elopement in my face and then Peg's husband, Castell, put me out of the house. There was nothing I could do to stop any of it.'

'I am sure that both girls will be perfectly safe with their new husbands,' she said, giving him an ineffectual pat on the shoulder.

'It was never their safety that was in question,' Hugh replied, staring at her as though he thought her a fool. 'I worry for their husbands. They have no idea what they have married into.'

This idea was too ridiculous to respond to, so she ignored it. 'Now that you no longer have to care for your sisters, you are free to do as you want.'

'I will never be free,' he said, shaking his head.

'You could marry, if you wished,' she encouraged.

'If I wished to marry, you would be the first to know,' he said, looking at her for the first time. 'But I do not.'

'And why is that?' she demanded. 'You are an innocent man, and we both know it.'

'I am not a murderer,' he agreed. 'But I lost my innocence the night my father died and I will never be the man you knew.'

It seemed he'd taken his father's death to heart in a way she could not begin to understand. 'The changes do not matter to me,' she said, taking the brandy bottle from the slack fingers and setting it on the ground.

'You cannot say that without knowing,' he answered, then paused, as if there was some secret he wanted to share.

'Then tell me,' she said, squeezing his hand in encouragement.

'Do you want the truth?' he asked with a

laugh. He turned to her, staring into her eyes until her mind went fuzzy and she was lost in the green depths of his, like a swimmer in a stormy sea.

Then he grabbed her, kissing her hard on the lips. His hands on her arms pinned her in place as he ravaged her mouth, his grip so tight that she couldn't have escaped even if she'd wanted to. His tongue thrust into her mouth in a demanding rhythm that was an imitation of something primal and frightening. After this, there could be no denying that he wanted her.

And, Lord help her, she wanted him in return. The feeling was wicked and all-consuming. If he let go of her now, she would sink to the ground and spread her legs for him, letting him teach her the meaning of his kiss under the open sky.

Then, as quickly as it had begun, it was over. He released her and laughed again. 'You want the truth? Well, here it is. I am mad. A madman heading a mad family. My father? My sisters? All mad. And I have no intention of breeding another generation of lunatics to occupy this house and torture each other with their lunacy. Now, give up the hope that there can be any more between us than there already has been.'

Then, he left her alone and returned to his house.

Chapter Eight

Now that Olivia was gone, the house was eerily quiet. He had not noticed how large the place was, nor how empty without even a dog underfoot to break up the solitude. It almost tempted him to reach out to Olivia to ask for one of the infinite number of puppies she needed to find homes for, since David Castell had foisted a mate onto the irritable Caesar the pug.

Almost, but not quite.

Instead, he threw himself into his work and interacted with society only as far as reading the gossip sheets that occasionally crossed his desk.

It appeared from them that Lady Rachel Graham was soon to be engaged to her cousin, Edward. At this news, Hugh could not decide if he was relieved or seething with jealousy. While he had done everything in his power to get her to move on from what they'd shared, that did not mean he had to like it when it happened.

But it did mean that it was probably safe to return to whatever part of society would have him. Like it or not, after his last repudiation of her, Rachel had selected a more sensible candidate for her hand and he need not fear any more clandestine meetings with her.

Despite that fact, he could not help a feeling of unease as he prepared to go out. He demanded a second shave and went through half a dozen cravats with his valet before declaring himself satisfied. The servant smiled in response, clearly assuming that it was a woman that had him so flustered.

Was it possible to be discomposed by a lack of women? Between the loss of his sisters and the feeling that Rachel was slipping away again, he was at sixes and sevens, unsure of what lay in his future other than silence and loneliness. Tonight, he would haunt the card room and avoid the ladies, ignoring the way they gossiped behind their fans as he walked by, and refusing any false congratulations about his sisters' marriages. And if he saw Rachel…?

Between seeing him with Martine and his drunken ravings in the garden, she was probably no more interested in seeing him than he was in trying to resist her. He must trust that the interludes they had shared recently were a thing of the past. For, no matter what the future held for them, he could not spend the rest of his life hiding away in his rooms.

In Rachel's opinion, her courtship with Edward was going far too well. She had assumed that, by the time things progressed to this point, she would have convinced Hugh that he must act or risk losing her. But with each passing day Edward became more convinced of her eventual acceptance, and she became less convinced that there was a way out of their impending marriage.

If she did not have another offer, her father would not accept a refusal. Perhaps, if she explained to Hugh what was at stake, he would take pity and marry her. He might have a mistress, and a conviction that his family was too unstable to reproduce, but that did not change the fact that he loved her. She would trust in that love as she always had, and she would find a way forward.

That night, they were attending one of the last balls of the season, yet another sign that her time was running out. Edward would be there, of course, and with luck she would see Hugh and could beg him to do the thing that they both wanted.

When she arrived in the ballroom, Edward was there to meet her, bowing low over her hand and claiming the waltz before working his way around the room and helping to fill the dance cards of the other young ladies present. He was a true gentleman, Rachel had to admit. And at least for now, his courtesy gave her time to think.

Hugh was here somewhere. She had heard people talking about him, disapproving as always. She scanned the crowd and saw no sign of him in the ballroom or the dining room. Then she found him on the veranda, standing alone and staring out over the darkened garden.

'I need to talk to you,' she whispered, glancing hurriedly around her to make sure she had not been heard by the other couples enjoying the night air.

'So, speak,' he said without turning round.

'In private,' she whispered. 'Somewhere we can be alone.'

'I do not think that is wise,' he said, still refusing to face her.

'Here, then,' she conceded with a sigh. 'As you may have heard, my engagement is imminent.'

'Congratulations,' he responded mechanically.

'I do not want your good wishes,' she snapped. 'I want help getting out of this.'

'Then, when the gentleman asks, say no,' he said with a shrug as if it made no difference to him how she answered.

She laughed bitterly. 'My father has informed me that a no is not an option. I am to marry by the end of the season, and Edward is my only suitor.'

'He seems like an unobjectionable young man,' he said, but she watched as his fingers that gripped the stone balustrade went painfully white.

'I do not love him,' she said, then waited for a response that did not come.

'Does any of this matter to you?' she snapped. 'Because you cannot have it both ways, you know. I will not be allowed by society to wait in stoic celibacy as you plan to. I have to marry someone, and soon.'

'Then all my blessings will go with you,' Hugh said.

'I want more than your blessing,' she replied. 'I want to know why you are still adamant that we cannot be together, now that your sisters are gone from the house. And do not tell me it is because you are mad. You are as sane as I am.'

She must have been growing louder as she spoke, for he was glancing around now, as if fearing they would be noticed. He looked back at the French doors behind her, which led to a darkened room. He opened them and pushed her through, following her into the room and latching the doors behind them.

Then he turned to face her. 'The problems in my life are far bigger than you can imagine, and they have not been solved by the absence of my sisters. If possible, they have grown worse.'

'Then let me help you,' she said, reaching for his arm.

He stepped back, out of her grasp. 'There is nothing you can do for me. And much that I would do to hurt you by our continued association. Remember the way your mother reacted when we danced?'

'And she was wrong. Nothing came of it,' she said.

'My reputation is the same as it was then,' he said with a sad shake of his head. 'In the eyes of the *ton*, you would be marrying a murderer.'

'But we know it is not true,' she reminded him. 'And that is all that matters.'

'That is but a part of it,' he said. 'My fears for the sanity of the family have not changed. My future is doomed and so will it be for any associated with me. I cannot force you to throw away your life on a hopeless situation.'

'And does what I want have no meaning to you?' she asked.

'You must trust that I know what is best for both of us,' he said in a patronising tone that made her all the more convinced that she was in the right.

Then a plan occurred to her that would solve the problem of Edward and help Hugh as well. He would be angry with her at first, but in time he would see that she was right.

'I am sorry,' she said. 'But you are wrong. And apparently it is up to me to prove it to you.'

She lunged at him, throwing her arms around his neck and planting a kiss on his lips. The suddenness caught them both off-guard and he stumbled back a step before reaching out to hold her and steady them both.

Then he kissed her back. And, as it always did when they were together like this, the world felt right again. His lips moved gently on hers, careful to leave no mark that would betray their activities. His hands stroked her body, grazing the sides of her breasts before gently gripping her shoulders.

She swayed against him, running her fingers through his hair and loosening his cravat. She wanted to stay like this with him for ever, showered in gentle kisses, feeling the heat of his body and the beat of his heart joining with hers.

Then she remembered that, if things went to plan, she could have this every day for the rest of her life. She just had to be brave and hope that Hugh was the man she knew him to be. So she pulled away from the kiss, gathered her wits, closed her eyes, took a deep breath to steady her nerves and screamed.

When she opened them again, it was to see a look of horror on Hugh's face. The kiss had wiped away all traces of the urbane and bitter peer who had pushed her into the room. It had rendered him young again, as vulnerable as she remembered him.

And he was hurt. He pushed her away from him, as if the touch could burn him, dropping his hands to his sides and clenching his fingers in the wool of his coat tails.

There was a pounding of footsteps in the hall outside and the door was thrown open, a crowd already forming to gawp at her in her disgrace.

She wondered if it disappointed them that there was not more to see. She and Hugh were standing in the room separated by at least five feet. Her clothing and hair were un-mussed, but with Hugh's ruffled hair and loose cravat it would appear something must have been going on. The biggest sign of scandal was the identity of the man she was with and the fact that he would dare be alone with a decent young lady.

The women in the crowd gasped and she heard her mother give a shriek of horror before sinking into a swoon. Edward was there at her side to catch her before she hit the floor. He stared over her head at Rachel, his face a mixture of disappointment and jealous anger.

From behind them, Rachel's father stepped forward and barked, 'Scofield, we will have words.'

Hugh's face darkened in barely contained rage and he turned and directed it at Rachel. 'That will not be necessary.'

Then he stiffly dropped to a knee, as if Napoleon himself had a pistol to his head. 'Rachel, would you do me the honour of becoming my wife?'

If possible, this shocked the crowd even more. Her mother was awake again and weeping openly, as if Rachel had been found dead and not simply compromised.

The rest of the people gathered were murmuring, alternating interest and disapproval. Disapproval of her? She was unaccustomed to anyone noticing her at all, much less having an opinion on her behaviour. And now it seemed she had done something that would make her the talk of the *ton*. Or perhaps it was Hugh they would be speaking of, as always.

'Rachel!' her father shouted from the doorway, obviously irate. 'Answer the man.' His tone made it very clear what the answer must be.

'Yes,' she said softly, staring down at the man before her, clear in his misery. This should be the happiest moment of both of their lives. But somehow she had ruined it, for he looked as though he had been happier when he'd been alone.

Hugh got to his feet. Then, without looking at her, he walked from the room.

She could hear her father calling after him about discussing the settlement, and the muttered reply that they would speak of it in the morning.

Hugh left the room, making his way through the crowd that had gathered and now parted like the red sea before Moses.

Or perhaps it was more like the faithful avoiding a leper. The people around him spurned his gaze, focused instead on the unfortunate girl he had almost ruined.

He wanted to shout at them that he had done nothing wrong. They had been having a simple conversation, in which he had been explaining that there was no way forward for them, when she had forced herself on him and decided without warning to bring the roof down on their heads.

As he thought of what had just happened, he was by turns elated and horrified. Marrying Rachel was all he had ever dreamed of for his future. The thought of her, in his house and his arms, was almost more than he could bear.

But not like this. He did not want to be manipulated into a wedding by society or by her. He had made up his mind long ago that what he wanted and what he could actually have were two different things. Even if he was sane enough to take a wife, and careful enough to avoid getting her with child, there was still the matter of his reputation, which would taint all things between them and make it impossible for her to be seen in society without the censure of women who would never be her equal. She had no idea what she had done in linking her life to his.

But that was his Rachel, always too impulsive for her own good. At one time, it had attracted him to her. Now, it only frustrated him.

He had to get out of here, away from the staring crowds, back to the peace of his own home and the brandy bottle. He drank too much, it seemed, but tonight was not the night to stop.

But now even that was proving illusive. Someone bumped into him, and he looked up, ready to apologise and go around, only to find that the other would not yield. It was the young man who had been dancing with Rachel earlier in the evening. He was glaring up at Hugh in a way he probably thought was intimidating.

Hugh stepped back, ignoring the gasp of the crowd, and staring back in silence to signal that the other man should either speak or move aside.

'You dishonoured Rachel,' the man-child said, refusing to budge.

'Graham. Edward, isn't it? We have not been formally introduced.' He added one part ducal hauteur to his tone and two parts irritated murderer. Normally, it was enough to make even the most persistent fellow back off and leave him alone.

The boy ignored it. 'I demand satisfaction, for Rachel and for the family.'

Hugh rethought his strategy. This was one of those rare situations where he could not just frighten the opposition away. He had to tread carefully to keep from making a disastrous situation even worse. 'It is not your place to demand an apology,' Hugh said in the mildest tone he could manage. 'You are not her father.'

'I am her cousin and Lord Graham's heir,' he countered.

'Well, you have no reason to take exception to me. I am marrying her,' Hugh reminded him, trying not to sound as testy as he felt. 'Beyond that, I do not know what you expect me to do.'

'To trap her into a marriage with the likes of you is no honour,' the boy insisted.

'Trap?' Hugh laughed. If they'd been talking about anyone other than Rachel, he'd have told the fellow the whole truth and withdrawn his proposal on the spot. But, angry though he was at her, he could not do such a thing.

'You are not worthy of her,' Edward snapped, clearly angered by Hugh's lack of response.

'Probably true,' Hugh agreed, trying to mollify him.

'Because you are a murderer.'

At this, the whole room stopped what it was doing and stared in their direction. No matter what everyone thought of the Duke of Scofield, no one had ever said the truth aloud to his face.

This was the moment when he could finally deny it. His sisters were out of his control, after all. Any further deaths need not be laid at his door. There was nothing he could do to protect Liv and Peg, guilty or innocent. He could free himself of the rumours, if he wished.

But he said nothing. Graham's words were an attempt to goad him into a duel, to make him fight to prove his innocence. And if his goal was to save Rachel's reputation, this man, of all people in England, was one that he could not fight.

'Are you not willing to defend your own

name? Then how can I trust you to defend Rachel?'

How indeed? He wanted to argue that it had never been his intention to drag her into this, and that in the end they would both be far happier if she thought better of it and refused his proposal.

But Graham took his silence for further insult. 'You have no answer? Let me answer for you.' Then he hauled back his arm and slapped Hugh across the face.

The sound of the blow rung loud as a bell in the silent room. Slowly, Hugh reached to rub the sting out of his cheek, trying not to laugh. It had been a weak attack at best, and he was tempted to announce that Rachel could have hit him the same way and brought the matter to an end before it had begun.

But the same action from another man was enough to have him arrested for striking a peer. To avoid that, Hugh could probably back down like a coward, apologise for something he had not done and withdraw his offer of marriage. It was clear that, if he did not marry her, Edward Graham would do so. Unless this matter was more about his own pride than it was about Rachel...

Or there was another way out of this. A more permanent way. Hugh could not be forced to deal with what he was not alive to see.

He smiled then, the sort of cold smile that had kept society in terror for two long years. 'Very well,' Hugh said. 'My second will contact you in the morning.'

Chapter Nine

'Were you mad?'

Her father was shouting again.

He had been doing so on and off since they had returned from the ball last night. It was an improvement on her mother, who had retired to her room with a case of the vapours and had been heard weeping for most of the night. Now, she sat in her usual chair across the table, eyes puffed and red, face wan and cheeks hollow, wearing an accusing look to silently remind Rachel that whatever happened now was all her own fault.

'You should have known better than to be alone with him, even for a moment. He is the least trustworthy man in England and you let yourself be taken in by him.'

Rachel let his voice wash over her, leaving her unmoved. She had succeeded in what she'd wished to accomplish, and the rest did not matter.

'It is no wonder that Edward called him out over what he did to you.'

'He did nothing to me,' she said, making her first contribution to the conversation. 'We were alone for but a few minutes.'

'But that is enough to ruin a reputation. And a man with a legacy such as his should know better than to...'

She could not help herself. She laughed. 'You are convinced that a man who would not stop at murder would be halted by fears for my reputation? As if the second sin is greater than the first.'

'You will not be laughing once you are married to the Bluebeard.'

'That is not accurate either. To the best of my knowledge, he has never been married before, much less murdered his wife.'

Her mother let out a wail of misery.

'Do not make light of the situation that you have caused. A good man is likely to die tomorrow, fighting for the honour that you casually threw away. But I suppose you like the idea of men fighting over you.' Her fa-

ther ended the statement with a derisive huff
to tell her what he thought of girls and their
foolishness.

'Do not blame me for what Edward did of
his own volition,' Rachel answered with a
sigh. 'If I had known…' If she had thought
he would do something as stupid as issue a
challenge, she'd have found another way.

Although she still had no idea what that
way might have been. Perhaps she should
have refused him properly before going to
talk to Hugh. Then she would not have left
him with any hope that she was likely to say
yes, had he asked.

For now, she turned to her crying mother,
reaching across the table to pat her hand. 'Do
not worry about me. I have known Hugh for
years and I am not the least bit afraid of him.
I know he means me no harm. And I know
that, despite what it looks like, he is not a
killer. I think he needs me.'

'He is a duke,' her mother reminded her.
'He does not need anyone or anything.'

It was not true, she was sure. No one had
ever needed her more. 'Then we should manage well together. Do not waste your tears
on me. I am going to be married to a duke.

That should be title enough to satisfy anyone's mother.'

Her mother made a scoffing noise and pushed away from the table, storming from the room and leaving Rachel alone with her father.

'That was most unkind of you,' he said, in a mild voice that cut far deeper than any shout.

'I know. But I do not like hearing people speak ill of him,' she said with a sigh, wishing she could make her family understand that this was not the disaster it appeared to be. 'I know he is not who you think he is. And I know that, after a period of adjustment, we will do well together.'

'After he has killed Edward,' her father said with a sneer.

The butler cleared his throat from the doorway and announced the arrival of Mr Graham, who had probably heard them speaking from the hallway, where he'd been waiting.

'Rachel will see him in the drawing room,' her father said, rising to leave the room. Before he went, he turned to her and whispered, 'You have made this mess and now you should be the one to deal with it. Please be kinder to the fellow than you were to your mother.'

As Rachel walked down the hall to meet her cousin, she struggled with what she was expected to say to him that would make any difference.

When she arrived in the room, he turned suddenly, as if she had interrupted his pacing. 'Rachel.' He reached for her, ready to console her.

She did not reciprocate, keeping her own hands firmly at her sides. 'Edward,' she said. 'What have you done?'

'Only what your father was too cautious to do,' he said. 'I do not understand why the family would allow this marriage to go forward when we are all aware of the danger you will be in.'

'I have made my decision,' she said. 'And I am content with it.'

'But what about me?' Edwards replied, giving her a wounded look. 'I thought that I... That *we*...' he corrected, proving that, as she feared, her own place in this was as an afterthought.

'I am not sure what you were expecting,' she lied. 'It was pleasant dancing and talking with you, Edward, but it was never any more than that. I would have explained to you, had you given me enough time. I never expected that you would get yourself into a duel with the Duke. I simply did not think you cared enough about me for that to happen.'

'I cared,' he insisted. But once again he forgot to add the 'about you' that would have made her believe she was anything more than a pawn in his plans to marry by the end of the season.

'If you wait, you will find someone you truly love, and you will see that it is better that way,' she said. 'But, if you do not stop this, someone might end up hurt, or worse.'

'That is the reason behind a duel,' Edward said. 'And I have no intention of crying off.' He was staring at her as if he thought she was simple-minded. 'Something had to be done.'

'And now, something has to be done to save you,' Rachel said, exasperated and starting for the door.

'Where are you going?' Edward asked, stepping in front of the door as if he could somehow control her.

'I am going next door to talk to the Duke,' she said.

'You can't do that,' he insisted.

'Why ever not?' she asked, honestly curious.

'It simply isn't done,' he said. 'There is your reputation to think of.'

'I am engaged to the man,' Rachel reminded him. 'I doubt, at this point, my reputation will get any better or worse based on a single visit.'

'But a duel is a matter between gentlemen and he will not want your interference any more than I do. Leave the details to the seconds,' he warned in the same dark tone he had used when speaking to Hugh last night.

'And if they fail?' she asked.

'Then you don't have to worry about me,' he said with a smile. 'I will prevail against this debaucher and you will have nothing more to fear.' Then he reached for her, as if she was to be the prize at the end of the contest.

She slapped his hands away. 'For the last time, Edward, you have no right to decide my future. You did not offer. If you had, the answer would have been no.' She stepped around him on the way through the door. 'And now, I will go to talk to Scofield about this, whether you like it or not. Hopefully, he will have more sense than you do.' If she could talk Hugh into marriage, perhaps she could talk him out of this duel.

Hugh sat in his desk chair, trying not to think about how the previous occupant would laugh to see him in this situation. The old man had never shown any affection for his children and seeing Hugh's life totally up-ended would have amused him greatly.

For himself, Hugh was more shocked than amused. But, after the events that had taken place in this very room two years earlier, he told himself he should not be surprised at how quickly things could go very, very wrong. Once again, his life had taken a sharp and unexpectedly disastrous turn and this time he was not going to bother to try and right it.

'I suppose you are wondering why I summoned you here,' he began, feeling unusually pompous as he faced his rather confused brother-in-law sitting in the chair on the other side of the desk.

'I assume it has something to do with Margaret.' David Castell had chosen the obvious answer to the question, and for a moment Hugh wished he could oblige him—and himself—by asking some probing questions about his sister's new life. Was she really as happy as she seemed? Was her pregnancy progressing without any issues? Despite what the man must think, he loved both of his sisters and cared about their welfare.

He would not have sacrificed as he had for them, had he not. He cleared his throat and pushed the distraction aside. 'On the contrary. This is a matter between us.'

'Between us,' Castell repeated, with an expression that clearly said there was nothing between them and therefore nothing to talk about.

'I wish a favour from you.'

'A favour.' Now he was likely thinking of the time that Hugh had sent men after him, threatening him with beatings or worse. Thus far, he had done nothing to earn a boon from this man. Any goodwill received from him would have to be offered on credit.

'This will go quicker if you do not repeat everything I say,' Hugh said with a sigh.

'Very well. What do you wish of me?'

'I need a second,' he said, relieved to have it out.

'A second for what?' asked the other man, still unable to grasp the reason for this requested visit.

Hugh continued as if he had not spoken. 'The challenge was issued last night, so I think some time this week would do. The sooner the better. All told, I should not need more than an hour or two of your time.'

'You mean to duel!' Castell said with an incredulous look.

'It was not my intention,' Hugh assured him. 'I was caught in a compromising situation with a lady and made an offer for her, as was to be expected. But the lady's cousin, who is also a suitor, took exception to that because of my reputation and wants me to pay with my life. You can try to negotiate an end to the thing, but I see no way out other than to go through with it.'

'And this role of your second. Would it not normally fall to a close friend?'

Hugh nodded. 'But since I do not have any friends…'

'No friend at all.'

'You are repeating again.'

'Not verbatim,' Castell replied, then added, 'As a newspaper reporter, words are important to me. And this situation needs all the clarity you can give it.'

'Very well,' Hugh allowed, then continued. 'I cannot think of a single man in London who would be willing to do this for me. In lieu of an acquaintance, I thought family would do just as well. And, since you married my sister and were so interested in my story at the start, I did not think you would mind being there at the finish of it.'

Castell responded to this with silence and raised eyebrows.

'Despite what the world may think, I do not murder every man who stands in my way, and I fail to see how killing this one will make life any easier for me. But if I do not shoot him...'

'Then he is likely to shoot you,' Castell finished.

'And step in as an honourable husband to the young lady at the crux of the matter,' Hugh finished. 'If you would be so kind as to speak to his second and agree on a time and location...'

Now Castell's look had changed to one of speculation. 'In honesty, I cannot say I care whether you live or die. But Peg is quite fond of you, despite all the trouble you caused her, and she would be sad to see you go. If I am to have any peace at home, I must expend at least minimal effort to keep you alive.'

'I expect nothing more from you,' Hugh said with a bitter smile. 'A single attempt at peace-making and an honest review of the events as you witness them will be all that is required.'

'I have never seen a duel before,' Castell admitted. 'It should be quite interesting.'

'I sincerely hope it is not,' Hugh replied, then shuffled through the papers on the surface of his desk to find the calling card that had been left with the butler that morning. 'The other participant is Mr Edward Graham. And here is the name of his second.'

Suddenly, there was a commotion from the hall, and Rachel burst into the study, one step ahead of the butler. The poor servant had given up trying to forestall her and announced her to the room with a sigh of resignation.

'You mean to duel my cousin,' Rachel said, ignoring the other man in the room and glaring at Hugh, as if any of this was his fault and not entirely hers.

'I meant to do no such thing,' Hugh reminded her. 'He was the one who challenged me. If he cannot get the idea out of his head, there is little I can do about it.' He glanced at Castell with a hopeless look. 'It seems our conversation is at an end. Please give my regards to my sister. And apologise to her for the current situation.'

Castell had the nerve to grin at him, as if he had some idea how much trouble a woman could cause, then exited the room with a bow in Rachel's direction before closing the door behind him.

Now, they were alone together again. Hugh stared at her, trying to get the nagging suspicion out of his mind that she was up to no good, as she had been on the previous evening. 'What brings you here?' he asked. 'Haven't you caused enough trouble?'

'I am here to end the trouble, not cause more,' she said, giving him an exasperated look. 'I want to put a stop to this nonsense that you and my cousin are planning.'

'And how do you mean to do that?' he asked, honestly interested.

'By showing you both how silly you are being,' she replied, which was really no answer at all.

'We will meet soon on some stretch of flat ground out of the city, with the intention of shooting each other dead. I cannot imagine a more serious situation than that,' he informed her. 'And do not take it into your own head to come charging between us, risking your own life to put a stop to it.'

'Why would you accuse me of such?' she said. 'I have come here *now* to end it. I do not want to wait until tomorrow or whenever.'

'Has your Edward agreed to that?' he asked with a laugh.

'He is not *my* Edward, and you know he did not,' she said bleakly, sinking into the chair in front of his desk. 'He would not listen to sense.'

'If he does not want to back down, there is nothing to be done,' Hugh said simply, pointing to the door.

'You can cry off,' she pointed out.

'And what, exactly, am I to apologise for?' Hugh asked. 'Proposing to you, or being alone with you? I am heartily sorry for both, but no one wants to hear that.'

Apparently, she did not either, for he saw tears forming at the corners of her eyes. For a moment, he almost felt guilty about it. But none of that was his fault. It was all down to her. And she would have reason enough to feel sorry once the shooting started.

'I never intended it to come to a duel,' she said in a whisper. 'I had no idea that Edward would behave so.'

It was clear then that she had no idea what she did to men with her attentions, twisting them around her little finger until they no longer knew which direction was up. He was an example of that himself. It almost made him pity her poor Edward. But it did nothing to change their present fate. 'Well, if there is a next time you decide to act rashly, stop and think better of it,' he said with a shake of his head. 'Now, there is only one thing that can be done.'

'And what is that?' she asked eagerly, jumping at anything that could change what was about to happen.

'You can refuse me and marry Graham. That is what he wants, when all is said and done.'

'Is that what you want?' she asked.

'It is the most sensible course of action,' he replied.

'But is it what you want?'

The question hung in the air for a moment as he tried to form the lie that would make her go away. But the words would not come. At last, he said, 'You should go.'

'Is that all the answer you can give me?' she asked, as if she could press the words out of his mouth when he was no longer sure what he wanted.

'I want this conversation to be over,' he said, sure of that fact at least. 'The duel will go ahead—tomorrow morning, most likely. There is nothing to do to stop it. Now, go back to your house and wait until someone comes to tell you the outcome.'

Chapter Ten

The next morning, Rachel rose and dressed before dawn, then called for a carriage to take her to Edward's rooms. She was waiting on his front steps when his friend called to drive him to the killing ground.

Edward took one look at her and shook his head. 'You are not coming along.'

'If it is my honour that is in question, I do not see why I cannot be there,' she said.

'Because what is to happen is not for a woman's eyes,' he said, huffing the way her father sometimes did when he was tired of reasoning with her.

In response, she laughed. 'You are not the head of the household yet, Edward. If I cannot convince you to call a halt to this mistake, then I mean to be there to see the results of it. It concerns me far more than it concerns you.'

'To me, it is a matter of life and death!' he retorted, amazed.

'It doesn't have to be,' she said, touching his hand. 'It is not too late to cry off. Don't you see that by this duel you are making it worse?'

Her cousin shook his head. 'I will do anything in my power to spare you from this marriage. Nothing can be worse than that.'

'I do not want to be spared,' Rachel announced, hoping that the truth would finally solve everything. 'I love Hugh and want to marry him.'

Apparently, the truth was not as important as what Edward believed, for he was looking at her as if she were an idiot. 'You do not love him, for several reasons. In the first place, you have no idea what it means to love. And in the second, if you did, you would not fix your affections on someone so base and dishonourable as the Duke of Scofield. He is a murderer and a despoiler of women.'

'That is ridiculous,' she said.

'Everyone knows it.'

'They think they know,' she argued. 'But there is no proof that he murdered his father.'

'Then what of Richard Sterling?'

'There is no proof of that either. Only supposition.'

'Then of the last charge, we have proof enough.'

She wrinkled her brow. 'And when has he ever despoiled a woman?'

'You screamed for rescue from him,' her cousin reminded her. 'If that is not reason enough to take up a pistol against him, I don't know what else is.'

'I did not scream for the reason you think I did,' she began, trying to come up with an excuse that would make sense to him. 'I was only startled.'

'You screamed because you were startled?' he asked with a raised eyebrow.

'And I wanted to be discovered so he would be forced to marry me.'

'If you needed to force him to marry you, then he has done something that he shouldn't,' her cousin responded, still stubborn. 'And was refusing to do the right thing in result of it.'

Unfortunately, that was closer to the truth

than she would have liked. But explaining the actions of the past would do nothing to stop her cousin's thirst for blood.

'When this is through, you will be free,' he reminded her.

'What does that have to do with anything?' she snapped, confused.

'If you cannot marry him, it will be best if you marry someone,' he reminded her. 'There will be scandal, else.'

'Someone?' she echoed, confused for a moment. Then, incredulous, she asked, 'Is this intended to be a proposal?'

'I'd have got out the words sooner or later,' Edward replied sheepishly. 'We will suit, you know.'

'I do not,' she said quickly. 'And, if you do propose, the answer is no.'

'You cannot refuse,' he said with a grimace. 'You were promised to me. It was all arranged.'

'It was what?' she demanded, shocked. 'I know that my father favours our match. But you told me that there was time for me to make my decision.'

'And I assumed that the decision would be the correct one,' Edward said, spoiling any good opinion she'd had of him. 'I did not think that you would run directly into the arms of the most dangerous man in London.'

'If I did so, it was my choice,' she said. 'That did not mean that you had to challenge him to try and win me back.'

For a moment, he was the cousin she remembered from childhood, uncertain, boyish and in far over his head. Then, he shook off the hesitancy, and obstinacy returned. 'There is no turning back from this. He must pay for what he has done.'

'He has done nothing,' she cried in a burst. 'It was me all along. I tricked him.'

Her cousin stared at her in amazement. 'Why would you do anything so foolish? He is a murderer, several times over. The letter said…'

'What letter?' she demanded.

At first he was silent, looking like a guilty little boy again. Then he blurted, 'A friend informed me that, before I arrived in London, you flirted with Scofield.'

'I danced with him,' she said, then added, 'Once.'

He ignored her excuse and continued. 'This friend informed me of your betrothed's crimes, enumerating them in a note. It said that he cannot be trusted with women. He abused his sisters horribly.'

'And who is this friend?' she demanded.

'The note was not signed,' he admitted. 'But…'

'You are risking your life and his on an anonymous letter?' she said, her hand to her throat, choking back the horror of it.

'Everyone knows…' he began.

'And everyone is wrong,' she said.

'Then come with me and you will see today,' he said, exasperated. 'Once the pistols are drawn, his true colours will be revealed.' Then he helped her up into the carriage and seated her beside his second, who looked as frightened as she felt at what was about to happen.

The sun was rising as they rode in silence towards an open field on the edge of the city. When they arrived, there was another carriage already waiting. Hugh stood with the man from his study the previous morning. They talked quietly as a nervous surgeon paced in the background.

When he saw her, Hugh's eyes narrowed

and he glared at Edward, his sombre expression changing to anger. 'Why is she here?'

'She would not be dissuaded,' Edward said with a shrug, then went back to his own preparations.

While the seconds were examining the pistols, Rachel walked over to Hugh, who was staring past her as if she didn't exist. 'This madness cannot go on,' she whispered to him.

'It is up to Graham to stop it,' Hugh said with the same blasé air that Edward had assumed. 'Apparently, I cannot marry you to satisfy him, and if I give you up I will be fighting your father.'

'I have tried to reason with him,' she said. 'But he received some sort of letter: an anonymous diatribe against you that pushed him to action.'

'While that is very interesting, there is little that we can do about it,' he said.

'There is one thing that you can do for me,' she said. 'Please do not kill my cousin.'

'Do you believe me a killer now?' he asked with a sardonic twist of his lip.

'I believe he is leaving you little choice,' she said. 'All the same, I beg you not to hurt him.'

At this, he laughed. 'Some men, when facing death, look forward to their betrothed praying for their safety. It appears that I am not so lucky.'

Inwardly, she winced. She had forgotten that he was alone in this, and she should be the stalwart on whose faith he could depend. 'I pray for your safety as well,' she said.

'And if you cannot have both, who do you choose?' he asked.

'Don't ask me to do so,' she begged.

'Then stay out of the way,' he said, and stalked towards the seconds. 'The sun is full up. Let us get this over with.'

Now that the moment had arrived, Edward looked like a scared rabbit, as if finally re-alising the gravity of what he had done. His second handed him a pistol with the quiet assurance that all was in order and that they could begin whenever he was ready.

Edward cast one more look of hopeless desperation in Rachel's direction. Then the two men stripped off their coats and stood back to back.

Hugh did not look at her at all, staring res-olutely ahead as they began to pace off the distance. She held her breath as they turned.

There was a single shot.

Edward stood shivering and holding a smoking pistol, obviously appalled at what he had done.

Hugh was still standing as well, a red stain spreading on his left shirt sleeve.

She made to rush to him but the man who was his second held her back. 'He has yet to shoot,' he reminded her in a soft voice.

And now he faced her cousin, who was unarmed and frightened and had wasted his only protection trying and failing to kill her lover.

The time stretched out silently, one agonising second after another, with the blood trickling down Hugh's arm. The expression on his face turned slowly into something strange and terrifying, making him seem every bit the cold-blooded killer that people thought he was. Edward let out a small whimper of fear and closed his eyes.

When it had reached the point where Rachel's own nerves were stretched to the breaking point, Hugh raised his weapon and fired, deliberately but harmlessly, into the air above his head.

And, for the first time in her life, Rachel swooned.

* * *

Being shot hurt like the devil.

But there was so much that was painful about this event that a bullet wound hardly seemed to matter. Rachel had come to him to beg for the life of another man, as if she thought he was some common butcher who would relish taking the life of any fool standing against him. If she did not believe in him, then he was truly alone.

The loss of blood was making him woozy, but he sent the surgeon to deal with Rachel, who had fainted at the sight of her dear Edward being threatened. He sneered at the thought of it then, with as much dignity as he could, sat down upon a nearby tree stump before he swooned himself.

'It is just a graze,' Castell assured him after ripping away his sleeve and making a brief examination of the wound. 'Once we have poured some brandy in you, we will pour some on it and the doctor will bandage you up, good as new.'

'You speak as if you have experience in the matter,' Hugh said, holding out his hand for the flask and taking a deep drink as the revived Rachel was led un-protesting to her cousin's carriage and driven away.

'Some small amount,' Castell admitted without elaborating. 'Now that I am married to your sister, I have promised to avoid gaining any more knowledge so as not to upset her. This is by far the most dangerous thing I have done in months.'

Did marriage really change a man that much? If it did, he was even more sure than before that he did not wish for it.

'That was a damned cold-blooded thing you did just now,' Castell said. 'There will be an article in my paper tomorrow about a pseudonymous peer facing down his accuser in an honourable fashion and taking no advantage of the unarmed and frightened opponent.'

Hugh sighed. 'I suppose there is no way to avoid the story escaping.'

Castell laughed. 'It amazes me that an innocent man is so intent on keeping the fact a secret. And we know you are innocent, Scofield. After watching you today, I would not say that there is no reason to fear you, but I do not fear that you will murder me or anyone else.'

'I have my reasons,' Hugh replied, concentrating on the sting in his arm.

'Peg feels the same,' Castell reminded him. 'She misses you and is eager to hear of your safety. She was beside herself when she heard of this duel and begged me to see you through it.'

Hugh's throat tightened at the thought of sweet Margaret and her concern for him, comparing it to Rachel and her worries for Graham. 'Tell her I am well,' he said, gritting his teeth in preparation for the surgeon's treatment of his wound. 'And tell her that I will see her soon.'

And with luck he would not see Rachel at all. Now that the deed was done, she was probably congratulating her Edward on his narrow escape, as he suggested a run for Gretna.

The duel had gone better than she had hoped, Rachel reflected. The man she loved was still alive and the matter of Edward's unwanted presence was settled as well. One did not shoot a peer and escape the notice of the law, so he would have to leave London for a while to avoid any prosecution. It was probably better that he be gone before the wedding, as she did not want him standing up in the middle of the ceremony and announcing an impediment or filling her father's ears with foolishness about Hugh's fitness as a husband.

And Hugh... She needed to talk to him as soon as she was able. She had fainted at the sight of the blood on his sleeve and the time he had taken before returning fire. It had been weak of her. As she had insisted on coming along, she should have had the strength to see the duel through to the end. She should have been there to be a comfort to Hugh and to tend to his injuries.

Instead, she had been carted off like an invalid in her cousin's carriage.

Sitting across from her, Edward was silent, finally sobered by what he had done.

'Are you content with the way things went?' Rachel asked, honestly curious to know the answer.

'Honour has been satisfied,' he said in the same ponderous tone he had taken to using when talking to her about her future. 'I will have to flee the city, of course,' he added with a groan of displeasure. 'You can come with me, to Gretna, where we will be married.'

'What?' she asked, sitting up and pulling back until she was in the farthest corner of the carriage, away from him and his second.

'This engagement to Scofield is not really binding. He cannot force you to marry him,' he said with a shrug. 'Since the duel did not go as planned…'

'And just what was the plan?' she asked, liking Edward less with each word he spoke.

'If I had truly prevailed, he would be out of the way permanently. I would still have had to flee the city, of course. But there would be no question of you going with me.'

'Well, there is more than a question on my part,' she said, looking at him in surprise. 'I told you before, I have no intention of marrying you, especially now that you have been foolish enough to embroil yourself in a mess that requires running from the law. Take me home immediately.' She gave the second a pointed look. 'It is your job to see that he acquits himself honourably. And if he, and you, do not turn this carriage towards my father's townhouse, I shall cry at the first stop—and every one after that—that I am being kidnapped.'

'That will not be necessary,' the second announced, and signalled the driver to take her home.

'You will regret this decision,' her cousin said in a dire tone. 'And when you do…'

'*If* I do,' she corrected, 'The matter will be between my husband and me. The fact that you wish to gloat over a thing which will never come to pass is all the proof I need that you are not the man you claim to be. Now, take me home.'

They drove the rest of the way in stony silence. Arriving at her family's townhouse, Edward put her out of the coach without offering so much as a hand to help her to the ground.

She went inside and had to face her parents, who could not decide whether to punish her for sneaking out of the house or demand a detailed description of the action she had witnessed. She assured them that, though they might think Hugh was the last man on earth she should marry, Edward was most assuredly worse.

Then she went to her room to try and write

a letter to Hugh. He deserved some sort of apology for the way things had gone today, and he certainly was not going to get it from Edward. In the end, she sent a carefully worded note enquiring about the wound in his arm and promising him that he would have no more trouble from her cousin.

She finished with an assurance that she would be no trouble either, was eagerly awaiting their wedding and hoped that he would answer to let her know he was recovering.

She signed it with a kiss and a splash of cologne, then dropped it in the pile of outgoing post, praying that it would not be long before Hugh forgave her and accepted that they would finally be together.

Chapter Eleven

To Hugh's surprise, Rachel did not run away after all. She sent him a letter asking about the wound that her idiot cousin had given him, an injury that he'd never have experienced if she had just taken him at his word and left him alone.

The letter was its own kind of hurt, for it reminded him of her behaviour on the day of the duel and how devoted she had seemed to her cousin. If *he* had been fatally struck, would she have spent any time weeping over his grave or would she have sent a weak letter of condolence to his sisters? After a quick read and a moment's indecision, he threw her current note into the fire and refused to answer.

The next day, he received a detailed missive from her father explaining what was expected from him with regard to the impending nuptials. It seemed that they would be proceeding as planned and pretending that the recent contretemps with the younger Graham had never happened.

But, despite following the instructions given, when his wedding day arrived Hugh was no more prepared for it than the day Rachel had tricked him into a proposal.

He had arranged for the special licence requested by Lord and Lady Graham, since he saw no point in having the banns read and allowing three weeks for society to gossip about the match. If it was to be done, better to do it quickly and give the world a chance to forget about it.

He had not bothered to invite his family to gather for what he was sure was a mistake, so he waited alone at the church for Rachel and her parents to arrive with a vicar who looked as frightened by His Grace the Duke of Scofield as the rest of London.

The poor fellow marshalled himself enough to give Hugh a brief lecture on the sanctity of marriage and asked if, under the circumstances, he might wish to confess anything that would clear his mind.

Hugh had not laughed so hard in weeks.

Then Rachel and her parents arrived, hesitating at the back of the church. He turned to stare at her, unable to help himself. She was wearing white today, a muslin gown sprigged with roses the same pink as her lips. And, despite her recent betrayal, he could not help wanting her.

How had something that should be right have gone so very wrong?

He reminded himself that it was never meant to be. She had trapped him into this marriage, which had never been his plan at all. He must not grow soft at the first sight of her, for there was a lifetime of marriage ahead of them and he had to be strong for all of it. There was no triumph here, and certainly no happiness to be gained by this union.

It was supposed to be the happiest day of her life.

But, with her parents' continual fretting and the fact that Hugh had made no effort to contact her, it was hard to keep her spirits up. Still, Rachel was willing to make the attempt, dressing with care and smiling all the way to the church.

Once she got there, things became even more difficult. When they entered at the back of the church, Hugh turned and looked at her with an expression as black as his reputation. It was not at all the sort of welcome she had hoped for, but she must trust that things would be better later, when they were alone.

The vicar glanced from Hugh to her with worried jerks of his head then gestured the Grahams forward so they could begin the ceremony. When he reached the request that any who knew why these two should not be joined speak, he stared out over the empty church, his gaze lingering at the entrance as if he was praying that someone would burst through the front doors and rescue them all.

She let out a sigh of relief as he received no answer, for she had feared that her mother would not be able to resist another fit of vapours. But the moment had passed, and they were getting married, and nothing and no one could stop it now. Only the vows needed to be said and then they would be joined for ever.

Beside her, Hugh looked every bit the dangerous man he claimed to be, simmering with rage at being forced to stand beside her. She would apologise for it later—every day for the rest of her life, if she had to—but if she had not done something she would soon have been standing beside Edward.

The thought made her shudder and the vicar noticed, casting another glance at her groom before asking if there was anything she wished to say.

She shook her head, then reached out to touch Hugh's arm in apology. He flinched and she remembered the wound hidden beneath his coat.

His mouth quirked in a sardonic smile as she withdrew. He then said his vows with a sarcastic snap to his voice, as if to remind her that each promise was delivered under duress.

She should be frightened, she supposed. He was doing his best to scare her out of the church. But she was where she was supposed to be, where he had promised she would be back when they had been in love.

She said her part without flaw, for she had practised it often enough in the quiet of her room, promising to love and to obey, then adding a silent caveat to the Lord that obedience did not mean she would stand for any nonsense in regards to supporting his claim of guilt. Like it or not, she would see to it that this marriage rehabilitated his ruined reputation. Her love would soften him, just as it had before, and the world would see him for the fine gentleman he was.

The moment had arrived for him to kiss the bride. He touched his lips to hers in a kiss that was quick, cold and unlike anything she had received from him before. Then he looked at her with an expression as frigid as his kiss.

'You have what you wanted. I hope you are satisfied with it.' And with that he turned and strode out of the church, not bothering to see if she was beside him.

The wedding breakfast at the Scofield townhouse was a small and dreary affair with only Rachel's parents for company. Neither of them wished to speak to her new husband and he showed no signs of wishing to speak to either of them.

It frustrated her that, though they were far from the *ton* and had only a few footmen for company, he insisted on playing the part that society had set for him, an unrepentant murderer who treated his own family as nothing more than potential victims of his mercurial temper.

Perhaps he thought it would be enough to send her running back to her parents' house. It did not matter to her because she was not afraid of him. Rachel had no intention of leaving now that she had what she'd wanted since the first time she'd seen him. So today, when he scowled, she smiled. He made veiled threats and she laughed as if they were the best jokes she had heard in an age.

In contrast, her parents were clearly terrified for her and for themselves, staring at the wine in their glasses as if they expected every sip to be their last. They spoke to her and each other in hushed tones, shooting glances in Hugh's direction to see if a careless word might be all that was needed to spur him to an act of violence.

She wanted to tell them that everything was going to be all right. For the first time in ages, she knew that her future was going as it should have all along. She had married the man she loved, and the man who she was sure loved her.

But, if that was true, why did he look so angry?

She reinforced her smile and gave her parents a reassuring nod as the meal ended. Hugh's expression was intimidating, of course, but she had seen the man underneath the mask and knew she had nothing to fear.

After pushing his plate aside, the Duke rose, then muttered a brief and cold farewell to her parents before retreating to his study. The minute he was out of earshot, her mother burst into tears. 'We cannot leave you here. We just cannot!' she cried, fumbling in her reticule for a handkerchief.

'If you wish to come home now that you have seen what it will be like, I do not blame you,' her father said in a surprisingly gentle voice.

'I thought that you had consigned me to my fate,' Rachel replied, trying to joke him out of his mood.

'This has gone far enough,' her father replied, now that he could speak freely. 'I know I told you that you must marry before the end of the season. But I am not so hard hearted as to expect you to live with that...' He raised his hand in a gesture meant to convey words he could not bring himself to speak.

She sighed. 'If I need you, which I promise I shall not, you are only one house away.'

'In the house where he murdered his father,' her mother said, then threw arms about her and wept in a way that made the few yards separating their lives seem like hundreds of miles.

'I shall be quite well,' Rachel said, carefully disentangling herself from her mother.

'We shall await your summons,' her mother replied, clearly expecting it within hours.

'I will write to you tomorrow,' she said, offering the only assurance she could think of.

'Or sooner, if you need us,' her father added, offering a brief hug of his own before they departed.

Now she was alone, Rachel went in search of her husband. But when she arrived at the door to the study it was closed against her, and her knock went unanswered. She tried the handle and found it locked, which left her to wonder if he was inside and ignoring her or already in some other part of the house. Perhaps he had even slipped out the back door while she'd been saying goodbye to her parents. She tried not to think of the beautiful woman that he had been meeting in Vauxhall, and the possibility that he might have already escaped his marriage to seek consolation with her.

Really, it should not matter what he did with his life when not with her. Wives were not supposed to make demands on their husband's time, or question how they spent it. If she had married Edward, it might have been no different.

Of course, it would not have hurt quite so much.

She sighed and turned her back on the closed door, reminding herself that there was little to do if he was not ready to speak to her. She must be patient. Now that they were married, she no longer had to worry about losing him. She simply had to wait until his anger cooled, and for that she had all the time in the world.

But that did nothing to fill the empty hours now. Since Hugh had not bothered to introduce her to the staff, she took the liberty of finding the housekeeper and requesting a tour. The woman took her round the house, giving her interesting details about each room before ending at the bedrooms.

The rooms of the two Bethune sisters were

unlocked for her and the housekeeper announced, 'We are not sure what to do with the contents. Neither lady has requested her possessions be shipped to her new home, nor has His Grace given us any instructions on what to do with them.'

'I will ask him what he wishes,' Rachel said, wondering if he would give her an answer. Surely he did not feel the need to punish his sisters for abandoning him? It was only natural that they find husbands and start their own lives and families.

'This is His Grace's room,' the housekeeper continued, opening and closing the door before Rachel could get a look inside. It was just as well, for she dared not show any familiarity with the room, though she had been there several times already.

Then the woman opened the door to the adjoining room. 'And this will be yours, Your Grace.' Her knees bent in apology as she said it, for the room she revealed was woefully out of date, the silk on the walls soot-stained and the rug threadbare. 'It has been some time since it was occupied,' she added. 'The last duke prioritised economy over fashion, even while the duchess was alive. And his son…'

'Made no provisions,' Rachel finished for the housekeeper. 'That is all right. Our marriage was sudden, and we have not had a chance to discuss the matter. I am sure whatever you have been able to prepare for me is good enough.' And it was true. For, though the hangings on the bed were out of fashion, they showed no sign of dust, and her maid had already unpacked her trunk and filled the wardrobe with her clothing.

The afternoon passed quickly and when it was time to dress for dinner Rachel chose a sophisticated gown of ruby silk with a bodice that displayed her breasts in a most flattering manner. She added the thick rope of pearls that her mother had given her for a wedding gift and went down to the dining room to greet her husband.

It was then that she learned she would be dining alone, for there was only one place set at the table. She ate in silence, acutely aware of the eyes of the servants as they did their best to impress their new mistress while ignoring the obvious snub from the master.

It made her wonder what it had been like for Hugh's sisters. Had he been taciturn and cold when they'd been in the house, or totally absent? Had they found some way to lighten his mood? Or had his bad humour worn on them, driving them to escape him by marriage?

The meal passed with no sign of her husband, as did the rest of the evening, which she spent in the main salon, just a door down from the shut and locked study door. Was he still inside? she wondered.

She made it as far as the doorway, standing with her hand on the knob and reaching out to knock with the other before losing her nerve and retreating to her bedroom to retire for the night.

Her maid had laid out her best nightdress, one that she had made herself specifically for her wedding night. She had worked on it for weeks, setting each delicate tuck and stitching down the inlays of Brussels lace in lawn so sheer that she shivered just to look at it.

Even when she'd known it was hopeless and they would never be together she had imagined herself wearing it for him. And now, when it appeared that the moment to join with him had finally come, where was he?

She waited for what felt like hours before

there was the sound of movement in the adjoining bedroom, the hushed voices of master and valet and the sound of the shutting door as the servant left.

She held her breath then and waited for the knock at her door that did not come.

Did he seriously mean to leave her alone on their wedding night? She could not help herself. She strode to the adjoining door and pounded on it. 'Hugh Bethune, you come in here this instant.'

The door opened with a yank that sent her tumbling into the sudden void. But she couldn't fall, for he was standing there as if he had been listening for her, just as she had for him.

He caught her and set her back on her feet. Then he said, 'What do you want?', biting out each word as if it pained him to say it.

'I should think that would be obvious,' she said, glaring back up at him.

His eyes raked her body, making her aware of the transparency of her gown. 'You mean to tempt me into your bed,' he said.

'Or into yours,' she replied, not wanting to seem too particular after all this time. 'You are my husband now,' she added, in case he had forgotten.

Hugh laughed in response, a sour sound, as if he could barely stand the thought. 'Through no choice of my own.'

'You chose me once and would have chosen me again, given enough time,' Rachel said.

'So that is what you think, is it?' he asked with a bitter smile. 'We will never know for sure, since you tricked me into it.'

'Not intentionally,' she said. It was an exaggeration at best for she had meant exactly what had happened.

'Liar,' he responded.

'I did not do anything that you did not want.'

'I wanted…' He stopped, as if he did not want to admit it, then finished. 'I did not want to marry. Ever. Not to you or anyone else.'

'And now, you are the liar,' Rachel said. 'When we were younger, you asked me dozens of times. You swore that we would be together for ever. But in the end, it was only a mistake that got you to the altar. Do you not understand what that meant to me?'

Now his smile turned cold. 'All young men

make promises of that sort and take what they can get from girls who are foolish enough to believe them.'

'That cannot be true,' she said, shaking her head. Her greatest fear, in the last two years, was that what she had trusted as truth was nothing more than the shallowest of lies. But she was sure she was not wrong about Hugh. 'When you kissed me, I felt—'

'You felt what I wanted you to,' he interrupted, his voice taking on a tinge of impatience. 'When I had no more time for diversions, I left you alone. I wanted you to find someone else. Someone…' For a moment, he seemed to soften, as if he had wished for something better for her. Then he gave a wave of his hand, as if conjuring a man who was all the things he was not and said, 'Someone else. But you have forced me to marry you. Well, I have news for you, Your Grace— you cannot force me to bed you.'

'But…' For a moment, she was not sure she had heard him correctly. Of all the potential issues she had considered, difficulty in getting her husband to bed had never occurred to her. 'You love me,' she said. She had assumed that would be enough.

There was a moment of silence before he laughed. The sound of it ripped across her heart like a dull razor. 'I *wanted* you,' Hugh corrected. 'But there are things I want more,' he said, arms folded across his chest. 'I want the Scofield line to die with me. There will be no children out of this union. And the best way to assure that is to stay away from you.'

Then he tugged the door out of her hand and shut it in her face.

Chapter Twelve

The next morning, Hugh was up at dawn and off to Hyde Park to ride before the rest of the *ton* crowded the Row. He wanted to gallop, to run free of the obstacles weighing him down. And for now the chief problem in his life was still asleep in the room beside his own.

He had not got a wink of sleep thinking of her lying a few yards away in a sheer gown. But he had managed to resist her—for one night, at least—by doing an unspeakable thing.

Now, he had to do it again, and each night for the rest of his life.

At first, he feared that his lies were as transparent as her nightgown and that she must know he loved her like his own life. But after she had gone back to her room and slammed the door between them, he had heard the quiet sobs emanating through the wall, carrying on until nearly daylight. He had lain awake in his bed, fists balled against the urge to comfort her, agonised by her suffering.

But it was fair, wasn't it, that they should both feel the pain of this marriage? If he was to be trapped in a hell of lust-crazed longing, the least she could do was be equally lonely and devoid of hope. If she did not already, she would soon wish to get away from him and might learn to enjoy the advantages of the title without relying on his affection to make their union complete.

One of them was going to the country. She would likely want to stay near her family, who lived in London all year long. But he needed to be near his sisters, at least until he could decide whether the disasters of the past were likely to repeat themselves now that the girls were supposedly happily married. Perhaps they could divide the year, with her in the country for the season, and him in town when Parliament was in session. To be separated from the gaiety of the London season was the last thing any woman would want, and a fitting punishment for the trickster he had married.

Of course, Rachel had never expressed any particular love of parties and balls. When they had first met, she'd enjoyed the garden best of all, and had been fascinated by his stories of life at the manor. And lately, she had been quite insistent that the only thing she wanted was to be married to him.

He gritted his teeth against the sentiment of it. While it was quite nice to have a woman who claimed to love him for himself and not his title, he could not afford to reciprocate that feeling. He was the murderous Duke of Scofield. The mad head of a mad family. There was no room in it for a sweet but devious girl who had loved him before he'd come into his destiny. His mind was made up. He would send her away as soon as he was able.

For Rachel, the sun dawned annoyingly bright and cheerful. Its light streamed through the windows of her new bedroom, brightening the colours on the faded rug and warming the bed linens. It was unfair that in a day starting so auspiciously she should be so lonely.

She had been utterly unprepared for Hugh's denial the previous evening. Of all things she had been sure of, it was that, once they had married, she would be waking in the arms of her lover. She had not imagined in a million years that he would reject the opportunity once the ring was on her finger. A part of her was still convinced that when she saw him again he would assure her that it had all been some terrible joke and that he loved her as much as she loved him.

Instead, she came down to the breakfast room to discover that the Duke had come and gone, off for his usual morning ride. As she had the previous evening, she ate alone, chewing mechanically on food that she had no taste for.

For how long would he be angry with her? Was this a temporary situation, or had he truly felt nothing all this time? He had told her he loved her often enough, right up to the moment his father had died. But had she just imagined the sincerity in his voice when he'd done so? Perhaps she had loved him so much that she'd created his half of the relationship, believing that his ardent actions were a sign of something much deeper.

If that was true, then her parents had been right all along. It would have been better not to feel too deeply when marrying. If she had done so, growing affection for her husband could have come as a pleasant surprise. Instead, like a limb after injury in battle, the love had been amputated from her life, leaving nothing but phantom traces and a strange numbness where her heart should be.

How was she to spend her days living with a man who did not even want to speak to her? Her pride refused to show the servants that she suffered. Nor did she want Hugh to see how much his words had hurt her. There would be no pity on that front, she was sure, so it was best to pretend that she was content until she could find some way actually to be so.

For the moment, at least, she was lonelier than she had imagined it possible to be and the feeling showed no sign of abating. She doubted anyone would have the nerve to visit and offer her congratulations. Even when the old duke had been alive, the Scofield townhouse was not the sort of place that one paid calls on. Now that he was dead, it was as if the house was cursed, and the *ton* avoided it.

But that did not mean she could not reach out to others. Maybe, given a little time, she could coax acquaintances into coming to see her. So, she went to the morning room to write letters.

It seemed pointless to write to her mother, given she was only a few steps away from her, but she had promised a letter to prove that she was not dead. What could she say that did not amount to an admission that they had been right and she totally wrong? She composed a short note to inform her parents that the household was well run, and that supper and breakfast had been excellent.

She pondered for some time what she could say about a husband who refused to be in the same room as her, then decided that a short line assuring them that living with Scofield was different from what anyone had expected summed up her marriage thus far.

After addressing and sealing the note, she decided to write to the two people who should be most welcome in the house, and who probably understood how mercurial Hugh could be. She addressed letters to each of her new sisters-in-law, apologising for their omission from the wedding, inviting them to visit and asking if they wanted to return for the contents of their rooms, and perhaps to visit with their brother.

From what she could gather, they had both departed under a cloud and married men that Hugh did not approve of. But if the poor lovelorn fellow whom she'd seen outside was any indication, Olivia had married in a way that would bring her happiness, if not status. Surely Hugh could not bar them from the family for following their hearts?

Then she thought of the way he had spoken to her the night before and wondered if he had a heart at all, much less the ability to empathise with the loves of others. But, if he was too cold to reach out to his sisters, there was no reason she should not. It had been ages since she had spoken to Liv and Peg and now that they were family she could not allow any estrangement to continue.

When she finished the letters, she took them to the hall to set on the salver that held the outgoing post. Almost as soon as she had laid them down, a footman picked them up and walked not towards the door but down the hall to the study where her husband was hiding.

'What are you doing?' Rachel asked, hurrying after him.

'His Grace has final say in what letters leave the house,' the footman said, puzzled as to why she would want to know.

'Not my letters, surely?' she questioned, giving him the sort of face that she thought a duchess would wear when setting down a servant.

'All letters,' he said firmly, ignoring her authority.

Before he could knock on the study door, she stepped in front of him and pounded against it. 'Hugh!'

The door opened and her husband stood, large and angry, filling the doorframe. 'What now?'

'Now?' she snapped, unable to resist striking back at him now that the opportunity presented itself. 'We have barely spoken since we left the church. Do not dare imply that I am imposing on your time.'

She could see by the look in his eye that he wanted to make some surly comment about the imposition of the marriage itself, but he did not want to air the family laundry in front of a servant. So, he stared at her without speaking, waiting for her to state her business.

'Your footman informs me that I cannot send a letter without your approval.' She took a moment to stare him down. 'I told him that was nonsense and that you have no intention of censoring my correspondence.'

Instead of answering, Hugh held out his hand for the letters and the footman handed them over. He glanced down. 'You are writing to my sisters.'

'I thought someone should, as they did not attend the ceremony or the breakfast. I assumed you would not want them to learn of the wedding by reading it in the newspaper.'

He sighed and looked past her at the footman. 'In the future, we will dispense with the need for me to review the day's post. Let my wife do as she wishes.' Had there been a hesitation before the word wife, or had that been her imagination?

'Very good, Your Grace,' the footman said, taking the opportunity to remove himself.

'Thank you,' she said when the servant had

gone, then added, 'Why did you find it necessary to censor the mail before?'

'Maybe I did not want them scattering *billet-doux* about London and then running off with the sort of men they chose,' he said with a shrug.

'Or maybe you caused the elopements by the way you treated them,' she countered. 'One of Edward's complaints against you was the way you treated your sisters.'

'Edward again,' Hugh said with a tone that implied more than two words could hold.

'More accurately, the person writing anonymous notes to him,' she replied. 'That was the person who helped precipitate the duel.'

'It was probably one of my sisters,' he said with surprising conviction.

'Certainly not!' Rachel said, amazed by the accusation. 'I am sure neither of them would want to see you injured, much less killed, if such a plan came to success.'

This was met with a silence that implied that was exactly what he believed.

'They could not possibly hate you that much,' she said, shocked.

'But you do not deny that they hate me,'

he replied with a smile. 'We simply disagree on the degree.'

Perhaps he truly was mad. Or perhaps there were problems in this family that she did not understand at all. 'Then do you not want me writing to them?' she asked, honestly confused by his reticence.

'Do as you please,' he said, his smile turning bitter. 'We both know that you will anyway.' And with that he went back to the papers on his desk, refusing to acknowledge her presence any further.

She glanced down at the letter he was holding, recognising the seal and guessing the contents. 'I am sorry to interrupt you, as you are obviously busy,' she said, trying to restrain her sarcasm, 'But, while I am here, I might as well enquire as to whether we will be attending the Earl of Folbroke's ball. You are holding the invitation in your hand, there. I will accept it for you, if you wish.'

'Who gave you permission to accept invitations?' he asked.

'I assumed no permission was needed, after the discussion on the subject of post we just had,' she said.

'I said you could write to whom you chose,' he responded. 'I said nothing about orchestrating outings.'

'You said nothing against it either,' she pointed out. 'And it normally falls to the wife to accept or refuse invitations.'

'They are only inviting us because they wish to gawk and gossip.'

'Then let them,' Rachel said with a firm smile. 'I would rather that they do it to my face than behind my back.'

'Have you no shame?' he asked, surprised.

'I have nothing to be ashamed of, and neither do you.'

'You cannot know that,' he said.

'Despite the way you are treating me, I know that you are not as bad as people think, and I refuse to live under the shadow of a lie,' she said, praying it was true.

'Very well.' He tossed the invitation in her direction. 'You may go where you want. But do not expect me to come along with you.'

'It will cause even more gossip if I arrive without an escort,' she pointed out.

'Perhaps you should have thought of that before asking to go,' he replied.

'Very well then,' Rachel said, tossing the

invitation back to him. 'Neither of us will go, which I suppose is just as you wanted in the first place.' Then she gathered what was left of her pride and left the room.

The nerve of the woman. They had been married only a day and she was already trying to dictate his evenings to him, making him dance to her tune just as she had with the proposal. If he did not stand firm, she would own his life as fully as she possessed his mind. He had not had a decent night's rest since the day he'd met her.

But, if he was honest, there was never any peace when it came to Rachel. He thought about her when he could not see her. He thought about her when he saw her again and, now that they were married, he thought about her constantly.

He drummed his fingers on the table, then looked at the direction on the invitation she had abandoned. Folbroke. He had intended to attend the ball in question even before the wedding. The smoking room would be full of fellow peers willing to trade support for the bill he had been working on nearly all session.

Of course, now that he was married, he would be required to bring his wife. He had wanted to give the world the illusion that he was capable of behaving himself in public for a few hours without running mad and committing mayhem. To leave Rachel at home would lead to rumours that she was afraid to be seen with him or, worse yet, that she was locked in a room somewhere and not allowed out.

He sighed and rang for the butler to summon Rachel back to the study. When she arrived, he had trouble meeting her eyes. Finally, he muttered, 'I have reconsidered the matter of this invitation. We will be going to the Folbroke ball after all.'

'Will we really?' she said. But, rather than enthusiastic, she sounded suspicious.

'You are correct that there is no reason we can't be seen in public together,' he said. 'In fact, there are certain advantages to it.'

'For whom?' she asked, her eyes narrowing.

It seemed that he had not appreciated her cooperation when he'd had it. Now he was going to have to persuade her to do what she would have done willingly a few moments ago. He took a deep breath and began. 'As part of my duties in Parliament, I need to be able to work with the other members.'

'To appear sane, you mean,' she said with a cool smile.

'I do socialise in some limited sense,' he said. 'You have seen me in public recently because of that.'

'And now you need me to accompany you,' she observed, and a calculating look came into her eyes.

'Because it would be strange for me to appear in public without my wife,' he admitted.

Rachel let out a small, triumphant laugh before covering her mouth to stop it. 'Our marriage will give you credibility.'

'Or take it away,' he admitted. 'Depending on how we choose to act when we are together.'

'This is too rich,' she said, her smile softening to something that raised the heat in his blood. 'You need me. I knew you did, of course. But it is nice to see that you are coming to realise it.'

'I need you to do what you have already

expressed an interest in doing. It will hardly require effort,' he said.

Rachel pursed her lips and shook her head. 'That was before. Now, the cost of my compliance has increased.'

'What do you want?' Hugh asked, resigned.

'Nothing too onerous,' she said. 'One dance at least. The waltz will be the most appropriate, I think.'

'Very well,' he conceded with a nod.

'And something else,' she said, considering. 'I cannot think what, as of yet. You will have to trust me not to demand the unattainable.'

'I am to trust you,' he said, as sceptical as she had been.

'If we are to have a successful marriage, you will have to learn to do so,' she said, still smiling.

'It was never my plan to be a successful husband,' Hugh reminded her, lest she become too comfortable with his cooperation now.

'Because you do not love me,' Rachel said, and for a moment she looked very near to tears. Then the moment passed and her jaw stiffened as she gave him a brutally efficient smile. 'As my parents continually pointed out to me, love is not necessary to have a successful marriage. It is not as if the oxen tied to the same yoke work together because they love each other. They have simply learned that it is easier for both of them if they are pulling in the same direction.'

Were they to be dumb beasts now, sharing a stable and keeping on their blinders? In his experience, that described the situation of many society marriages. But he had never imagined a situation with Rachel that would be so cold. Still, it was better to have expediency than to be continually at war, and he must learn to accept that it was the best they could manage.

'Very well, then,' Hugh said. 'If you will accompany me to this ball, I will allow you to collect the debt at the time of your choosing.'

'And do not forget the waltz,' Rachel reminded him.

'And a waltz,' he agreed, trying not to smile back at her.

'Very well. We shall go to the ball as man and wife,' she said.

'Duke and Duchess.'

'I will not disappoint you,' she replied. And

for a moment he saw a flash of the old, eager Rachel before she smothered it with a frown and hurried from the room.

Chapter Thirteen

Progress had been made.

If she could not get Hugh to admit that their marriage wasn't a mistake, she had at least got him to agree that, in some small way, she could be useful to him. That had to be better than the complete disdain he had showed for her on their wedding night. And it made her feel like less of a fool for wanting to marry him in the first place.

Maybe she had hoped to be lovers when she had dreamed of Hugh in the past. But perhaps there were a host of other feelings involved in the union between man and wife. Helpfulness, for example. Companionship, for another. Her father had spoken highly of security. And, though she had teased her mother about it being better to be married to a duke than a common man, she had to admit that it might be better to be an unpopular duchess than to be no duchess at all. She supposed she would find out the truth of that at the Folbroke affair.

The ball was still a week away and would likely be the last major social event of the season, which meant she would not get another chance to prove to Hugh that she could manage herself in society without embarrassing herself or him. She must make sure that it went perfectly.

This was clearly a case for a new gown, something worthy of a duchess. Rather than moping about the house alone, she decided to spend the afternoon on Bond Street and to visit her *modiste* to discuss a new wardrobe befitting her new title.

Of course, it was not until she arrived there that she remembered she had no idea whether her husband would be willing to pay her bills. Surely one gown would not bother him, especially if it was for an event that he specifically wanted her to attend?

As she was looking through the dressmaker's sketchbook, she felt a strange feeling on the back of her neck and turned to find the other customers looking away quickly as if they did not want to be caught staring. She turned her attention back to the designs, holding first one fabric swatch and then another against the page, trying to decide which would suit.

But it was difficult to concentrate because the silence of the shop made it too easy to overhear the conversations around her.

'The men fought over her.'

'And the murderer married her.'

The comments were delivered in awed whispers that stopped whenever she looked up. She supposed it was too much to expect that the duel and her sudden marriage would go unnoticed. But she had never imagined that the *ton* would manufacture stories about her, as they had with Hugh.

Now, as she moved about the room selecting laces and trims, the other ladies gave her a wide birth. One woman even exited the shop to avoid her.

Apparently, it was as Hugh had said when he'd first warned her that they could not marry—his reputation had marked her to some as untouchable. He spoke from experience, for he had been going through this for the last two years. He might pretend that it did not matter what people thought of him, but in truth he was the loneliest man in London.

Until now. She must remember to include friendship in her list of marital virtues. Perhaps, once he stopped being so angry, he would remember that they had once been friends.

She smiled to herself and then acknowledged the gossips with another smile and a benevolent nod. Hugh Bethune might refuse to admit to the fact that he needed her. But, now that they were married, he need never be alone in this exile again.

The next morning, Hugh rose, exhausted from another sleepless night. To have the woman of his dreams so close and yet so far away was wearing on his nerves and keeping him awake, wondering if and when he might be too tired to resist.

It appeared sooner rather than later. When he went downstairs, prepared for his morning ride, he found that the servants had saddled two horses and his wife, sleepy but stunning in her red habit, was stumbling down the main stairs to go with him.

'You were not invited,' Hugh said as he turned away from her, reaching for his reins.

'Does one need a voucher of some kind to go to Rotten Row?' she said with false naivety. 'I never have in the past.'

'I meant that you were not invited to go with me,' he amended pointedly before he mounted.

'Then we do not have to ride together,' she said, stepping up on the mounting block that the servants had set for her. 'We will simply ride at the same time.'

'I thought I made it clear that I have no desire to be with you,' he said, hoping that a brutal set down might send her scurrying back to the house.

'On the contrary,' she said. 'You told me you did not love me. And that emotion is hardly required for us to take a ride together.'

'All the same, I prefer...'

'That I remain in the house, as your sisters did?' Rachel finished. 'Well, I prefer that we be seen in public together, to assure the gossips that I have not been murdered on my wedding night. You do not have to enjoy my presence. But, for the sake of my pride, I ask you to tolerate it, at least until the honeymoon is over.'

It was pointless arguing with her, for she had made an excellent point. There was nothing to be done to stop the rumours that were spread about him. But he could take some small measures to minimise gossip about her by proving that their marriage was cordial and she had no reason to fear him. So he set out for the park and she followed a few paces behind him, just as she'd described.

The presence of her there was annoying, like an unreachable itch between his shoulder blades. He wanted to turn around and stare at her, drink in the sight that he had wanted for so long.

Instead, he kept his eyes resolutely forward until they reached the park. Once there, she came up to ride at his side, where she was much harder to ignore.

'I do not come here to converse,' Hugh said through clenched teeth.

'I never said you were required to speak to me,' Rachel replied, giving him a brilliant smile. 'But, should someone notice us, it will seem less odd if we ride together in silence than if I trail behind you, looking abandoned.'

It was probably true. 'Very well,' he muttered. 'Ride where you like.' Then he kicked his horse into a canter.

She followed him easily, laughing as a lock of hair escaped her hat and whipped her face.

Despite himself, he glanced over to admire her, and could not help the way his heart lifted as she kept pace with him. She sat a horse as if she'd been born in the saddle, and he imagined for a moment what it would be like to ride with her through the fields around his estate, stopping to rest under the big oak out of sight of the house...

He pulled up short as his mind wondered what would occur next.

'Is something wrong?' Rachel asked, stopping as well.

'No,' Hugh said, shaking his head to dislodge the strange ideas taking root in his mind. This day was just as he'd imagined it when they'd been together years ago. Then, he had not been able to keep a horse in London, and these rides had been a dream. But in that dream he had always ridden with her.

He had found his dream. Why could he not manage to enjoy it, as a normal person might when having a nice day? Why was he trying so hard to spoil perfection?

He watched as another rider passed them, spurring carefully around and turning his head so as not to acknowledge the presence of a pariah. If the new Duchess of Scofield noticed the snub, she gave no indication of it. Instead, she smiled at the road ahead of them as if she could see a future that he could not.

Perhaps, for just a little while, he could allow himself to ride into that happy place with her. They needn't speak, they needn't plan. They might just exist in the moment.

But then he remembered who he was and what he had done, and the moment was gone.

When they returned to the house, Rachel retired to her room to change from her habit and revel in her success.

The ride had gone better than she'd expected. Of course, her husband had spoken but a few words. But they had not been particularly angry ones. Eventually, he had accepted her presence at his side and it had been a pleasant morning, though a trifle early for her tastes. She yawned. But pleasant all the same.

'Rachel!'

When she heard the shout, she was rear-ranging a bouquet of flowers on the bed-side table and trying to make the room seem fresher and more cheerful than it was. But the daisies only made the blue walls seem greyer and she had come to suspect that, without a coat of paint and a new carpet, the place was quite beyond hope.

'Here,' she called back. Now she could hear the thumping of determined footsteps coming up the main stairs. Before she could stick her head out of the door, her husband appeared in the doorway, a piece of paper balled in his fist.

'What is the meaning of this?' he demanded, waving it at her but offering no explanation.

She shrugged and waited.

'I opened the morning post and was sur-prised to find a bill from a Madame Giselle for a new ball gown.'

She nodded. 'I went to Bond Street and bought a gown for the ball you want me to attend.'

'I did not give you permission to spend my money,' he said. 'I did not even give you per-mission to—'

'Leave the house?' she said with a laugh. 'Do I need your permission for that? I am your wife, not your sister.'

'I...' Was it her imagination or was he blushing? 'I am aware of that.' There was an awkward pause as they both remembered the torrid kisses that they'd shared in the past, and what could happen now if they were so inclined. Then he broke the spell, saying, 'I just thought that we would discuss your spending before you took it into your own hands.'

'At the time, I was unaware we would be discussing anything,' she said, trying not to be annoyed. 'You were not speaking to me, and I was wondering how I was expected to manage the house with no input from you at all.'

'It was never my intention for you to manage the house,' he informed her.

'Because you did not intend to be married to me,' she said with a sigh. 'You made that quite clear on our wedding night. But we are married, and there is no changing the fact, even if you wish it otherwise. And you must admit, it is usually the wife's job to take over the running of the household.'

'That has nothing to do with the purchase of a ball gown,' he pointed out.

'I know I have no right to ask it of you,' she said. 'But I will need some money for personal expenses beyond the household budget.' She did not know why it had not occurred to her that he would be difficult over that. His father had been a well-known skinflint, and it appeared that Hugh had picked up some of his habits. 'If it bothers you, I will send the gown back.'

Of course, then she would have nothing to wear to the ball. She thought for a moment, then went to the dressing table and removed her pearls from the jewellery case. 'If you wish to be reimbursed for the money I spent, I have these. I will sell two or three of them at a time, which will cover the cost of the gown and any other things I might buy. There should be enough pearls to last for several months before anyone notices the difference in the necklace.'

He looked appalled at the suggestion. 'Good God, woman, I am not going to make you sell your pearls to pay for a new gown.'

'Then what do you want of me?'

There was a moment of silence, as if he had

trouble finding the right words to answer the question. Then, he took a step in her direction and stumbled over a worn spot on the rug.

'Be careful of that,' she said, too late to do any good. 'The carpet is not in very good condition.'

He glared down at the floor, even more irritated than he'd been before. Then he looked around him, taking in the sad state of the room.

'It has been rather a long time since anything has been done to this room,' Rachel supplied. 'The whole house could benefit from redecoration, but this is the worst.'

Hugh was silent a moment longer. Then he shook his head with disgust and said, 'Take what money you need and redo this room. The rest of the house as well, if you wish. In the future, all bills submitted to my bank will be honoured. Do not concern yourself over the price.'

It was not exactly an apology. Really, it was the opposite of one. It meant that, while he admitted there was a problem, he refused to consult with her about it. He wanted her to change things, but not to bother him. She would have no reason to talk with him at all, which was not what she wanted. All the same, she said, 'Thank you,' and smiled, doing her best to conceal any disappointment she felt.

He nodded and left her to pass the rest of the day in solitude.

But it seemed that he felt some guilt at his neglect of her. That evening, he came to eat in the dining room. And, though he sat at the far end of the table with six feet separating them, it was less like being married to the ghost of the man she had known and more like being with the irritable man he had become.

She helped herself to a thick slice of roast beef from the platter that a footman held for her and said as casually as she could manage, 'It is good to see you, Your Grace. These last nights, I wondered if you might be dining somewhere other than at home.' She held her breath, awaiting the answer.

'I had a cold meal in the study,' Hugh said, focusing on his plate.

'You were not with your mistress, then?' she asked, trying to sound as if it did not matter to her how he answered.

He choked on his wine, then sputtered, 'What made you think that?'

'The woman in Vauxhall was very pretty.' She looked at him over the rim of her glass. 'I assumed that you and she…' She gave a shrug that she hoped was as worldly as that of a duchess's should be.

'It is not your place to assume things about my relationships with other women,' Hugh said in a tone that announced the conversation was over.

He had used the plural and not the singular. Did that mean there was more than one woman to be jealous of? She hoped not, but there was little she could do in any case. She sighed. 'I will not have to assume. I suspect I will be told directly of any relationships you have outside of ours. You are the frequent topic of the *ton* gossips, you know.'

'I take no notice of such things and neither should you,' he said in a firm tone. It was the sensible answer to all gossip, she supposed. But she had already noticed that it was hard to ignore.

A thought occurred to her. 'And I suppose, when you are with your mistress, that you are intimate?'

'This is not something that one discusses

with one's wife,' Hugh said, putting down his glass.

'But we are not *actually* husband and wife,' she reminded him.

'We are married,' he reminded her.

'But you have not bedded me,' she countered. 'Because you do not love me. And you say you do not want children.'

He sliced off a large piece of beef and chewed industriously.

'Does that mean that you are in love with her?'

'The two things have nothing to do with each other,' Hugh snapped.

'So you can lie with a woman you do not love,' she said, verifying her suspicions on the subject.

'Rachel,' he said in a tone that warned her to ask no more questions.

She ignored it. 'But, when you bedded your mistress, how did you keep from getting her with child?'

'That should be none of your concern,' he said.

'And yet, it is. I should think that it is a matter of concern for all married women. And it is not as if we are told such things before we are married. I would think that one's husband is the logical person to ask.'

'You would be wrong,' he said, taking a gulp of wine and signalling that the glass be refilled.

'If there is a way that you and I—'

'I thought I made it clear to you that would not happen,' he said, finishing another glass.

'Hypothetically,' she replied, giving him the most innocent look she could muster.

'It requires restraint,' he said through gritted teeth. 'Restraint that I do not believe I would have, should I be with you.'

'Well, that is flattering, I suppose,' she said. Flattering and unsatisfying. But, if he feared a loss of control, perhaps he'd not been as unaffected as he'd claimed to be on their wedding night. She changed the subject. 'I don't suppose you have thought about what we might do together, other than the things that you have already forbidden.'

'What do you know of these other things?' He sounded shocked.

'There are many diversions in London during the season,' she said with a sigh. 'And I am not planning always to stay in the house, as you wished your sisters to. I have done nothing to earn such restrictions.'

'Diversions,' he said with a relieved sigh. 'What do you wish to do?'

'I thought it might be quite nice to go to the theatre.'

'Then go,' Hugh answered without looking up.

'I thought perhaps we could go together. The Duke of Scofield has a box at the Theatre Royal, does he not?'

Hugh grunted in a way that she assumed was an affirmative.

'That is very handy. We will not have to bother purchasing tickets, like my parents do,' she said with a smile.

'I do not like the theatre,' Hugh said gruffly, sounding like a little boy being told to finish his vegetables.

'How strange. I remember you used to quite enjoy plays, although you seldom could afford to go to them.'

'I do not any longer,' he said, focusing on cutting his meat as if the job required supreme concentration.

'Why not?' she pressed, giving no quarter.

'People stare,' he said simply.

It surprised her. For all his claims that he ignored gossip, this was the first evidence she had that he did not like the life that he had chosen for himself. She must proceed with caution or it would sound as if she was blaming him for a very real problem that was only partly of his making. 'I suspect that they will stare even more when I go to the theatre alone.'

'You will not be going alone,' he said sharply.

She smiled back at him. 'I thought not. It is always more enjoyable to go with a companion.'

'I did not mean…' he began, then stopped, as if unsure of what he did mean.

'I am sorry,' she said, surprised. 'Did you mean that I should not go to the theatre? You will have to give me a reason, if you are delivering edicts of that nature. After all, you do not have to keep me confined to the house to keep me from running away. I came here freely and, if I am to be a prisoner, surely you can accept my parole and be assured that I do not plan to leave you in the first week?'

He sighed, then corrected himself. 'I meant you will not be alone because I will accompany you.' He tossed his napkin aside and rose from the table.

'Where are you going?' she asked, surprised.

'To dress. There is still time to catch the last act of whatever it is that you are so eager to see.'

'All right, then. I will meet you in the hall,' she said, racing for her room to beat him.

As he waited for Rachel to finish dressing, Hugh was longing for his unfinished roast beef. To admit to that fact made him seem much stuffier than he should be at his age. It would be even more churlish to complain about missing his dinner when he had gone out of his way to avoid it the night before.

But it had not been the food he was avoiding, it had been Rachel, who seemed to think it was possible to salvage a normal life from what he could offer. Their marriage was only days old and she was already tired of the solitude that his life demanded of her. The only way he could prove to her that isolation was for the best was to subject her to the curiosity of the *ton* until she went fleeing back to her own sitting room and whatever entertainments she could find there.

Then she appeared above him, hurrying down the steps towards the front door in a rustle of gold silk, one hand resting against her bosom, the other trailing elegantly down the mahogany banister, a brilliant smile on her face. His throat tightened as he took her arm and led her to the carriage in silence.

They arrived at his box in the theatre, much to the surprise of the footman left to tend it, and candles were hurriedly lit for them so that it was possible to read the programme.

As he had expected, the audience declared them more interesting than the action on the stage, and stared openly as Hugh helped Rachel to her seat. Women were whispering behind their fans about the new Duchess, probably the fact that, after so much time with him, she was still alive and unharmed.

For her part, Rachel was unmoved by the attention, focusing on the stage where Puck had just turned Bottom into an ass. The only possible sign of nervousness was her hand toying with the long string of pearls that hung about her neck, and her lips moving silently, as if in prayer. Then he looked more closely and could see she was reciting the lines along with the actors.

He smiled. They had entertained each other many times when they'd been younger, reciting Shakespeare back and forth over the garden wall, like Pyramus and Thisbe in this play. And now, here they were again. He searched for the lines and found them ready in the back of his mind, as familiar to him as the woman next to him.

If he made the effort, for a few hours his life could be exactly as he'd imagined it two years ago. He was married to the woman he loved and they were sharing their favourite story. He signalled to the footman to put out the candles, plunging the box into darkness, and making it harder for the crowd to spy on them. Then he settled back in his seat to enjoy the play.

They were quiet in the carriage on the way home. But it was a different sort of silence than Rachel had experienced on the way to the theatre. Then, Hugh had seemed irritable, as if he wished to prove that the evening would be a disappointment. Now, he was satisfied, and she might almost say happy.

'Did you enjoy the play?' she asked.

He grunted again, but a trace of a smile spoiled his attempt at gruffness. 'It has been a long time since we last read it, hasn't it?'

'We must not wait so long again,' she replied.

'Did the crowd bother you?' he asked, looking past her as if afraid to meet her eyes.

'At first,' she admitted. 'But I expect every duchess has to put up with a certain amount of attention.' This had been worse than that, of course. She had heard the whispers when she went to the ladies' retiring rooms during the entr'acte and watched as a few women had deliberately turned away from her. She had ignored it then, and she was not about to allow it to hurt Hugh by association. She smiled. 'But the play was delightful, just as I knew it would be.'

'True,' he agreed, and she felt him relax in his seat.

'And you were there,' she added, smiling. 'I trust that this did not interfere too much with your plans to stay separate from me?'

'It did no harm,' Hugh admitted.

'And do the crowds bother you?' she asked.

'Yes,' he said without hesitation. 'It is tiring to pretend it doesn't matter. And if I am not careful I am goaded into making things worse than they need to be.'

'Like the duel,' she said with a nod.

'Like the duel,' he agreed. 'I did not mean to do anything that would hold you up to ridicule.'

'I have myself to thank for that,' she said with a sigh. 'As you are quick to point out, this marriage was not your plan.'

'There is nothing to be done now,' he concluded with a shrug.

It was not the affirmation she had hoped for, but at least he did not seem as angry as he'd been before. Rachel sighed quietly, tired but satisfied. She could tell Hugh felt the same, for he had stretched his legs across the floor of the carriage until his shoes brushed against her skirts. She did her best to appear relaxed, not wanting to scare him away from what little contact he was willing to give.

And he had already unbent further than she had expected him to. The evening had been so nice that she had almost forgotten how eager he had been to avoid it. Now, he was smiling, probably thinking of the play.

His smile really was beautiful. Perhaps she'd had too much wine tonight, for she could not help herself from sliding across the body of the coach to sit beside him. 'The story was very romantic, was it not?' she asked, unable to stop the silly smile on her face as she stared up at him.

'One might call it that,' he said, his smile fading as he stared down at her, hunger warring with suspicion in his eyes.

'I remember when a few lines of Shakespeare were enough to move you to kiss me.'

'That was a long time ago,' he reminded her.

'You did promise to let me pick my reward for going to the ball.'

'But that has not happened yet,' he reminded her.

'It is not as if I mean to back out of the ball. I have a new gown, after all.'

He sighed in frustration, but there was still a trace of a smile on his lips that encouraged her.

'I am not asking you to love me,' she said softly. 'It is just a kiss. And how much trouble can we get into in a moving carriage?' she added, trying to pretend she did not know the answer.

'I should not find out,' he said, wrapping an arm around her and drawing her close.

A hundred thoughts rushed through her head along with the desire to assure him that she would settle for whatever he would give, and that a peck on the cheek would be enough, if only he would forgive her for this marriage.

Instead, she waited in silence to see what would happen next.

He turned his head to her, touching her chin with a finger to tip her face up to his. 'I should have learned from the past,' he said. 'You would drive a priest to break his vows with that mouth. What hope do I have?' Then his lips came down to brush hers.

It was delicious, but it was not enough. He must have agreed, for he did not pull away. Instead, his arms tightened about her and the tip of his tongue traced her barely parted lips, asking for permission to kiss her properly.

She relaxed into him, opening her mouth with a sigh and inviting him in. The gentle play of his tongue against hers was heaven, making her forget everything else about the past weeks, leaving nothing but the feel of him, finally holding her as he used to.

'And this is why I cannot trust myself around you,' he said, his head sinking to her throat. 'One kiss will turn into a dozen.'

'Will it really be so bad if all we do is kiss?' Rachel asked, gingerly reaching out to stroke his hair as he kissed her.

'You are so hard to resist,' he whispered. 'And in this gown…' His hands reached to cup the under sides of her breasts until the nipples crested above the neckline of her bodice.

'Then don't,' she said, leaning back into the squabs of the seat and letting him take them into his mouth one at a time. He had kissed her there before, when they'd been younger. But then he had been gentle and she had still been learning the pleasures of the flesh.

Tonight, after years apart, he was eager and not afraid to be rough. The stubble on his chin raked against her skin, awakening nerves that she didn't know she had. And when his teeth grazed the hardened buds sensation shot through her body, pooling in her core.

As if he sensed what he needed, his hand dipped beneath her skirts and possessively roved up her thigh until it settled in the delta between her legs. She was on the brink of true happiness. The lightest brush of his fingers would be enough.

Then the carriage drew to a stop and his hand withdrew. The footmen were coming to open the door and she yanked her dress up to cover her breasts and smoothed her hair, embarrassed. Then she remembered that she was married, and their behaviour was not nearly as shocking as it would have been a week ago.

Beside her, Hugh was quiet, his eyes and his mood dark. He followed her into the house, then walked to his room and slammed the door without another word.

Chapter Fourteen

That night, he dreamed of loving Rachel.

That was the problem with a single kiss. It led to more, and yet more, and then a night of dreams and seeking release in solitude that felt lonely instead of satisfying.

He did not want to be alone in his room. He wanted to open the door between the two of them and finish what they had started together. It was why he had avoided marriage in the first place, knowing that he could never be with her in the way he wanted to.

The next day, he skipped his ride and went back to his study, and even he had to admit that he was hiding, just as she had accused him of doing. It seemed his denial of love for her had been only partially successful. If last night's dinner conversation had been any indication, she was already testing the boundaries of what could and could not be done by people who were not in love. He must hope that his noncommittal answers had convinced her that his needs were still being met by a mistress and that he did not require a wife for satisfaction.

He had hoped to distract her carnal curiosity with the trip to the theatre. He had not expected to enjoy it as he had. With the light low in the box, watching the actors on the stage, he had felt human for the first time in ages. For two hours, he had been like any other audience member, wrapped up in the story playing out in front of him.

Then it had ended and they had gone back to the carriage, and in the dim light and close surroundings it had been too easy to forget himself. As they'd kissed, he'd felt human again. It did not matter to Rachel if he was a duke or the keeper of a madhouse. When she looked at him, she saw only the man that she loved.

The temptation of it was both delightful and terrifying. If he recanted his lie and asked her to run away with him, taking nothing but the clothes on their backs, she would do it.

They could start again, somewhere else, and leave his problems behind. He could forget it all.

And do what? Even the humblest tradesman had a skill of some sort with which to support his family. But that man could no more become a duke than Hugh could stop being one. He could not imagine a life where he was not Scofield. What would he do with his time?

He could not leave his sisters behind either. If one or the other of their foolish husbands was murdered because of his carelessness in letting them escape, the death would be on his head.

There was a knock on the door and the butler entered with a calling card. 'Mr Solomon to see you, Your Grace,' he said with a slight raise of his eyebrow to indicate that he did not like riff raff cluttering the receiving rooms, even when they were family.

Since Mr Solomon had been an employee before he became a brother-in-law, Hugh could hardly blame him. 'Bring him here.' It would be easier to speak to him in the study and to remove any sense that he was entertaining an equal.

A short time later, Solomon was brought before him and the butler withdrew, shutting the door behind him.

'It surprises me to see you here,' Hugh began, giving the fellow a thoughtful look. It seemed that marriage suited him. The restlessness in his character that had been there before was now missing.

'It surprises me to be here as well. I had thought, now that your sister and I are married, that there would be no more trouble between us.'

Hugh looked up at the man standing in front of his desk, allowing the silence to stretch an awkward few seconds before gesturing to the chair and giving the fellow permission to sit. 'Believe me when I say, Mr Solomon, you are the last thing on my mind.'

'Then do me the courtesy of your full neglect,' the other man responded. 'In short, stop trying to assassinate me.'

'What?' Hugh snapped to alert.

Solomon held his hands out as if shielding himself from objections. 'I know that Margaret and her husband are convinced that it is not you that was behind the murders.'

'How generous of them,' Hugh said in a dry tone.

'But we all suspect that you know more about the identity of the killer than you are saying. If it is someone in your employ, or some acquaintance, or some woman that you feel honour-bound to protect…' He paused dramatically.

Hugh reached for the decanter on his desk and poured himself a brandy. Then he thought on it and poured one for Solomon as well. 'I have no idea what you are talking about.'

Solomon pulled away his cravat and revealed a long, thin bruise about his throat. 'Someone set upon me with a garrotte when I was walking home from my club last night. And, two nights before that, I was very nearly pushed off a bridge and into the river.'

'Someone is trying to kill you,' Hugh said numbly. It was just as he had feared. But there was very little he could do about it now other than to trust that the fellow was fast on his feet.

'That is what I have been trying to tell you,' Solomon said in a tone that suggested he was surprised that he had to explain himself. 'And I want it stopped.'

'It is not me,' Hugh said, and realised that it was the first time he'd spoken those words in two long years. 'It was not me. It was never me.' As the evening with Rachel had been, the phrase was liberating. He felt another dangerous rush of freedom.

'Your lover, then?' Solomon suggested. 'Peg and Castell claim that there was someone else in the house the night that your father was killed. A mad woman.'

'Where did they get that ludicrous idea?' Hugh snapped.

'The housekeeper confirmed it.'

'Then I shall have to have a talk with her about her loose tongue,' he said, letting the old menace creep back into his voice before he could stop himself.

'This is not about what your housekeeper revealed,' Solomon said quickly. 'It is what we learned subsequently. We know you tried to have this woman committed.'

'I… How…?' He shook his head, wondering how they had found information that was safely locked away from the family. 'You are sorely mistaken if you think this has anything to do with…' What was he to call Rachel now? The answer was obvious and yet foreign to him. But was there a need to keep the past a secret?

He took a breath. 'What I am telling you now is not something I wish commonly known. I am now married to the woman who was in this house the night my father died. She had nothing to do with the murder. We were together the whole time.'

'Your wife,' Solomon said thoughtfully. 'That will be a relief to your sister, who has been beside herself with recent news about you and the fact that she was not invited to the wedding. She has received a letter from the new Duchess and was unsure whether you wished her to answer.'

'I am sorry for that,' Hugh said awkwardly. 'I did not think…' He had not thought that she would want to come back after the way he had treated her. But apparently, he had been wrong.

'I will convey your apologies,' Solomon replied, leaning forward to take another sip of his drink. 'And what about the letters to the asylum that were found?'

'Where and by whom?' Hugh asked, his eyes narrowed.

'Margaret and her husband discovered them in your mistress's apartment.'

He had not kept Martine in almost a year but had not bothered to rid himself of her apartment as the rooms came in handy when he did not want to upend the household by returning home late.

'I suppose I have the annoying scribbler Castell to thank for the discovery of that space?' he said. It was probably unfair of him to speak so of someone who had just helped him, but there had been a time when Castell had been set on proving him a murderer, and the fellow had been a damned nuisance then. 'I suppose this explains why he has left me alone since they married.'

'They were under the impression that you did not want to see them, since you did not answer Peg's letters,' Solomon replied.

'True as well,' he agreed. 'I have handled things badly.'

'But that does not answer my question about the asylum.'

'I do not think you will like the answer I have for you. And that is that you need look no further than your own house for the one I sought to contain.'

'Olivia?'

'Or Margaret. I have never been sure. Perhaps I should get a cell beside them, for if I were to commit them there would be little reason left to enjoy my life in freedom. But, if you are experiencing mysterious attacks, I would question your wife for the source of them.'

'Then insanity must run in your family, Scofield, for I could not think of a more ludicrous idea.'

'You may think what you like. I know I did not kill our father. And there were only two other people in the house on the night it happened.'

'Three,' Solomon reminded him.

'Rachel had no reason to kill the Duke,' Hugh said. 'More importantly, she did not have time. She was barely in the house before the screaming started.'

Solomon continued to look sceptically at him. 'I do not care what you think. I know your sister as well as my own heart and she is as sane as you or I. Even if she was not, she would never do such a thing.'

'Then Margaret,' Hugh said automatically.

'Have you ever asked her? Either of them?' Solomon asked.

'If they were innocent, I did them no harm in treating them with caution. And if they were guilty?' He tried not to shudder. 'How could I live with their confession? I looked at asylums. But I would not kennel a dog in the best of them, much less send a member of my family. And if they were found and prosecuted...'

Solomon was staring at him as if he could not quite understand what he was hearing. 'You may think this is the logical answer, but that does not make it true. You have to have more evidence than supposition.'

'I have more reason to suspect them,' he said. 'But believe me that, if you love your wife, you do not want to know it. You could not live with yourself if you knew.'

'It would not matter to me,' Solomon insisted, 'Because I am sure that I was attacked by a man. Not even a mad woman would have the strength that I felt in the hands that gripped my throat.'

'If not them, and not me, then who?' Hugh asked, honestly perplexed.

'That is an excellent question,' Solomon replied.

'Until we can find an answer for it, do not travel alone,' Hugh said. 'If necessary…'

'You will set a guard on me?' Solomon finished, amused.

It would be embarrassing for Hugh to admit that he had been thinking something very like that.

'I have been fine thus far,' Solomon replied. 'I will be careful. And if I learn anything I will tell you of it immediately.'

'I suppose I cannot ask for more,' Hugh said, rising and escorting him to the door. 'Send the best to my sister.' *And do not let her kill you,* he added silently.

Then he went back to reading his mail.

Chapter Fifteen

He had been married to Rachel for almost a week, and it seemed they had achieved a sort of truce. In many ways, it was like not being married at all. She did not question his movements, as she had on the night they had gone to the theatre, probably because she had convinced herself that he was still keeping Martine.

He made no effort to disabuse her of the mistake. He dined with her on some evenings and disappeared to his club on others. He told himself that these absences were to remind her that she had no claim on his time or his heart but, though they were painful, they were for his benefit as well. Sometimes, the temptation of having her near grew too much to resist and he had to get out of the house.

He tried not to think about what had happened in the carriage. It had been a lapse in judgement that preyed on his mind, especially when he was alone in his room at night. There was some consolation in the fact that Rachel had moved down the hall to a different bedroom while her room was being repainted. Unless he meant to roam the halls in his nightshirt, she was temporarily out of reach until such time that he could relocate her to his estate in Suffolk and get her properly out of his life.

The thought should have given him some relief. Instead, he felt even more uneasy, as if the distance would be an insurmountable gap and not a day's travel. It was ridiculous. They were married now. And, though it was unwise to see her every day, moving her to the country would not cut her out of his life. He could see her whenever he wished.

But he wished to see her all the time.

Since this had proven unwise, it was best to continue with the original plan.

But she was also very good at making him wonder why he wanted to be with her at all. One day, when he came home from a day spent at the club, instead of the peace and solitude of his study, he found a footman there, balancing on a ladder in the window, waving a tape measure at the curtains.

'What the devil are you doing?' he shouted, causing the man to step back and almost tumble to the floor.

'Her Grace's instructions,' the man said, clinging to the draperies for stability. The old fabric ripped in his hand and the gash left a scar of sunlight across the carpet.

'Rachel!' Hugh shouted. The word and the volume were familiar in his mouth, as was the sense that he was losing control of his life with each day he spent with her.

'Hugh,' Rachel said, appearing in the doorway and smiling at him as if she had just discovered gold. 'You are back so soon.'

'What is going on here?' He gave an expansive wave.

The footman took the gesture as his cue to leave and darted down the ladder, under Hugh's raised arm and out of the door.

As he passed, Rachel snatched a paper and pencil from his hand and looked approvingly at the figures on it. 'We are measuring for new draperies. I was hoping to surprise you,' she said, and her smile seemed to grow even brighter at the prospect.

'I do not like surprises,' Hugh said, giving her his sternest look. 'And I do not like people meddling with my study.'

'You gave me permission to redecorate,' she reminded him.

'Not my private space,' he snapped.

'Your space?' she said, arching an eyebrow. 'Tell me, when was the last time anything was done with this room?'

'I do not know,' he muttered. It was likely the same time as the late duchess's rooms, a renovation so far in the past that there was no way he would remember.

'Then, really, it is not your room at all,' Rachel said firmly. 'It is your father's study. You just inhabit it.'

'My father is dead,' he said, as if any of them needed to be reminded of the fact.

'And you did nothing to change the room after that happened other than clean up the mess,' Rachel said with a shake of her head.

The answer to that stuck in his throat. He could remember how it had been to be working those first weeks in the shadow of the old man's ghost. To step over the threshold was enough to fill him with dread. But he had bullied through the trouble with raw nerve and brandy, and it had been easier recently. Or so he'd told himself.

She did not give him a chance to affirm or deny but pressed on. 'You are working at the desk where the body was found, walking on the same carpet...'

He remembered his first sight of the room, with the body still slumped over the desk, and tried not to shudder. 'It does not bother me.'

She reached out to the decanter of brandy that sat beside the desk and tipped the liquor in the bottle to show it was three quarters empty. 'Things are well, I am sure.'

'I have more than enough reasons to drink,' Hugh snapped. 'You, for example.'

He had meant to say that the loss of her had made him over-imbibe. But the words had come out wrong. And now the coldness of the first days had returned to her voice and there was a faint sense of injury in her reply. 'Then I will make sure that the decanter is filled when the redecorating is finished. But I assumed with the end of the season you would not be needing the room as much as you have. Unless you mean to continue hiding in it, of course.'

'I was not hiding,' he said, though that was precisely what he had been doing those first days. He could not understand why he was fighting with her now, for he had no reason to love the room—which was not comfortably shabby, as he'd told himself, but dreary, tattered and full of terrible memories.

'Of course not,' Rachel said in a voice dripping with irony. 'On our wedding night, you preferred to eat a cold supper at a dead man's desk than have dinner with me.'

She made it sound foolish and childish and he hated to admit that she was probably right. 'But I am eating with you now,' he said.

'Occasionally. And barely speaking to me when you do,' she snapped.

He had thought the silence comfortable compared to the dinners he remembered with his family, that had been nothing but arguments and threats from start to finish. But, apparently, she was not satisfied with what he could offer. 'At least we were not arguing, as we are now,' he replied.

'We are arguing because I did exactly what you gave me permission to do,' she reminded him.

'Then I should not have given you permission to do anything,' he said, exasperated.

'You are trying to treat me as you did your sisters, controlling every element of my life.' Rachel shook her head. 'Just as your father did to you, when he was alive.'

'I am nothing like my father!' He had not meant to shout. But then, he had not meant to give anyone the impression that his motives were the same as the last duke's. He took a breath. 'It is not my intention to control each element of your life, nor did I mean to be as tight-fisted as my father. I was leaving this room the way it was because it gave me comfort.'

'I do not believe you,' Rachel said, staring into his eyes as if she could see into his soul. 'Perhaps you could fool someone who does not know you as I do. But I know that there was never any comfort in this house when your father was alive and I do not see why you would find it now.'

She was right. Without meaning to, he was becoming his father. Even without the excuse of having two sisters to watch, he was controlling and tight-fisted. He had stayed in this room, drinking to forget the faint stains in the rug and the sight of his father's body. He had allowed his wife to move into a room that was hardly fit for habitation, refusing to see that twenty or more years had passed since it had been cared for.

And, because she was Rachel, she had said not a word of complaint. She had even offered to sell her wedding gift to pay for a new gown.

The wedding gift she had got from her parents. He had got her nothing. He had not even bothered to send for the jewellery in the lockroom at Scofield Manor.

He could not help that he had been angry at the way this marriage had come about. But, if he expected her to perform the duties of a duchess, the least he could do was treat her better than his father had treated his mother.

He closed his eyes and took a deep breath to clear his head.

'I am sorry. I do not mean to act the way I do towards you. In my sisters' cases, I had reason to be cautious.'

'You were an overprotective brother,' she

said, completely misunderstanding the situation. 'But they are both gone now, and happily married. You don't need to worry about them any more.'

'I will never stop,' he said, remembering Solomon's visit and the recent attacks.

'Your diligence does you credit,' she told him, patting him on the arm. 'But things are quite different, now that I am here.'

'Of course,' he said, surrendering with a sigh. 'If you wish to redecorate, then do as you will with this room. It does not matter to me what it looks like.' If it kept her distracted until the end of the season, then he was a fool to complain.

She beamed at him and he felt his heart lurch in his chest. 'You will not be sorry.' Then, before he could stop her, she rushed to kiss him lightly on the lips and ran from the room.

It was wrong to think of each interaction with Hugh as a battle, but Rachel could not help but think that she was winning the war. Though he had been shocked to realise her plans for his study, after she had pressed him on it he had agreed that something needed to be done.

She shivered. Even the thought of what had happened in that room frightened her. It was a wonder that he could think at all when sitting in it.

To break the chill, she stepped out into the garden. There was no reason that she should let the palpable gloom of a single room ruin an otherwise beautiful day. Taking the bench under the oak tree, she tipped her face up towards the dappled light of the sun shining through the leaves and closed her eyes.

Then, from behind her, someone cleared their throat. When she turned to look, she saw a man standing at the back gate, watching her through the wrought-iron bars. They stared at each other for a moment in silence as she tried and failed to remind herself that the correct social response to such rudeness was to cut the stranger dead by ignoring him.

Then, as she watched in shock, he reached through the bars of the gate and manipulated the loose latch, as she had done many times, and let himself into the garden.

'I beg your pardon,' she said sharply, trying to muster an outraged stare that would put this stranger in his place.

'And I beg yours, Your Grace,' the man said with a deep bow. 'I needed to speak with you, and I could not think of another way to arrange it.'

'Other than to invade my private garden, you mean,' she said, watching uneasily as he approached. He did not look like a threat, and his hands were held in front of him as if to prove his harmlessness.

'Might I have a moment of your time?' he asked, stopping a few feet away in the shadow of a shrub,

'I do not know you, sir,' she said, looking back towards the house for help.

'And if you did, I doubt I would be welcome here,' he admitted. 'My name is Alister Clement, and when I was courting Lady Olivia your husband did everything possible to frighten me away.'

'Olivia is no longer here,' she said, rising to go inside.

'I am aware of that,' he said, taking a step to follow her. 'I feel her absence with each beat of my broken heart. But my concern now is with you.'

'With me?' she said, too surprised to send him away without a hearing.

'Surely you must know of your husband's reputation?' he asked in a disapproving tone.

'Since the accusations are not true, it is not something that concerns me,' she said with a chilly smile.

'You believe your husband is innocent?' Now he was the one who was surprised.

'I do not believe,' she said. 'I know he is innocent.' She gave him what she hoped was a confident smile, pleased to finally meet the gossip that trailed after Hugh with the contempt it deserved.

'How can you be sure?' he said, his head tipped to the side as he awaited her answer.

She considered for a moment. The only truth that mattered was one that she had no intention of sharing with her friends, much less a man that she had just met. Then she realised that there was a truth just as important that he would understand if his heart was as broken as he claimed.

'I know that Hugh is not guilty because I know him. I love him. He is not the man that people think he is. And I will no longer stand for people whispering behind my back, much less walking into my private garden and making accusations.' She smiled at him again, quite proud to be taking the initiative on this rather annoying problem.

'It surprises me that your husband is not equally insistent on his innocence,' Clement said with a sarcastic grin.

'Perhaps he thinks it is beneath him to answer to every person who wants to spout nonsense about his reputation,' she said, hoping that this was the case.

'If it is not him, then he should be conscious of the fact that the murderer is still out there and might strike again.'

She had never thought about that. If the last duke had been a victim, might Hugh be in danger? Surely, if he was, something would have happened by now? 'Thank you for your interest. I will warn my husband of the risk.' She glanced at the gate to indicate that the conversation was over.

'I have not come to warn him,' Clement said with an exasperated shake of his head. 'You are the one that is in trouble. You have married into a cursed family. You need to beware.'

She could not help herself. She laughed.

'Me?' Then she saw Clement's offended look and realised he was probably not used to having his concerns tossed back in his face. She sobered and said, 'I had not thought of that. But I suppose it is possible. I will take care, Mr Clement. And thank you for your warning.'

'If you need anything…anything at all… please come to me. And for the sake of all that is holy, trust no one.' He reached out to her and pressed a calling card into her hand.

'If I need your help, I will write,' Rachel said, glancing towards the gate again. 'And now, I think it wise that you leave before my husband notices your presence.' She did not want to use Hugh as an excuse, but something told her that he would not be happy if he realised Mr Clement had visited.

The fellow nodded. 'Farewell, Your Grace. And take care.' Then he was gone and she was alone again.

Chapter Sixteen

When Hugh returned from his ride the next day, the house was ominously quiet.

When his sisters had first gone, he'd found the lack of noise depressing. But now that Rachel was here the silence worried him even more. She had forgone the morning ride, mentioning that she had other plans for the day, but had given him no hint of what they might be. It likely meant she was up to something that would destroy what little peace he had left.

His fears were confirmed when the servants directed him to the green salon, where his wife was entertaining a gentleman visitor.

A gentleman. And the doors were closed. The jealousy that rose in him was as hot and strong as it was irrational. Unable to help himself, he grabbed the door handles and pulled, barely resisting the desire to shout, '*Aha!*' as he stood in the opening, staring at her and…

He was not sure what he'd expected but it was certainly not Mr Pilkington of the Bow Street Runners, hat in hand and being served tea by the Duchess of Scofield.

'Rachel,' he said, trying to keep his tone calm, as one would when finding a loved one staring into the teeth of a rabid dog. 'Are you aware who you are entertaining?'

'Of course, darling,' Rachel said, giving him a radiant smile that left him foggy-headed at a moment when he needed all his clarity. 'This is one of the inspectors who was here the night your father died.'

One of the inspectors indeed. He was the chief inspector and the bane of Hugh's existence for weeks afterward, grilling him with endless questions and making it quite clear that the answers were not satisfactory.

'And to what do we owe the honour of this visit?' He directed this to Pilkington, who was staring at him with the same narrowed gaze he had used that night.

'I invited him,' she announced, clearly

proud of her brilliant idea. 'I did not think you would mind.'

'Because an innocent man has nothing to fear from the law,' Pilkington announced in a ponderous tone.

'Of course not,' Hugh said, feeling his mouth go dry.

As if she could sense it, Rachel pointed to the tea and said, 'Shall I call for another cup?'

'That will not be necessary,' Hugh said, hoping the moisture he needed to speak was not sprouting on his brow.

Now she was looking between the two of them, as if trying to draw together a conversation. 'Did you know that Mr Pilkington has no further suspects in the case?'

'I assumed, if he was doing his job and had found the murderer, he'd have informed me of it,' Hugh replied, holding Pilkington's gaze as it narrowed even further.

'There has only ever been one suspect,' the officer replied without blinking.

'And yet, so little evidence,' Rachel said, clucking her tongue. 'You admitted to me now that you had nothing other than Hugh's presence in the house on that night.'

'And the threat he made at dinner,' Pilkington added.

'But people have often heard him make such threats before and since. And yet, the people he threatened are still alive,' she pointed out.

'Not all of them,' Pilkington responded. 'Two were murdered.'

'And could that not also be a sign that someone is trying to make him seem guilty?' she suggested in a reasonable tone.

At this, Pilkington was silent, probably too busy locked in his staring contest with Hugh to give an answer. Fortunately, two years as a duke had given Hugh the gift of the superior glare and he used it now to the best of his ability.

'Was that a nod, Mr Pilkington?' Rachel asked innocently. 'I don't believe I heard your answer.'

'It is possible,' the man admitted slowly. 'Other explanations are far more likely.'

'But the likely answer is not always the right one,' she said, helping herself to a biscuit.

'Do you have some evidence to support

your claim?' Pilkington enquired with a raised eyebrow.

'No more than you have to support yours,' she replied.

'But I have an instinct about such things,' the officer admitted.

'And I am a woman, and therefore naturally intuitive,' Rachel replied with a smile. 'I am also married to the man you are accusing and can find no trace of murderous violence in him.'

Hugh was tempted to announce that she must not be looking very hard. If he could have murdered the Runner with a glance, it would have been done long before now.

'While a witness to his character is a fine thing, it surprises me that His Grace cannot speak for himself,' Pilkington replied with a note of triumph.

'Because I do not dignify such things with a response,' Hugh said automatically.

Rachel sighed. 'I said he was not violent. But I will admit that he is stubborn. Or perhaps there is another name for it, when one is a duke. Imperious?' She considered the word as she sipped her tea.

Now the Runner looked at Rachel with the

same penetrating stare he had tried on Hugh. 'You are disappointing me, Your Grace. I had come here in hopes that you had some information to give me pertaining to the murders. But it appears that is not the case.'

'And I invited you here to see if you had any real information about the crime. Apparently, that is not the case.' She gave him another of her perfect smiles. 'You may finish your tea. But, after that, this interview is at an end.' Then she gave him a look that was as worthy of any duchess he had seen, staring the man down until he bolted his tea and excused himself.

When they had heard the front door close and were sure that the Runner was gone, Hugh closed the salon doors and exploded. 'What was the meaning of that?'

'I wanted to know if the Runners had more information than they'd let on.' She smiled as she refreshed her cup. 'Even after two years they have no idea who committed the crime because they are too intent that it is you.'

'I am aware of that,' Hugh said. 'And just what made you think I would allow that man back into this house?'

'I did not think I needed permission to entertain a guest,' Rachel said, batting her lashes at him and feigning innocence.

'Pilkington was not a guest. He is an adversary,' Hugh said with a snarl.

'Not mine,' Rachel replied, her expression unchanged. 'And I had your interests at heart when I summoned him. I think it is for the best that we know what he knows. And that he knows that I do not believe a word of the speculation about you.'

'I do not need your help,' Hugh said firmly. The last thing he needed was for her to upset the delicate balance of his life and set the Runners looking for the real murderer.

'That is the problem with you, Hugh,' she said, shaking her head. 'You are always so insistent that you do not need me, and yet you do. You are certainly not doing that well on your own.'

'I was doing perfectly well,' he insisted, trying to remember a moment of the last two years that had felt like a success.

'Well, then, I am not,' Rachel said with a stubborn set of her chin. 'I cannot bear to see you suffer as people accuse you of something you have not done.'

'I am not suffering,' he insisted. But why did his voice not sound as confident as it once had?

'Do not lie to me,' she said, her eyes as narrowed as the Runner's had been. 'It is bad enough that you will not tell the whole truth. But do not lie.'

'I am used to things the way they are,' he said. That was much closer to the truth, at least.

'Like the study,' she said. 'But things are changing. Your sisters are both gone and I am here now. And I refuse to allow you to take the blame for something you did not do.'

'I would rather it be that way than that they learn the truth,' Hugh said with a sigh.

'And what is that, exactly?' she asked. 'We both know that you are not the killer. But that means that the real murderer is walking free and might kill again.'

'I will not let that happen,' Hugh said, knowing he had already tried and failed.

'If he has killed one Duke of Scofield, he might kill another. Now that I have you, I cannot bear to lose you.' The sudden impact as she threw herself into his arms was enough to knock the wind from his lungs.

He held her. How could he resist? It had never occurred to him that she might be worried for him, and it was both flattering and inconvenient. He did not want her exposing truths that were better buried in an attempt to help him. 'Do not worry about me,' he said, kissing the top of her head and pausing to inhale her scent. 'I have lived this long without incident. I doubt there will be a problem in the future.'

'But what if there is?' she insisted. Her face grew pale, and her eyes seemed to grow even larger as she looked up at him. He was losing himself in the blue depths of them, and in her fear that something might happen before they had spent even one night in each other's arms.

'It will be all right,' he assured her, dropping his head and kissing her. And for a moment everything was all right. She nestled close to him, the gentle friction of her body raising old memories of passion-drugged hours and the future he had promised her when he'd still had hope.

Her arms stroked his back, both comforting and seeking comfort. 'As long as we are together, nothing else matters.'

He nodded, then carefully disentangled

himself from her arms, fighting to regain control. 'We will be all right,' he repeated. 'But please, do not try to help me again. Things are fine as they are.'

'I will try,' she said with a sigh. But, when he looked into her eyes, there was a spark of unquenched rebellion waiting for the moment she forgot her promise and tried again.

He loved her.

He had not said it in so many words, but she could feel it in the way he held her. Even he had to admit that things were better, now that they had each other. But the feeling raised almost as many questions as it answered.

If he loved her, why had he insisted he did not? Or, as Edward had said, was she just confused as to what it meant to be in love? And did he feel the same for his mistress as he felt for her? Worse yet, was the feeling stronger?

And what was she to do about Hugh's desire to leave things as they were? He must know that it would be impossible to do as he wished. If she had not meddled, they would not be married, and he would still be sitting alone with a brandy bottle in his father's study.

She nodded in approval as a pair of footmen hung the last panel of the drapes at the study window. The afternoon sun streamed into the room, bringing out the colours on the Aubusson rug she had chosen.

She took a deep breath and smiled. Even the air felt better, like lemon and beeswax from the freshly polished bookshelves that would be behind the new desk. She ran her hand lightly along the neat row of journals bound in red leather, the date of each year embossed in gold on the spine.

Then she paused. There was a book for 1812 and another for 1814. The current year had been sitting on the surface of the desk. But 1813, the year of the old duke's death, was missing.

'Your Grace,' the butler called from the hall. 'Are you ready for the new furniture?' Two more servants were grunting under the weight of the mahogany desk chosen to replace the old one.

'In a moment.' She took note of the papers on the surface then stacked them carefully on a library table on the other side of the room. Then, she turned her attention to the drawers, pulling them out and stacking them beside the papers, so she might transfer the contents. The first three opened easily but the last one resisted.

Then she noted the little brass lock, which was barely protection at all if Hugh meant to keep the contents secure. She pulled a hairpin from a curl and went to work. The drawer yielded easily and she pulled it out, ready to put it with the others.

Then she looked down. The missing journal sat on top a stack of papers. She stared down at it for a moment, trying to resist. Then she scooped it up, dropped it into her pocket and went back to the rearranging of the room.

When he returned home for the day, Hugh went to his study and paused at the door in amazement. In the few hours he had been gone, the room had been transformed from the familiar into a place he did not recognise.

The draperies, the carpets and the furniture were all new. He knew the chair by the fire as a mate to the one he found most comfortable when in the salon. The new paper on the walls was his favourite shade of green.

How had she known? They must have discussed personal preferences at some point in the past during the times when they had shared everything with each other. It embarrassed him that he could not recall what she had said to him on those occasions, for it was clear that she had memorised his words for exactly this moment.

As he entered the room, he felt immediately at ease. He could hear the sound of birdsong from the garden outside, no longer deadened by the hangings on the window. The rug under his feet was soft and clean. The stuffy hunt paintings on the wall had been replaced with scenes of the places he had visited on his grand tour. This room was so obviously for him that he did not want to leave it.

'Have the renovations been completed on Her Grace's bedroom?' he asked a passing footman.

The boy shook his head. 'She wanted this done first, and quickly, so that it did not disturb your work.'

'I see,' Hugh said softly. If she had wanted his life to be undisturbed, she might have done nothing at all. But he had to admit, now that he saw the finished project, she had been right to try and change his life. He had not noticed how the sight of the study had depressed him until she had removed the problem.

As she often did, she was putting his needs before her own. He smiled. It might have been nice if she had allowed him to voice his own desires, or even decide what they were by himself. But he had to admit, she had chosen well.

He stepped further into the room and ran a hand over the highly polished wood of the new desk. The papers that he had left on the surface of the old desk had been replaced in approximately the same place on the new one. Alongside them rested a key ring with the small brass key that would unlock the drawers of the desk.

He fitted it into the lock and opened it, surprised to find the contents of his old desk had been transferred to the new.

Almost all the contents, at least.

He ran a quick hand through the papers, searching for the red leather journal that should be in the left-hand side, but finding nothing.

'Rachel!' He rose and went to the open doorway, searching both ways down the hall. She stepped out of the salon, slowly walking towards him, the journal in her hand and a shocked look on her face.

'Hugh?' She held the book out to him, as if asking for explanation.

'How did you get that?' he demanded.

'I opened the drawer,' she admitted. 'But I did not think…'

'That I would mind your rifling through my personal things?' he finished for her.

'I did not intend to read it. But it is the journal for the time we were together. And I could not resist seeing what you had said.'

'That is also the year my father died,' he reminded her. 'You looked at that, didn't you?'

'There was nothing to see,' she said hurriedly, proving that she had indeed looked.

'After I wrote the story, I tore the pages out and burned them,' he said with a shudder. 'I did not want anyone to see what I had written there.'

'This makes you look guilty,' she said, holding the book out to him. For the first time since they had reunited, her face was full of doubt.

'And that is why I kept it locked in a desk drawer,' he replied with a laugh. 'I did not intend for it to be read by you or anyone else.'

'I cannot un-see what I have read,' she said. 'But you can explain it to me.' She came into the study and dropped the book on the desk. 'Your secret is safe with me, whatever it is.'

'Even if I have done something unspeakable?' he asked, watching her closely.

'I am your wife,' she said, holding out her hands to him. 'I can help you, if you let me.'

He looked around the room, searching for a way to avoid the conversation that he knew was coming. But it wasn't the same room, the one that had held his secrets for so long. It was as if she had reached into his heart to create a safe place where he could be the man he was meant to be.

He could refuse to speak of it. But, until she had read the journal, her faith in his innocence was the one true constant in his life. If he did not tell her the truth, her imagination might create something even worse than what he had actually done.

Now she followed him into the room and shut the door behind them, leaning against the panels as if she feared he could grab her and put her out.

'Tell me the truth,' she said. Then she waited.

Chapter Seventeen

She never should have opened the drawer,
much less read what she had discovered there.
Now, instead of enjoying the redecorated
study, Hugh seemed to have aged ten years.

'You think you understand what happened
here the night my father died. But you only
do to a point. Much happened after you were
gone and I made sure that the people who
knew of it could never speak a word of it.
Are you really sure you want to share the
knowledge?'

'I was here that night and it changed my
life, as it changed yours,' Rachel said, staring into his tired green eyes. 'I want to know
the real reason that you rejected me and are
rejecting me still. If our vows in the church
mean anything at all to you, know that I own

a share of whatever it is you are hiding. Give it to me.'

He gave her an anguished look, as if this burden was the last thing he wished to give her. Then, he began. 'The night of the murder—before I met with you—I argued with my father at dinner over money.'

'Everyone knows that,' she said with a dismissive wave of her hand. 'The servants spread the tale almost immediately.'

'But no one mentioned that it was not the least bit uncommon. As a family, we argued often and over everything. Sometimes I thought that the old man enjoyed seeing us at each other's throats. My sisters wanted money as much as I did and that night they were arguing over a dress. Peg had been wearing Olivia's gowns about the house and angling for a season. There was one gown, a green net, that was in particular contention. Olivia claimed that Peg had ruined it.'

'What does any of this have to do with your father's death?' she asked.

'The night it happened, as I was going up the stairs to wait for you, I saw one of my sisters in a green dress going into my father's study.'

'Which one?'

'I am not sure,' he said with a shrug. 'Father refused to spend money on candles if it was only family in the house and did not keep the halls lit. That night I did not see much more than a flash of blonde hair and a swish of that green skirt before the door closed.' He gave her a sad smile. 'Since we were up to no good, I did not want to see her any more than I wanted her to see me.'

Rachel had not thought of it at the time, but the house had always been uncommonly dark when she'd visited it. All the same, there was nothing about what he was claiming that seemed worthy of melodrama. 'So you saw one of your sisters going to wish your father goodnight,' she said with a shrug. 'There is nothing so mysterious about that.'

'When I was called downstairs to see the body, there was a green spangle in the blood on the desk. No one noticed but me. I hid it.'

Rachel laughed, for she could not help herself. 'You are not accusing your sisters of the crime of murder?' It had to be a coincidence, or a mistake. Nothing more than that.

'I did not want to,' he said. 'It was Olivia who found the body and she was wearing a blue dress when she did so. It was different from the one she had worn at dinner. And Margaret was wearing her nightgown when I saw her next. Neither one wore green.'

'I can see why you did not tell the Runners such a tale,' she said. 'It would have seemed more dishonourable for you to accuse your sisters.'

He gave her an exasperated look. 'People have been hanged on less information than that. I had my suspicions, but the Runners wanted it to be me. They could not prosecute without evidence, so I held my tongue and let them believe what they liked.'

'And is that all?' she asked, unimpressed.

'If that had been all, I'd have chosen to forget, assumed it a trick or a mistake. But the next day a maid came to me with a scrap of the gown, stained with blood and charred from burning. She said she found it in the fireplace of an unused guest room.'

Rachel frowned. There was likely an explanation for it, but she could not think what it would be. 'Did you go to your sisters to ask about it?'

'Later, after things had settled, I asked them both. Olivia claimed to have given it to Margaret, and Peg said she did not know what had happened to it.'

'Strange for a dress that they liked well enough to fight over,' she admitted.

'I wish that were all,' he said, shaking his head as if he did not want to continue. 'The next night, the maid that came to me with the dress was found dead on the lawn. Strangled with Peg's hair ribbon.'

'I heard nothing about this!' Rachel said, shocked.

'Because I saw to it that you did not,' he replied, sinking into a chair and burying his face in his hands. 'I did not call the Runners. I made the footman who had found her get a cart from the stables. Then I drove to the Thames and dumped the body.' He shook his head again and reached for the brandy bottle that sat on the side table, pouring a glass for Rachel as well.

She took it and drank, letting the liquor burn its way down her throat, and gasping for air.

'And that is the sort of man you have married,' he said with a bitter laugh. 'One that treated a family servant as if she had no value at all.'

'The poor girl,' she whispered. 'Did no one ask after her?'

'The butler assured me that she had no family. Even so, the poor thing deserved more than I gave her. I pensioned the butler and sent the footman that helped us home to his family with references and a heavy purse. And then I set to keeping my sisters out of society so that what happened to their maid would not happen to anyone else.'

'You punished both of them?' she asked, shocked.

'What else could I do? The evidence conflicts. And I have searched for years for a clue that did not point to them. Everyone in the house can be accounted for. One of them did this, which means one of them is surely mad. And if one is mad, then perhaps both are.' He was shaking his head again. 'Perhaps I am as well. I can assure you, I am not as sane as I was when I began this and madness often runs in families.'

'But surely, since nothing has happened in two years…?'

He laughed. 'Less than one year. Despite my efforts to contain them, Olivia has been meeting men in secret. Her suitor Richard

Sterling was found in the river with a knife in his back.'

'It could have been a coincidence,' Rachel suggested, not really believing her own words.

'Coincidences happen too often in this family,' Hugh said with a bitter smile. 'The *ton* has no problem believing that I was the one that killed him. And I have no trouble believing it was one of my sisters. Probably Liv.' He paused. 'I cannot manage to believe Peg capable. But that is because I am too soft, not because she could not manage it, if she thought she was protecting her sister...'

'And now they are both married,' Rachel said.

'And Liv's husband has been attacked on the street,' Hugh added, taking a drink. 'The man might as well have dug his own grave by marrying into this family. And you...' He reached out to take her hand. 'If I have put you at risk...'

'What reason would anyone have for hurting me?' Rachel asked, then took another sip of the brandy and tried not to think of one.

'What reason would they have to leave you safe? What reason has there been for any of this?' Hugh asked with a shrug. 'That is why I fear madness. Sane people do not solve their problems with wholesale butchery. Their actions cannot be predicted.'

'And you have been taking the blame all this time?'

'Because nothing could be done to me,' he said in a tone that made it all sound very logical. 'The protection of the peerage does not extend to my sisters. And I have seen the sort of places that they could be remanded to, should charges be brought. Horrible prisons, and hospitals and asylums nearly as bad. And then there is the hangman's noose. I don't know if my influence could save them.'

'Surely it would not come to that?' she asked, not wanting to believe.

'I do not know how else it will end,' he said. 'And now they are both out of my house and I have no control over them at all. I have but to wait for their husbands to discover what sort of family they have married into. Solomon has already been here, complaining of attacks on his life. It is not over,' he said with another shake of his head.

'You did your best,' she assured him.

'And it was not good enough. Now that I have lost control, it is beginning again.'

'And there is no reason to believe that it is a family problem. You are not affected,' she said, still not wanting to believe.

'And there is no way to prove that it is not,' he said. 'I do not think I am likely to run mad and kill as my sisters might, but I am prone to nightmares, black moods—melancholy and hopelessness that never seems to lift. I did not want to risk your future by intertwining it with mine but, now that it has been done, I refuse to bring a child into the world only to have it suffer as I am suffering.'

It did not make his rejection of her any easier, but it at least made sense.

'You understand what this means for us,' he said. 'It is why I do not want to take the risk of lying with you. Whatever this is, it must end with my generation.'

'I understand,' she said, still not sure that she did. 'But that does not mean that we cannot be friends.'

'Friends?' he said, as if the word was alien to him.

'I am not afraid of you. I never was,' she reminded him. 'I understand you better than anyone else in the world. And we are married, after all. I should think that makes us friends.'

He laughed. 'You make it sound easy. It is not. At least, not for me. My past friendship with you led to nothing but trouble.'

'Surely it was not that bad?' she asked, biting her lip to fight back the sob forming in her throat. If he could speak thus of their past, she wondered if she had truly understood anything that had happened between them.

'I took advantage of your innocence and you wasted your future because of it. Now you have roped yourself to me and there is nothing I can offer that will give you the future you deserved to have. That is why I would prefer it if distance is kept between us. Anything more will make our lives more complicated than they need to be.'

'It is almost the end of the season,' she reminded him. 'Perhaps it will be easier when we are out of London.'

'We?' he said, his eyes darkening.

'In the past, you have retired to the country at the end of the season,' she reminded him. 'Except for last year, when you remained...' She blushed, for the statement made it clear how closely she had been watching him during their separation, mooning after him from a few yards away.

'Because of my sisters' needs,' Hugh said. 'I thought it best to stay here.' Then he cleared his throat. 'This year, there is no reason you cannot go to Suffolk. I suspect there are many improvements you will need to make on the house. It has been some time since there has been a lady in residence. Not since my mother was alive, and she died at Margaret's birth.'

'Are you sending me away?' Rachel demanded, shock in her voice.

'Not away,' he muttered. 'The estate is mine, after all. You like riding. The gardens are very fine, and larger than the one we have here. You will be very happy there.'

'I did not marry you for your property,' she said, unable to hide the hurt from her voice.

'And I did not marry you to listen to you argue,' he said, then changed his tone. 'It will be easier for both of us if we are not together.'

'Because you are afraid that your children will be mad,' she said.

'Because I am afraid,' he agreed, unashamed to admit it. 'Now that I cannot watch out for my sisters, I had hoped for a small degree of peace in my life, and I will not find it sharing a house with you.'

'I see,' she lied, then added, 'But the season is not over just yet. We will have two weeks together at least. I am sure we can learn to make the best of it.'

He smiled back at her, clearly relieved that she was agreeing after only a small amount of argument. 'I think we can both control ourselves, now that I have explained what is at risk.' Then, before she could make an objection, he held out a hand for the journal she had been holding. When she offered it to him, he locked it in the drawer of his new desk, then sat down and contentedly began shuffling his papers as if all the problems they had discussed were settled.

Without another word, she left the room. She had much to think about and even more to do.

After her departure, Hugh leaned back in his chair, suddenly weak. Perhaps it was the wound from the duel that was still bothering him, or perhaps it was simply the conversation they'd had and the weight that had been lifted from his spirit.

Someone knew.

She had always known part of it, of course. But her conviction of his innocence had been more of a problem than a relief. What was the good of having an alibi when one did not dare use it? The assumed truth of what had happened here had clung to him like mud. But the reality was worse and he had not wanted to expose her to it.

But now? He had told her everything, and she had not left him. He could not manage to express the feeling of waking each day, for years, and fearing that there would be another death to cover. Or the dreams that plagued him of the feel of cold, dead flesh and the final splash as a body slid into the river. How could she understand or forgive a thing that he could not forgive himself?

But she had listened, and she had not run.

It was as if he had been bound so long that he had lost all feeling. And, suddenly, someone had cut one of the ropes. Sensation was flooding back into his dormant spirit.

And it ached.

The sudden return of feeling made some hurts even more acute. What was he to do with a wife that he wanted but could not have?

Would it ever be possible to speak freely to her whenever he wanted and have her listen, as she had today? Of all the things he missed about the old times, he'd forgotten how much he liked talking with her.

He had been so intent on the journal and its contents that he had forgotten to thank her for what she had done in the study. When he looked around him, the space was as comforting as a hug. Now that the book was locked away again, it was as if the problem was contained and he was free of it.

And, though it was bittersweet, in a week or two he would be free of the continuous temptation that was Rachel. His life would be lonely but safe. He could not hope for much more than that.

Chapter Eighteen

Rachel stood in the doorway of the Duchess's suite, staring in approval at the servants hanging paper and taking down the old draperies. She had done much good since coming here and would do even more, given the chance. But she could do nothing for Hugh if he carried out his plan to cart her off to the country like so much unwanted furniture.

Two years ago, when she had convinced him to allow her into his rooms, she had been impulsive to the point of foolishness, but they had never been discovered. When she had tricked him into marriage, he had been angry. But, with time, she was proving that he had no reason to hate her. Even if he was no longer willing to love her, they were just as well suited as they'd ever been.

Today, she had shown a similar lack of foresight when she had gone through his desk drawers. But it had come out right again and precipitated a revelation that Hugh had managed to keep hidden from everyone else.

She could not deny that her impulses sometimes led her to wild and unladylike activities. But she meant no harm, and it seemed that her instincts were good. Everything worked out for the best.

Which led to the question of what she should do now. She could allow Hugh to proceed with his plan and abandon her in Suffolk, alone and unloved. And he would be here, lonely and in the same city as the exotic beauty from Vauxhall Gardens.

It was probably unworthy of her to be so jealous. But she had seen the way that woman had looked at Hugh, like a hungry lioness staring at a meal. It would be extremely unwise to leave him alone with her.

She glanced out of the window into the peace of the garden and was surprised to see Mr Clement sitting on the bench under the oak tree. He seemed to notice her and raised a hand in welcome, beckoning her to come down and speak.

She hurried down the back stairs and out through the kitchen door to find him still waiting, a smug smile on his face, as if he felt he belonged there. He gestured to the empty dog house. 'I must say, this space is much nicer now that Olivia's dogs are gone from it. I miss her quite horribly, but it would be a lie to say I miss those dogs.'

'You really are not allowed here, you know,' Rachel said with a worried shake of her head and a glance at the study where Hugh might be.

Clement sighed. 'I have treated the space as my own for so long it is difficult to let it go. Olivia and I met here, you see.'

She nodded, thinking of her visits to Hugh, and wondering if his sister had had the nerve for such intimacies under an open sky where anyone might have seen them. She suspected not. But that did not make her time with Clement any less precious. 'But, in the end, she did not choose you?' The question was part commiseration and part a reminder that what this man had shared in was over.

'Solomon came along,' Clement said with a

frown and a shake of his head. 'He was here and everything changed.'

'And Olivia…' Rachel said, thinking of all Hugh suspected about her. 'Were her affections for you not true?'

'They seemed so,' he said, shaking his head. 'I do not know what Solomon could offer that I could not. But he came and everything between us changed.'

He might not know but, having seen Mr Solomon, Rachel was able to speculate. While Mr Clement might claim to be miserable at the loss of Olivia, it was Mr Solomon she pictured when she thought of one suffering from a broken heart.

But today, she gave Mr Clement's hand a pat and tried encouragement. 'I am sure you are sad for now. But there will be other women, and other loves.'

'Not for me,' he said firmly. 'Never for me.' His jaw was set and his expression cool. He looked as Edward had when he'd insisted on the need for a duel, as if his will had been thwarted and he had no real interest in the reason that the woman he'd chosen had not chosen him.

'Well, Olivia no longer lives here,' Rachel

reminded him as gently as she could, wishing he would go away and take his bitterness with him.

'Are you aware of her new direction?' he asked, staring at her expectantly.

It was in the house in her writing desk. But what would it do for the poor fellow other than give him an excuse to haunt someone else's garden? A white lie would be a mercy. She shook her head. 'Hugh and his sisters are estranged, and he would prefer that I not try to heal the breach.'

'That is most unfair of him,' he said.

'He is the master of the house and there is little I can do without his permission.' Another lie. But she much preferred that he think it was Hugh's idea to keep him away from Olivia and not her own.

Clement reached into his pocket and offered her another of his cards. 'If you discover her location, please contact me. If only so that I may see her one more time.'

'Of course,' she agreed weakly, trying not to shiver as he excused himself and exited through the gate, latching it behind him as if it were his own property.

* * *

That night was the night of the long-awaited Folbroke ball, her first official appearance as the Duchess of Scofield. She dressed with the same care she had on her wedding night, donning the gown that her *modiste* had guaranteed was designed to set tongues wagging. It was blue silk a shade deeper than her eyes, with skirts sprinkled with diamante stars and a bodice cut lower than anything she had worn in public before.

She looked in the mirror and smiled. It was not the *ton* she meant to attract with this daring ensemble. If Hugh did not notice her tonight, he was as dead as his father.

There was a knock on the door and her maid appeared, arms laden with several jewel cases. 'His Grace said they are yours if you wish them and to take what suits you.'

'Thank you,' Rachel said, trying not to frown. She had imagined Hugh draping her neck with sapphires, his touch hot on the skin of her throat and his breath tickling her ear as he whispered his appreciation of her looks. But apparently he could not be bothered and she was to do it herself.

She refused to let the maid see her displeasure. 'Let us see what he has sent.'

She rejected emeralds as the wrong colour, and the pearls as too common. But the third box held a rather simple necklace of silver chains adorned with a single diamond drop that rested in her cleavage and drew attention to her breasts. After Rachel put it on, they dressed her hair with matching silver combs and diamond pins.

Her look complete, she stepped back from the dressing table to admire herself. She looked older than she had just a day ago, sophisticated and knowing, very like a married woman and not the scared virgin that she was. Most importantly, she looked how she imagined a duchess should look.

If she could do nothing else for Hugh, she could make him proud when they were in public together and be the sort of woman he deserved to have married—one who was gracious and beautiful and who held her head high above the rumours that people wanted to spread. There would be talk, of course. There always was when Scofield went out in public. But perhaps this time people would find something good to say about him.

Her preparations finished, she went downstairs to wait for her husband, praying that he had not changed his mind about the whole affair.

As his valet put the finishing touches on his evening clothes, Hugh tried not to think about the night ahead. The outing was likely to be a disaster, but there was nothing to be done about it but force his way through.

He was used to the censure of society and could take it or leave it alone, as he needed. But it had never been his intention to put Rachel through the gossip and snide comments that had become a matter of course for his appearances in public. Knowing what it would be like for her had been one more reason to avoid any chance at a relationship between them.

Her trips to Bond Street and the theatre had given her a taste of what was to come. Unfortunately, the only way to teach her was to let her experience the full derision of the *ton* when attending a ball. Somehow, when one had dressed in one's finest and was feeling well, the whispers hurt more than the idle murmuring that happened at other times.

He let his valet place an emerald stick pin in his lapel and then trotted down the stairs towards doom.

He was halfway to the ground floor before he noticed the vision awaiting him in the hall. The blue silk clung to her body, barely covering her soft white breasts. Diamonds sparkled in her black hair like stars in a night sky. And suddenly he was two years younger and seeing her with all the carefree hunger he used to. His heart was in his throat; it was impossible to speak.

Apparently, she had no such trouble. 'I did not think I'd be ready before you,' she said, staring up at him where he was frozen in place on the stairs. 'I was afraid you'd changed your mind.'

'No,' he said, and slowly continued his descent, trying to appear as if he was in control of his own life and not ready to offer it to her. 'I gave my word.'

'Of course,' she said, as if just realising the significance of his promise.

'We do not have to go, if you have changed *your* mind,' he assured her. 'We can stay in.'

She laughed at the idea. 'With you in the

study and me alone in my finest gown? No thank you. I have had enough of that.'

That was not what he'd imagined at all when he'd suggested it. Instead, he could picture himself, his head in her lap, telling her how he had missed her as she stroked his hair. Then they would go upstairs to his bedroom and he would show her all the things he had promised so long ago.

But then he remembered that there could be none of that, regardless of whether they stayed in or went out. Either way, he was trying to keep his distance, if only to preserve what was left of his sanity.

'We are going out, are we not?' she said. His silence was clearly making her suspicious.

'Of course,' he replied, signalling the footman to summon the carriage, leading her out of the open door and handing her up into her seat. They rode in silence to the ball, and he hid in the shadows on his side, still amazed to find himself married to this goddess.

She had tricked him into it, of course. But tonight he had to force himself to remember that he had ever been angry. Would it really be so bad to succumb to her charms? They could not have children, but perhaps they could come to some understanding. At dinner before the theatre, she had been curious about the pleasures of the flesh that had had nothing to do with procreation. If he could remember to withdraw, they could enjoy all of them. But, if he did not want to embarrass himself in public, if was not something he should be thinking about now.

They arrived at the Folbroke townhouse and Hugh took Rachel's arm, escorting her in and listening to the audible gasp as the footman announced the Duke and Duchess of Scofield. Hugh felt no flinch from the woman at his side, to her credit, and when he glanced down at her, her expression was as serene as if she had walked at his side for a lifetime and not less than a month.

The hostess took her hands as they reached the receiving line and announced her eagerness to meet the new Duchess, and without thinking Hugh searched her face for traces of sarcasm, but it seemed that the countess was sincere. As was her husband, who greeted him with a smile.

Then they passed through the receiving line and came out on the floor surrounded by the other guests. Rachel dropped his arm and readied herself to disappear into the crowd.

'You are leaving me,' he said, surprised.

'We are married now,' Rachel reminded him. 'We can enjoy each other's company any time we wish.' There was a slight and awkward pause after the suggestion, to remind him that the amount he had wished of her company was minimal to non-existent. Then she added, 'And I was under the impression that you had business to attend to that did not concern me.'

'But I thought…' What had he thought? That she would need his protection? She did not seem to think so. He could not claim that he wished to fill her dance card, since he had only grudgingly promised her a single waltz. But suddenly the display of marital *ennui* that he had intended seemed contrived and unnecessary.

'The gossip around me can be vicious,' he said at last.

'But we know it is unfounded, and I will pay it no mind,' she said with a superior look worthy of the wife of a peer.

He smiled back at her, reaching for her hand and raising the gloved knuckles to his lips. He allowed himself to linger over her hand a moment, savouring the warmth of it against his cheek before releasing it, and saying, 'If you need me, I shall be close by.'

'Do not forget that you have promised me the waltz,' she said, holding out her dance card for him to sign. 'Do not think you can escape to the smoking room for the whole night.'

They parted then, or at least attempted to, as he found himself unable to leave, standing in a corner of the ballroom, watching as his wife moved easily from group to group, equally as polite to those who approved and those who did not.

Beside him, he heard a laugh. It was Belston, a fellow peer who, while not exactly a friend, showed no sign that he noticed the cloud that hung over the Scofield title. 'I never thought I would see the notorious Duke of Scofield besotted by a woman.'

'I am not besotted,' Hugh snapped, refusing to take his eyes off Rachel.

'And over his own wife, no less,' the other

Duke said with a snigger. 'I know the pain of it. I am so afflicted myself.'

'I have no idea what you are talking about,' Hugh muttered.

'Of course not,' Belston said, still grinning. 'But I fear your intimidating reputation is a thing of the past. After tonight, the *ton* will keep whispering about Scofield, of course. But who can think totally ill of a man with such a charming wife?'

'Thank you,' Hugh said absently, still not sure that what had been said was a compliment. Was that really all it took to change the tide of public opinion? Rachel was as charming and as beautiful as he could wish in a duchess. When he had married her, he had never thought she might be useful, for he had not imagined that she would be seen in public any more than his sisters had been.

But he had kept his sisters in isolation for an entirely different purpose. There was no reason that he could not go about with Rachel all he wished…other than the fact that the nearness of her frightened him in a way it never used to. The last two years of his life had been about rigid control of himself and of others, but suddenly he had joined his life to a woman so uncontrollable that he never knew what she might do next. He could not decide whether to be angry or delightfully surprised.

For the first time in memory, the dangerous Duke of Scofield smiled.

All things considered, Rachel had to admit that it was better being a duchess than it had been when she'd been plain Lady Rachel. There were the usual whispers of scandal, because of her husband, but she was also in the awkward position of being a person so august that the majority of the women—the ones who had not bothered to meet her when she'd been a lesser member of the peerage— were now afraid to speak to her without an introduction.

Fortunately, her hostess was a charming and pleasant woman who seemed more amused by the rumours than anxious to spread them, and she made sure that the other guests were presented to her, parading them past Rachel as if she were a bear in the Tower of London.

In response, Rachel made sure she was

equally charming and pleasant, and not at all
the sort of woman one would expect to marry
a murderer. Between Lady Folbroke's support
and her own positive attitude, the women,
who had probably planned to shun her, were
not quite sure how to go about it.

But she did notice that her dance card remained empty other than the single scrawl
of 'Scofield' next to the waltz. Though the
other ladies had declared it safe to speak to
her, gentlemen, both single and married, gave
her a wide birth, unwilling to do anything
that might attract negative attention from her
husband.

When the waltz started, Hugh reappeared,
dutifully ready to dance her around the room.
And, as he did, she understood the reason for
the boycott.

'You are scowling,' she said, trying not to
laugh.

'I beg your pardon?' he queried, turning
his attention back to her and away from the
single men ringing the floor.

She tapped his shoulder with her fan. 'You
look like a dog guarding a bone. Surely you
must realise that I am not going anywhere
and do not need protecting?'

His expression gentled and he relaxed into the rhythm of the dance. 'I am simply concerned that you will not be received as you should.'

'Of course,' she said, rolling her eyes.

'We can go home whenever you are ready,' he said, but he looked concerned rather than angry for a change.

'Then I may force you to stay until dawn,' she said with a laugh. 'I am having a delightful time.'

He frowned at her in confusion.

'Would you prefer that I be miserable?' she asked.

'Of course not,' he said quickly.

'Because you seem to view outings such as these as a form of punishment.'

'It is probably foolish of me to be so difficult,' Hugh admitted, sounding almost contrite.

'Probably,' Rachel agreed. 'Have you forgiven me for wanting to accept this invitation? Despite your fears, the company has been most diverting.'

'There is nothing to forgive,' he assured her. 'I simply did not want you to be as unhappy as I was.'

'As you were?' she asked, staring up into his eyes. 'And am I to take that as a sign that you are happier now?'

Would it be a mistake to admit that she was right? It had been so long since he had been happy that he was not sure he recognised the feeling. Finally, he cleared his throat and said, 'Recently, there is much that has changed around me. And you are the cause of it.'

'Because you are no longer alone,' she said.

'But I am afraid that you will be,' he replied, giving her hand a light squeeze.

'Not as long as I have you.' She smiled and returned the gesture. 'Now, give me another dance. I do not want to sit down until the sun rises.'

Rachel came close to getting her wish. When they staggered back to the carriage after more dances than she could count, there was a rosy glow in the sky that grew brighter as they drove towards home. She sat on the seat opposite him, unable to help the smile on her face, and unwilling to curb the wicked thoughts flitting through her mind.

He must have shared some of them, for he

was smiling as well, and shaking his head in warning.

'Did you have a good evening?' she asked, smug.

'Better than I've had in a very long time,' Hugh admitted.

'Because of me,' she said with a proud nod.

'You may have had something to do with it,' he replied.

'Perhaps, next season, we can throw a ball of our own.'

'No one will come,' he said quickly, but his smile did not fade.

'Then it will be just the two of us, drinking all the champagne and dancing all the dances.'

'I cannot imagine a better evening,' he said with a sigh. Then the carriage drew to a stop at their front door and he helped her down…

And went through the front door without her.

She gave her skirts a frustrated swish and hurried after him, but he paid her no mind, continuing up the stairs to his room and blowing her a kiss before shutting the door against her.

She continued on to the next door, her

freshly remodelled room. The silk on the walls was her favourite shade of blue, as were the curtains on the bed and the windows. But none of it brought her any happiness because she was still alone. There was one way that a night like this should end and it was not lying alone in one's bed, scant yards from the man who could change everything.

Without bothering to call her maid, she slipped out of her gown, shift and stockings, letting down her hair one pin at a time until the curls tickled her bare shoulders. The diamond necklace remained, swaying in invitation between her breasts. She stared at it in the mirror, fascinated.

Then, she pulled on the nightgown that she had chosen for her wedding night and covered it with a silk wrapper before walking across the room and opening the connecting door that led to her husband's room.

She glanced into the room on the other side of the threshold to see Hugh, bare chested, sitting on his bed and pulling off his boots. He froze, staring at her, then he gathered his dignity and said, 'Is there something that I can help you with?'

She smiled. 'No. I was just…' She stepped

back from the door. 'I find the room rather close tonight and thought an open door might help.' It was a transparent lie and she waited to hear him suggest an open window, or even unlatching the hall door.

Instead, he continued to stare.

She unbelted the wrapper she was wearing and let it fall to the floor. 'That is somewhat better.'

His boot dropped to the floor with a thump.

She turned and walked back towards her bed, letting her hips sway in invitation. Then she reached to her throat and undid the top buttons on her nightdress. She stretched, feeling the bodice slip on her shoulder and her skin chill at the exposure to the night air.

There was the thump of a second boot.

Her breath caught in her throat.

'Rachel.'

She had grown used to the tone he used when calling her name, and the faint upward inflection to indicate that she had done something to displease him. But this time his voice was softer, and held a warning note, as if there was danger in front of both of them.

'Close the door.'

She undid another button then turned and

walked slowly back towards his room. 'This door?' Rachel braced her spine against the door frame and stretched for the door handle to widen the gap at the front of her gown.

He had seen her breasts before—in their hurried grappling in his room two years ago—but never decorated in diamonds when all the night and the rest of their lives lay before them. If only one of them could find the courage to act.

He sighed at the sight of her, breathing slow and deep, as if trying to regain control.

She took a breath of her own and undid the last button. She shrugged out of her nightdress, letting it fall to the floor as the robe had done. Then she stood before him, naked for the first time, stepped away from the door into his room and closed it behind her, exactly the opposite of what he had asked for.

'Rachel,' Hugh said again with amused resignation.

'It was a lovely night, wasn't it?' Rachel tempted.

'Not as lovely as you,' he admitted.

'I don't want for it to end,' she said, staring into his eyes.

'I told you before...' he warned with a sigh.

'That you did not love me,' she said, then forced herself to smile and continued. 'But you do want me. And, for tonight, that is enough.'

She walked towards the bed, trying not to shiver as her nipples tightened from the cold air against her bare skin. When she reached the bed, she sat beside him, so close that her arm brushed his and warmth flooded into her again.

He touched her cheek, stroking a thumb along her jawline. 'You don't know what you are playing with. It is known all over London that I am a very dangerous man.'

Rachel laughed. 'Not to me,' she said, turning her head to bite the pad of his thumb.

'There is madness in my family,' he reminded her, his voice serious, though he did not withdraw his hand. 'It should not be propagated.'

'Propagated.' She tasted the word. 'You make it sound like we are about to plant tulips.'

'It is not a joking matter,' he said. 'Time has changed me. I am not the same man I was. I was not worthy of your hand then and I am not worthy of your body now.'

'Then how about my lips?' she asked, closing her eyes and tipping her face up to receive his kiss.

There was a pause of only a moment. Then he groaned and she felt his cheek rub against hers, the stubble rough on her skin. He turned his head and their lips met, softly at first, then hungrily, as if it was possible to make up for all the lost time in a single night.

Her tongue found his and they kissed, as he had taught her two years ago—deeply, as if life itself depended on the contact. His hand tightened on her shoulder, a finger hooking in the necklace she still wore and tracing down the length of it to settle against the pendant between her breasts.

She pressed a hand flat against his chest, fingers spread. 'I have dreamed of this moment since you left me,' she whispered. 'Every night, I touch myself and I wish you were beside me.'

He groaned and pulled her body tight to his, pushing her back to lie on the bed. 'I am lost without you. But I cannot trust myself with you. What am I to do?'

'Give in,' she murmured.

He needed no further urging. He struggled out of his breeches and re-joined her on the bed to take her in his arms.

She stole a look down the length of him, both shocked and amazed at so much bare skin. Before, when they had been together in this room, she had revealed far more than she had seen. Now she could admire his broad chest and the fascinating trail of hair that led down his belly, directing her eyes to his erection.

He tipped her face back up to look into his eyes, which were full of mirth at her curiosity. 'Soon,' he whispered and kissed his way from her lips down her shoulders as his hands stroked her breasts.

She sighed then, leaning into him to enjoy the weight of his hands on her and the gentle flutter of his tongue on her collar bone. She let her hands rove through his hair, cradling his head against her body and urging his lips lower to take her nipple. When he did, the feeling arched through her and left her with no thought beyond the pleasure of the moment.

And then, his mouth continued its journey south, circling her navel before delving into it. Then Rachel remembered something he had promised to do when they used to meet in secret, something that had sounded too wicked to be possible. His mouth was between her legs now, searching, finding, kissing, driving her mad.

She remembered the first time he had brought her to climax with a few easy strokes of his hand and a caution to be still, lest anyone hear them together. She had wondered then if it was exciting because it was forbidden. But this was even better and she needn't be quiet. She could scream in ecstasy if she wanted or come on a whisper.

As if he could sense her dilemma, Hugh laughed against her skin, nipping and licking until she dissolved into uncontrolled moans and gave herself up for him. Then he rose from between her legs and hovered over her for a moment before urging her to spread her legs.

She reached for him, holding him at the

waist, guiding him to her. His fingers stroked her now in the place where she was wet and eager, spreading the lips of her sex and murmuring that he did not mean to hurt her.

She closed her eyes, braced herself and felt him slide into her as if they had been formed to join by God. It must have been so, for why else would it feel so good? He was taking her to heaven with slow thrusts of his body, cupping her bottom and urging her to move in harmony with him, equal and opposite.

She could feel the climax approaching like a wave building far out at sea. Her body tightened on his as her nails dug into the flesh of his back and his pace quickened. Then he whispered in a passion-drugged voice, 'I mustn't…'

Unless he meant that he mustn't stop, she did not want to hear it. He had spent far too much time telling her what was wrong and avoiding this moment, something that was clearly right. So she kissed him, hoping that he would forget. He responded, just as she knew he would, as hungry for her as she was for him.

Then, suddenly, he was gone. He broke the

kiss, freed himself from her arms and her body, then rolled away and turned his back to her, spending in the sheet with a quick jerk of his hand.

For a moment, he did not move, neither reaching for her nor moving further away. She could hear his breath growing more even as the last of the passion drained from him and his blood cooled. Only then did he reach for her, his hand settling between her legs to try and finish what he had started.

This was what he had meant about control and how he prevented children with his mistress. He had claimed that he could not love her in the same way because he would not be able to control himself.

Apparently, he had lied.

Tonight had proved that he was more than capable of resisting her, even in the throes of passion. He had denied her her due as his wife—the completion of the act. Apparently, when the moment came to decide, he had found she was no different from one of his whores.

She evaded his hand, rolling away and trying to ignore the ache in her body, the longing to be touched and to feel the rush of ecstasy that she knew he could bring her to. She had told him that desire was enough, that love was not needed. But she was wrong.

His hand settled on her hip and his lips grazed her ear. 'Are you sure?' He stroked her side, then settled his hand over her breast. 'We need not be finished, if you are not done. And if the first time did not hurt…'

'It hurt,' she lied. Or was it a lie? She hurt in spirit, if not in body, a pain that she did not know how to explain. To avoid conversation, she curled inwards, hugging her stomach and pulling her knees up to her body.

His hand withdrew, settling on her shoulder. 'I understand. I will give you time. As much time as you need.'

'Thank you,' she whispered.

And then she waited for the words that would salvage the night. If only he would tell her he loved her, she would know that there was hope.

Instead, he kissed the back of her neck and said, 'We have all the time in the world now. I had planned that you would be on your way to Suffolk by the end of the week. But now…'

'Nothing has changed.' She rolled to the

edge of the bed and swung her feet to the floor.

'You want to go?' he asked, surprised.

'The season is ending.' She refused to look at him. 'There is no reason to remain in town.'

'I cannot accompany you,' he reminded her. 'Not until I am sure that Solomon is safe from my sister.'

'That is all right,' she said, putting on the false smile she had used for the few women who had snubbed her at the ball. 'Now that we are married, we need not live in each other's pockets. As you have told me before, the manor is just as much your property as this house. It will almost be like being together.' The words were coming too quickly, falling over each other, as if she was trying to convince herself as much as him.

'If that is what you wish,' he said, sounding as confused as she felt.

'That is what I want,' she confirmed, rising now and going towards the connecting door.

'Where are you going?' Now he sounded hurt.

'Back to my room.' She opened the door now and scooped the silk robe off the floor, wrapping her body in it and hiding from his view. 'I have to begin packing tomorrow and need to get some sleep.'

'Of course,' he said. His voice was distant, as if they were separated by miles and not just the length of the room. 'Sleep well, my dear.'

'And you,' she said, shutting the door.

When she had gone, Hugh settled himself into the small, warm spot where her body had been, trying to fix the best of what had just happened in his memory so he might never lose it.

Like so many of the important moments of his life, he had bungled this badly. But this time he was not even sure what he had done. She had been near to orgasm, just as he had been. But by the time he had finished, he had lost her in body, mind and spirit.

He should have known better. But he had expected lying with her to have something in common with previous life experience. He had bedded women before. But he had kissed them as well and, as kisses with Rachel had always been better, it should have been a warning that when the moment came to withdraw he should stay.

But giving himself to her in that way had felt too dangerous, and not just because of the risk of children. It would be like an outpouring of the spirit to come inside her, as if he'd have been giving up his very soul. And, since he was not even sure he had a soul after all that had happened, he certainly did not deserve the divine redemption of the angel he had married.

As it had been her first time, he should have been the generous lover he had promised himself he would be. Instead, it seemed he had hurt her without noticing. He had been selfish, used her for his pleasure then turned from her to finish. In the moments that had taken, he had lost her.

Perhaps it was for the best that she leave. It would be easier on both of them if they did not see each other for a while. She would have more freedom to do as she pleased. And he would have his old life back, such as it was. There would be no great joy, but neither would there be a continual risk of succumbing to passion and producing children as mad as him and as uncontrollable as their mother.

But why did something that sounded rational, right and in control feel completely wrong?

Unable to answer the question, he rolled over to his own side of the bed and tried to sleep.

Chapter Nineteen

The next morning, Rachel considered getting up to ride with Hugh, to prove that she still had her pride. Then she pounded her pillow and rolled over, giving it up as a bad job. It would take more than a fine habit and a dust of powder to make her look other than what she was: a woman who'd had more tears than sleep.

Last night, she had run from him when a more experienced woman might have stayed to fight. She had announced that she would go away, just as he'd wanted, but some part of her had hoped to hear him contradict her. He could have asked her to stay. He might have said he could not live without her.

She was being a fool. She doubted the mystery woman from Vauxhall would have played coy in the same situation. Instead, she'd have said what she wanted, and used her body to see to it that Hugh never let her go.

And she might do it still if Rachel retreated from London at the first sign of defeat. But what else could she do?

She rang for chocolate and toast to be brought to her room. Then she splashed her face with cold water and instructed her maid to begin the packing. If she wanted her marriage to work, she had three days to persuade her husband that he loved her and could not live without her. As it had taken two years to get this far, it seemed an incredibly short amount of time to bring about a miracle.

And then there was the matter of her investigation into what had happened on the night Hugh's father had died. But, as the Bow Street Runners had proved worthless, what was she to do on her own?

The matter was decided when she opened the afternoon post and found a note from Lady Margaret Castell, announcing that she and her sister would be visiting tomorrow and were eager to reacquaint themselves with their new sister-in-law. She must get them to open their minds as well and prove that Hugh's suspicions were not correct.

Promptly at ten the next morning, Rachel heard a knock on the front door and the butler announced that Lady Olivia and Lady Margaret had been shown to the green salon. She called for tea to be laid and went to meet them, suddenly anxious.

It was not bad enough that Hugh had filled her mind with suspicions about the sanity of his family. When they had played together as children, the girls had been her social superiors and she had never quite overcome her awe of them. Now she had married Hugh, she was the mistress of their childhood home. How would they receive her when much of society had turned their backs on her for marrying their brother?

When she came into the room, it was hard to think of the two elegant ladies sitting there as having once been her childhood friends, Liv and Peg. Margaret had changed even more since last Rachel had seen her. Judging by the gentle swell of her stomach, she would be a mother in a few more months.

'Welcome,' Rachel said, sitting down and

gesturing the servants to serve the tea and cakes. 'It is so good to see you again after all this time.'

'We were rather surprised at your invitation, Your Grace,' Lady Olivia admitted in a formal tone, 'As we are under the impression that our brother has still not forgiven us for eloping.'

'Please, call me Rachel, as you used to,' she began, smiling in what she hoped was an open and friendly way.

'It has been some time since we have talked together,' Margaret said, smiling back at her.

'Two years at least,' Olivia agreed and frowned. 'We can blame Hugh for that.'

'Well, do not worry about Hugh's welcome today,' Rachel assured them. 'I am sure he did not mean to ban you from the house.'

Of course, she had not actually warned him that they would be coming today. But she was sure enough that he would not mind their presence, should he notice it. 'I am sure he is most concerned for your welfare and happiness,' Rachel said, trying to dispel the worried looks the sisters were giving her. 'He wants the best for you, though I will admit he sometimes does a bad job of showing it.'

Now the girls were passing doubtful looks between them, as if remembering everything he had done to keep them contained, and wondering how any of it could have been for their own good.

Rachel reached for her tea. 'But he is not the only person in the family now. I thought I would make it clear that I hold no animosity towards you and am eager to see any breach there might be between your brother and the pair of you healed.'

'That is most generous of you,' Olivia replied, taking her cup. 'I will admit that I wondered, when we were not invited to the wedding.'

How was she to answer this? Rachel cleared her throat. 'It was a hurried affair. I was rather more concerned that the groom attended than worrying about guests.'

'We read the news of it in the scandal sheets,' Margaret said with a giggle. 'And my husband told me of the duel,' she added in a more sombre tone.

'I was most impressed that Hugh managed to persuade a girl to be alone with him, much less allowed himself to be caught that way,' Olivia finished.

'It was mostly my doing,' Rachel admitted. 'But when one is in love…'

'Love?' Both the girls spoke in shocked unison.

Rachel nodded. 'It is quite hopeless, I am afraid. I have been in love with him since we were girls, though I did not tell you, for fear that you would tease me. There is nothing I can do to change my feelings for him.'

The two stared at each other, still in shock at this revelation, and Lady Olivia admitted, 'We were wondering if, after less than a month with Hugh, you called us here to ask for sanctuary.'

'And how does he feel about you?' Margaret blurted, then looked down into her tea cup, embarrassed.

'He swore he would never marry, you see,' Olivia informed her. 'He is still in love with someone from his past…'

'That is me!' Rachel announced, then blushed as she remembered that he had denied just such that emotion on their wedding night. 'Well, at least… He made promises of marriage before your father died.'

'Then you are…' The two girls looked at

her, alarmed, then stared towards the door, as if eager to depart.

Then Margaret seemed to gather her nerve and asked, 'Were you here, in the house, on the night that our father died?'

'I was in your brother's room,' she admitted. 'Hugh did not do it, if that is what you are concerned about. I was with him when the body was discovered. We heard the screams from downstairs.'

'Then you were not the one who screamed first?' Margaret asked, a confused look on her face.

'I do not understand,' Rachel responded.

'Before Olivia got to the study, there was a scream,' she replied. 'We had learned of your presence in the house—though not your identity, of course—and we assumed that it must have been you who screamed.'

'It was not,' she said with a sigh. 'I came straight to your brother's room and did not leave until after the crime was committed. I am his alibi and he is mine.'

There was a moment of confused silence. Then Margaret said, 'You can offer no other information on the identity of the killer?'

Rachel shook her head.

Olivia's expression dropped in disappointment. 'We assumed that, when and if we found you, you would have the answer to the whole thing.'

'I was rather hoping that you could answer questions for me,' she said, trying not to sound threatening. 'The night of the murder, was one of you wearing a green gown?'

'The green net with the spangles,' Olivia said with a sigh. 'I have not thought about that for years.'

'So it was you?' Rachel asked, surprised that the truth would be so easy to find.

'No,' Olivia said. 'By that time, Peg had ruined it and I had given it to her.'

'And I had no idea what happened to it,' Margaret said. 'I assumed the maid stole it when she ran away.'

'Your maid ran away?'

'Right after the murder,' Olivia said. The pair of them were looking at Rachel with large, guileless eyes, and it was clear that they were either the best liars in England or completely innocent of the crime Hugh accused them of, for they had no idea that the maid was dead.

Rachel continued cautiously. 'The night

your father was killed, your brother saw a woman wearing a green gown going into the study. He assumed it was one of you.'

'Us?' The girls laughed in unison.

'What utter nonsense,' Olivia added.

'Why did he not simply ask us what we were doing at the time of father's death?' Margaret said.

'I assume it was because he thought you would lie,' Rachel replied. 'And it is true that, unless you can account for each moment of the time between supper and the discovery of the body, we cannot actually prove that you are not guilty.'

At this, the two girls looked at each other for a long, silent moment, then Olivia admitted, 'We have never asked him for the same reason. It was only when we learned of the presence of a mysterious woman in the house that we realised who must have been guilty. But, if it was not you...'

'Then why was he trying to have you committed?' asked Margaret.

Rachel gave a nervous cough. 'I assume, if an asylum was suggested, it was for one or both of you.'

'Us?' Margaret looked thoroughly insulted.

'When I see Hugh next, I will box his ears. The place he considered was quite horrible. I saw it myself.'

'He did not send you there,' Rachel reminded her. 'He kept you in the house instead.'

'We were little better than prisoners here,' Olivia agreed.

'It was because he feared that you would kill again. Your maid did not run away. The body was found in the garden and hidden.'

At this, the two girls sobered. 'Poor Bess,' Margaret whispered.

'And, when Richard Sterling was killed...' Rachel began.

'He thought it was me,' Olivia finished, her face clouding with anger. 'I still have nightmares about that night. And all this time he thought it was me.'

'Since you were equally sure that it was him, it is hardly fair of you to be angry,' her sister replied.

'He treated us horribly,' Olivia reminded her.

'It was not so horrible, really. I suspect father would have been almost as strict. And, if things had been different, we would not have found the husbands we did,' Margaret finished softly.

'While I do not want to minimise how hard this has been on the two of you, I rather hoped that one of you might contribute something that would make matters clearer,' Rachel said, staring from one to the other. 'The culprit is not Hugh, nor was it me. But there were three murders, and someone must have done them. Did you see anything at all that night?'

'I went straight to my room after dinner,' Peg said quickly.

They both turned to look at Olivia.

'And I changed into a darker gown that would not be seen from the windows and met Alister in the garden, as I did every night,' Olivia said, her voice slowing with each word. She was staring at them, staring at her. 'But it could not have been him. I watched him leave and latched the gate behind him.'

'The latch is loose,' Rachel said. 'I have seen him open it myself.'

'And the dog would not have barked because he never barked at Alister,' Margaret added.

Olivia shook her head. 'It could not be him.

It simply could not. I have known him for years. What reason could he have had?'

'Father refused him,' her sister reminded her. 'And if the maid saw him in the study and screamed...'

'It could not have been Alister,' Olivia repeated, but this time she began to shake.

'Rachel? What the devil is going on?' Hugh was standing in the doorway, staring at the three of them, especially at the shocked Olivia, who looked near to fainting.

'Alister Clement was in the house that night,' Rachel said, offering no other explanation.

'What do you know of Alister Clement?'

'He has been to visit me in the garden,' Rachel said, surprising everyone. 'He claimed to be a family friend. He was looking for Olivia's direction.'

'Clement,' Hugh said, considering. 'The man didn't have the nerve to elope with Liv. I doubt...'

'He found the nerve once Peg was out of the way,' Liv said, her voice turning bitter. 'He didn't want her to live with us. He didn't want the dogs, either. He just wanted me.' Now she looked sick.

'It would explain Sterling's death,' Hugh said thoughtfully.

'And the maid must have known something,' Rachel finished. 'She was the one to accuse the two of you,' she added.

'If it was Alister, then Liv is still in danger,' Peg said, reaching out for her sister and trying to rub some warmth into her shaking hands.

'As is Solomon,' Hugh said. 'Has he experienced any more attacks?'

'Attacks?' Liv repeated in a whisper. 'What are you talking about?'

'He probably didn't want to worry you,' Hugh said, ringing for a servant. Then he scribbled a quick note at the writing desk in the corner and handed it to the footman when he arrived. 'I am sending for him to come here so that we might get you safely to the country. We will deal with the fellow once we know you will not be hurt.'

'He never meant to hurt me,' Liv said in a strangled voice. 'It is Michael who is in danger.' She stared at her brother with pleading eyes. 'Please do not let him do anything foolish.'

'I will think of something,' Hugh said, then

reached in his pocket for a flask and poured a bit of brandy into Olivia's empty cup. 'Drink. It will steady your nerves. And we will need you to be strong for what may lie ahead.'

Chapter Twenty

While they waited for Michael Solomon to arrive, Peg took her sister up to her childhood bedroom, insisting that she lie down for a nap, leaving Hugh alone with his wife.

He turned to her with what was becoming a familiar feeling of exasperation and said, 'You should not have meddled in this.'

'Meddled?' Rachel asked, hands on hips and an equally exasperated expression on her face. 'I may have found an answer to the killings that you could have found long ago if you weren't so set on controlling everything in your reach.'

'I do not…' he insisted. The only thing he had to control right at this moment was his temper.

'You already knew I invited your sisters

for tea. It should not have been a surprise to you that they actually decided to come,' she pointed out.

She was right. All the same, it had been a surprise. He'd thought, once they escaped, they would never return here.

'And I talked to them about a matter that concerns us all, just as you could have,' she finished. 'I know your father did not feel that he need listen to anyone else in the family...'

'I am not my father,' he snapped.

'Of course not. But I think sometimes, when you do not know what to do, you behave in a way you think he would approve of.'

'My father was a dictatorial miser,' he said. 'Is that what you think of me?'

'I think you would do well to talk to your sisters,' she said quietly. 'And to trust them, though you were not raised to do so.'

The words stung, though she'd said them gently enough.

'You have no right to lecture me on how I choose to manage my family.'

'Your sisters are grown women and did not need to be managed,' she said, a little more insistently.

'And I suppose next you will be telling me I have no right to decide what is best for you?'

'You have made decisions that affect me because you were afraid of the madness in your family,' she reminded him. 'And now it appears that there is another explanation for what has been happening around you.'

'And until that matter is settled you are going to Suffolk,' he replied, relieved that this, at least, they agreed on. 'And you will be taking Olivia with you. If you are right in your suspicions about Clement, I do not want you anywhere around the man.'

'He did not mean any harm to me when we spoke,' she said.

'And you did not tell me that you have seen him,' he countered, finding his anger again.

'Because I did not think it was important.'

'Because you did not think I would approve, more like,' he replied. 'If that is so, you are right. The man had no right to be trespassing on the property, even if he was not a murderer.'

But what if he was the killer? What if the answer had been right under his nose all along and he had been too proud and too stupid to look for it?

He shook his head to clear it. There would be time enough for recrimination later. Now was the time for action. 'I am not going to let anything happen to you.'

'I am not afraid for myself,' she insisted. 'Clement killed your father. Suppose he decides to kill you as well?'

'He has made no move to do so in two years,' he said with a shrug. 'And, if he is the killer, he does not know that we have discovered the fact. There is no reason to believe that anyone other than Olivia and her husband are at risk. But I will feel better once I know Clement has been caught and has confessed.'

'I have a suggestion,' she said, smiling as she did just before she did something that left him fuming.

He braced himself and gestured for her to continue.

'You should give Alister's card to Mr Pilkington and tell him what we have found. Tomorrow, as planned, we pack my things and send them to Suffolk, along with Olivia, dressed in one of my gowns and wearing a veil. Her husband can accompany her as an outrider, disguised in Scofield livery. You can accompany them as far as needed to be sure they have not been followed.'

'And you?' he asked.

'Will remain in the house so as not to spoil Olivia's disguise.' She smiled. 'If you like, you can put a guard on the house to protect me.'

The plan made a surprising amount of sense. If Solomon agreed, it would be good to see the pair of them safely out of the city before Clement realised they were gone.

'Very well,' he said. 'I will broach the idea with Solomon. In the meantime, continue your packing and explain the plan to Olivia. If they are agreed, we will carry it out tomorrow morning.'

The next day, the carriage was brought round with as much ceremony as possible and loaded with trunks and boxes while Rachel helped Olivia into one of her best day gowns and fixed a thick veil to the brim of the matching bonnet.

Olivia reached out a gloved hand and clasped hers. 'Thank you for this, and for what you have done for Hugh.'

'What have I done for Hugh?'

'You believed in him when no one else did.' Olivia glanced out of the window to where her brother was talking with the coachman. 'He has been very alone all this time.'

'It was his choice to be so,' she said softly, wondering if he would ever change. 'He thinks he can control everything, and that leaves no room in his life for others.'

'I had not thought of him in that way,' Olivia said, surprised.

Rachel thought of how he had been when they'd been in bed together—rigid and disciplined at the moment when they should both have been free. 'You don't know him as I do.' She sighed. 'But let us not think of that now.' There might be a lifetime to contend with that, and she was not sure she could stand it.

So, she focused on completing the transformation of Olivia into a copy of herself. With the veil pinned in place and the disguise complete, she led Olivia through the largely empty house to the front door. The majority of the servants had been dismissed for the day and told that, with the departure of the mistress, there would be no need to lay a hot supper. But in reality it made the departure of the Solomons easier to keep secret.

Then Hugh returned to the house to escort his sister to the carriage, staring out of the window at the yard. 'The guard that Pilkington has promised is not yet in place.'

'He is probably waiting until the carriage has left so as not to make the departure appear suspicious.'

Hugh nodded but said, 'I do not like it.'

'I will be well,' she said, touching his arm.

'I will follow the carriage until we are free of the city and I am sure that they have not been followed. Then I shall return to you.'

'And we will plan what to do next.' She clasped his hand.

'We most certainly will not,' Hugh replied, pulling away from her. 'You will have no part in what happens next. It is far too dangerous.'

'Mr Clement has no reason to suspect me,' she said.

'And I do not mean to give him one. For once, leave the rest to me.'

She sighed. 'Very well.'

'And, while I am gone, you are to do nothing, you understand? Nothing at all.'

'I am not a fool, Hugh,' she said with a shake of her head.

'I do not think you are,' he said softly. Then he reached for her to kiss her goodbye.

She hesitated for only a moment, then she wrapped her arms around him and kissed him back.

'I will be back tonight,' he whispered, touching her cheek. And then he was gone and she was alone.

She sighed, touching her lips and hoping that she had understood the unspoken message he had left there. If Clement was the killer, there was no reason that they might not have a perfectly ordinary marriage and love each other as husband and wife should. At the very least, he might finally forgive her for the way they had married and admit to his feelings for her.

Or, perhaps what he had given her thus far was all he had to give. If that was the case, she did not know how she could face the future. She had hoped for so much more.

She sighed. Of course, he would have to come back for anything to happen at all. And that return was a few hours from now, at minimum. How was she to spend the time? She went into the library, searching through the books for one that might hold her interest and staring out of the window into the empty garden. There was still no sign of Pilkington's guard, but that man was likely to be an unnecessary precaution, now that Liv and her husband were safely away.

Would it really do any harm if she waited there for him to return? It was not leaving home, after all. But, when she rose to go, she had the strangest sensation as she walked down the hall. It was as if someone was in the house with her.

Then she heard it. A rustling noise was coming from the study. She stepped through the open door to discover Alister Clement rifling the contents of the desk.

He looked up and for a moment their eyes met in silence. Then he drew a gun from his pocket and was across the room before she could think to scream.

'You are supposed to be gone,' he said in a dry, disinterested voice.

'What are you doing here?' she said, backing away until she felt the wall flat against her back.

'The real question is why you are not Olivia,' Clement said with a shrug of impatience. 'She came here with her sister yesterday and did not leave. I had hoped to find her above, in her room.'

'She stayed the night and has gone back to her house,' Rachel replied. 'She was not feeling well after tea.'

'Then who was in the carriage that left for the country this morning?' Clement asked with a raised eyebrow.

'Just my maid,' she said, glancing behind her towards the door.

'In a fine gown and bonnet and with all that luggage?' he said, still sceptical. 'I think it far more likely that you sent Olivia away to keep her safe from me.'

'Why would I do that?' she said, trying to keep her voice calm and slow. 'I thought you were her friend.'

'Because you have discovered the truth,' he said with a sad shake of his head. 'This is most inconvenient. Not at all in line with my plans. And, now that you have seen me, I cannot allow you to tattle.'

'What would I want to tell anyone?' she asked, forcing a smile. But when he looked at her his eyes were devoid of any respect, instead glinting with cold amusement.

'I think we both know the answer to that,'

he said. 'You would want to tell that fool of a husband of yours that I killed his father.'

'He already knows,' she said. There was no point in allowing him to think she was alone in the knowledge. 'He knows and he will be back any time now with a man from the Bow Street Runners.'

Clement smiled and applauded, giving a small nod of approval. 'And I am sure you were the one to tell him. No one has suspected me in all this time. It is impressive that you have discovered the truth, but unfortunately the information comes too late to do you any good.'

'I have guessed most of it…' she said, praying that Hugh would come. 'But not all. How did you get past the dog and into the house?'

'I was in the garden with Liv after supper, and the dog was so used to our visits that he did nothing but wag his tail,' he said. 'When she went back to the house, I waited at the kitchen door and her maid let me in.'

'The maid,' she said with a nod.

'She was quite infatuated with me. And I may have made promises that I had no intention of keeping.'

'But that does not explain why the Duke had to die,' she said. 'What did he ever do to you?'

'Do not waste energy feeling sorry for the man,' Clement replied with a smirk. 'Even his son knew that the world was better off without the old miser. As to my reasons for getting rid of him, I asked for Olivia's hand and he refused me. So, I entered the house as the family was getting ready for bed and paid a visit to his study.' He made a stabbing motion and shrugged. 'I thought, perhaps, his son would be more receptive to my suit. Unfortunately, he wasn't.'

'And what of the maid?' Rachel asked in a choked whisper.

'She assumed that we were to have a liaison. The silly creature even stole one of Olivia's dresses to impress me. She followed me to the study and discovered the truth. She screamed and nearly brought the house down on us. It took some quick thinking on my part to hide the two of us long enough so I could escape in the confusion.'

'This was all about marrying Olivia?' she said, surprised. 'It is a wonder you did not kill Hugh as well. After all, he refused you, just as his father did.'

'It was better to leave him alive and under a cloud of accusation for the crimes I committed. He looked guilty enough when Richard Sterling was found in the river.'

'You did that as well?' She was not really surprised.

'Olivia showed signs of favouring him over me,' he said. 'I could not have that.'

'And why did you kill the maid?'

'She knew too much.' He gave a shrug. 'She witnessed the crime and thought that it entitled her to my full attention. She expected me to run off with her the next day. She thought to blackmail me into it.' He laughed. 'Did she not understand what I was capable of, even after she witnessed it?'

'So, you killed her,' Rachel said, struggling to contain her horror.

'With the ribbon she stole from Olivia's troublesome little sister.' He shook his head. 'Until the last moment, she imagined that we would be together. She should have known that she was never my goal.'

'You love Olivia,' Rachel said.

He gave her a dubious look. 'As much as I can love anyone. At one time, I wanted her luscious body. But, now it has been despoiled by that wretch Solomon, I want my revenge. Thus far, he has proved surprisingly hard to kill. But one day he will be careless and I will end him.'

'You cannot go about exterminating everyone who gets in your way,' she said, amazed.

'So far, it has been a surprisingly successful strategy,' he said. 'And when Scofield's wife is discovered dead it will only confirm what everyone knows: that he is a man that murders any who get too close to him. Perhaps, this time, he will be brought to justice.'

'You will not use my death to discredit Hugh,' she said, still unsure what it was she could do to prevent it.

Mr Clement smiled, as if picturing the dark future that awaited them. 'I fail to see how you will stop me. As the bodies mount, Scofield's reputation will no longer protect him. Even the House of Lords cannot ignore his crimes. With him hanged, there will be no one for Olivia to turn to except me.'

The idea was mad, of course. If Olivia

loved her husband as deeply as Rachel did Hugh, there was no way that widowhood could make her forget him and turn to another for comfort. But it would be a mistake to taunt a madman, so she held her tongue.

He looked at her and sighed. 'But we have talked too long, Your Grace. I think it is time that you tell me where the carriage was headed. And then we must say goodbye.'

'With what you have planned for me, there is very little incentive to help you,' she said, trying to be brave.

'I know from experience that death can be quick and painless, or slow and painful.' He gave her another mad smile. 'I would advise you not to aggravate me.'

'Then I would ask one thing of you first.'

'I suppose a last request is not out of the question.'

'Do not let me die in here. I have just replaced the rug and it would be a shame to ruin it.'

He laughed then, the sincere sound of mirth at odds with what he was contemplating for her. 'How can I refuse the wishes of a lady in her own home? Very well, Your Grace. In what room do you wish to finish this?'

She thought for a moment, trying to decide. 'The green salon, I think.'

'Very well,' he agreed, gesturing with the gun in his hand. 'Lead the way.'

She walked slowly through the door and down the hall towards the salon, listening for the sound of anyone that might save her. But there was nothing but the sound of their footsteps echoing on the marble tile of the hallway. When they arrived at the salon, she hurried into the room ahead of him, slamming the door in his face.

The act bought her only a moment, but she used it to the best of her abilities. By the time he opened the door, she'd grabbed a vase from a nearby side table and threw it at him.

The blow was enough to startle him and he dropped the gun, which discharged as it hit the rug, sending a ball into the plaster beside the fireplace.

He lunged for her then, clawed hands reaching for her throat.

She backed away and her hand flailed behind her, grabbing a poker from the fireplace and bringing it down hard on his head.

He staggered back, more shocked than hurt, then advanced again.

She screamed, praying that someone would hear her. Then she swung again, harder this time. And then again, as he fell to the floor.

And then, she rushed across the room to the bell-pull, tugged it and collapsed.

Hugh followed the carriage, riding at Solomon's side in silence, his mind focused on the woman he'd left behind.

He should not have left Rachel alone, if only because he knew how much trouble she could get into when he was not watching. She had promised to stay in the house and do nothing other than wait for his return. How could she manage to circumvent an instruction as simple as that?

'Turn back.'

Solomon's voice dragged him from his reverie.

'We are far enough along to manage the trip by ourselves. Let me protect my wife and you can protect your own.' The other man was looking at him with a wry smile.

'If you are sure…' Hugh said, glancing at the road behind him.

'When you have been married as long as I have,' Solomon said, 'You will learn that it is impossible to keep control of everything around you.'

'You have been married barely a month,' Hugh said, smiling.

'And I learn something every day,' Solomon replied. 'Now, go back to London and see to your wife.'

'I will send you word when the Runners have arrested Clement and it is safe to return.'

'Fair enough,' Solomon said, and spurred his horse to catch up with the carriage.

Meanwhile, Hugh turned his horse towards London.

It was almost evening when he arrived at the townhouse. He dismounted and handed his reins to the groom that had accompanied him, then entered through the front door, calling for Rachel.

There was a feeble answering cry from the salon.

He hurried to the door and found her at the windows trying to pull down the drapery cord, an unconscious Clement on the floor at her feet.

'Rachel!'

She looked up at him, her blue eyes wide with panic. She rushed to him then, throwing herself into his arms.

He caught her and held her as she trembled against him.

'I swear, this time I did not do anything. I stayed in the house just like you told me to.' She was muttering apologies into his coat, her arms linked around his waist, swaying against him as if she could barely stand.

'Did he hurt you?' Hugh asked in as calm a tone as he could manage.

She shook her head. 'He wanted to, but I hit him with a poker.'

The man at their feet was moaning, as if consciousness was returning, so Hugh set his wife gently aside. 'Run to the mews and see if you can find a groomsman or two to help me settle this fellow. And send someone to find Pilkington. I am sure he will be interested in your story.'

Then he picked up the pistol that lay on the floor near Clement and grabbed the poker in his other hand for good measure. As Clement sat up, Hugh gave the man a sharp poke in the ribs, sending him skittering towards the nearest wall. 'If you know what is good for you, you will stay down, Clement.'

'Or what?' Clement laughed. 'You will kill me?'

'Perhaps that is what you hope to hear,' Hugh said in a calm, cold voice. 'But then, you would not live to stand trial for the murders you have committed. Do not think you can goad me to fatal violence when justice is close at hand. I am not the man people believe me to be. You, of all people, should know that. But the Runners will not care if you are whole or damaged when they take you away, and if you give me reason to act you will live to regret it.'

Rachel returned then with two grooms and a stout rope. The Runners arrived a short time later, and Hugh sat beside Rachel, holding her hand as she related the gruesome story that Clement had revealed to her. The inspector listened in silence, then signalled that the suspect be manacled and escorted from the room.

Before he left, he turned to Hugh, head bowed in respect. 'I apologise for my misunderstanding of the situation, Your Grace.'

Hugh resisted the urge to laugh in response

and tell him that a few words could not make up for the trials of the last two years. But then he turned and looked at Rachel, who was looking at him with the same devotion as always, and Pilkington's former opinion of him did not seem so very important. So, he dismissed the man with a smile and a nod.

Then, he was alone with his wife.

Rachel stared at Hugh as the door closed, eager to see what his reaction would be now that he was finally free of the rumours that had circulated about him for so long.

But, before she could ask, he had pulled her from her seat on the divan and wrapped her in his arms for a passionate kiss. 'I should never have left you alone.' He paused just long enough to murmur the words against her throat. 'When I think that I might have lost you…'

'It is all right,' Rachel murmured, trying not to tremble. 'I was not hurt.'

'But you could have been,' he said, running his hands lightly over her body as if to reassure himself that she was real and whole. 'If anything had happened to you because I was too foolish to find the truth of this…'

'Do not say that word,' she replied, placing a finger on his lips. 'You are nobody's fool.'

'And you, as always, are too good to me,' he said, kissing her hand. 'We could have been together all this time.'

'Is that what you truly wanted?' Rachel asked hopefully.

'More than life,' he replied, slowly backing her towards the divan.

'On our wedding night—'

'I lied,' he interrupted before she could finish. 'I wanted to hurt you so it would be easier to push you away. As I said before, I was a fool.' He turned then and sat, drawing her into his lap. 'But a fool in love,' he added, adjusting her so that she was sprawled on top of him.

'You love me,' she whispered, relieved.

'And you love me,' he said softly. 'You have been telling me so with every fibre of your being, even when I deserved it least, and defended me when I would not defend myself.'

He was tugging at the hem of her dress now, pulling it up over her knees, so she tugged it down again. 'We mustn't,' she said, surprised to see a roguish glint in his eyes that had not been there for years. 'Not here, at least,' she amended.

'The servants are gone and we are finally alone,' he reminded her. 'We can do whatever we want, wherever we want.'

'How utterly shameless,' she said, but she could not help smiling.

'We have nothing to be ashamed of. We are married, after all. And if you sit thusly, there will be no question of discomfort, as there was the last time.' He leaned back in his seat and adjusted her so she straddled his hips. 'You will be in complete control of what happens.'

She wondered if she should explain that the last time had not been painful in the physical sense. And then, she realised what he had just said. 'You would relinquish control?' she whispered, amazed.

'I have learned that letting you do what you want can be pleasurable for both of us,' he said, kissing his way along her jawline.

'And is this true of other women?' she asked, her breath quickening as he undid the buttons on the back of her gown.

'You are worrying about Martine again.' He growled against her skin. 'Other than that brief visit in Vauxhall, I have not seen her in over a year.' His hand came down to cup her bottom, pressing her hips to his. 'And if you are very good, or perhaps very naughty, I will do things with you that I never considered with her.'

The suggestion sent a thrill through Rachel and she reached between her legs to the buttons of his breeches.

He gave a grunt of approval and pushed her dress off her shoulders, running his hands over the bare skin he'd exposed. The room was chilly, but her body was hot from his touch and she wanted to shed every last stitch of clothing, to be near him as she had been in bed.

But that would take too long. His gentle kisses had reached her breasts and a rush of heat passed through her, settling between her legs. She bundled her skirts out of the way and settled over him, reaching between them to touch his manhood and guide it into her body, which was wet and ready.

He entered her with a long, slow thrust and they were one again, as she had always hoped they would be. He stilled then, waiting. Waiting for her.

At first she revelled in the sensation, afraid that movement might spoil what they already had. Then she realised that by flexing her thighs she could control the thrusts, just as he had promised. So she braced her hands on his shoulders and moved, writhing against him as he palmed her breasts, urging her on.

The tension was growing between them, and Rachel could not resist the opportunity to reach between them and touch herself, driving her body to grip his, drawing him in as she moved around him. She could feel him nearing a climax as well. His breathing quickened and his body shook with trying to prolong the inevitable.

Then, when she was teetering on the brink and feared he would push her away, he drew her closer, coming into her in a rush of heat that tipped her over the edge too.

It was as wonderful as she'd always known it would be. She kissed him then, free of the fears that had haunted her since they'd married.

He did not bother to withdraw but laid his head on her breast and sighed happily. 'Rachel,' he said, and there was none of the usual frustration in his tone.

'Hugh,' she replied, tugging on his cravat.

'I should write to Solomon and tell him they are safe.'

She sighed and climbed off his lap, taking his hand and pulling him towards the writing desk. 'You have time for a short note before bed time.'

He smiled in surprise, swept her off her feet and into his arms. 'Or I can write to him tomorrow.' Then he carried her towards the stairs and her room.

Epilogue

'Rachel.' They had been married for months, and still Hugh could not manage his wife. At the moment, she was balancing on a ladder, hanging a kissing bow in the doorway of the Scofield Manor library, paying no heed to the risks she was taking.

'The guests will be here tomorrow,' Rachel reminded him. 'And I cannot trust the footman to hang this straight.'

Since it was pointless to argue with her, he went to steady the ladder. 'Think of the baby,' he warned, laying a protective hand on her stomach.

'The baby and I will be fine,' she assured him, giving the satin ribbons a final tug. 'We are not made of glass.'

She was probably right. But the fact that he

was to be a father was still a novelty to him, and he could not help feeling protective. 'Next time you wish to hang decorations, come to me for help.'

She smiled and stepped down to the floor again. 'I just want everything to be perfect for the house party. It is Christmas, after all, and I want it to be special.'

'I am sure that it will be fine,' he assured her. 'Some of the people are only coming to gawk at us.'

'They have no reason to,' she reminded him. 'Since the arrest of Mr Clement, I have never met so many apologetic acquaintances eager to get on our good side.'

He smiled. 'I doubt that it will make a difference to some people. They have believed the worst for too long. But it is easier for me to manage now that I know the truth.'

'You will see the change by next season,' she said with a smile. 'When we throw a ball, people will be clamouring for invitations.'

'Rachel,' he said in a tone of mock warning. 'Who gave you permission to hold a ball?'

'You will, I am sure, if I ask when we are in bed tonight,' she answered with a grin.

He grabbed her then and kissed her, for she was right. In or out of bed, he could deny her nothing.

The sound of the first guests arriving came from the hall. Rachel grabbed his hand and tugged Hugh into the hall to greet his sisters and their husbands and the newest addition to the family—his niece, Emily Castell.

He stared in amazement at the infant squalling in Peg's arms, still finding it hard to believe that his youngest sister was now a mother. As far as he knew, Olivia had not been similarly blessed. But then, she and Solomon had been married only a few weeks longer than Rachel and him. It was early, yet.

Rachel hugged each of the girls in turn, cooed at the baby and smiled at her brothers-in-law. She was a warm and genuine hostess and he could not help but be proud of how easily she managed.

For Hugh, it was somewhat more difficult. Castell and Solomon looked at him with polite curiosity and each offered a greeting. 'Scofield.'

He smiled back at them, reaching out to shake their hands. 'Gentlemen, welcome to my home.'

At this, Solomon could not help but laugh. 'I am sorry, Your Grace, but I never thought I would hear those words from you.'

'Then I doubt you will expect these words either,' Hugh replied, pausing to gather his nerve. 'Please call me Hugh, as your wives do. We are family now, after all.'

His guests fell silent as they tried to digest his offer, and then the room broke into laughter along with Solomon.

'Is my hospitality so strange as that?' Hugh asked, confused.

'As strange as if my dog began to talk,' Olivia said, showing him no mercy.

'You are the dangerous Duke of Scofield, after all,' Peg added with a stern expression. 'The unsmiling terror of London.' Then she handed him the baby, who burbled happily in his uneasy grip.

While holding a child, he did not feel the least bit dangerous. He felt terrified at what was to come. But it was a happy sort of terror, if such a thing could be, full of possibilities as well as risks. He beamed down at the child and said, 'You may call me Uncle Hugh, when you are able.'

'As I have been telling everyone who will

listen, Hugh is not the least bit dangerous,' Rachel said as he passed the child back to her mother.

'I cannot afford to be dangerous.' Hugh smiled at his family. 'My wife will not allow it. And you must know, gentlemen, that there is no point in arguing with a woman who loves you once she decides to change your life. And now, let us all go in by the fire and enjoy what I am sure will be the best Christmas ever.'

* * * * *

COMING SOON!

We really hope you enjoyed reading this book.
If you're looking for more romance, be sure to
head to the shops when new books are
available on

Thursday 23rd
June

To see which titles are coming soon, please visit
millsandboon.co.uk/nextmonth

MILLS & BOON ®

Coming next month

THE DEBUTANTE'S SECRET
Sophia James

'I like rules and manners because these are the only things that keep the world from chaos.'

He laughed at her comment and the sound was not kind.

'I cannot tell you what the secret of a successful life is, Miss Barrington-Hall, but a sure way to failure is to try and please everyone.'

'You think that is what I am doing?'

'Aren't you?'

She took in breath and answered him.

'Perhaps your way of pleasing no one has its flaws as well, Mr Moreland, for the illicit and forbidden have their drawbacks.'

'Ahhh, but they are much more fun, Esther.'

Her name was said informally and in a tone that made her heart lurch. She was prepared for neither his wildness nor his passion, and he knew it.

'I think, sir, that we have come to the edge of patience with each other, but I would like to thank you for the confidentiality you have kept concerning my past.'

'How little you know me, Miss Barrington-Hall.'

She frowned and stood her ground.

'Do you allow anyone to, or do you send people off as soon as they might guess something you may not wish them to know?'

'I've always found distance has its advantages because people can often be disappointing.'

Squaring her shoulders, Esther answered him. 'Nothing hurts more than being disappointed by the one person you thought would never hurt you.'

'Your mother?' Now he looked at her with more interest.

But she was not drawn in to making a confession. 'After disappointment there comes hope.'

'Hope to make a good life?'

'Yes, for without it one is lost, and I have been.'

These words had him stepping back.

'I am sure things will improve markedly, Miss Barrington-Hall, for you are the belle of the season with a choice of fine upstanding suitors who will do everything possible to make your life a happy one.'

She could see him retreat almost as a physical thing, a man who knew who he was and would never change. People had disappointed him, that much was for sure, so he had stopped trying to fit in to expectations and walked a path that was far from her own.

Then he was gone, lost into the throng of people on the busy street. Out of his company she felt the loss of what might have been. Once he had said to her that he wanted her to like him, but now...

Continue reading
THE DEBUTANTE'S SECRET
Sophia James

Available next month
www.millsandboon.co.uk

MILLS & BOON

THE HEART OF ROMANCE

A ROMANCE FOR EVERY READER

MODERN

Prepare to be swept off your feet by sophisticated, sexy and seductive heroes, in some of the world's most glamourous and roman[tic] locations, where power and passion collide.

HISTORICAL

Escape with historical heroes from time gone by. Whether your passio[n] for wicked Regency Rakes, muscled Vikings or rugged Highlanders, [?] the romance of the past.

MEDICAL

Set your pulse racing with dedicated, delectable doctors in the high-p[res]sure world of medicine, where emotions run high and passion, comfo[rt] love are the best medicine.

True Love

Celebrate true love with tender stories of heartfelt romance, from the rush of falling in love to the joy a new baby can bring, and a focus o[n] emotional heart of a relationship.

Desire

Indulge in secrets and scandal, intense drama and plenty of sizzling h[ot] action with powerful and passionate heroes who have it all: wealth, st[?] good looks…everything but the right woman.

HEROES

Experience all the excitement of a gripping thriller, with an intense r[o]mance at its heart. Resourceful, true-to-life women and strong, fearles[s] face danger and desire - a killer combination!

To see which titles are coming soon, please visit

millsandboon.co.uk/nextmonth

PROMISE TO OBEY

When Jessica is charmed by Lucas
Coleman into accepting a job at grand
Upton Hall, she is not expecting to have
to provide full-time care for his autistic
son and asthmatic daughter, as well as the
sharp-tongued Lady Grace, who is recu-
perating from hip replacement surgery
— and she certainly did not expect a
marriage proposal from her employer. But
where is the children's mother? Fighting
her attraction to the beguiling Lucas, she
is determined to keep her head. A disastrous affair with a London doctor has put
her off men; but when he descends on
Upton Hall, determined to win her back,
Jessica's life is thrown into turmoil.

Books by Stella Whitelaw
Published by The House of Ulverscroft:

CATS' TALES: A TREASURY
DESERT STORM
WEAVE A LOVING WEB
THE OWL AND THE PUSSYCATS
NEW CAT STORIES
MIDSUMMER MADNESS
PORTRAIT OF A MURDER
MONEY NEVER SLEEPS

STELLA WHITELAW

PROMISE
TO OBEY

Complete and Unabridged

ULVERSCROFT
Leicester

First published in Great Britain in 2013 by
Robert Hale Limited
London

First Large Print Edition
published 2015
by arrangement with
Robert Hale Limited
London

A catalogue record for this book is available
from the British Library.

ISBN 978–1–4448–2258–8

Published by
F. A. Thorpe (Publishing)
Anstey, Leicestershire

Set by Words & Graphics Ltd.
Anstey, Leicestershire
Printed and bound in Great Britain by
T. J. International Ltd., Padstow, Cornwall

This book is printed on acid-free paper

To

My beautiful Rosie who dozed in the
filing tray, keeping me company while I
wrote this book.

Acknowledgements

As always, overwhelming thanks to Dr David Thomas. I bombarded him with questions, every one of which was answered in detail and with patience. If there are any medical mistakes, then they are entirely mine.

The staff of the Tourist Office at Worthing and at Brighton for helpful information.

And again, the libraries at both Oxted and Worthing for endless assistance and encouragement.

And to the editorial team at Robert Hale who are always so friendly and kind. It's a pleasure to work with you all.

Won't you come into the garden?
I would like my roses to see you.

Richard Brinsley Sheridan
1751–1816

1

'Hello? Is there anybody there? I think someone is supposed to be meeting me.'

Jessica Harlow's voice carried along the empty platform. Dried leaves scattered like little insects. Dead geraniums drooped in flowerpots, like exhausted dancers at the end of a long ballet.

Jessica came out of Eastly Station and stood on the forecourt, still wondering if anyone was going to meet her. She was already regretting her decision to accept a three-month private nursing contract at Upton Hall. This place was out in the wilds, masses of trees, and it was beginning to rain.

She stood under the inadequate ironwork porch of the station entrance, peering through the fine drizzle at the bleak view, wondering where she was. It was all hills and woodland, hedges and fields. It was part of the South Downs but even that meant very little. She was a town girl, born and bred in North London. This green countryside was alien. She could barely recognize a rabbit. They had long ears, didn't they, and hopped about, Beatrix Potter style?

It was a forlorn view and she was getting wet and cold. Her shoes were poor protection and her toes were squelching. There was an anorak in her case but it would be foolish to open it in this weather. Everything inside would get wet.

There wasn't even anyone she could ask for the whereabouts of Upton Hall. The station was unmanned with only a machine for tickets. There was no one to help with her wheelie case and travel bag, no bus stop, no taxi. Surely they didn't expect her to walk? Which way, left or right?

'I might as well give up and take the next train back,' she said aloud. 'If there is ever a next train from this godforsaken hole.'

She huddled into her damp clothes. Her smart navy suit and high heels were glistening with raindrops. Her fine tawny hair was already clinging to her cheeks like a wet curtain. She could feel the fringe catching on her eyelashes. She was going to make a fine impression in this state.

There was a discreet cough from some-where. 'Please don't do that,' said an amused voice, deep and resonant. 'I've come out in this damned awful weather to meet you and my mother will be furious if I don't return with you in tow.'

It was not easy to take in the meaning of

the words. She was adrift, like someone on a treadmill, pumping toxic fumes. There was no way out.

Jessica turned to find a tall stranger standing a few yards away in the rain, not suitably dressed either, checked blue shirt soaked, jeans creased, dark hair plastered to his head. He was regarding her with cool courtesy but Jessica refused to be cowed. He was good-looking and probably knew it. His jaw-line was firm and dominant. He was someone who was used to getting his own way.

'You are Miss Harlow? There can't be two young female passengers alighting at Eastly Station today. We get about one a month in a good year. That's our allocation. Southern Railways don't make their profit out of us.'

'I'm Jessica Harlow,' she said. 'I'm here to nurse Lady Grace Coleman of Upton Hall after her hip replacement operation.'

'My mother.' The tall man moved closer and held out his hand. 'I'm Lucas Coleman, son of Lady Grace. Glad to meet you. And father of the two children you are also going to keep an eye on. You're going to save the day for us.'

'The children, yes. Not usually my domain,' said Jessica, shaking his hand. 'But I can do that. Keep an eye on them if you are away.'

'I'm often away,' said Lucas Coleman, enigmatically.

I bet you are, thought Jessica. A playboy, if ever I saw one. He looked like a dissipated layabout, someone who lived off his mother, who never did a day's work. She probably kept him to run errands and meet visitors at the station. 'Can we go now?' she went on. 'I'm getting soaked. Do we have to walk?'

'Heavens no,' said Lucas Coleman, abruptly. 'We are quite civilized out here. We've moved on a bit from the horse and cart days.'

Jessica hadn't noticed the car. It was behind him, parked at some distance against a hedge, a low slung machine in glistening metallic blue. Too low to get into with any dignity. Still, it was a vehicle of sorts. She pretended to be interested, put on her enquiring face.

'Great looking car,' she said. 'What is it?'

'A Porsche Boxster, Spyder class, very fast, very reliable. Lovely vehicle. Are you interested in cars?'

'No,' said Jessica. 'They are merely a means of getting about.'

'I agree,' said Lucas smoothly. 'There's far too much importance attached to status cars these days. But I do like this one. It's fast and suits my purpose.'

He opened the door for her and Jessica lowered herself into the low-slung seat. The

4

dashboard was like an aircraft cockpit with dials and knobs and blinking screens. She struggled to find a seatbelt further down in the depths. She heard Lucas Coleman heaving her case and bag into the boot. The rain was becoming a blanket. She couldn't see anything through the rivulets of water on the windscreen.

This was going to be a disaster. Jessica could already feel that everything was going wrong. She should not have accepted the offer but she had three months to fill before she took up a new hospital appointment in Sheffield. This represented her mortgage repayments and other commitments. She had to keep earning money and the terms on offer were good ones. Lucas Coleman wanted someone to take care of his mother, Lady Grace, when she came out of hospital.

Lucas folded himself into the driver's seat and fastened his seatbelt. Jessica had a chance to look at him more closely. Not that she cared about men anymore, not after Fraser Burton. Fraser had shattered her fragile confidence, and he had done it unforgivably in public, but the experience had made her become a stronger woman. Not many men could do that. It was an evening she wanted to forget.

Lucas had a good-looking face but it was

rigid with a lack of emotion. She wondered what had happened to cause this reserve. At this rate she would never know. There was no way she was going to dig beneath that cold exterior. She'd let him drive her to Upton Hall and then she need never see him again.

'And the children?' she began. 'How old are they? What are they like? You didn't say much about them in your letter.'

'Lily is five and Daniel is seven, going on eight. He'll have his birthday in a few weeks' time.' It was a blunt statement.

'We must have a party,' said Jessica, exhausted already at the thought of jelly and games, party hats and crowds of noisy children.

'I doubt it.'

What an odd answer. Didn't most children have parties on their birthdays? Every child deserved a birthday party.

'We could go to McDonald's. Is there a McDonald's nearby, at Brighton or Worthing? They do great parties. They lay on everything. Daniel would enjoy it.'

'No, thank you, Miss Harlow. We'll talk about this later.'

Jessica shrank back into the low seat. What kind of father was he? All children wanted a party on their birthday.

It was a long and winding drive, leaves

brushing the top of the car, rain streaking the windscreen. Jessica had no idea where they were. He could be driving her to the end of some remote moor, a forgotten quarry or desolate headland. She was absolutely in his hands. There was no knowing if he was who he said he was, or where he was taking her.

She thought of the book she was reading. A crime novel with an abduction and a victim who was never found. A little unsettling.

Jessica felt a surge of panic. Panic was a recent thing. An unrealistic fear. It was all part of the aftermath of the faithless Fraser. The man had almost destroyed her but she was fighting back. She was clinging tight to the seatbelt now as if they were on the point of crashing over Beachy Head.

'There's no need to be so tense, Miss Harlow,' said Lucas Coleman. 'I can drive this beast. I know what I'm doing. We are not going to land upside-down in a ditch. You're safe in my hands.'

'Sorry,' said Jessica, trying to relax. Her skirt was damp, clinging to her legs like a wet sandwich. 'It's been a difficult day, such a long train journey. So many changes. I'm feeling really tired.'

'Shall I play you some music? To soothe your shattered nerves? How about Rod Stewart in his most nostalgic mode? The

7

Great American Songbook. *It Had to be You.* It's one of my favourites.'

He slid in the CD and pressed the starter button. The soft opening notes and rasping voice of the maestro were a perfect contrast. Jessica felt her breathing slow down in time to the music. Maybe she could survive these three months after all. It was not forever. The time would fly by if she kept busy. A hip replacement patient could not be that difficult and she could easily manage two small children.

'Cheer up, Miss Harlow. We'll soon be there,' he said. 'Upton Hall is only a few more miles, to the right, behind the trees. This damned rain.'

'I'll believe it when I see it.'

'My mother may be a dragon but she doesn't bite.'

'I do bite.'

'Then you may have met your match with my mother, Lady Grace. She's a fighter. She gives as good as she gets, just like you.'

Was there a glimmer of laughter in his voice or had she imagined it?

Jessica was beginning to wish she had stayed at home or turned back after one bleak look at Eastly Station. This fancy sports car was no consolation, nor was its cool looking owner. It was starting to rain in earnest, the windscreen wipers hardly coping. The hills were swathed in fog like a creepy Johnny Depp film.

She felt Lucas shiver in his wet clothes. He switched on a heater.

'Why are you soaked?' she asked. 'Didn't you know it was raining?'

'I was late meeting you, so I didn't stop to get a raincoat. Then I found the petrol was low so I had to make a detour to fill her up. I didn't want to run out of petrol with a special passenger on board. You wouldn't have believed such a tall story, would you? Running out of petrol in a leafy lane?'

'I doubt it,' said Jessica. 'I've heard it all before.'

'I was very late in last night, early hours, so I hadn't checked.'

Late in? Party? Out clubbing? Girlfriend or girlfriends? Jessica sighed. She guessed that any one of those might be true, probably all three. He looked the kind of man with a string of doting women friends and he'd said nothing about a wife. She wouldn't be joining the queue. She had learned her lesson. No more men for her after Fraser. From now on it was going to be work and more work.

She watched his hands on the steering wheel. They were strong and capable hands with long tapering fingers, nails cut short.

The smooth hands of an artist. He'd never done a day's work in his life, that was obvious. She wouldn't waste any sympathy on him, even if he was trying to be pleasant.

'Thank you for meeting me,' she said, in an effort to bridge the gap, but not using his name. Her wet clothes were clammy and uncomfortable. She needed to be dry and warm. 'I appreciate your kindness.'

'Don't worry,' he said, his silvery grey eyes still cold and blank. 'You won't see much of me, day or night. I'm a creature of uncertain habits.'

He was putting her straight, right from the start. Lucas Coleman was out of bounds. She needn't harbour any romantic thoughts about the heir to Upton Hall. She was, after all, the hired help. The temporary hired help.

'Don't worry,' said Jessica, deliberately repeating his phrase. 'I won't get in your way. I shall be far too busy with your family. It looks as if I shall have my hands full with two children and a convalescent.'

She turned away, staring out of the window at the passing countryside. It was a blur of trees and branches, swaying in the wind. What on earth had she let herself in for? It was going to be a battle of staying power.

'Miss Harlow,' said Lucas Coleman, eyes fixed on the road ahead. 'Let's get this sorted.

You are only employed to work here, to help the family though a difficult period. There is no ulterior motive.'

'I don't understand what you mean.'

'I don't have any designs on you. Even though you are quite pretty. If a drowned rat can look pretty.'

2

Lucas Coleman drove the last two miles from the station with occasional small talk that passed for conversation. Jessica was cold and wet and not listening. She appreciated that the man was trying to put her at her ease, but she could only wonder what on earth had possessed her to come out here to the wilds of the country. There was nothing but fields and hills in the pallid light. Civilization was receding fast.

'Do you drive?' he was asking.

'Yes, of course. Doesn't everyone?'

'While you are with us, you can have use of my mother's car. It's a vintage Vanden Plas Austin Princess, and she's very proud of it. In fact, I think she loves it more than she loves her family. It's got little picnic trays in the back that let down, with a place to stand your drink. Very posh.'

'Useful for picnics,' said Jessica drily.

'Automatic gears.'

'I can change gears.'

'I'm sure you can. Automatic takes a little getting used to. I've stalled it a couple of times. A bit tricky to start.'

12

'It's surprising that your mother lets you drive it then.'

'She didn't know,' he said.

Jessica was beginning to think she had brought all the wrong clothes. It looked like Wellingtons, jerseys and anorak weather. The windscreen wipers were working overtime. Upton Hall would probably be unheated and her bedroom like ice. She should have brought winceyette pyjamas, bed socks and a hot water bottle.

'Does it rain every day down here?'

'This is the wet season,' he said, as if they lived in Asia.

'I hope you are not expecting me to wear uniform all the time,' she said.

'No, of course not. The kids would think they were in hospital. Just wear your own clothes. Be comfortable and warm. Lots of layers.'

This sounded ominous as if he was warning her that Upton Hall could be a chilly house. Well, she would soon change that. This fit and healthy looking man could flex his muscles chopping wood for a fire. She'd soon find him a couple of trees. There were plenty around.

'What about my hours of work,' Jessica went on, relentlessly. 'Your letter didn't say anything about my time off.'

'Didn't it? How very remiss. I should prefer

it if you were with the children every weekend, both Saturday and Sunday, but you can certainly take time off during the week. They are both at school and the school bus picks them up at the end of the road. But there is always Lady Grace to look after. I don't want her left alone for any length of time, not so soon after her operation.'

'Patients usually recover quickly from a hip replacement. They need to keep moving. It's not like the old days with endless bed rest.' It didn't sound as if she would have any time off. Jessica wished she had asked earlier.

'As you think fit and proper,' said Lucas, a renewed coolness entering his voice. 'But I would remind you that you are employed to look after my mother and whole days off to go gallivanting to the shops are out of the question.'

'I wasn't planning to go gallivanting.'

'Then we can work something out.'

'Surely you could be around too, occasionally?' said Jessica, with a note of sharpness. 'There are times when you could look after the children and your mother and I could have an afternoon off. A few hours perhaps?'

'No, I'm not,' he said curtly, closing the subject. 'We're nearly there. Look out for tall chimneys through the trees. This is Upton Hall.'

All Jessica could see were trees. They were driving through an avenue of close trees, the canopy of dripping leaves overhead like a cathedral roof. Her spirits fell. She didn't even know what kind of trees they were. This was going to be disastrous. She could feel the despair growing. She was already homesick for her little London flat and wanted more than anything to turn round and go back to its safety. Then she remembered that she had let it to a friend of a friend for the whole three months, banking the rent. There was no going back.

'Upton Hall,' he said, with a degree of pride and utter masculinity. 'The home of the Colemans for over a hundred years.'

Upton Hall was impressive, standing within the lea of a low pastured hill, sheltered on two sides from the worst of the wind. It was a two-storeyed stone building with leaded windows, with a tall tower at one end with wide curved bay windows, crenulated like a mock castle. The front door was of heavy oak, flanked by two columns and a porch of slate. Virginia creeper was turning to russet on the walls, warming the austere lines of the house.

'It's . . . it's very grand,' said Jessica, eventually, unable to find the right words. She had a hundred sudden impressions, crowding in. 'How old is it?'

'It's a Victorian folly, built onto a medieval farmhouse and stables, we think. The farmhouse is at the back, part of it now the new kitchen, a utility room and garages. It's rambling inside. You'll get lost.'

'I'm lost already,' said Jessica.

Upton Hall was awesome, so much larger than anything she had ever seen before. But its grandeur had a certain gentleness, a timeless warmth.

The unhappiness in her voice was not lost on Lucas. He bent forward, his fiery, silver grey eyes for once tinged with concern. 'Cheer up, Miss Harlow. You'll love it once you get used to it. Upton Hall will grow on you.'

Jessica did not believe him. Nothing was going to sway her or make the next three months any easier. She would have to grit her teeth and get on with it. The handsome Lucas Coleman could be as pleasant and welcoming as he could manage, it would not make any difference. She hated the countryside, she hated trees and especially she hated wet trees, dripping everywhere.

'Does it ever stop raining?'

'Occasionally. We put out the flags and eat in the garden.'

'Even in winter?'

'Especially in the winter.'

Now he was laughing at her and that made the arrival even worse. The sooner she escaped to whatever damp bedroom was to be hers, the better. She would lock the door, become distant and withdrawn and go into a Jane Austen decline.

Lucas stopped the car in the curved drive and climbed out. He went round and opened the car door. Jessica was struggling to undo the safety belt.

'Let me do that for you,' he said, bending over her. For a second his unruly dark hair brushed her face and the shock was electric. The freshness of soap and water with his own manly scent was overwhelming, scant inches away. For a second Jessica could not breathe. It was an endless moment.

'There. It's an awkward one, too far back. Damned designers.'

He straightened up and held out his arm to assist her. The passenger seat of the Porsche was so low down, again Jessica was struggling. She had to use his arm as a lever, to get herself out of the seat. She was angry for being made to look such a fool when she was normally so calm and efficient. It washed over her in a turbulent wave. She brushed back wet hair from her face.

'Thank you,' she said, trying to regain her composure. 'Damned stupid seat,' she went on. 'Built for a midget.'

'And you are about five foot seven. I do agree. I have the same problem.'

Now that Lucas was standing beside her, she realized that he was over six feet. He would have to fold himself up to get inside the car. He was already getting her case out of the boot and carrying it towards the front door.

He turned round, seeing her hesitation. It was a long, challenging look.

'Are you coming, or have you changed your mind already?'

Jessica did not know what to say. He was giving her a chance to back out. Say yes, and in twenty minutes she could be sitting on a wet platform, waiting for a train back to London, if there were any trains back to London at this time.

'I'm coming.'

It didn't sound like her at all. Some other person was speaking. Some strange woman that she didn't know. The real Jessica Harlow had gone into hibernation.

⋆ ⋆ ⋆

The hall floor was tiled with black and white squares. A curving staircase led to the upper regions. Busts of Greek philosophers stood

18

on marble pillars and portraits of ancestors in oil glared down from the walls.

Someone had put bursts of wild flowers on side tables and their scent was overwhelming. The huge vases looked antique and valuable.

'Mrs Harris, the housekeeper,' said Lucas, putting down her case and bag. 'She has a mania for picking flowers but no sense on how to arrange them. It requires a special skill. Perhaps you can do flowers. Let me show you round.'

He opened a door to the left. It was a long, gracious room in ivory and pale blue with a grand piano, armchairs and more portraits. 'The sitting room,' he announced. 'My mother uses it when she has bridge parties.'

Jessica could not imagine anyone sitting there and feeling comfortable. It was stiff and unused. A room that was kept for best and best never happened.

Lucas turned right off the hall. 'The library. No overdue fines.'

The room was wall to wall leather-bound books, ninety-nine per cent unread. But Jessica spotted a small clutch of modern novels on a side table. It also had a computer at a desk overlooking the drive. The several armchairs were deep and inviting, well used. There was a small wine cooler in a corner.

'Can you use a computer?' he asked.

'I'm not from outer space,' she answered, biting off each word.

'You may use this one. Remind me to give you the password.'

Lucas nodded, then opened sliding doors in a wall between the bookcases. 'This leads into the dining room. So if we hold a party, we can use both rooms. Unfortunately, we rarely hold parties. Such a pity. This house was made for parties.'

The dining room was beautiful with eau de nil walls, toning carpet and curtains. More portraits on the walls. A long polished walnut table that could seat at least twelve people. Jessica hoped she would not have to eat here.

'How do you talk to each other?' she asked. 'With walkie-talkies?'

'No,' he said. 'We don't sit marooned at either end. We sit together, here at the top. It's really pleasant. Nearer the kitchen, so the food is always hot.'

He took her up a few steps into a strangely bleak area, white-washed walls and low ceiling. There was nothing in it, apart from a stone inglenook fireplace. The floor was made up of huge slabs of uneven slate. Their size was amazing.

'We think this is the oldest part of the house, perhaps even before the farmhouse. Maybe it's all that is left of some medieval hall. This middle post has been dated back to 1412. All the rest has gone.'

The post was thick and blackened, gnarled and sturdy enough to hold up a roof. Lucas stood with his arms laced easily round the post in an embrace, something he had done since a child. He was looking at the post fondly.

'How do they know how old it is?' Jessica asked.

'They took a core sample,' he said. 'It's the tiniest plug of wood. They can tell the date by the year rings. It's very clever and very accurate.'

'No graffiti?'

'Not on our rings.'

'I'm relieved.'

They went back into the hall and began climbing. The stairs divided halfway and Lucas took her first to the left. 'The kid's bedrooms are in this wing. They have a bedroom each, a family bathroom, and their nanny's room is next door.'

'Do I have the nanny's room, then?' Jessica felt this was to be her place in their life. She was the nanny, single bed, no radiator, no fire, cramped and soulless.

'No way, Miss Harlow. Follow me.' He led her across the wide landing. Jessica reckoned they must be nearing the tower. 'My mother has the front bedroom in the tower. It's a beautiful room with big windows that look out onto the garden, the best in the house. You are in the guest room, next to hers. It's called the Primrose Room. I think you'll like it.' He threw open the door.

It was as big as her entire flat in London with pale yellow walls and cream paintwork; buttermilk damask curtains with matching cover on the double bed. A sofa covered in saffron velvet toned with the carpet; a desk by the window, and an upright chair with upholstered seat in the same velvet. The room was warm and radiated light. 'En suite through there,' Lucas added, pointing to a far door.

Jessica went over to the window. The view was of rolling hills and dappled fields, the hedges and crops of trees like a painting. Nothing moved. It was so still, emptiness and clarity stole the scene. It had even stopped raining. So unlike the rooftop view from her North London flat of ugly buildings, refuse bins and scaffolding, parked lorries and neon street lights.

'Thank you,' she said with genuine warmth. 'I love the room.'

Lucas did a mock sigh of relief. 'Glad to have got something right at last.'

'So where's your room?'

Jessica had not meant to ask but it came without thinking. She did not want to bump into him in the night. Coming home late from a party.

'I have a makeshift sort of room, somewhere to bunk down, over the garage stables. I'm not here much. You won't bump into me in the night,' he added, reading her thoughts. 'You may want to tidy up before meeting my mother. She's very particular. I'll bring up your case.'

The buttercup tiled bathroom was as pretty as the bedroom. Jessica had another sigh of relief. She was going to be so comfortable here. Some of her misgivings faded, her spirit recovering. But she still tested the lock on the door.

She was dishevelled by the wind and rain and all her subtle make-up had disappeared. She set to and repaired the damage so that Lady Grace would get a good impression. Her high-heeled shoes were muddied and she changed into a pair of flat black suede slip-ons. Her wet jacket was hung behind the bathroom door to dry.

She tucked her white shirt into the plain navy skirt, added a red patterned silk scarf to her throat and she was ready to face the dragon.

'So you are the nurse who is supposed to look after me and make sure I do all the right things,' said Lady Grace with a decided lack of grace. 'You're a bit too young and skinny for my idea of a nurse. Are you properly trained? Supposing I fell?'

'I'm stronger than you think,' said Jessica.

'You don't look strong enough to lift a bedpan.'

'I should hope you are bathroom trained.'

'I'm convalescing after a serious operation, I'll have you know. I need a great deal of care and attention.'

'Hip and knee replacements are routine these days and highly successful,' said Jessica. 'You'll be as right as rain in no time, and free of pain.'

Lady Grace snorted. 'I'm certainly not free of pain yet. I need regular medication.'

'I can do regular medication,' said Jessica calmly.

'Any idiot can pop a couple of capsules and fill a glass with water. I don't need your help.'

'I'm glad to hear it. I shall be free then to make sure you eat the right foods and take the right amount of exercise. Exercise is the key. It will all help to make your recovery quick and painless.'

'I can do all of that by myself, thank you, Nurse, Matron, whatever you are,' said Lady Grace. 'Well, if you have got to stay, I suppose I'll have to get used to it. What am I supposed to call you?'

'Jessica will do fine,' said Jessica.

'I don't like fancy names. I shall call you Jess.'

Jessica fumed. She hated her name being shortened. It made her sound as if she was a dog. A shaggy dog at that.

Lady Grace was indeed tetchy and short tempered. She was sitting in an armchair by the big bay window in her bedroom, dressed in a fawn skirt and blue twin set, a double string of pearls at her neck. Her fine grey hair was drawn back into a French pleat and pinned with combs. She had a certain pallor after her operation and the lines on her face were not all bad temper and impatience.

'Shakespeare didn't think Jessica was a fancy name,' said Jessica. 'He used it in one of his plays, *The Merchant of Venice*. Jessica was the daughter of Shylock, in love with Lorenzo.'

'Makes no difference. I'll still call you Jess, Shakespeare or not. Never could stand all that rubbish. Shakespeare indeed.'

Jessica let it pass. There were more important things to discuss. She had a feeling that Lady Grace was not moving about much or doing any exercises.

'How are you getting on with the exercises they gave you at the hospital?' she asked. 'Have you got the printed sheet?'

'They are too painful so I'm not doing them,' said Lady Grace. 'Getting from my bed to this chair is all I can do at present.' She nodded towards the window. 'I like the view. It's perfect, don't you agree?'

Jessica moved towards the bay window. She could appreciate the glorious countryside now, hill upon hill of the South Downs, once deeply forested, now for grazing sheep and growing corn. The view from this window was of the gardens which she had not noticed, arriving in the rain in Lucas's low-slung car. The rain had flattened some of the flowers, the heavy heads hanging with abandon to the elements. But the droplets were glistening in the late sun and the garden looked magical.

'It is indeed a beautiful garden, a beautiful view,' said Jessica. 'You'll be able to walk round it very soon. Once we get you downstairs.'

'I can't go downstairs!' Lady Grace was aghast. 'I can't do stairs. Far too painful. I can barely reach this chair.'

'The more exercise you do, the less painful it will be,' said Jessica patiently. 'The long

26

term success of this operation depends on the patient strengthening the leg muscles that hold up the hip. So, regular exercise.'

'I'm not just the patient,' said Lady Grace indignantly. 'I'm Lady Grace Coleman, not a nobody. I know what I can do and what I can't do.'

Jessica held back a sharp retort. She paced the bedroom, judging its size. It was a big room, decorated in a style of thirty years ago, heavy walnut furniture with dark rose flowered curtains and toning carpet. Silver-backed brushes lay on the dressing table with an old-fashioned glass powder bowl and puff. A single tube of Max Factor dark red lipstick and bottle of clear nail varnish stood beside a large bottle of Elizabeth Arden eau de cologne.

'You have a beautiful room, too,' said Jessica. 'But it will become your prison if you don't get some exercise. I suggest you walk from one side of the room to the other once every hour, holding onto something. Then tomorrow you can walk to the landing and back and perhaps try one or two steps of the stairs.'

'The stairs? Are you trying to kill me, young woman? I can't do the stairs. My son, Lucas, will have to have one of those new-fangled stair lifts put in.'

'On the contrary, I'm going to get you downstairs and into the garden. You won't need a stair lift, I promise you. It would spoil that lovely staircase. You need lots of encouragement and a positive attitude.'

Lady Grace swung round in her chair and the sudden movement was painful. She gasped, her fury overriding the pain.

'I won't be spoken to like this. You can leave my house immediately. Lucas can get another nanny for the children.' She sat back, her face reddening, her hands clutched together.

Jessica searched the bedside table for prescription painkillers. She couldn't find them. But Lady Grace's leather handbag was on the floor by the bed. She opened it and a packet of painkillers, with her name from the hospital dispensary, was inside. She fetched a glass of water from the adjacent bathroom and took two tablets to Lady Grace.

'Here you are. These will help. You shouldn't lean forward in a chair or in bed for the first couple of weeks. The hospital told you that, didn't they? And you need a high-rise toilet seat. I'll get one for you.'

'You've been in my bathroom,' Lady Grace spluttered.

'That's right,' said Jessica. 'I'm a nurse. I go in bathrooms.'

'Not in mine, you don't.'

The air was strained and Lady Grace abruptly fell silent.

'I'll go and make some tea. I think we could both do with a cup of tea,' said Jessica. She had to get away from this exasperating woman.

'Is that hair colour natural?' was her parting shot.

'It's certainly not a wig,' said Jessica.

Jessica escaped to the peace of the landing, her heart pounding. She had never, in all her days of nursing, had such an impossible twenty minutes with a patient. She could easily grab her coat and her case and walk back to the station. It might take an hour, two hours. But Jessica knew she couldn't walk out on a difficult patient: Lady Grace needed her or that operation would have been wasted.

Jessica took several deep breaths to steady herself.

This prickly old woman needed help. The hip replacement would not be a success if she refused to exercise and she would be back to square one. Back to constant pain and unable to get about at all.

It was a challenge. Jessica could not resist a challenge.

★ ★ ★

Mrs Harris, the housekeeper, was busy in the kitchen supervising the children's tea. The scene was pleasant and homely. Jessica noted the big Aga range pumping out heat and moved towards it. This was somewhere to get warm.

'Hello, Mrs Harris. I'm Jessica Harlow, nurse of sorts for the next three months, looking after Lady Grace. I think she would appreciate a tray of tea, if you have time. Something to calm her nerves. She is a little frayed by my arrival.'

'Of course, Miss Harlow. I'll take a tray up to her ladyship immediately. Perhaps you'd like some tea yourself. You could join the children.'

'That's exactly what I shall do,' said Jessica gratefully. 'And no need to call me Miss Harlow, Jessica will do.'

She sat down at the kitchen table, aware that the two children had been listening to the conversation. They looked at her expectantly. Now she was going to meet them and make friends. She hoped that they were not as prickly as their dragon grandmother.

'Hello,' she said, turning her attention to the little girl. 'And who are you?'

The little girl was squirming in her seat, her eyes bright with excitement. She was about five years old, a little on the plump side, but as pretty as a picture with a riot of dark curls and bewitching lashes that were outrageously long.

'I'm Lily,' she said, wriggling. 'I'm five. I go to school now.'

'Nice to meet you, Lily.' She shook a sticky hand with a solemn dignity. 'You must show me some of your school work. I'd like to see it.'

'Do we call you Jessica Willdo?'

Jessica laughed. The first genuine laugh of the day. It lit up her face and she was transformed. Her true face was often hidden behind professional calmness. But when she laughed, her periwinkle blue eyes sparkled like gems and her mouth curved into an irresistible shape of happiness.

'Jessica Willdo, will do.'

'I like you already,' said Lily, still chewing on her jam sandwich. 'I like you better than our last nanny. All she did was smoke all the time and watch television.'

'First of all, Lily, I will put you straight. I am not your nanny. I am a nurse who is here to look after your grandmother after her operation. But at the same time, I'll be around for you both, keep an eye on you. You can come to me any time, ask me anything, and we'll do things together.'

'What sort of things?'

31

'For a start, I thought we might go to Worthing and see what's there, walk on the beach if the tide is out. You'll need your Wellington boots.'

Lily jumped up and down in her chair, wheezing. 'Can we go now, Willdo?'

Jessica laughed again, so much that she nearly spilt her tea. 'It's far too late, poppet. We'll see about tomorrow or the next day.'

She turned her attention to the boy who had not said a word. He was concentrating on his tea. She noticed that he had lined up the jam, the butter dish, and a jar of Marmite in front of his plate, like sentries. His cup of tea was exactly in line with his plate and he had put the spoon rigidly straight by the saucer.

'Hello,' she said gently. 'I'm Jessica. Who are you?'

'Who are you?' he said.

'I've just explained. I'm Jessica, a nurse who has come to look after your grandmother after her operation. Nice to meet you.'

'Nice to meet you.'

Lily piped up, her mouth lined with jam, 'Daniel doesn't say much. He likes being alone. He doesn't like people.'

Jessica noticed the lack of eye contact. Daniel would not look at her. There was no communication between them. She tried again. It might be initial shyness.

'I'd like us all to be friends while I'm here. It could be such fun. I have lots of plans.' This was not true, but she had time to make some instant plans. 'We'll do all sorts of things together. And I know that someone soon has a birthday.' There was no response. 'You don't want to be stuck in the house all the time, do you?'

'All the time,' said Daniel.

Alarm bells were ringing in Jessica's head. The repetition of her words. His whole posture had not moved. He lived in another world, no contact with this one. He was cutting his sandwich into exact squares and lining them into rows. He then ate them in order. At least, he was eating, methodically.

'Never mind, Daniel. We'll talk another time.'

'Another time,' he said.

Jessica finished her tea. She was not hungry. The emotion of the last few hours had drained her appetite. Perhaps later, she would poke around and make herself a cheese sandwich.

'Willdo?' asked Lily, still wheezing as she started on a big slice of home-made sponge cake, 'are you going to put us to bed? Are you going to read us a story?'

'I guess I can do all that. What story would you like me to read?'

'The one about the baby mole who couldn't find his way home in the fading light.' Lily was perfectly sure about her favourite story.

'That's a new one on me,' said Jessica. 'And what's your favourite story, Daniel?'

This threw the boy off balance. He was seven, coming on eight, and looked a lot like his father. He was going to be lean and tall, incredibly handsome, break a few hearts one day. He had no answer to that question. He drew swirls on his plate with smears of Marmite. He did not look at her.

'Perhaps you'll tell me later,' said Jessica, throwing him a lifeline.

'Later,' he said.

★　★　★

Jessica stood outside the house in the falling dusk and wondered where she would find Lucas. He said he had a room over the stables. She had no intention of going to his room but she might find his car parked in the stables.

She wasn't angry but she was annoyed that Lucas had not been straight with her. He had got her down here to Upton Hall on false pretences about the children and there was no way he was going to escape her tongue.

She had an anorak over her shoulders because the trees were still spilling their raindrops. The garden scent was heady and the landscape was mesmerizing her. She wondered if she could cut some flowers and put them in her room. A few wouldn't be missed. She loved fresh flowers. She always bought herself a bunch in a market.

The peace of the garden was soothing, the mist spinning round her like a cocoon. Perhaps she would be beamed up to some alien ship and transported to an Elysian community. It would be peaceful there.

'Have you survived?' Lucas was coming out of the mist, clad now in Wellington boots and worn anorak, his hair still plastered wet to his head. He looked breathtakingly handsome. 'You don't look too shattered. How did you get on with the dragon, Lady Grace?'

'I think I won,' said Jessica.

'First round to you, then.'

'Do you have the walker frame? Surely the hospital issued one for your mother to use? She needs it.'

'It's downstairs, in a cupboard. My mother won't use it. Says it makes her look a cripple. It does look a bit like sheltered housing gear.'

'She will be a cripple if she doesn't get some exercise. Can you resurrect it and take it upstairs? I shall get her to use it.'

'Your word is my command.' Lucas bowed his head in mock deference, looking grave, almost grim. 'I obey the dragon-slayer.'

'Daniel and Lily,' said Jessica, changing the subject.

'My two delightful children.'

'You didn't tell me.'

'Tell you what?' He looked defensive, a hard set on his face, but still someone in charge. He looked over her head, out into the garden.

'You didn't tell me that Lily was overweight and asthmatic and that Daniel is autistic. They both need trained help.'

'And aren't you exactly the right person to do that?' said Lucas, coming so close that she could barely stand straight. 'I looked into your qualifications. You've done a lot of work with difficult children. I don't want them regimented and put into specialist centres where children are numbers and shuffled about like pieces on a chessboard. I want them looked after at home. I want you to change their lives.'

'In three months?' Jessica was astounded at his impudence.

'However long it takes.'

Jessica took a deep breath and moved away from his closeness. Rain was dripping off his nose. His tongue came out and licked away a drip. A sharp, guilty thrill ran through her and he caught the change of expression.

'You'll stay?' he asked with a sudden sweetness, mentally on his knees but not physically on his knees. There was an unexpected warmth in his eyes.

'I suppose I'll stay,' she said reluctantly.

'Thank you, Jessica.' Lucas brought his hands out from behind his back. He was holding a bunch of freshly cut yellow pom-pom dahlias and white daisies. 'I thought you might like these for your room. I think you like flowers.'

'Thank you,' said Jessica, taking the flowers. 'But there is one more thing I must ask you. What about your wife? Will she be here too, telling me what to do, ordering me about?'

His face froze. 'No,' he said. 'Forget my wife. She's not likely to interfere in any way.'

'How can I be sure?'

'You can take my word.'

He snapped out the words and walked away. His back said don't ask me again. It was a wall of ice. Jessica was suddenly afraid.

She walked slowly back into the house, wondering what she had taken on.

3

It was a long time before Jessica got her breath back. Lucas had tricked her into this job and that made her really mad with a complex mixture of emotions. She had been gullible, not asking the right questions, taking all he had said at face value.

But she could also see his point of view as a father. He cared about his children and he knew they both needed help. No nanny was qualified to take on the complex task. And would she have come if he had told her the truth? Probably not. She would have said that she didn't know enough about autism and that Lily needed a dietician, not a nurse.

She was here now and she would have to make the best of it. She might be able to make the smallest difference, but at least she would get Lady Grace up and downstairs. Even if she had to fight that lady for every step of the way.

It was going to be a fight. Two strong wills in opposition. Jessica might end up feeling a fool, but she knew she could genuinely make a difference.

Bathtime with Lily was hilarious. The

family bathroom had been converted from a small side bedroom. It was plain cream tiled, but there was plenty of space and a comfortable Lloyd Loom basket chair to sit on, and there were more ducks than the Royals could shoot in a day. Lily blew enough bubbles to launch herself into space. Jessica was glad of a plastic apron. It was ages since she had towel dried a little girl, and the small cuddly, sweet smelling bundle was delightful. So different from washing a sickly child in the antiseptic confines of a hospital ward.

'You are going to read me a story, aren't you, Willdo?'

'Of course,' said Jessica. 'I always keep my word, if I can.'

'And you are not going off down to the pub after we've gone to bed?'

'No, I'll be here. Wherever did you get that idea from?'

'The nanny before the last one was always down the pub.' Lily giggled. 'We called her Ginger Beer because of her hair and the pub. She was always down at the pub drinking ginger beer. And she had ginger hair.'

'That wasn't very kind. She might have been drinking champagne.'

'She wasn't very kind. She wouldn't read to us at all.'

'Perhaps she couldn't read very well.'

'I can read. Only small words, of course. Daniel can't read properly yet.'

Daniel bathed by himself in awkward silence. He didn't want a story but Jessica noticed that his door was left open so that he could listen to the baby mole story. Lily managed her nightly inhaler dose with a careless regard to the correct procedure. It was more gasp and puff and blow. Jessica made a mental note to show Lily tomorrow. She wondered if anyone had ever checked.

'Goodnight, Lily, sweet dreams,' said Jessica, tucking her in. 'Sleep tight.'

'Night, night, Willdo. I like having you here. You will stay, won't you?'

Again that anxious note as if Lily was used to being let down. Perhaps nannies came and went. It seemed they did.

'Don't you worry, Lily. I'll be here tomorrow.'

Jessica switched on the dim battery light on the wall and half closed the door. Mrs Harris had told her that Lily had nightmares if she was left in the dark. Jessica wondered what the nightmares were about.

Jessica looked into Daniel's room. He was already in bed, huddled under the clothes, only the top of his head showing. He also had a dim light on the wall.

'Goodnight, Daniel, sweet dreams,' she

said. 'You can stay up a little later tomorrow if you like. You don't have to go to bed at exactly the same time as Lily.'

There was no answer. But she hadn't expected any.

She tidied up the bathroom, leaving nothing on the floor that they could slip on, in case one of the children got up to use the bathroom in the night. She gave her hair a quick smooth, tucking away the damp ends, and went across the landing to Lady Grace's bedroom. After a polite knock on the door, and a moment's pause, she went in.

Lady Grace was sitting on the edge of the bed, looking distraught and dishevelled. Her hair had escaped from its neat French pleat.

'Where were you when I wanted you?' she cried out, her voice low and full of pain. 'I've been calling and calling.'

Jessica knew this was not true. She would have heard. The children's bedrooms were only across the landing. And the baby mole story had been read in a hushed silence.

'I'm here now, Lady Grace. What do you need?'

'I need to get to the bathroom, idiot. I can't make it without help.' She was struggling to stand up but making a poor job of it. 'You know that.'

'My name is Jessica by the way, not idiot.

41

Take my arm and I'll help you to the bathroom. Lucas is going to bring up your walking frame which you will find a great help. You can lean on it as two extra legs.'

'I'm not using that damned contraption.'

'Oh yes, you are. You'll be surprised at how much support it gives. No need to tell anyone. Use it in secret if you like. Hide it in the bathroom. Give it a name. Call it Fred. Fred is a nice name. Unless you actually know someone called Fred.'

Jessica saw a fractional quirk to the woman's lips. It was the nearest Lady Grace ever got to smiling. She would never show that anything amused her. A bit like Queen Victoria. It was slow progress to the bathroom, and once safely there, Jessica left Lady Grace on her own. She knew further help would be an insult to her dignity. She heard water running and thought it safe to leave her.

Jessica took the tea tray down to the kitchen. Mrs Harris was busy preparing supper. She was a comely woman in her late fifties, with greying hair still tied back in the ponytail of her youth. Jessica could imagine her in the carefree flower power days, dancing to the Beatles barefoot in a long flowing dress with flowers strung in her hair and round her neck. Very rural and poetic. Mr Harris had been lucky.

'I'm doing you and the master a cold buffet on the sideboard in the dining room, with a tureen of hot leek and potato soup. Will that be all right, Miss Jessica?'

'Perfect. Is Mr Lucas still around then?'

'He's fiddling with the Austin, I expect. Making sure it's all right for you to drive. He'll probably give me a lift home if it's still raining, though I've got my bicycle. I live in the village, you see. Dove Cottage, down by the green.'

'I didn't know there was a village.'

'It's called West Easily which is the daftest name, proper Sussex, that is. We've got a lot of daft names. Some people collect them. It's only a few houses and cottages, a church and a pub. The mobile library calls once a week. There's a small grocers shop. My brother, Ted, runs the shop. You can get most things. Here at Upton Hall, we have a weekly delivery from that Avocado firm, ordered on the Internet. Newfangled shopping. How can you tell what you want from a photo?'

Jessica moved over to the Aga and lifted her hands towards the warmth. It was raining in earnest again, large drops pelting onto the path, spurting brown earth.

'Always ask me if you want a lift home, Mrs Harris.'

'That's real kind of you, miss. Thank you.'

'And Lady Grace's supper?'

'I'm doing a tray of the same for her ladyship. It's her favourite soup.'

'I'll help you carry it up.'

'Thanks. I always hate carrying soup upstairs in case I spill any.'

'Why not take it in a lidded jug and pour it out when you get there?' Jessica suggested, seeing a bowl of hot soup sliding everywhere on a disaster course.

'Now that's an idea. Why didn't I think of that?'

'It's an old hospital trick,' Jessica grinned. 'Hot soup is dangerous.'

It was quite a procession taking supper up to her ladyship. Jessica privately adjusted the title to her battleship. Lady Grace was sitting in her chair, looking regal and triumphant. She had tidied her hair.

'I shan't be needing Fred,' she said with a straight face.

'He's handy to have around,' said Jessica, equally straight faced.

Mrs Harris looked bemused but immediately began laying a small table which she lifted across to the armchair. A white lace cloth and silver cutlery appeared.

'Your favourite soup,' she said.

'I don't have a favourite soup,' said Lady Grace, reverting to normal.

'Leek and potato. You said it was your favourite.'

'Pour, not talk, Mrs Harris. It's getting cold. And please draw the curtains. It looks dark and miserable outside. I don't want to look at it.'

Mrs Harris did as she was told. Jessica wondered how long she had put up with her employer. Maybe work was hard to get in West Easily. Or perhaps there was another reason she stayed. Some dark secret that she knew nothing about. Jessica thought about the possibility of a secret, but quickly gave up.

It was none of her business.

Lady Grace dismissed both women. 'But I'll need you later,' she added, nodding towards Jessica.

Jessica checked on the children who were both fast asleep. She noticed that Daniel's toys were all lined up in rows. And his shoes were in rows. A sad young boy, living in a world of his own.

She changed into a cornflower blue tracksuit for supper, as her skirt and shirt were still damp from bathtime. There was no need to dress up for Lucas Coleman and it was going to be a snack supper. She would be warm and comfortable. She wandered into the dining room, not knowing if it was the right time.

Lucas was already there, struggling with opening a bottle of wine. He'd screwed the corkscrew in diagonally so the cork would not come out. He looked annoyed then amused. He peered at the bottle.

'I'm hopeless. Can't do anything properly,' he drawled calmly. 'Are you any good at this?'

'I'll have a go,' said Jessica, jerking her gaze away. She withdrew the corkscrew and started again, making sure it went in straight. Then she folded down the levers and the cork came out, ruined in shape but out. She noticed that it was a very good New Zealand Merlot from a vineyard in Oyster Bay, wherever that was.

'Efficient at everything. I hope you've put opening wine bottles on your CV,' said Lucas, pouring out two generous glasses. 'None of this precocious sniffing and tasting business, please. I know what corking means. It's going to be good.'

The glasses were elegant old crystal, their fine cut catching the light and flashing sparks through the red wine. She couldn't put a price on their worth, but it would be a lot. She would not be able to afford them.

'I wouldn't care if it was the cheapest super-market plonk in these glasses,' said Jessica, relaxing a few degrees. 'They are beautiful.'

'I'll remember that,' said Lucas. 'In case I'm ever hard up.'

The soup tureen was already on the sideboard, standing on a hot plate. There was an array of salads and cold meats and a cheese board. Suddenly Jessica was hungry. She had not eaten since breakfast and that had been a hurried affair, using up bits and pieces from the refrigerator before leaving her London flat.

'Let me serve you,' said Lucas. 'You look worn out. Sit down.'

He had changed too. He was in black jeans with a black polo necked shirt, very casual but still smart. His hair hadn't seen a comb and was all over the place, drying itself from his shower. Instinct was telling Jessica not to look at him. It was too dangerous and too much of an effort.

Jessica did not argue. She let him bring her a bowl of soup. The china was beautiful too, almost too old to use. It was cream with a turquoise and gold border. The side plate matched, a brown roll on it, ready to crumble. A slab of butter was on a silver serving dish. None of those horrid little packets that were hopeless to open. Jessica sighed. It was all so civilized. She craved civilization after years of NHS hospital routine and crowded canteens. It was a seductive delight.

'Are you regretting it?' Lucas asked, sitting

opposite her at the top end of the long table. 'Do you still want to go home?'

The soup was good, hot and creamy with a delicate taste. Mrs Harris knew how to make soup. Jessica did not answer straight away. She was too hungry.

'I don't know,' she said eventually, with a surge of confidence. 'You did trick me and I'm annoyed about that. But I can understand why. No one in their right mind would have come if they had known all the problems.'

'No one but you. You are different.'

'That's not the point. I still have to deal with these problems. And deal with them every day. It won't be easy.'

'Does that mean you are going to stay?' He was staring at her as if trying to hypnotize her answer, sweep away her defences. She could sense his anxiety overflowing like a flood. But he still had an air of coolness. A Coleman would never plead or beg. He had inherited that trait from his mother.

'It goes against all my good judgement, but yes, I will stay. I can see that your mother, Lady Grace, needs a firm hand. She is the most awkward patient I have ever had and she will dislocate that new hip if she is not careful. Daniel is difficult. He lives in a world of his own, sees the world through a different lens. I'm not sure how I can help him. Little Lily is a delightful child but she is going to put on weight in a big way if she doesn't change her eating habits. An obese child will have health problems later. And she doesn't know how to use her inhaler.'

'I didn't know that she didn't know. I thought someone had shown her.'

'Did you ever think of checking? And you should have seen the cake and jam she put away at teatime. She should have been eating fruit. An apple or a banana. There's not even a fruit bowl in the kitchen.'

'Not a fruit bowl?'

Jessica laughed. 'Ah, now I know. So that's where Daniel gets it from.'

'Gets what from?'

'Repeating the last phrase of whatever is said to him. It saves him thinking or having to say anything. There's a word for it: parroting.'

'It's better than not speaking at all,' said Lucas, helping himself to a second bowl of soup. He offered some to Jessica but she shook her head. She stood up and served herself some salad and cheese. She rarely ate meat but made no fuss if meat was offered. She had refined a neat way of pushing it around the plate as if she was eating it. She could not bear to eat something which had once lived.

'Would you allow me to do the weekly shopping order from Avocado? That's not the proper name, is it? Mrs Harris couldn't remember what it was.' Jessica hoped this was not too pushy but Lucas nodded in agreement.

'Please order what you think fit. It's a Brighton firm. You'll see the link on the computer under Favourites. My card is registered with them. It will pay for anything. Order crates of apples, grapes and oranges. Whatever you like.'

The good wine was making her feel warm and mellow. She tried not to look at Lucas in case her thought processes stopped working. She was looking forward to sleeping in that pretty primrose bedroom, her body now aching with tiredness. But first she would have to see Lady Grace to bed, and that would be another battle.

Jessica wanted to know where the children's mother was in all this, but it was obvious that Lucas had no wish to give her that information. He said nothing about their mother. They talked about the garden and cars and other mundane matters, never touching on anything personal.

'My mother has made a complaint,' Lucas said eventually, helping himself from the cheeseboard while stabbing at an olive.

'Complaint number one.'

'So what's new?' Jessica sighed. 'I'm sure she complains about everything.'

'You went into her handbag without permission.'

'Oh, my God. She was crunched up with pain and then complains when I try to find her prescription painkillers. I don't believe it.' Jessica was astounded.

'Apparently she considers that an invasion of her privacy.'

'Like she might have a packet of condoms in there or a stash of ecstasy?'

'Hold on, easy, easy there. I know she is difficult, but I would be grateful if you could try to remember that she is an old fashioned lady in many ways. Her handbag is a fortress of privacy. No one is allowed to look in it.'

Jessica took a deep breath, worried she might tremble with indignation. 'I will try to remember in future. Her tablets will be where I put them.'

'Thank you.'

Lucas made fresh coffee for them and brought it through from the kitchen. He was not the usual helpless male. He could make good coffee. Perhaps he had been on his own for a long time, somewhere else.

'I've brought in the walking frame and given it an antiseptic wipe down. No hospital germs. I know how important it is that my mother doesn't pick up any infection. The early days are tricky ones,' he said.

'I wish your mother would understand that. You could speak to her. She doesn't seem to want to know that exercise is vital. The stronger she gets, the less pain she will be in. It can't be that she enjoys being in pain.'

'I think in a strange way she enjoys the attention,' said Lucas, stirring a black coffee. 'She hasn't got much else left in life to enjoy, poor soul.'

'That's nonsense,' said Jessica briskly. 'She has lots to enjoy. The Sussex coast, theatres, having friends in, walking, swimming. You said she liked playing cards. Swimming is excellent for hip replacements because the water is a support.'

Lucas looked appalled. 'You'd never get my mother to go swimming. It would be equal to a total eclipse of the moon.'

'You'd be surprised what I can get people to do. And it would be good for Daniel and Lily too. Daniel would find a kind of freedom in the water, freedom to be himself, not having to talk to the water. And the exercise would help our tubby little girl immensely, especially if I buy her a very pretty swimsuit.'

Lucas sat back, laughing, those silvery eyes

twinkling for once. 'Well, I wish you luck. How about a wager? I'll take you out to dinner at the Grand Hotel in Brighton if you get my mother into a pool. Champagne if you get her to swim more than three strokes. A length would be an impossibility.'

'Done,' said Jessica. 'Tell them to put the champagne on ice.'

A small sharp ringing sound broke into the moment of equality. Lucas took his mobile out of his pocket and answered the call.

'Yes? OK, I'll come right away. You could take all the necessary pre-op scans and X-rays for me to look at. Sedate him lightly in preparation. I'll be there in about twenty minutes.'

Lucas switched off and got up abruptly, leaving his half drunk coffee. He lifted his hand in a half gesture of farewell.

'Sorry,' he said. 'Work calls. Motorbike RTA. Nasty one. I'll leave everyone here in your good hands. Enjoy your evening.'

Jessica sat back in total shock. The professional jargon was not put on. Lucas had already forgotten she was even there. She heard the front door close and then the low throb of his powerful Porsche Boxster pulling away out of the drive.

She did not understand what was going on. He'd said nothing about himself or any commitment anywhere. Was she supposed to make guesses?

She got up and took the coffee cups out into the kitchen. Mrs Harris was ready to leave with her coat and hat on, prepared to cycle home. She took the tray from Jessica.

'Don't worry, miss. I'll clear up in the morning.'

'I can put these in the dishwasher and food in the refrigerator. Mr Coleman has had to hurry off somewhere.'

'He's not just Mr Coleman,' said Mrs Harris, shaking her head. 'It's Dr Coleman. Didn't you know that? He works at that famous hospital in East Grinstead, the Queen Victoria, where the burnt pilots were taken in the war. He's a plastic surgeon: then he's called Mr Coleman. He puts faces back together again.'

Jessica listened in silence, hating herself.

'A plastic surgeon? I didn't know that,' said Jessica weakly. She remembered how she had thought he was a playboy, being kept by his mother, running errands for her. No wonder he had little time for his children.

Suddenly another name came into her head. She had heard it somewhere before. Sir Bernard Coleman was a famous surgeon. He must have been the husband of Grace and father of Lucas. It made her cringe, the way

54

she had been making waves and saying she wanted this and wanted that, proper time off. Lucas had not said a word, quietly keeping his peace, letting her rant on.

About twenty minutes, he'd said. She hoped there weren't any speed cameras on the roads. It would surely take longer than that.

'Don't you worry, miss. He may not come back tonight so I'll leave you to lock up. I'll give you the code for the alarm. He has a room at the hospital where he can doss down for a sleep. See you in the morning.'

'Thank you, Mrs Harris. It was a lovely supper.'

Jessica was all alone in the big house except for a grumpy patient upstairs and two sleeping children. Jessica cleared the dining room and stacked the dishwasher. Then she made some hot milk to take up to Lady Grace. She braced herself for the battle ahead. Whatever happened she was going to make sure she won.

⋆   ⋆   ⋆

It was late before Jessica had Lady Grace safely in bed, clean and comfortable. Lady Grace had objected to the pillow between her knees but Jessica explained that it was to prevent her crossing over a leg in bed and rotating the new hip.

'Didn't they strap a foam pillow to your knees when you were in hospital? They call them knee immobilizers, to stop you bending the hip. A pillow is for the same purpose. It's not forever. Only till your new hip is stable.'

'I don't need a pillow. I won't cross my legs,' said Lady Grace, exasperated.

'You don't know what you might do in your sleep,' said Jessica.

'I shan't sleep a wink,' she decided.

'I'll leave the bedside light on, in case you want to read. And here are your spectacles.' Jessica put them where Lady Grace could reach them.

'I don't know where my book is. I can't find it.'

'I expect it's the one on the floor beside your chair. This one.'

'I don't like that one. It's very stupid and badly written.'

'When the mobile library calls at West Eastly, I'll get some new books for you. Tell me what you like to read and your favourite authors. Tomorrow you are going to start walking for real. And exercising. Straight leg raising is a good one.'

Lady Grace didn't answer. She closed her eyes with a pained expression. Jessica decided she was being dismissed and left the stuffy bedroom with relief. Tomorrow she would open some windows. Another battle ahead.

Jessica locked the house, discovering so many unexpected doors, it took ages. The alarm was simple to set. If Lucas returned, he could get to his room over the stables without coming into the main house. Then she checked on the children again. All was well.

Her primrose bedroom was a refuge of peace and privacy. She was exhausted physically and emotionally. She slumped onto the sofa and stretched out her aching legs. She flexed her muscles to ease the cramp. She could fall asleep right now, but she knew she would wake in the early hours, stiff and uncomfortable.

Instead she wallowed in a bath of really warm water, letting the heat take out the ache. Geranium bath oil filled the air with its fragrance. Again she fought off waves of sleep. She didn't want to wake up in a cold bath, all wrinkled like a dried prune. Time to pull the plug and hope the noise didn't disturb Lady Grace.

Jessica dried off and wafting talc around, wrapped herself in a big towel. She had only brought her usual pretty silk night garments, not warm enough for the wilds of the country. But the bed was comfortable and in no time, her own body heat had warmed it. She fell asleep almost immediately, lulled by the quietness. Where was the traffic, the buses, the sirens, the nightly concert of London street noise?

Had she been washed onto some desert island and was the only person living there in a bamboo hut, the wavelets of sea a watery lullaby? Her dreams had no answer. Her dream was a sunburst of happiness. She smiled in her sleep.

★ ★ ★

She was awoken by a sudden heavy lump landing on her stomach. She was awake instantly, visualizing some disaster, ceiling falling down, plane crash, satellite plunging from the sky.

'Willdo! Willdo! Wake up, it's morning. You said you would still be here.'

It was Lily, jumping up and down on the bed with wild abandon, her pyjamas half undone. Her face was bright with excitement.

'So I am still here,' said Jessica sleepily. 'I said I would be.'

'But you are not up. You are in bed. We want you up.'

'I might be able to get up if I didn't have an elephant sitting on my stomach.'

Lily fell about giggling on the bed and Jessica struggled to sit up. Her peach silk nightie was half off her shoulders. She ran a hand through her flattened hair.

'What's the time?' she asked.

'I don't know,' said Lily. 'I can't tell the time.'

Jessica felt about on the bedside table in the dim light for her watch. She could not believe her eyes. At first she thought that the hands had got stuck on their circuit. The hands were luminous and bright.

'It's only six o'clock in the morning, you imp,' she said. 'I'm not getting up this early. Dawn is for the birds.'

'But, Willdo, we want you to get up.'

'Well, Willdo won't.' This was a little too complicated for Lily to understand and she continued to pound the bed with her feet and her hands, singing to herself. Jessica lifted the side of the duvet so the little girl could climb in. 'You can stay for a while if you promise to go back to sleep for one hour.'

'I promise.'

Lily climbed in and snuggled up. 'Tell me another story about that poor lost baby mole.'

'No,' said Jessica, closing her eyes. 'I said, go back to sleep.'

The door to the yellow bedroom was still open. Jessica was aware that someone had come in. She could barely force her eyes open even if it was an intruder. She sort of recognized the tall dark figure in wet clothes.

'I do apologize,' said Lucas, hesitantly. 'I was checking on the children and heard this rumpus. It sounded like a herd of elephants.'

'It was one elephant.'

His eyes roved over her bare shoulder and the peachy silk barely covering her softly rising breasts. Jessica crossed her free arm over the bare skin, wishing he had not seen her so exposed. She couldn't handle the yearning emotion.

'Lily can't tell the time,' she explained.

'I wish I had the same excuse,' he said, his eyes sweeping over the empty space the other side of her. He looked very tired. He had not been to bed at all.

'How is the motorbike rider?'

'He doesn't look like a young Brad Pitt any more. But he will live.'

'You must be tired.'

'I am. I've been up all night, working on the boy. You must know what it's like. I'll say goodnight or is it good morning? I've no idea.'

Jessica wanted to be near to him, touch him, tuck him up into bed. But of course, she couldn't. There was a limit to her nursing duties. Nothing in her contract said that she had to put him to bed. 'Do you know the way?'

'North, I think.'

Lucas closed the door behind him. He stood for a moment outside on the landing, uncertain of what he should do. He knew what he longed to do, but it was too early, too soon. He would have to wait.

Jessica listened to his footsteps fading away. They sounded like a man so tired he had almost forgotten how to walk. There was nothing she could do. But she could make life at Upton Hall easier for him. That would not be too hard. As long as she kept her thoughts to herself.

Lily slept soundly beside her, breathing shallow. Where was the child's mother? Why was she never mentioned? It was like a shadow in the room, a shadow with no shape.

4

Mrs Harris was cooking a full English breakfast, bacon, eggs, mushrooms, tomatoes and lashings of fried bread. Jessica cringed at the pans of food sizzling on the stove top. Lily and Daniel were already demolishing bowls of crunchy cereal.

'Come and sit with me, Willdo,' cried Lily, waving happily. She was proudly wearing her new navy and cream school uniform.

'I'll take your grandmother's breakfast up first,' said Jessica. 'What does she usually like?'

'A lightly boiled egg, bread and butter, coffee,' said Mrs Harris. 'The tray is all ready.'

The egg will be more than lightly boiled by the time I get upstairs, thought Jessica. It'll be half cold and starting to congeal.

Jessica was wearing slim indigo jeans this morning with a crisp white open-necked shirt. If she was going to be walking her ladyship, running around with Lily and hunting for Daniel, she needed to be in activity clothes. She took the tray quickly upstairs. She had already helped Lady Grace to wash and dress and now she was sitting regally in her arm-chair by the window.

'You haven't changed,' she said. 'I told you I don't like jeans on my staff.'

'I'm not on your staff,' said Jessica. 'I'm employed by your son, Dr Coleman. He has no objection to what I wear. I shall be running about all day.'

Lady Grace sniffed. 'Bring the table over here and put the tray down. I don't like my breakfast cold. Mrs Harris knows how I like my egg.'

'You could have your breakfast downstairs in the dining room.'

'Nonsense, I can't do the stairs.'

'Today you are going to walk along the landing and down the stairs to halfway where the stairs divide. There will be a chair for you to sit on and rest. Then you will come up the other stairs, along the landing again and back to your room. How does that sound? It's not very far.'

'It sounds ridiculous. This egg is cold.'

'I'm not surprised. It was lightly boiled. You should know that a lightly boiled egg cools very quickly. Would you like something different? There's a full English breakfast cooking on the stove. Would you like some scrambled egg?'

'Leave me alone, you idiot girl. I can

manage my breakfast by myself.'

Jessica returned to the kitchen in time to catch Mrs Harris piling up plates of fried food for Lily and Daniel. She took the plates aside.

'That's far too much food for a five year old and a seven year old,' she said.

'Lily always eats hers and Daniel leaves what he doesn't want.'

'Let's see what they would really like,' Jessica suggested. She went back to the children who were wondering what was happening. She sat down beside them.

'There must be things you like and things that you don't like,' she began. 'You don't have to eat everything that is put in front of you. Tell me what you don't like, Lily. Think about it carefully. I'd really like to know.'

Lily wrinkled up her nose. 'I don't like yucky mushrooms and hard meat.'

'You mean the bacon?'

Lily nodded. 'Ba-con.'

'Well, I never,' said Mrs Harris. 'I never knew.'

'And what about you, Daniel?' said Jessica, turning to the boy. He was thrown. Jessica hadn't given him anything he could repeat as an answer. She helped him out. 'Do you like bacon? Mushrooms?'

He shook his head.

'But you like eggs and fried bread?'

'Fried bread,' he breathed. The morning was new and young. He was not into speaking at all yet. He wanted peace and quiet. He wanted to be left alone.

'There you are, Mrs Harris. They've told you what they like.'

'Well, I never,' said Mrs Harris again. 'What about you, miss?'

'I'll have the same.'

'And I'll have everything that's left over,' said Lucas, striding into the kitchen, his eyes raking over her gently. 'I'm famished. There's nothing wrong with my appetite. Shall I join you?'

A few hours' sleep and Lucas had recovered. This was the normal doctor/surgeon self-imposed sleep deprivation routine. He looked casual in ancient brown cords and a sweater that needed mending at the elbows. He still hadn't put a comb through his hair. And it needed cutting.

Jessica had a wild, unreasoning elation that he had joined them in the kitchen for a family breakfast. He chatted away to the children, to Mrs Harris, to herself as if everything was normal. Jessica nearly forgot the time, mesmerized by his voice.

'The school bus,' she cried. 'You've only got five minutes to get ready.'

'But I haven't had my toast and honey,' Lily protested.

She hustled them into their coats, checked their school bags, and then ran with them out onto the drive. Daniel was away like the wind but Lily was panting and wheezing. Jessica slowed down.

'Have you got your inhaler?'

Lily looked vague as if she had never heard the word before. 'I dunno.'

Jessica searched the schoolbag and found the inhaler at the bottom. It felt light and empty. She checked the expiry date. She took Lily's hand and started walking. 'Now breathe with me slowly,' she said. 'In . . . and out. Again, in time with me, Lily, in . . . and out. Big slow breaths. That's the way.'

By the time they reached the waiting bus, Lily's breathing had settled. Jessica smiled at the driver. 'Thank you for waiting,' she said. 'We had a little problem.'

'Anything for you, miss,' he grinned back.

'Will you be here when we come home?' Lily asked as she climbed the bus steps, looking back anxiously. 'Willdo, please, will you be here?'

'I'll be here,' said Jessica. 'We're going to play some games in the garden, remember? I've some new ones to show you.'

Lily smiled happily. 'Games in the garden,

Willdo? And you promise?'

Jessica waved the bus out of sight, unaware that Lucas was standing behind her, hands in his pockets, rocking on his heels.

'Ah, the Jessica magic,' he said lightly. 'New games in the garden.'

Jessica started. She had not expected an audience. 'Not really,' she said. 'It's keeping a promise.'

'And do you always keep your promises?'

'It depends on what they are,' she said, as they began walking back to the house. He adjusted his step to match hers. 'If it's a promise that's been forced out of me, then I should not hesitate to break it.'

'And have you made a promise to Lady Grace?'

He was sharp. He knew that there was no way Lady Grace would do anything without a very large carrot. And Jessica had discovered a carrot.

'I've promised to play cards with her this afternoon if she will walk a short distance with me this morning.'

'Ah, cards. She's an addict. Whist, bridge, poker. She'll beat you.'

'Winning isn't important; it's the playing that matters.'

Lucas's arm went round her slim waist. It was casual, unexpected. 'And what are you going to promise me, Willdo, if I am very good and walk with you and do everything that you say?'

Jessica was lost for words, reluctant to break the spell. She wished he had not begun this teasing. She could hear the electricity humming in the wires overhead, the wind rustling the trees, the faint engine of the school bus. But her heart was pounding even louder. She twisted herself out of his grasp.

'Now that would be telling,' she said, deliberately evasive.

He drew away, putting space between them. He began to pull at a loose thread in his sweater, seemingly unaware that it needed mending.

'So what do you plan to do this morning?'

She was glad that the conversation had reverted to mundane things. 'I have to unpack my things. Everything will be horribly creased. Then I want to check the children's clothes and see if they have swimsuits. I could do this anytime. I'm really putting off the moment when I have to confront Lady Grace and get her walking.'

'Do you need any help?' He sounded genuinely concerned. 'How about a whip or a gun? I think we've got an old airgun in an attic somewhere.'

She was immediately drawn to his easy

banter. She could cope with this. It gave her time to look at the structure of his face and the imprint of Daniel echoed in the fine bones. She thought of the motorbike boy and shuddered. Accidents were always dreadful, but facial injuries could be devastating. She wondered what it would be like to look in the mirror and see a different face staring back.

'Any medieval torture implements in the cellars?' she asked.

'I daresay I can find a few screws. My mother probably put them there.'

Jessica laughed and Lucas was fascinated by the change in her features when she laughed. Her smile was dimpled and delightful, her rosy lips enchanting, her teeth perfect. But it was the deep-blue eyes that drew him more than anything. They sparkled like sapphires, like gems; priceless. How appalling if anything happened to these beautiful eyes. He could not replace them.

'You will be careful when you drive, won't you?' he said without expression.

'Of course, I'm always careful. It's the other drivers who are careless and impatient. Especially those without any tax or insurance.'

'Will you have time this morning for a quick trial drive in the Austin, just to get used to it? I could come with you. Twenty minutes at the most. But I do have to go back to the hospital to check on my patient.'

Jessica did quick mental calculations, some part of her alarmed at being so close to him in the front of the small car. 'Thanks. I think it's mobile library day at the village. I could get Lady Grace some new books. And some for the children. Did you know that Daniel can't read properly yet?'

'He's having special help at school. His writing is poor as well. It's all over the place.'

'I could do a little work with him, every evening, five minutes say. Nothing too arduous. Little and often, one to one, often works the best.'

'Thank you. That might help. It's an epidemic, you know. There never used to be so many autistic children. Daniel seemed to develop normally for the first eighteen to twenty-four months then he somehow lost his skill. It's a regression in ability. Some autistic children never speak, but Daniel can if he wants to. He has a limited vocabulary.'

'He repeats back what you've just said,' said Jessica.

'It's called echolalia or parrot back. He either repeats back immediately or maybe hours or days later, completely out of context, in an unrelated situation. Sometimes he picks up a phrase from the television or an advert and says it over and over again. It's very strange.'

Lucas's strong features were fractured with anguish. This was his son, his first born, and he shuddered at the thought of the boy's future.

'We know autism is on the rise. There's no explanation. He hates noise, bright light, crowds. It makes him worse.'

'Autistic children often have some talent in a totally different and unexpected direction. We've simply got to find what it is that Daniel can do,' said Jessica, aware that Lucas's pain was as raw as her own. 'He will have some talent. We've got to find it. Perhaps his guardian angel will guide us.'

Only her pain was the emotion of being discarded ruthlessly, and in public, by the man she thought she had loved. The humiliation of it was still vivid in her mind. It would take years for the memory to heal. How innocent she had been that evening. Led to the slaughter. In an expensive red silk dress. A dress that she had later bundled up and thrown away.

Lucas's strong fingers suddenly laced hers in a firm grip. 'Thank you, Jessica. I think I've found Daniel's angel.'

Jessica laughed again but this time most of her sparkle had gone.

'Lily won't think so when she finds that I have cut out cakes and jam at teatime. It's apples and pears from now on. She's consuming well over eighteen hundred calories a day at the moment. She's becoming a plump little girl.'

'She'll grow out of it. I like Mrs Harris's home-made cake.'

'You can eat as much as you like. There's not a superfluous ounce on you.'

Lucas grinned. 'And how would you know, Miss Willdo? When have you seen any of my superfluous ounces?'

Jessica coloured. The words had come out without thinking. She turned away and hurried indoors. 'Walkies time,' she said, trying to cover her embarrassment.

'Shall I bring a lead?' Lucas asked from the foot of the stairs.

'I need determination more than a lead.'

'Call for help if my mother stabs you with a hatpin.'

★　★　★

It took over an hour to talk Lady Grace into taking the few steps out of her room and onto the landing. She complained all the time of the pain, her stiffness, her back, her leg. Jessica gathered her patience and persuasive

72

skill. It was exhausting.

Eventually with the aid of the walker, Lady Grace did manage to walk the length of the landing, peering into Lily's bedroom. It was a bit untidy.

'That child's bedroom is a disgrace,' she said. 'Chaos.'

'That's why you need to be up and about,' said Jessica. 'To take charge of things again. The more exercise you take, the less pain there is.'

Lady Grace snorted. 'You're merely saying that. You've no proof.'

'I'll get you some proof.'

There would be a self-help book in the mobile library, Jessica felt sure. She would get one today.

The journey back was marginally faster as Lady Grace had seen her mid-morning coffee arrive. She sank back into her armchair by the window, pushing the walker away. Jessica sorted out the blood-thinning medication.

'Don't forget we're playing cards this afternoon,' said Lady Grace. 'The cards are in the sitting room. I'll tell you where they are kept.'

'After you have done your straight leg exercises,' Jessica said. 'They are very boring but necessary. You could listen to music or watch television at the same time if you like.

We could find some decent music on the radio.'

'I don't allow television in bedrooms. Not character building.'

It was going to be a busy day.

Jessica hurried down to the kitchen, hoping to catch Lucas before he went back to the Queen Victoria Hospital. But he had gone. His patient came first as was to be expected. She poured herself some coffee from the percolator and sipped the reviving caffeine gratefully.

'I needed that,' she said. 'Thank you.'

'I could hear you having a time of it upstairs,' said Mrs Harris. 'I didn't interfere. I hadn't done Lily's bedroom, more's the pity. I'd better do it now before her ladyship starts into me.'

'You put up with a lot,' said Jessica.

Mrs Harris nodded. 'Sometimes we have to. That's life.'

'Where's the nearest swimming pool, Mrs Harris? I really want to get Lady Grace into the water. Walking in the shallow end of a swimming pool is one of the best exercises after a hip operation. Because the water is buoyant and holds you up, there's very little stress on the hip. She would enjoy it.'

Mrs Harris said nothing. She knew about Lady Grace's aversion to water.

'A pool would be a good idea,' Jessica went on.

'She'd say the water was too warm, too cold, too wet,' said Mrs Harris, going upstairs. She paused halfway, lowered her voice. 'Yet she used to be a champion swimmer. Used to swim in the sea, off Brighton beach, any weather, I'm told.'

Jessica found a copy of Yellow Pages and roamed through, looking for leisure centres. Brighton and Worthing were both unsuitable, having large pools. Lady Grace would certainly refuse to go anywhere that members of the public might be using at the same time.

Lucas was a puzzle, one minute kind and charming, and the next cold and aloof. Perhaps one day he would tell her what had made him so unfathomable. There was no antagonism between them but she never knew where she was with the man. He was unpredictable. And yet so attractive. But he was the last thing she wanted. There was no place for another man, however good-looking, in her life.

She had to keep him at a distance.

He could be dangerous. One move from him and she might find herself unable to forget him. He had spirit and texture and soul. Not many of those about.

There was a range of keys hanging from

75

hooks near the kitchen door. Jessica glanced at the labels. There were more keys than doors. One of them was the key to the vintage car waiting for her in the garage and this was a good time to try it. She knew how to drive and it was not far to the village. If Mrs Harris could cycle the distance, she could drive it.

It was a small, low-roofed car with sleek lines, not what she had expected at all. She thought all Austin cars were saloon, family cars. This was a neat shape, park it anywhere, with a walnut dashboard, leather seats and the famous picnic trays at the back. She slipped into the driver's seat and switched on the ignition, took off the hand brake. The car shot into life, almost taking the garage doors with it.

Jessica stamped hard on the foot brake, was flung against the wheel, no seat belt fastened. She gasped. She had not realized that automatic gears need very gentle handling to ease the car away.

She sat back, regaining her breath, slowly fastening the seat belt, hoping she had not bruised her ribs. Lucas had been right. Automatics take some getting used to. Good thing that there was no one around watching. She tried again, easing the car away with only a couple of little jerks. Once moving, the car was a dream. She loved it. She drove slowly out of the drive and onto the road.

Left or right? She could not remember which way they had come yesterday. Well, she only had two choices and the village couldn't be far. So she went right.

It was a quiet, leafy lane, twisting and turning so she drove carefully, hoping to see the village of West Eastly come into sight, cottages, pub and church. A male pheasant hopped across the road, its long tail feathers gleaming. If she was going the wrong way, then the station would appear. If she saw anyone, she would ask for help.

There was no one around, not a soul. Only a few grazing sheep and they weren't much help. She doubted if they had any sense of direction. This was not the time to panic. Surely she could not get lost in such a small place?

She drove on. More leafy lanes, no signposts, nothing to say where she was. The hills looked all the same. There were no houses. At this rate she was going to end up in Brighton or Worthing or maybe back on the M27.

She was lost. She had no idea where she was. Surely Mrs Harris didn't cycle all this way from Dove Cottage to Upton Hall? Jessica glanced down at the milometer but the figures were no help. It was more than ten minutes ago that she left Upton Hall, turned right at the end of the drive and now she could be anywhere.

She slowed down, worried about petrol. She had not checked. Always check on your petrol before setting off, the driving instructor had said, many years ago.

She drew into the next lay-by and turned off the engine, taking stock, hoping that someone would drive by. If she heard a car coming, she would flag them down and ask for directions.

There was a throb of a car in the distance, coming closer, maybe too fast to stop for her. Jessica stood clearly on the side of the road, her hand up in the air, hoping for a Good Samaritan. She prayed that it would be someone helpful, articulate and English.

It was. Someone very articulate. The car braked.

'What the hell are you doing out here, Jessica? I told you to wait for me. I said I would come with you, the first time you went out in the Austin. I suppose it was you who nearly took the garage door off? And now you are lost. Well, it serves you right.' Lucas glared at her.

Jessica stood shocked by the onslaught. She didn't deserve this. Her intentions had been the best. She had intended to get some books for Lady Grace and find out how to renew Lily's inhaler prescription. Not exactly in line with robbing a bank or stealing the church silver.

'Yes, sir, I am lost,' she said, briskly. 'All these lanes look the same. I'm hardly to blame if your council doesn't spend any money on signposts. It must be because of some literacy deficit among the locals.'

Lucas was still glaring at her. 'Did you turn right coming out of Upton Hall?'

'Yes, I turned right. I'm not stupid.'

'Then right again at the fork?'

'What fork?'

Jessica could not remember any fork. The lane had been twisting and turning. She had been concentrating on driving round the bends, keeping to the left.

'There's a fork after the third bend. It takes you directly to West Eastly. A child could follow it.'

'There was no signpost.'

'It's in the hedge.'

'Overgrown no doubt.'

Jessica was tired of the argument. At least Lucas could not refuse to see that she got back to Upton Hall. 'I think I should return,' she said. 'Lady Grace may be needing me. We've got a lot to do.'

'She may well indeed. A pity you didn't

think of that when you took off in the Austin, not telling anyone where you were going.' Lucas was still fuming.

'Shall I follow you?' she asked, recovering some dignity.

'Yes. I'll lead.'

'Please drive at my speed, not like a bat out of hell.'

He was about to make a retort but thought better of it. He sat there, engine turning, while Jessica got back into the Austin. She was very careful, trying not to do a jerk start. She handled it smoothly, pleased with herself, and lined the Austin up behind the Porsche Boxster. Piece of cake.

It was a slow and careful procession back to Upton Hall. Lucas was deliberately going at a snail's pace to irritate her. Any locals would have thought it was a funeral. Any slower and the Austin would stall.

Jessica smiled to herself. She would let Lucas have his little joke and say nothing. But she was relieved when she saw the tall chimneys of Upton Hall coming into sight. Somehow she had done a tortuous circle.

She parked the car in the stables, next to the Porsche. The garage door was not exactly coming off. He had been exaggerating as usual. Lucas was nowhere to be seen. He had not waited to see if she was all right.

She went into the kitchen, hoping Mrs Harris would not mind if she made a cup of tea. Her throat was dry and a cup of tea would be welcome.

The kitchen was empty, everywhere tidy, no coat or hat on the door. Mrs Harris had gone. Jessica immediately thought something awful must have happened to Lady Grace in her absence and she had been taken to hospital in an ambulance.

She raced up the stairs and rushed into the tower bedroom. Lady Grace and Lucas were sitting by the window. There was a glass decanter of sherry on the table and Lucas was pouring a small amount into a delicate sherry glass.

'Don't barge in like that, young lady,' said Lady Grace. 'Please knock.'

'I thought you had had . . . an accident . . . fallen or something,' said Jessica, getting her breath back.

'I'm talking to my son. Kindly leave us alone. We have something to discuss. Something important.'

'Of course,' said Jessica, turning to leave. 'I'm making some tea. Would you like a cup?'

'No, thank you. I'm having my afternoon sherry,' said Lady Grace.

'But I'd love a cup,' said Lucas, leaning back and laying on the charm. 'I've just had a maddeningly slow journey. The traffic these days and learner drivers.'

'Better slow and safe,' said Jessica, 'than fast and flashy.'

Lady Grace glared at Jessica and she retreated, smiling to herself as she closed the door. At least she had had the last word.

★   ★   ★

Mrs Harris had an urgent dental appointment and Jessica made the children's tea when they got home from school. She found some Bramley apples in the orchard and stewed them with honey and raisins. She made cheese, tomato and lettuce sandwiches with celery sticks to crunch on. No doubt there would be complaints from little Miss Sugary Sweet-tooth. No jam and no cake for her today.

Lily surprised everyone by saying she liked this tea. 'I like this sandwich,' she said, holding the celery stick between two fingers as if it was a cigarette. 'Have you got a light, miss?'

'Got a light?' repeated Daniel.

'I'm not the nanny before last, the one who smoked,' said Jessica. 'Hurry up, then we can play in the garden before it gets dark.'

'I want to play in the dark,' said Lily,

jumping up and down. 'I like the dark. It's all spooky.'

Daniel said nothing, He was lining up raisins on the rim of his plate before eating them. It was a slow and deliberate procedure.

Lucas came in the kitchen with his cup and saucer. Lily was pretending to smoke the celery stick, giggling and coughing. 'Have you got a light, mister?'

'Bad habits already, young lady?' he said, gravely. 'We shall have to watch you. I'll get you a nicotine patch.'

Lily blew out pretend smoke and started coughing again. Jessica fetched a glass of water from the tap. She drank it and the coughing eased.

'Is there another inhaler for Lily?' Jessica asked. 'I think her current puffer is nearly empty. We're going to have a lesson this evening on the best way to use it.'

'I keep Lily's inhalers in a safe place. I'll get one for you before I go back to the hospital,' said Lucas, closing the dishwasher door.

'Another RTA?'

'No, I had a list this morning. I'm going back now to check on them. They should be in recovery or transferred to their rooms by now.' He spoke in a vague manner, miles away, mentally going over what he had to do.

83

'I'll catch a quick bite at the canteen. Don't wait supper for me.'

Jessica discovered that Mrs Harris had left a cold supper tray for Lady Grace and all she had to do was heat some soup and take it up. She would have soup and another sandwich.

They played in the garden till the light began to fail. Jessica could only remember how to play *He* and *What's the Time, Mr Wolf?* Lily threw herself into both games with a complete disregard for the rules. Daniel didn't understand what they were doing but enjoyed shouting *What's the Time, Mr Wolf?* Jessica noticed that his motor skills were not co-ordinated and he ran awkwardly, sometimes almost falling.

They danced and sang *Ring-a-Ring a-Roses*, which seemed to help his co-ordination, because they were inter-acting together. He didn't know the words. Lily sang loud enough for two.

When she took Lily upstairs for her bath, Jessica told Daniel that he could stay up for another half an hour as he was older. He didn't react.

'What's the time, Mr Wolf?' he said.

'Bedtime,' Lily shrieked.

At this rate they would have Lady Grace banging on the floor with Fred.

★ ★ ★

It was quite late before Jessica took her supper on a tray into the library and settled herself into a comfortable armchair. Lady Grace had had her supper and was settled with a book.

One of the bookcases had a false door which opened and revealed a medium size television set. It was an older model but the picture was clear with a good signal and Jessica was happy to watch any programme.

She was lulled into deep relaxation with the undemanding programme, a pleasant supper by herself, a strenuous day and the fresh air activity. She was dozing off, halfway to a rambling dream about trains, when she was jolted awake by a tiny noise.

Lucas was switching off the television.

'Late night film,' he said. 'Were you watching it?'

Jessica shook her head. 'No, I wasn't. I fell asleep. What's the time?' She nearly added, *Mr Wolf*.

'It's after midnight. Cops and robbers film, very violent. Not at all suitable for a young lady to watch.'

She struggled to sit up. 'Heavens. I'd better clear up the supper things.'

'Leave it for Mrs Harris in the morning,' said Lucas. He was looking at her with an expression that was impossible to fathom, his eyes full of warmth. 'You don't look nearly so fierce when you are asleep,' he added.

Her heart began to beat faster as he came over to the armchair and held out his hand. He smelt fresh and manly. It was a heady scent. 'Would you like me to tell you a bedtime story?' he asked.

'What story would it be?' she said, her throat going dry. He helped her to her feet. She was quite unsteady.

'I thought Beauty and the Beast would be appropriate.' He paused. 'Since I am so handsome and you are quite beastly at times.'

Jessica began laughing quietly and that broke the spell. They brushed against each other as they went out of the room. There was no madness in the moment, only a brief recognition of the contact, then moving apart.

'Goodnight, Willdo,' said Lucas, pausing again in the hallway, on his way to the stables. 'Do I get a goodnight kiss?'

'Sorry,' said Jessica. 'That's something Willdo, won't do.'

5

Jessica drove down to Worthing sea front with Daniel and Lily strapped into the back seat. She prayed that she would not get lost or lose the children. It was a straightforward drive, nothing complicated, lots of visible signposts. She immediately found somewhere to park along the front and put money into the meter.

The size and expanse of the sea front was like tearing apart sky curtains and seeing a vast blue seascape moving in every direction. There were four miles of promenade to walk on (or cycle if you weren't caught), acres of sand and shingle when the tide was far out, the pier to perambulate on if it was high tide and the waves were lashing the high shoreline. The smell of ozone was a reminder of seaside holidays. The screeching seagulls set up a raucous welcome

'It's the sea. I love it, I love it,' said Lily, jumping up and down with excitement, her hair bobbing about. 'I want to paddle. Willdo, can we paddle?'

'Of course,' said Jessica. 'Let me lock up the car, get our towels and the backpack, and we'll be away down the beach. We'll find somewhere out of the wind. Would you like that, Daniel, to go on the beach?'

'Go on the beach,' he said solemnly.

They wore canvas trainers going down the slippery slope of the shingle but once free of the pebbles, they shed their shoes and ran over the wet sand, splashing through puddles, fording rivulets, skirting rocks, making for the tiny waves that lapped in the far distance. Jessica had a job keeping up with the children.

Daniel ran ahead, sensing freedom, sensing the elements that demanded nothing of him. Water made him free from a world he did not understand. No one wanted to talk to him. The lapping of the wavelets was a gentle sound. He had an unusual burst of energy, legs awkward, arms waving erratically.

They were all wearing shorts and vest tops, even Jessica. Her shorts were cut off jeans with a frayed edge. Lady Grace had been outraged.

'My grandchildren don't wear such skimpy clothes. I demand that you put them into something decent. Hasn't Lily got a frock?'

'They are going on the beach and they are going to get wet. I'm taking along dry clothes and fleeces in case it gets chilly. Would you like to come with us? It's not far in the car.'

'Good heavens, no. I don't want to walk along the front with Fred. Most improper. I might meet someone I know.'

Jessica and Mrs Harris had come to a new and amicable arrangement. Mrs Harris was to have every other afternoon and evening off. In return she would look after Lady Grace on the afternoons when Jessica wanted to take the children out. It was more time off than Mrs Harris had ever had before. Anyone could see she was pleased the way she fussed round the kitchen, cleaning surfaces that were already clean and sparkling. It was like an unexpected lifeline.

'It'll make a real difference,' she said warmly. 'Having a bit of regular time off to myself. It's always been difficult to get away and those other nannies were useless to leave in charge. No good at all, drinking and smoking. I'd like to go to the village hall afternoon Bingo. I might win a fortune one day.'

Jessica had made real progress with Lady Grace but it had not been easy. The first time she had made it down the stairs and into the sitting room, Jessica called for celebration drinks and Lucas had opened a bottle of champagne. Lady Grace had been flushed with pride, but alarmed by the thought of the climb back upstairs. A few minutes in her beloved walled garden gave her renewed courage to make the climb. She picked a few roses for her room.

'You can do it,' said Jessica encouragingly. 'Well done. You've proved that.'

'You're such a bully,' said Lady Grace. 'And yet you are so slim. I don't know how I put up with you.'

'Because you know I'm right. Exercise is the answer. You might not admit it but the pain is not so bad these days, is it?'

'I still need my painkillers.'

'I know that but not so many,' said Jessica, preparing the blood thinning medication. 'I'm the guardian of your painkillers. Custodian, keeper, steward.'

'You do talk a lot of high-falutin' nonsense. Get me a cup of tea, please, Jess. And those roses need dead-heading. Look at the poor things.'

'I'm not here to do gardening.'

'I shall have to bribe you.'

'Difficult, but you could try.'

★   ★   ★

Lily got the wettest. She had no fear of the water and was soon paddling and jumping over incoming waves, splashing through puddles. The tide was on the turn and they were surprised how the expanse of wet sand began to disappear under the incoming sea. They had the sense to obey Jessica and return back to shore.

Daniel was more interested in what the tide was bringing in with it. So many shells and bits of seaweed, dead fish and driftwood. He was scavenging in the pools, collecting all sorts of bits and pieces in his bucket. The shells were so interesting and so intricate. He was completely immersed in his treasure hunt.

Jessica had brought a magazine to read on the beach but she didn't get past page three. A book would have been better but she dare not take her eyes off either child for more than a moment. She might get lost in a good book.

Irrational fears crowded her mind: drowning, abduction, fish hooks.

The day before yesterday she had taken the children to the mobile library on its weekly visit to West Easily. They had never been before and were amazed at the choice of books. Jessica had found some new books for Lady Grace which were accepted with reluctant gratitude. Daniel settled on a book with colour photographs of animals which he liked a lot. Lily chose more books than she could carry and insisted on carrying them across the green to the car.

'Let me take some of them,' Jessica offered.

'I want to carry all my books from the library myself,' Lily insisted.

Now they were enjoying themselves on the beach as children should, running about here and there, digging wet sand, collecting shells. Lily was filling her lungs with clean coastal air, not coughing or wheezing at all. Pure sea ozone.

As the waves edged them nearer and nearer to the shore of shingle, it was not quite so much fun. Bare feet on sharp stones is *ouch* time. They were slipping and sliding on a shelf of wet pebbles. But Jessica had brought plastic flip-flops for them to wear and the discomfort was soon forgotten. They had a picnic tea higher up on the beach — plenty of cheese sandwiches, apples and pears, yogurts, cartons of juice. They ate every crumb, then shook it all down skimming pebbles into the waves, watching the greedy seagulls diving into the deeper water for their fish suppers. Daniel was quite good at skimming. He watched the bouncing pebbles.

'Wow! Daniel's pebble bounced four times. One more go, everyone.'

It was two very tired children whom Jessica drove home to Upton Hall, drowsy and wet and sandy. Lily went to sleep on the back seat. Daniel sat close, examining his treasures. His romp on the beach had brought a colour to his cheeks. His hair was stiff with sea water.

'Did you enjoy the beach, Daniel?' Jessica asked. 'It was fun, wasn't it?'

'Fun,' he said, from the depths of his bucket.

'You've both brought half of the beach home with you,' said Jessica later, as Lily's bath water filled with a swirl of sand. 'I shall have to wash your hair.'

'Please don't tug my hair.'

'I'll try not to, poppet. Hold this little towel over your eyes.'

Lucas appeared in the doorway, tousled and leaning on the doorway, as if he didn't have the strength to hold himself up. Jessica wanted to soothe away the fatigue, wipe away the pain, let him fall asleep in her arms. She shook away the devastating thoughts, wishing her emotions would calm down. They were burning her up. He was not her responsibility.

'So you've had an afternoon on Worthing beach? Some people are lucky,' he said laconically. 'Some people have to work, day and night.'

'I was working,' said Jessica.

'We had a picnic tea on the beach and we didn't even have plates!' said Lily, who thought this was the best part. 'We ate out of a box!'

'How civilized,' said Lucas, raising his dark eyebrows. 'It could catch on, eating out of boxes. No washing up.'

'As long as you bring them home,' said Jessica.

Lucas agreed. 'Did you bring your litter home, Lily?'

'We did.'

But Lily's attention had already wandered elsewhere. 'Are you going to have your supper with Willdo, Daddy? She will look after you, when she has put on some clothes. She will make herself look very nice, in a frock.'

Jessica was still in her cut-off denim shorts and vest top. They were indeed skimpy and clung damply to her soft curves. Lucas could see the shape of her breasts and he could not wrench his gaze away. They were too enticing, so deliciously feminine, made to be touched and explored.

And those long tanned legs were asking to be stroked. Lucas moved away with barely concealed impatience, the tension between them rising. 'Supper sharp at eight, Jessica, is that all right?' he said curtly. 'And Lily is right. Put some clothes on. You look positively indecent.'

Jessica gave him an ironic, distant stare.

'Most medics are used to half-clad women. It goes with the job.'

'I do faces, not bodies,' he said.

Jessica went to an extreme. She made sure every inch was covered. She put on a baggy cotton jersey and black trousers and a waistcoat and scarf. Her slip-on black shoes completed the camouflage. She combed her fringe well over her eyes and brushed her hair onto her shoulders.

'The only part of me showing is my nose,' she said as she went into the dining room. Supper was waiting on the hot trays.

'Quite a nice nose,' he said, without looking at her. 'I could do a bob or a tuck but you don't need it. Mrs Harris has left us a beef casserole with lots of vegetables. It's very hot and smells delicious. Would you like some wine? I've managed to open the bottle this time.'

'It's the practice you need.'

'I'll remember that and keep practising.'

Jessica took a small helping of the casserole, avoiding the tasty chunks of dark meat. But she had plenty of vegetables, broccoli, French beans, carrots, mashed potatoes. There was home-made blackcurrant cheesecake afterwards.

'I see that you are avoiding the beef,' said Lucas. 'Is there a reason?'

'I don't much like eating animals. Not exactly a vegetarian, but near. I occasionally eat fish, but mainly because I think fish have a chance to get away.'

'Not in fish farms.'

'I know,' said Jessica, realizing this was merely polite conversation. He was not really interested in what she said. He was so self-contained, a passionate introvert. 'It's getting all too complicated these days. I won't know what to eat.'

Lucas was almost too tired to eat. He pushed away his plate. 'Do you mind if I tell you about today? I had a little girl in this morning, her name's Maggie. She was attacked by three Rottweilers. They tore at her face and broke her jaw in three places. She's a mess, but alive.'

Jessica caught her breath at the horror of it. 'Poor little thing. How dreadful. Is she going to be all right? What did you do?'

'For the moment I've done what I can. She'll need some skin grafts when the injuries have healed. Her mouth is damaged. It's going to be a long haul.'

Jessica was always shaken by injuries to innocent children. 'Can we do anything for her? Does Maggie need anything?'

Lucas thought for a moment. 'If Lily has any spare books or toys, they might help

Maggie. She's going to feel really bad these early days and needs distraction. She only has a disabled grandmother who lives quite a long journey away.'

'Would it be of any help if I came and read stories to her?' Jessica heard herself saying. The offer came out without any thought of how it could be organized or when she might have time. She would have to drive to East Grinstead and back. Perhaps there was a train. She realized her offer was near impossible. There was Lady Grace to think of, as well as the two children. They were her responsibilities.

'That's very kind of you, Jessica, but I don't see how it can be worked out. Let me think about it. Some of Lily's toys might be acceptable.'

He pushed away his slice of cheesecake, unable to finish it. He looked at Jessica over his glass of wine. He wondered how she would take his news. He was knotted with tension, rigid, yet restless.

'I have something to tell you,' he said, his face changing oddly.

'So, tell me.'

Jessica wondered why he was suddenly so serious. His eyes clouded and he pushed his unruly hair back. It was easy to see that he didn't know how to begin.

'I have been thinking about it for some time,' he said. 'It's been a long time since my wife, Liz, died. They used to call us the three L's, Lucas, Liz and Lily. We were a lively threesome.' He didn't include Daniel, she noticed. How sad.

Jessica froze. No one had ever said anything about Mrs Coleman as if she never existed. Jessica dare not say anything for fear of breaking the spell. Lucas was finding it difficult, that was clear. She let him go on.

'It was a car accident, late at night. Crash with an articulated lorry on the M25. Instantaneous death. Horrific. They were both killed outright.'

His voice was without emotion. He could have been reading a weather forecast to an unseen audience of millions. There was nothing in his expression either. Yet he was talking about his wife, mother of his children. He was staring into his glass of wine, as if seeing the carnage again in the pool of red.

'Both of them?' Jessica said, after a moment's hesitation. It seemed like prying, opening a painful wound. The room was still. Nothing moved. The oil portraits looked down on them in stony silence. Maybe they had heard it all before, centuries ago. It was the same old story.

'Did I say both?' He stared at her.

'Yes, you did.'

'You misheard me. I said nothing of the kind. And anyway, it's none of your business. Now I've lost my train of thought. Don't interrupt.'

Lucas ran his fingers through his hair, making it even more untidy. Jessica was afraid to say anything that would disturb him.

'But what about your two children, Daniel and Lily?' she asked, at last. The silence had a positive quality. Jessica knew this was about years of anguish.

'Lily was only a baby, barely six months old. Liz didn't like having babies, losing her figure and all the pain. She didn't like children at all and had no patience with Daniel. Daniel hadn't been diagnosed as autistic but we knew something was not right. She was quite happy to leave them both with me. At least she left me the children. That was something. More than something. It was a blessing.'

'I'm so sorry,' said Jessica. 'I know words are inadequate but I am sorry. You must have been really hurt. And it was a difficult time.'

'Well, not any more,' he said, injecting some false cheerfulness into his voice though his face was set in gloom. 'Things are going to change. You see, I have decided to get married again. I'm going to take the plunge.

Yes, very soon, Jessica. I have made up my mind. It's a good idea, isn't it? Don't you agree?'

Jessica couldn't think of anything to say. It was a good idea but she was thrown by the thought of having to adapt to another woman living in the house. Lucas deserved someone to help him, to look after him. He worked so hard, such long hours. He needed someone loving to come home to.

'Yes, it is a good idea,' said Jessica, taking a firm hold of her doubts. His words were stealing away the happiness of the day, the colours fading. 'You need someone to look after you and it would be good for Lily and Daniel. They need stability. I hope this woman is kind and caring. They need a lot of love.'

He poured out some more wine and gulped it down.

'Yes, she is kind and caring, very good with children. A bit bossy at times, used to getting her own way, but I daresay I can cope with that. I think Lily and Daniel will be pleased. As you say, they need lots of love and mothering. And I'm sure she's the kind of woman who will give them that.'

'So do we drink to the happy day?' said Jessica, raising her glass. Her hand was trembling. She was frightened by the depth and power of her own feelings. She could no longer smell the fruit of the grapes. 'Have you fixed a date?'

A flicker of a smile crossed his lined face. 'Unfortunately, no date in view. You see, I haven't even asked her yet. I still have that bridge to cross. And I'm out of practice in the proposal stakes.'

'Well, you'd better hurry up, get things moving,' said Jessica, engineering some sort of enthusiasm. 'Such a paragon might be snapped up by someone else. She sounds too good to be true. Make your move.'

'I do agree with you. She may well have some ardent suitor waiting in the wings. I don't really know. I know very little about her, actually.'

Jessica was lost. She did not understand what Lucas was saying. He was going to marry someone that he knew little or nothing about? It was absurd. She rallied her good sense. He may not want her advice but she was going to give it.

'Forgive me, if I'm speaking out of turn, but this sounds crazy. You can't marry someone who you know very little about. This isn't one of those dating agencies on the Internet, is it? It could lead to all sorts of disasters. She might be completely fraudulent, years older than you, foreign, merely

101

wanting to marry someone to get hold of a British passport. Don't do it, I beg of you.'

The tension broke and Lucas grinned. 'Internet dating? I hadn't thought of that. I might try it next if this falls through. Well, I'd better get it over quick then. Jessica Harlow, fantastic nurse, glamorous nanny, funny Willdo from the wilderness, will you marry me? Will you become my lawful-wedded wife?'

Jessica said no, of course, straight away. What else could she say? It was all too sudden. They didn't know each other. It was a ridiculous idea.

'No way, sir, Lucas, Mr Coleman. Is this some sort of joke? Are you making fun of me? Well, I'm not laughing. It's not even funny.'

'Please think it over,' said Lucas, pouring coffee. 'Get used to the idea. It might grow on you. We get on pretty well together.'

'Don't you reckon on it,' Jessica said. 'Why me?'

'Because you are eminently suitable. A very good nurse. Excellent with children. Not bad-looking at times. Quite the arm candy, I could say, if I ever need a glamorous escort. I do have various medical dinners and functions that I am supposed to attend. You'd look pretty good, wearing the right clothes.'

'Thank you,' said Jessica, icily. 'You

certainly know how to make a woman feel good. Did you take a correspondence course on courtship? I should ask them for your money back.'

'Then you'll consider my proposal?' Lucas was looking at her keenly, his silvery grey eyes suddenly fierce and glittering. 'I mean it. I want you to marry me.'

'I didn't say that,' Jessica said.

'You nearly did.'

'Please listen, Lucas,' she said, dredging the words from somewhere. 'Marriage isn't just a convenient arrangement. It has to mean so much more. It's between people who love each other, who can't bear to be apart, who want to live the rest of their lives together.'

'I know,' he said smoothly. 'But we are different. We have both been hurt, badly, in the past. I don't know what happened to you, but it's there in your eyes, the hurt and humiliation. So this could be second best for both of us. I'm offering you security, a pleasant home, status in society, two children who need you. I'm not asking anything for myself. No midnight romps in bed or early morning quickies. Nothing more than an obligatory kiss on the cheek in public. I ask for nothing more. Could you manage that? It might not be too hard a duty to perform.'

Jessica was breathing hard. Lucas was

offering her a lifeline, a way out of the swamp she had been wallowing in, throwing a life-belt to a shipwrecked woman. But where was the love she had always dreamed about? Where was the gallant knight in shining armour, riding to rescue her? He must be somewhere on the horizon.

'It's your choice,' he went on, finishing his coffee. 'Please listen to your heart. I'll leave you to think about it.'

He got up from the dining table and came round to her side. He pulled Jessica to her feet. He steadied her hip against his body and his mouth touched her lips. There was nothing inexpert about his kiss. It was warm and gentle, incredibly familiar. She was trapped in his arms.

'Goodnight Jessica,' he said in a deep, slow and husky voice. 'Don't make me wait too long.'

Jessica did not sleep well, tossed and turned. When she awoke the next morning, she wondered if she had imagined the whole strange proposal? Lucas had been overtired, drinking wine on an empty stomach. He might regret it this morning, if he remembered it at all. Maybe he had also had a few whiskies before the wine.

The light streamed through the window, turning the primrose to gold.

But Lucas had already left for the hospital. She heard the Porsche Boxster leaving at some inhuman hour. She had wanted to talk to him about Daniel's coming birthday. There had been no response from Daniel himself. The concept of birthdays did not register. Time and age meant little to him.

When she put her head round his bedroom door, Daniel was already up. He was sitting on the floor in his pyjamas, all his treasures from the beach lined up in front of him. He had one of his school books on his knee and he was busy drawing on a blank page. It was the drawing of a shell, in great detail, very small and intricate. Unlike his handwriting, which was all over the place, this drawing was perfect.

'Time to get washed and dressed, Daniel,' she said.

He didn't answer but kept drawing.

Lily on the other hand, had dressed herself in shorts and T-shirt, ready to go to the beach. She had decided it was going to be the beach again. The T-shirt was on inside-out but what did that matter, and she had odd socks on.

'Have you practiced your inhaler this morning, Lily?'

She shook her head, dark hair bouncing around. 'I have to breathe slowly,' she said. 'Do it properly.'

'That's right. Let's do it now. Sit down and check inside and outside the mouthpiece to make sure it's clean and clear.'

'All clean.'

'Shake the inhaler. How many times?'

'Four or five times. To mix all the stuff up inside.'

Lily held up the inhaler and breathed out slowly which she did not find easy. She always wanted to breath in again quickly, scared of not having any air in her lungs, of starting to gasp.

'Don't panic. Hold your breath. Put the mouthpiece in your mouth and press down on top of the canister to release a puff. Then you can breathe that in. Breathe it in slowly. Well done, steady now. Don't rush.'

'Not rushing.'

'Now do it again, Lily. Excellent. You've got the hang of it now. Put the cover on firmly. Next time we'll clean it with a dry cloth or tissue.'

'I'm getting better at it,' said Lily happily. 'Now can we go to the beach?'

'Not today, Lily. We're going to do something quite different today. I'll get you a peak flow meter so we can check how you are doing.'

'Is that like a parking meter?'

'In a way, yes. It tells us if your airways are

relaxed. If they are, then you get a high score.'

Jessica had a new idea. She was fast running out of new ideas. 'Over breakfast, I'm going to tell you about a little girl called Maggie who is in hospital.'

'Is it a sad story?'

'It's a true story and quite sad.'

Mrs Harris had breakfast ready in the kitchen. She had adapted to the healthier eating without any problem. It was poached eggs this morning, and fruit. Jessica did the ordering now after discussing the family's needs with Mrs Harris first. There was far less cooking involved, lots more fruit and salads.

Lady Grace resisted all change. She ordered her own menus every day and Jessica had no wish to be involved. It was the children that she cared about and Lucas. She knew what hospital food was like, even in the staff canteen.

It was exercises first this morning. Lady Grace always tried to get out of them. She thought up new arguments every day. It was like a game show.

'I don't need to do them every day,' she protested. 'I shall get ugly, bulging arm muscles like an athlete. As long as I walk a bit, I'm doing fine. You must admit I have made excellent progress, Miss Know-all.'

'Indeed, Lady Grace. Your progress is good. It's remarkable when you have argued every step of the way. You must admit now, that regular exercise is the answer. So let's start. Let's put some music on. Straight leg first.'

'Do we have to? I don't like that music.'

'Yes, we do. Think of that lovely glass of your favourite dry sherry when you get downstairs. Then your walk round the garden. The roses are magnificent. I've even done some dead-heading. I'd like to know some of the names.'

'I know all the names.' There was no thank you for the dead-heading.

'I'm sure you do. Your memory is amazing.'

Sundays were not easy. No school. Lily and Daniel were at home all day with Lady Grace demanding constant attention. But today Jessica told the children about Maggie, the little girl who had been bitten. She didn't go into too much detail but said that they had been three fierce dogs and she was in hospital.

'She's very lonely and she hasn't any toys or any books. And I thought we could make Get Well cards to send her, lovely pictures with glitter and ribbons.'

'Yes, yes, we'll make lots of cards,' said Lily, immediately brimming with enthusiasm. 'And she can have some of my toys.' She raced upstairs to her bedroom, turning floor and cupboard chaos out into more chaos. Jessica sat back and laughed. Lily was a bundle of energy, despite her weight.

'Lily is such a funny little girl,' she said to Daniel. She was hoping he might reply.

He didn't look up. He was already drawing on some cardboard which Jessica had found. It was an old chocolate box lid on its way to the refuse collection. He was absorbed in what he was doing.

When Lucas returned from the hospital that evening, there was a box of goodies for Maggie, toys, a teddy, books and cards. Lily had been busy all day making cards for everyone. She had gone into serious card production. She had made a large pink one for Maggie with silver angels and stars, lots of glitter and ribbons. She had also made a hospital one for Lucas with rows of beds, on which she had written 'I love you, Daddy.' Jessica had helped with the writing.

Lady Grace got a card on which Lily had drawn a picture of her doing a cartwheel down the stairs. Not exactly tactful, Jessica thought, nor appreciated. Lady Grace had sniffed and said, 'Very nice, dear.'

'At least you got a card,' said Jessica.

Lily's card for Daniel was a secret. 'For his

birthday,' she whispered to Jessica. Mrs Harris was presented with a card covered in photographs of food cut out from a magazine. It said: To the Bestest Cook.

'I'm amazed at that,' said Mrs Harris.

Even Jessica got a card. It was more glittery angels and stars and inside Lily had written 'I love you', copying the writing on her father's card.

'Thank you, Lily,' said Jessica. 'I shall treasure your card. I'll put it on the mantelpiece in my bedroom.'

'So you can see it when you wake up.'

'Every morning when I wake up. It's the first thing I shall see.'

Lucas was the first to spot the near identical message. He was not slow in spotting the implication, though he had said nothing about the previous evening.

'These cards should stand together, don't you think, Jessica?' For once, his silvery eyes were twinkling. 'They were made for each other. The same message.'

It wasn't easy to find the right reply. It made her realize how strong he was. The dark stubble on his chin was her undoing. He looked so vulnerable.

'You didn't have time to shave this morning,' she said. 'Was it a busy night?'

'Saturday night drinking always brings a

wave of emergencies,' he said, passing a hand over his chin. 'Bike accidents, car accidents, falling down stairs, falling off balconies. No one has any sense of balance on a Saturday. It's a wonder anyone is still standing upright.'

Daniel got up off the floor and brought over his card for Maggie. He had been working on it all day, not letting anyone see what he was doing. He had folded the chocolate box lid so that it became card shape. The front said Terry's All Gold Milk Chocolates on a swirling gold and blue pattern.

Daniel said nothing but indicated that the card should be opened. Jessica opened the card and drew in her breath sharply.

The inside was covered with intricate drawings of shells, all in rows, every kind of shell in every position. Some were the ones he had collected from Worthing beach, others were dreamed up shells. The pencil lines were fine and delicate. They reminded Jessica of ancient Japanese art. She handed Lucas the card.

'I don't think you need worry about Daniel's future,' she said. 'This is his future. He is a born artist. He will be able to make a living from his work.'

Lucas took the card and studied the drawings. 'They are perfect,' he said, nodding. He smiled at Daniel. 'All the more reason to give my son the stability of a loving family. Don't you agree, Jessica?'

Jessica could not look at him. Lucas could not dictate her future in that cavalier fashion. When she married, it would be for love. Not convenience.

6

The revelation that Daniel could draw tiny objects with exquisite detail amazed and raised everyone's spirits, except Daniel's. He was unperturbed by the fuss.

'I can't draw like this,' said Lucas.

'Very few people can. Each shell is quite perfect.'

'My grandmother used to paint, delicate watercolours and pastels. She did mostly wild flowers. There's a little book of hers up in the attic somewhere,' said Lady Grace, modestly accepting her place on the talent tree. 'He's obviously inherited the gift from my side.'

Daniel made no response. Jessica longed for some kind of communication with the boy. Every evening she spent some time with him, helping with his writing practice but still his words and letters had no coherence. His b's looked like p's and m and n were interchangeable. S was always curved the other way round. In a funny way, it was readable, like an ancient Persian or Egyptian script. She could read it. His alphabet was re-invented, drawn backwards, upside-down, sometimes he added a completely new letter shape. ^ and > were two of them. They meant something.

'You probably had another grandparent who lived on the Easter Isles,' said Jessica. 'But I suppose it won't really matter in the future if you can't write a letter. All letters will be via the Internet. And when you become really famous, you can employ a secretary. I think you should learn to use the Internet.'

Daniel looked marginally interested as Jessica moved over to the computer in the library, switched on, logged into Yahoo, the free server, and began signing Daniel in as a new user.

He went and stood behind her, watching what she was doing, not saying a word. There was no way of judging if he understood the process.

'This is for sending letters. Now what do you want to be called?' said Jessica. 'Daniel Coleman is your real name but it is a bit too long for an email address. And it might be already in use. What do you think about DanCole?'

Daniel shook his head slowly. 'DanCo,' he said. 'DanCo.'

'I like that,' said Jessica. 'DanCo. Very neat. Let's see if it has already been used. Let's hope it's available. It is! Good, now that's your email address, Daniel. I'll write it down for you. And you will need a password, something secret that only you will know, that you have to type in this space, every time you switch on.'

Jessica thought this might be a real headache but Daniel understood and typed something in without hesitation. She couldn't see what he put. Whether he would remember it was a different matter.

'Now you can send emails to your friends.'

'No friends,' he said.

'You could send one to me, now and again,' said Jessica. 'I'm your friend. This is my email address. JessHar@yahoo.co.uk. I'll type it in for you and add it to your contacts. Watch me. Any time you want to say something to me, you can send me an email letter. I'll show you how to do it. Does that sound good?'

'Good.'

'And here is my email address at the hospital,' said Lucas. 'You should have that in your contacts.'

Before she went to bed that night, she checked on her emails. She had eight emails from DanCo. She tried not to laugh but it was a success of sorts. At least he had got the hang of how to send emails. It took ages deciphering their content. They were mostly incoherent ramblings, weird spellings and incorrect typing, but there were snatches which made a lot of sense.

'Paper 2 poot markz on.' 'I have no Mummy.' 'Skool iz bad.' 'U help me.' And so it went on . . . reams of Daniel's thoughts.

It was heart-breaking. Jessica showed the emails to Lucas when he came in from the hospital. Lucas was dropping with sleep. It had been another long day. Jessica knew that he still had some reserve energy or she would not have waited.

Lucas became both elated and dejected. 'Daniel's got the hang of email already? That's terrific. It's the way to the twenty-first century. OK, they are practically unreadable but he will get better in time. My spelling is just as bad.'

'But look what he is writing,' she said. 'This is what Daniel really thinks of his life. How can we help him? We must help him.'

Lucas gave her a penetrating look and took hold of her hand. It was a magical touch. His fingers were firm and warm, his thumb circling her palm. 'You know what you can do. Say yes, right away, Jessica. That would solve one of his problems. He would have a mummy. That's what he wants. You would be so right.'

'It's not that easy,' said Jessica, marvelling at the touch. How would this touch feel all

116

over her body? She went weak at the thought, skin shrivelling, sliding away. 'You're talking about me making a commitment for the rest of my life. How do I know what I want to do with the rest of my life? I can't make that sort of commitment to someone I don't even know.'

'We could make it a marriage contract,' said Lucas, slowly. 'If you would prefer something that is less of an emotional commitment. I realize that a life-long marriage would be unfair to such a young and beautiful woman as you. You deserve something better. Would a ten-year marriage contract be more acceptable? I promise that I would set you free at the end of it. That would cover Daniel reaching eighteen and Lily over fifteen. It sounds feasible to me.'

Jessica was shocked to the core. She snatched her hand away. 'I can't believe that you could be so callous. A marriage contract with a time limit? As if anyone could just turn off care and affection for your children at the end of so many years and walk away. You simply have no idea.'

'I thought it would make it easier for you to decide. For you to know that it was not forever.' Lucas was trying to control his anger.

'Well, I have decided and the answer is no.

No, no, no. There is no way that I am going to marry you. So you can forget it.'

'I don't believe you for one moment, Jessica,' said Lucas, his eyes darkening. 'Your head says one thing but your eyes say something quite different. And that kiss last night — there was something special about it and you know that. You are not totally immune to me. You have some feeling for me and my children.'

'For both your children, yes. I care about them. For your awkward mother, I have a lot of sympathy. But having feelings for you, definitely not. I don't have a scrap of feeling for you, Lucas Coleman. I feel nothing for you at all. I rarely see you and I hardly know you. When you come in, you are usually half-asleep, wet and exhausted. We exchange a few polite words and that's that.'

'That's true,' said Lucas, with a touch of mockery. 'We don't know each other. A few suppers and family breakfasts hardly count. I suppose I should give you the chance to know me better. I don't remember when I last had a day off. We could go somewhere together, get to know each other.'

'It won't make any difference,' said Jessica vehemently. 'You can't turn on feelings with a few hours of making small talk over a candlelit dinner.'

'I wouldn't talk at all,' he said, hiding his laughter. 'I'd simply let you find out what a really nice person I am.'

'In a day?' Jessica scoffed. 'It would surely take months.'

'I'll wait months.'

'And only on clear days, no rain, no fog, no sea mist.'

'I can't guarantee the weather but I can guarantee my undivided attention.'

'Oh, such sweet words. Clever words, too. They don't sway me.' Jessica marched away, trying to still the hammering of her heart.

★   ★   ★

Lucas was as good as his word. He reorganized his work schedule and arranged to take a whole afternoon off. Mrs Harris was happy to give the children their tea when they came in from school, and keep a friendly eye on Lady Grace.

'I thought you might like to go into Brighton to buy Daniel's birthday present. I need to find something suitable. You could help me,' Lucas said. 'Is that a good idea, Jessica? Would you like to come?'

Jessica was not sure what tempted her most. She'd like to wander round Brighton. She'd also like a drive in his Porsche Boxster with the roof down. But she'd really like the chance to buy Daniel something nice for his birthday. She did not admit to herself that she might want to enjoy some time with Lucas.

He was ready for her on the dot of two o'clock. He had changed into black jeans and an open necked black shirt. His hair still needed a cut but he looked devilishly handsome. The car was at the front door waiting. A fresh breeze combed the gardens, sending waves of scent from Lady Grace's roses.

Jessica had tried not to make an effort, to show that she didn't care a jot about going out with Lucas, but she looked wonderful in slim white linen trousers and a belted flame-red shirt, her hair tied back with a red scarf. She threw a navy fleece into the back of the car.

'You'll need a coat for coming back,' she said. 'Summer is on its way out. It'll be chilly.'

Lucas nodded, hurried back into the house and returned with the same well worn sweater that needed mending. 'Sorry, that's all I could find,' he said, seeing her dismayed expression. 'Donkey's years old.'

'I'll mend it one day.'

'No wife of mine is going to mend clothes,' he said.

'I'm not your wife.'

'Not yet.'

It was an exciting drive. Jessica loved the speed of the car on the main M27 dual carriage road to Brighton that allowed some speed. They sped through the over-lit tunnel that cut under the South Downs. Lucas was an excellent driver and she felt perfectly safe in his hands. It was such a different day to her arrival in the rain. A September sun was flinging burnt golden rays of sun down onto the earth, a sort of last gesture before autumn set in and decay began the tombstone slide. Jessica put on her sunglasses to cut the glaring light.

They drove in through the genteel residences of Hove. There were so many beautiful elegant Regency terraces, Brunswick Terrace and Adelaide Crescent, white and curving houses with big windows and ironwork balustrades. They had the long ago stamp of past elegant living, long dresses, bonnets, carriages.

'They are mostly flats now,' said Lucas. 'Very sought after and expensive, I expect. A lot of show business people live down here, television and theatre stars, because of the decent train service to London. Keep your eyes open. This is spot the celebrities time. They are everywhere. Some have a small dog.'

Parking was apparently a nightmare in Brighton but Lucas had an arrangement with the Royal Sussex Hospital. He had a visitor's pass.

'I never normally use it for a private visit,' he said. 'Mostly when I'm called to see a patient or assist in some surgery. But today is special.'

Jessica had not been to Brighton for years, since childhood, and it had changed beyond recognition. It was all shops and boutiques, crowds of visitors and tourists, overflowing with pubs and wine bars. Lucas had to take her arm or they would have been separated by the milling throng of tourists. Lucas was steering her through the narrow passages and cobbled streets of The Lanes.

'The Lanes used to be the paths between an area of allotments or gardens,' he said. 'Can you imagine what it was like when Brighton was just a small fishing port? It was really tiny. It used to pay its taxes to the crown in fish.'

The shops were a mixture of fancy boutiques, ancient antique shops, expensive jewellery shops, music collectors' havens. The oldest shops, with faded paintwork, were held together with dust and cobwebs. Their old books and records dying in untidy piles. The past struggling to survive in the modernization.

Jessica could have lingered for ages in The

Lanes but time was already flying and Lucas had promised her tea somewhere special and Jessica wanted to be touristy and go on the Palace pier.

Jessica spotted it first. It was a specialist shop that sold artists' materials. This was exactly what she wanted. Lucas guessed what she was thinking.

'Daniel's present? This is it. Right first time,' he said.

They spent some time in the shop, exploring all its wonders, remembering that Daniel was at a very early stage in his exploration of drawing and it would not help to push him too hard with expensive equipment or give him bewildering choices. Everything had to be slowly, slowly.

Jessica found some good quality sketching paper, 140 gsm. She bought pads in two sizes, large A3 and a small A5 sketch pad for him to carry around. She also bought a packet of heavy coloured paper, blue, pink, green and pale yellow, which Daniel might find interesting to use.

Lucas browsed through a collection of instruction books which helped very young artists with their initial efforts. Not that Daniel seemed to need any help. He was an instinctive artist. Lucas bought a paperback on How to Draw Everything and a hardback called Sixteen Drawing Lessons which seemed overly complicated for Daniel. But the pictures were beautifully produced.

'That's quite enough books to begin with, isn't it?' he said. 'We don't want to swamp him with loads of different ideas or a different media.'

'Quite enough,' agreed Jessica. She was enjoying his casual friendliness. 'I think he might like some decent soft pencils too.'

They found a packet of eight sketching pencils from 6B to 2H. They added a soft putty eraser. Lucas was tempted to buy an artist's satchel.

'No, Lucas, not yet,' said Jessica, hastening to damp the thought. 'It makes his drawing all too organized. Let Daniel find his own bag. He'll have his own ideas. He'll find something strange that is all his own.'

The girl assistant was obviously smitten by Lucas and his easy manner and wanted to know everything about Daniel. Perhaps this was work experience and she would make notes. It took them ten minutes to get out of the shop. The girl stood in the doorway, watching them walk away. She gave a brief wave, cursing her bad luck not to have met Lucas first.

Tea was a calorific cream tea in a crazy, picturesque tea room called Mrs Kipling's where everything was home-made. By this time they were both ravenous as neither had had time for lunch. They went upstairs where the tables had lace cloths and they served on pretty china, which was a change from thick white mugs that most places seemed to go for these days.

'This is so lovely,' said Jessica. 'A choice of tea, a choice of milk, even a choice of jam. I'd like strawberry jam, please.'

'Pot of tea for two, Earl Grey, semi-skimmed milk and strawberry jam with our scones, please,' Lucas ordered. 'And a plate of your delicious cakes.' It even came with a pot of hot water for their second cups.

Jessica sat back into her chair, enjoying the atmosphere of the tea rooms. It had been a wonderful afternoon, doing normal things with Lucas.

'Civilization is rare these days,' said Lucas. 'I often used to come here when I was a student. I had to save up.'

'Was Brighton one of your favourite clubbing places?'

He grinned. 'You obviously know about students. We were all broke so we used to take food and beer down onto the beach and stay there to watch the dawn come up. What did you do when you were a student nurse?'

'Nothing so exciting. We were mostly too

tired. Sometimes we'd go to a disco or a party. People drank too much, as they do. It wasn't always fun.'

Jessica tried not to think how much she was enjoying herself in Lucas's company. He was sitting close by. They were together. They agreed about most things. He was being amusing and informal, pleasant to get along with. There was no pressure. Jessica relaxed into the warm feeling of togetherness.

'Have we got time to go on the West Pier?' Jessica asked.

'Unfortunately I fear we're a few years too late,' said Lucas. 'The West Pier has collapsed into the sea after two fires, a violent storm, neglect and more neglect. It was once a very elegant Edwardian pier with a concert hall and ballroom. There's only a gaunt wreck now, standing out to sea. People take photographs and paint pictures of it. But we could go on the Palace Pier, if you like noisy entertainments.'

'That's where I meant, the Palace Pier. Yes, I'd like to be very touristy but I draw the line at wearing a funny hat.'

'Absolutely no funny hats,' said Lucas, paying the bill for their tea. 'And I refuse all scary rides. I've no head for heights. I might be an embarrassment.'

Palace Pier was non-stop entertainments,

both sides crowded with side-shows and kiosks selling candy floss and seaside rock, fortune tellers and bars. Everywhere smelt saccharine sweet. The domed amusement arcade rang with loud music, clinking coins and money squandered on machines in search of instant riches. Jessica won a white rabbit with long ears for Lily after three goes on a crane machine.

'I suppose we ought to go on something,' said Lucas reluctantly, as they walked round the thrill rides and the roller coaster. 'But I can't see anything that my delicate constitution would cope with.'

'Especially after that big cream tea.'

'Exactly. Now I wouldn't mind a go at that rifle shooting range. What about you, Jessica?'

Jessica shook her head. 'No eye for it.'

Lucas did have an eye and a nonchalant way of shouldering a rifle. He won a cowboy hat for Daniel. So each child had a present.

It was turning chilly, the sun already sinking. There was no feeling of being at sea on the Palace Pier yet they were a third of a mile out over the water. They watched the seagulls wheeling and diving in formation. The birds were tracking a fishing boat returning, waiting for the gutted bits to be thrown overboard. Jessica pulled on her fleece. Lucas had left his threadbare jersey in the car. He tucked his arm into hers, smiling down.

'I'm afraid you'll have to keep me warm,' he said. 'A brisk walk to the car and then home to Upton Hall? Is that all right with you?'

Jessica nodded. 'We don't want to be too late because of Mrs Harris.'

It struck her that she sounded like a much married wife, showing concern about a baby-sitter. She didn't want Lucas to think she was getting ideas. One pleasant afternoon did not a marriage make.

'I hope I haven't been clamped or towed away,' said Lucas as they climbed the steep road to the hospital car park. 'I shouldn't have parked there today.'

'Why shouldn't you? You haven't done anything really wrong.'

'It's not a question of right or wrong: I have the wrong make of car. One look at this beauty and officials go berserk. I'm a target for every fine invented. If I haven't broken some by-law, they'll invent one.'

'That's not fair.'

'I'm sure, as you will have discovered, a lot of things in life are not fair. I should be driving a clapped-out Volvo. The Porsche is my one indulgence and I've earned it. I like the speed. As you've probably gathered, I've no time for shopping for clothes or CDs or DVDs or any other trappings.'

The cool scent of a crisp autumn heralded the end of the last day of the summer. Evenings would be cooler from now on. It had been a pleasant afternoon, wandering about, but that didn't mean Jessica wanted to marry him.

'I'm going into the hospital a bit later tomorrow morning,' he said, as they drove through the tortuous back streets of Brighton, searching for the main road out of the town. The tall white Regency houses of Hove sea front were melting into shadows. A sea mist was folding the beach into a shroud. 'You might like to come with me. I'm sure young Maggie would enjoy your company for half an hour. You could read to her some of your famous bed-time stories.'

'I'd like that but how would I get home?'

'You could leave my mother's car at Easily station in the morning, and get a train back to there. A bit complicated, but worth the effort. I think you'd have to change trains. Maggie's grandmother can't get down to visit her. It's such a shame.'

'What about Lady Grace?'

'I'm sure she could do her exercises on her own for once.'

Jessica was happy to go and read to Maggie

but the return journey would be a long one. She remembered that first train journey down to Eastly and shuddered at the thought of enduring part of it again. At least there would be a car waiting for her at the station, her current little car. That would be a big improvement.

Was this what it would be like as Lucas's wife, having to do wifely things like visiting patients or going to see ailing ex-patients? She knew Lucas was a conscientious doctor and surgeon and his wife might find herself acting as a second string. Jessica did not object to this. As a nurse, she knew the importance of visits and family contact. Young Maggie would be feeling strange and lonely by herself, face stitched up, in pain, feeding tube attached.

'It's going to rain,' said Jessica. A mantle of purple light was bruising the sky as rain clouds gathered. 'Thank goodness you put the roof up.'

'The holiday brochures call this part of the coast *Sunny Sussex*. But they always forget to mention the rain. And the wind. It can be ferocious. We get gales of up to seventy miles per hour. Almost impossible to walk in or cross a road. The twittens become wind tunnels. It can take your breath away.'

'Thank you for the lovely tea,' said Jessica,

getting the gratitude bit over in case she forgot. 'Wonderful home-made cakes. Very calorific.'

'The first of many,' said Lucas politely.

Soon the windscreen was weeping with rain. How could Lucas see to drive? He must have laser eyes to do that intricate surgery, and he used the same laser eyes to pierce the curtains of rain.

It slowed down their return journey, although several madmen overtook them on the M27, despite the fact that they could barely see ahead.

'The Monopoly game with death,' said Lucas. 'Move to Intensive Care,' he added as another impatient driver swept passed them, his wheels spraying up dirt and water. Lucas switched on the spray washers to clean the windscreen.

Jessica was tense, the base of her spine aching. His driving was perfect. It was the jolting of the road surface that did not help.

It was a relief when they turned off the busy dual carriageway and found the quieter side roads and twisting lanes that would take them to Eastly. It almost felt like coming home when Upton Hall loomed into sight among the dripping trees.

Lily and Daniel came rushing out into the rain carrying big umbrellas. Lily's face was alight with excitement. Daniel was having trouble keeping his umbrella open. It was threatening to turn itself inside out.

'You're back! You're back,' she shouted, as if they had gone on an expedition to the Himalayas. 'Have you brought us presents from Brighton?'

'What a greedy little girl you are,' said Lucas, bending himself in half to get under the umbrella she was holding up. 'Why should we bring you presents?'

'Because you love us!'

'Do we? Who said so?'

Jessica dodged under Daniel's umbrella, helping him to get the mechanism to stay up. 'This is an awkward one,' she said. 'It never works properly.'

He nodded, not meeting her eyes. But she did feel some sort of awareness from him. It was different to his normal indifference.

They stood in the hall, both wet, trying to remember what it was like to be warm, the children clamouring around them, wondering if there were any presents.

Lily loved her floppy-eared rabbit. 'A wabbit! A wabbit,' she shrieked. It was going to be a noisy evening.

Daniel was also taken by his cowboy hat. He put it on immediately and went to bed wearing it.

Lucas disappeared to his study. Paperwork, he said. It was never ending.

It was late when Jessica came downstairs after putting the children to bed and checking on Lady Grace.

'No cards this afternoon, then,' said Lady Grace, sitting up in bed, reading. 'Better things to do?'

'We'll play cards tomorrow afternoon,' said Jessica, not forgetting about her visit to read to Maggie. It was going to be difficult to fit everything in. But she had promised.

Lucas was wandering about downstairs, talking on his mobile phone. He looked apprehensive and Jessica felt an urge to put her arm round him. She watched the changing expression on his face with a sudden chill.

'OK, I'll come right away. You were right to call me.' He switched off his phone. 'I'm afraid you'll have supper on your own. It's young Maggie. She's running a high temperature. Not good news. I don't like it. I'll have to go back.'

'You'll need an anorak. It's still raining,' said Jessica. 'I'll make you a sandwich to take with you. It won't take a minute.'

'I haven't time for a sandwich.'

'I'm the fastest sandwich maker in the West,' said Jessica, speeding into the kitchen.

Minutes later she was in the porch, standing back from the rain, with a packet of cheese and tomato sandwiches. She tucked them into his pocket as Lucas shrugged himself into his anorak.

'You're going to make somebody a wonderful wife,' he said, brooding.

Suddenly he moulded her slender body to him. Jessica ached with the warmth of his closeness, his rampant attractiveness. His eyes lingered on hers for a second too long. Neither of them could stop the tidal wave of feeling.

Lucas had no idea what he was doing, being swept along. He could drown in her sweetness. Jessica was so lusciously willowy and slender. It was an agony as his lips touched her mouth briefly. His fierce kiss was burning with undisguised longing and desire.

'Oh, Jessica, if only you knew,' he murmured.

'Drive carefully,' she said against his cheek.

Then just as suddenly he was gone. Jessica had not had time to respond to his kiss. She stood in the porch, shattered and trembling, and it was not because of the rain. This was the moment that Jessica realized that she loved him.

She had not admitted it before, but now she knew.

It was dark and she was glad that no one could see her face. This was a secret that she had to keep to herself. Even if she loved him, she could not marry a man who did not love her, who wanted only a token wife to care for his mother and his children. It was not a bargain she could accept.

He'd said he wanted nothing else. He would go elsewhere for the pleasures of the body. And that kiss had been telling her that he would go elsewhere. Perhaps to a nurse or a grateful patient.

She shuddered at the thought. As before, he was asking too much. She was a human being with real feelings.

Jessica went back into the kitchen, still trembling. At least she had put the best Stilton in his sandwich. No meanness in her heart.

7

Jessica took a sandwich and a mug of tea into the library and switched on the television. She did not really want to watch any programme. She wanted to relive every step of the afternoon but knew it would be a dangerous occupation. Lucas was someone she should blot from her mind, and fast.

Poor Maggie. Instead, she should think of that little girl, still not out of the woods from her frightening experience. But Lucas would do all that he could with his skilful hands. The whole team would be there at her side. Jessica had lived through trauma many times in different wards. It was always an alarming situation, especially with sick and vulnerable children.

She didn't take in a word of the programme. It was a mindless sound track running through her head and disjointed figures moving across the television screen like puppets. Wallpaper television.

It was pointless staying up any longer. Lucas was not coming home. He would spend the night at the hospital, near Maggie, fighting for her.

Jessica went round locking up the big house, making sure all the windows were closed. She activated the alarm. It was a bit scary and still raining. The gardens were trapped in darkness, rain slicing through the night with relentless obstinacy.

She checked on the children. Lily was asleep with Floppy Ears, as he was now called, cuddled in her arms. Daniel had placed the cowboy hat on his pillow and Jessica gently removed it, putting it beside his bed, where he would see it first thing when he awoke in the morning.

If only she could get through to him. It would be such an achievement.

'Goodnight, young man,' Jessica whispered.

'I suppose you're going to bed,' said Lady Grace, still sitting up in bed, propped up with pillows, reading a new library book. 'All that gallivanting about. Tired you out, has it? Young people have no stamina these days.'

'Brighton is so bustling and crowded. Masses of people. It's hard work finding room to walk on the pavements.'

'It's all those gays and lesbians,' said Lady Grace. 'They flock there, filling the place up, taking all the accommodation.'

'They have a right to live somewhere,' said Jessica, drawing the heavy curtains. 'Would you like some hot milk?'

'Yes, please, Jess. And two digestive biscuits. And make sure the milk is hot. I can't stand lukewarm milk. It's disgusting. That skin forming on the top.'

★   ★   ★

Sleep did not come easily. Jessica tossed and turned as if her bed was a ship at sea, making a nest of all her worries and fears. Dawn was filtering eerily through the sky before she fell into a deep sleep. Those few hours were not enough and Jessica awoke at her normal time, groggy and thick enough to spread on toast.

Lily was hopping about on the landing with Floppy Ears. 'I'm taking him for a walk,' she told the world. The world wasn't listening.

'Take him for a very long walk,' groaned Jessica, turning her face into the pillow. There was no way of getting out of it. The household was waking up. She could hear Lady Grace's strident bell. This was a new idea so that her ladyship could command attention at all times.

Jessica stumbled into the big front bedroom, still pulling on her bathrobe.

'Hello,' she said, blinking sleep from her eyes. 'This is a bit early.'

'I've lost Fred.'

'You don't need Fred to get out of bed. Fred is for long journeys. Do it slowly as I've showed you. Swing your legs over the side of the bed and feel the floor firmly first before putting your weight on your legs. Stand still for a few moments before starting to walk.'

'I prefer using Fred,' she insisted.

Fred was left overnight in the bathroom. Jessica hauled out the walker and took it round to Lady Grace. But she stood it some feet away from the bed.

'Here's poor Fred, banished as usual. Now, get out of bed as I showed you and then you can have Fred,' she promised.

Lady Grace pulled her bed jacket round her. 'You are a tyrant and a bully, Nurse Jess. I don't know why I put up with you. You're supposed to look after me, do what I say. I'm your employer.'

'I'm supposed to be getting you through your hip replacement. Because you know, even if you won't admit it, that this is doing you a lot of good,' said Jessica, her good humour returning with wakefulness. 'Look who can get downstairs now? Look who has been out into the garden to admire her roses?'

'I'd have done that anyway, with or without you, young minx.'

'Of course,' grinned Jessica. 'By installing an expensive stair lift. I'm sure you'd rather spend the money on a dozen crates of the best extra dry sherry.'

Lady Grace simply grunted and swung herself out of bed. She could do it quite well. She grabbed hold of Fred as if he was the staff of life. Maybe it was confidence she needed first thing in the morning. Or attention.

'And stop those noisy children stamping about out there on the landing. You know I can't stand noise in my delicate state. I shall get a headache. Take them out to play or whatever you're paid to do.'

'Sure, they'd love to go out and play, half dressed, at seven o'clock in the morning. Grass damp with dew, trying to rain, before a crumb of breakfast. Anyway, rabbits don't stamp. They hop.'

But Jessica did take Lily off to the bathroom where it was difficult to stop Lily brushing Floppy Ears' teeth. 'He doesn't need his teeth cleaning,' said Jessica, rescuing the creature from a watery grave in the washbasin.

'But look, he's got big pointed teeth.'

'He doesn't eat anything.'

Down in the kitchen Mrs Harris had arrived and was taking off her hat and coat. Jessica escaped into the warmth, still in her bathrobe, to beg for a cup of tea. The kettle was singing on the Aga as she knew it would be. The kitchen was a haven.

'This is going to be some day,' Jessica said. 'I have that gut feeling.'

'I hope you are wrong,' said Mrs Harris, wrapping herself in the flowered overall she insisted on wearing. 'I don't want one of those days. Lady Grace nearly drove me round the bend yesterday. She was in the worst of moods. Jealous because you had gone out with Lucas, I reckon. I can always tell.'

'I'm so sorry,' said Jessica, contrite. 'We went shopping for Daniel's birthday presents.' She didn't mention the cream tea or the walk on Palace Pier, or the drive home, or the kiss. Definitely not the kiss.

'And you both deserved some time off, some time together.'

Jessica wondered about that last comment. Some time together? Surely Mrs Harris was not part of the marriage conspiracy? No, it couldn't be. She was far too open and honest.

'I don't know how you have put up with Lady Grace all these years,' said Jessica, curling up on a kitchen chair with a cup of hot tea cradled in her hand. 'You could have got a job anywhere. Maybe housekeeper in one of the big hotels or another big house. You are such a good organizer, so efficient. Great cook.'

'It's a long story, miss. I won't bore you

with it. All lost and gone in the past now. Nothing left.' Her voice was emotionless, it also said: *don't ask me.*

Mrs Harris sat down, her drink of tea in her own special cup. She always used the same cup, a 1981 Diana and Charles bone-china wedding cup, their faces and royal logo entwined. No one knew why she had the cup. It was the finest bone china, almost too good to use. Yet she used it every day. She always washed and dried it carefully by hand. It never went in the dishwasher.

She saw Jessica looking at the cup and smiled.

'Yes, I know. It's lovely, isn't it? I should keep it as an heirloom, stand it on a mantelpiece, but I prefer to use it everyday. It reminds me, you see, of someone I used to know very well, someone who gave it to me. So it's a very special cup.'

Jessica held her breath. Was Mrs Harris going to tell her one of the secrets of Upton Hall? The house was full of secrets. It echoed with secrets, corridors filled with ghosts. She thought of Lily's mother, Liz, and her strange disappearance. The wife that Lucas lost. The wife who died needlessly on the M25. Lucas had not told her everything. He had been hiding something.

'It's beautiful,' said Jessica, sipping the

142

reviving tea. 'And how much better to use your cup everyday, rather than leave it on a shelf to be dusted once a week. Theirs was a very sad love story. A sad fairy-tale.'

'That's what he said,' Mrs Harris said. 'This is going to be a sad love story, he said to me, when the engagement was first splashed all over the newspapers. He was a man of great emotional depth. He knew exactly how people felt. It was an instinct. No one knew how much he suffered, mostly for other people.'

Jessica knew what she had to say. It was obvious. She could not stop herself.

'Is that why you loved him?'

Mrs Harris nodded. 'Yes, of course, miss, That's why I loved him. We had loved each other for years, on and off. Since our schooldays really. He always carried my satchel home from school. Sometimes I had no lunch and he shared his with me. We went dancing together on Saturday nights, then to open air pop concerts, lived in tents, deep in the mud. He looked after me, then he went away to study medicine. He had the brains, a skill, a talent that he had to use. He had to go.'

'Then what happened?'

'I got married. Bloody fool. I was out of my stupid mind. Some foolish romance that meant nothing. Somebody I met at the flicks. I knew as I was walking down the aisle in my white satin wedding dress and veil, all done up to the nines, that it was a horrible mistake. I thought: this is the wrong man. But it was too late. I had to go through with it. My mum had paid for everything, you see, the church, the cars, the reception. She would have been livid if I had backed out at the last moment.'

Jessica did not know what to say. This was a story she had heard so many times, patients confiding to her in the still of the night, finding relief, often their last night in this world. People make mistakes. The kitchen was quiet, splinters of light like diamonds. Even the children were quiet, somewhere in their rooms.

'It didn't last. He drank, he was useless, clumsy. I left him. It was the only sensible thing I did. Then I got this job at Upton Hall. I was broke and needed the money. It was like heaven opening to me again. He was here, but with a classy aristocratic and demanding wife. I didn't mind too much. I was near him. I could look after him because she didn't look after him. Especially after Lucas was born. She didn't want any more pregnancies, couldn't go through that pain again.'

Mrs Harris was sitting with her hands

144

round her precious cup, staring into the past. Jessica did not move. She knew who Mrs Harris was talking about.

'Sir Bernard?'

'Yes, he was knighted for his work and deserved it. He was a great surgeon and he was a wonderful man. I did everything I could for him. He needed a woman to love him and look after him. I always loved him. He remembered those schooldays and gave me this cup and saucer. They are all I have of him.'

'But you have other memories?'

'Oh yes, miss. I have many good memories. He made me promise to look after Lady Grace if anything happened to him. It was not an easy promise to make, but I agreed, thinking it would never happen. No one knew that he had worked himself to the bone, that he would collapse and die at the hospital. They brought him home to Upton Hall and I was the one who washed and dressed him and held his cold body in my arms. She wouldn't even look at him.'

Jessica was shattered, her mouth turned to sawdust. She could imagine the suffering. She could not bear the thought of Lucas working himself to the bone, of him collapsing and dying at the hospital as his father had done.

What could she say? There was no way she

could comfort this woman, after years of putting up with Lady Grace, all because of a promise she made to a man she loved. Mrs Harris had devoted her life to that promise.

'Mrs Harris, you have carried out your promise,' said Jessica earnestly. 'Sir Bernard wouldn't have wanted you to devote your entire life, chained to Lady Grace's every whim. It's not fair. There's still time to find yourself a new life, new friends, even a new happiness.'

Mrs Harris got up and started to rinse her precious cup and saucer.

'Well, I really appreciate the regular time off that you are giving me now. That's enough for the moment. It feels like a proper bit of freedom.'

'You ask for all the freedom you want,' said Jessica. 'I think you have fulfilled your promise to Sir Bernard, many times over. He sounds a special man and would understand.'

'That's nice of you to say so,' said Mrs Harris, starting to lay the table for breakfast. Jessica yawned, ready to drop off. 'Remember, school today, miss.'

Jessica raced upstairs with a second cup of tea. She had a quick shower to wake herself up. As she was dressing in jeans and a warm jersey, her phone rang.

'Hello?'

'Jessica?' It was Lucas. He sounded a long way away, as if he was holding the phone at a distance. 'I'm afraid your visit here is off for the time being. Maggie is in intensive care.'

'Oh, that's bad news. How is she doing?'

'Not good,' he said. He sounded as if he had been up all night. 'I don't know when I'll be home. Maybe tonight, maybe tomorrow.'

'Take care, Lucas,' said Jessica. She didn't know what else to say. She knew Maggie was in good hands. She knew he was doing his best. Any comment would be trite and hackneyed. 'I'll look after everyone here.'

He rang off without another word. He would be home when he could. All she could do was wait, trapped at Upton Hall beneath ashen skies. It was going to be a wet day. The clouds were already spilling token droplets.

They had to run through the rain for the school bus. Jessica managed to persuade Daniel that a cowboy hat was not part of the school uniform, and Lily also had to be persuaded that Floppy Ears did not need to learn to read.

'We can teach him at home,' she promised. 'You and me, together.'

Lady Grace was determined to have a difficult day. Jessica was so afraid she would dislocate her new hip. It was one of the major complications following a hip replacement.

147

She kept attempting to bend her hip past a right angle, pointing towards the other leg.

'I've told you before,' said Jessica, containing her exasperation. 'You simply mustn't do that. A dislocation is a painful event. During the three months healing period, thick layer tissue is forming round the new hip, and this tissue is helping to keep the hip in place.'

'I thought it was screwed in,' said Lady Grace with a grimace.

'They use a plate and screw if there's a major fracture. There's lots of different methods. I believe your stem was cemented in. A press-fit stem is hammered in and tends to be used for younger patients as their bone is less likely to fracture in the procedure. A cemented stem doesn't last quite as long, but long enough for you.'

'Good heavens. Cement? I wasn't told it would be cement.'

'It's orthopaedic cement. Not the road works stuff.'

'Indeed I should hope not. But I'm not sure if they got it right. One leg seems to be shorter than the other.' She peered down at her feet. She was wearing sensible flat shoes with cushioned soles, and hated them intensely. Her wardrobe was full of smart court shoes in every colour and style which she wanted to continue to wear.

Jessica tried not to sigh. Nearly all hip patients had this worry. At some time they seemed to think their legs were not a matching length.

'Now that is something the surgeon is very careful about, but it's not as simple as you might think. Your real leg length might be different to the apparent leg length,' said Jessica, seeing that this was an explanation that could take hours. Leg length was obviously going to be Lady Grace's newest complaint. It made a change from everything else she complained about.

'They don't feel equal,' said Lady Grace. 'And they certainly don't look equal.' She wriggled her feet slightly, trying to judge a comparison.

'It all depends on whether the pelvis is level or tilted. That can make a difference as to how your legs feel and look. It's very confusing. Be assured, the surgeon made precise measurements and did his best to get it right.'

'His best might not be enough. I'm not at all happy. The operated leg feels shorter.'

'Then you must mention it to your surgeon at your next appointment. Most patients can tolerate a tiny difference, perhaps a centimetre, that's a fraction more than a quarter of an inch. It's a small price for getting rid of the pain.'

'I certainly shan't tolerate it,' said Lady

Grace emphatically. 'I can tell you that. Please phone my consultant this morning and ask for an immediate appointment. I insist on seeing him.'

'If you say so, Lady Grace. But it really isn't something to worry about.'

'I'll worry about what I want to worry about, young lady. It's my leg. Make that phone call now.'

Jessica escaped from the bedroom, leaning against the door outside, getting her breath back. No wonder employees at Upton Hall rarely stayed long with the Coleman family, whatever status, nurse or nanny. Lucas was lucky to keep Mrs Harris. The good woman had her own reasons, and loving someone for years was always the best reason in the world.

This was a slight dilemma. An imagined difference in leg length was not exactly an emergency. Jessica would not hesitate to phone the surgeon's office if it was something like a dislocation or a clot. That would be an emergency. She couldn't phone Lucas. He would not appreciate a call about leg length.

Caffeine might provide an alternative answer. She went into the kitchen and made herself a black coffee. She had the room to herself and stood by the Aga, warming her hands. So many hospital staff rooms had been icy, the chilliest room in a big building. She

150

remembered pacing with her hands tucked under her armpits, trying to bring her fingers back to life after a long night shift. She remembered Fraser finding her there and warming her hands for her.

She thought he had been sent from heaven. An angel in green theatre gear.

Fraser had been her life for two years. She had been young and inexperienced, new to everything. It had been so easy to fall in love with Fraser. He was ruggedly handsome, tall and fair, Sir Lancelot material without the horse. He made her heart thud, her senses reel. His lips were lingering and passionate. She drank in the scent of his masculinity, expecting this happiness to last the rest of her life.

But it didn't happen. She shut her mind to the evening when he humiliated her in front of all her friends and colleagues. For a moment she hung onto the back of a kitchen chair to steady herself. The memory was so vivid. She swam to the surface.

'Swimming,' said Jessica to herself. It was not the perfect answer but it would help. Swimming was the best exercise for a hip replacement and Lady Grace might feel more equal leg-wise after a few swims.

But Lady Grace wouldn't go to a public pool that was for sure. Both Brighton and

151

Littlehampton had excellent swimming facilities. Mrs Harris had said Lady Grace once swam in the sea off Brighton, so she must have enjoyed swimming once.

Jessica wanted to take both children swimming too. She had a gut feeling that Daniel would love the water. It might give him another sense of freedom, a world of his own without talking. And roly-poly Lily would benefit from more active exercise. As long as she did not insist that Floppy Ears had to learn to swim.

Mrs Harris had left the local newspaper open on the kitchen table. It was a good balance of local news stories and advertisements. But it was the advertisements that drew Jessica. Her agile mind was already juggling with words. She thought of the film, *Desperately Seeking Susan*. Would an item headed Desperately Seeking Water do the trick? She pulled a pen and pad towards her and began to play with words.

★ ★ ★

The day flew by but still no sign of Lucas. Jessica went around in a state of permanent anxiety. She was fielding awkward questions about appointments from Lady Grace without actually telling a lie.

152

The evening was melting into darkness before she heard the sound of his Porsche Boxster coming into the drive. He had been gone almost twenty-four hours. He came into the house, dishevelled and rubbing the dark stubble on his chin.

Jessica flew to him. She could not stop herself. For a few seconds, he was hers alone. They stood together and he rested his head against hers in complete exhaustion. Jessica was silent with delight, a fine flame running under her skin. Then both the children arrived and even Lady Grace hobbled into the hall. They moved apart, unsteadily.

'How's Maggie?'

'She's all right,' he said, wearily. 'We saved her. But we nearly lost her.'

'Thank goodness. I knew you would save her. I knew she would come through. You must be so relieved.'

'It was a fight. Touch and go. At one point, we thought — '

Lady Grace pushed herself forward on Fred, interrupting. 'I've been trying to phone you all day, Lucas. Your phone must be out of order. I couldn't get an answer.'

'I switched my phone off, Mother. They are not allowed in the operating theatre. I had major surgery in my own theatre, and was supervising my senior registrar in the theatre next door. And when I had a moment, I popped into theatre three to help out with the odd minor procedure. Hardly time for social phone calls.'

His voice was cold, distant, without feeling.

'Not even from your own mother?'

'Not unless you had fallen down the stairs.'

'I could hardly call you if I had fallen down the stairs,' Lady Grace said curtly. 'That's obvious.'

'But the angelic Jessica would have called the main switchboard and they would have got a message through to me. Though by that time, knowing how efficient she is, Jessica would have you in an ambulance taking you to the Royal Sussex in the fast lane.'

'Daddy, Daddy, I think Floppy Ears will have to have an operation,' said Lily, holding up sick rabbit. He did look pretty sick after the frantic day he'd had.

'Oh dear, that's very serious. Shall I have a look at him after I've had some supper? Meanwhile keep him warm and sedated.'

'Seat-dated.'

Lily rushed off to wrap Floppy Ears in numerous blankets and shawls. She thought sedated meant sit him in a chair near a calendar. He sat, propped up, for the rest of the evening, exhausted by all the fuss.

'One of my legs is definitely shorter than

154

the other, Lucas,' Lady Grace said, trying again to catch her son's attention. 'I insist on seeing my consultant immediately.'

'If you say so, Mother,' he said, his voice as dry as sandpaper. 'I will make an appointment for you tomorrow. Now, I should like some peace and quiet.'

Lucas stood still and quiet. He was ready to drop, drained by the day.

Daniel had not said a word in all this. But now he came up to his father, serious and confiding. 'Peace and quiet,' he said in agreement.

'That's it, Son,' said Lucas, smiling at him. 'At least you understand.'

'It's not good enough,' said Lady Grace.

'Tomorrow,' he said firmly.

Lucas went into the sitting room, taking off his coat, dropping it onto the floor. He threw himself down onto the sofa with a groan, stretching out his long legs. Jessica saw how tired he was and, without a word, knelt down to take off his shoes. His socks were damp with green sweat from the theatre boots. She took them off too, and began to massage his feet with firm and gentle movements.

She could look at his face, drink in all his features, print them on her mind. His eyes were closed and those absurdly long lashes fluttered on his cheeks. His mouth was lightly parted and she glimpsed the white of his teeth as he breathed out. Any moment now he would be asleep.

She lifted his legs up onto the sofa and he settled into a more comfortable position. Her hand brushed the roughness of his chin as she shifted a cushion under his head. The temptation to touch him was almost too strong. She wanted to kiss his love-soft face, to breathe in his breath, lay her head on his chest and listen to that strong heart beating.

There was a fleecy throw on one of the chairs and she covered his bare feet with it. Jessica stood back as daylight flickered and faded from the room. She switched on a nearby lamp and left him in the rosy gloom. The moment was too precious to lose. If she stayed a moment longer, she would have knelt by him again and whispered three words into his ear.

She realized that she did love him. It was a strong, passionate feeling that swept aside all previous doubts. But she could not tell him. She would never be able to tell him.

That would not have been wise. Even if he couldn't hear.

8

Jessica never heard Lucas crawl into his own bed, somehow remembering the way to the stables. He disappeared from the couch, only a dent in the cushion to remind her of his presence.

The children had long gone to bed, including the now mortally sick rabbit, so she let Mrs Harris go home.

'I can do myself some supper and a snack for Lucas if he wants it,' she said. 'There's no need for you to stay.'

'If you don't mind, miss. There's a programme I'd like to watch on the telly.'

Lady Grace was climbing the stairs quite well, although Jessica always made sure she was close at hand. Her ladyship was in a better mood now that an appointment was promised.

'My son knows best, you see,' she said. 'You don't know anything.'

'That's why he's a surgeon and I'm a nurse,' said Jessica.

'I think I'll read for a bit. Hot milk at nine o'clock, please. This is quite a good book. I'm surprised that you found such a good writer.

Perhaps you'll remember the author's name for the future.'

'I certainly will. I've read all of his books,' said Jessica, as she closed the door. She leaned against it for a moment. She was learning to maintain a calm composure in the face of all verbal assaults.

It was warm and cosy in the kitchen. She dragged the old rocking chair closer to the Aga, and settled herself with an egg, tomato and lettuce sandwich. This was her peace and quiet. Somewhere warm with a book and a sandwich. She seemed to live on sandwiches. The warmth spread through her and all the worries of the day faded. Lucas was safely home and that was all that mattered. He was here, somewhere, sleeping alone in his room in the stables. A room which she had never seen.

He had not mentioned this ill-planned marriage arrangement again. Maybe he had accepted her decision. She regretted nothing. Marriage was for two people deeply in love, who could not bear to be separated, who were twinned together in mind even when they were miles apart.

But she had to let him go. Lucas should go back to his medical environment and find a suitable woman to love. Perhaps another surgeon would set him afire. A woman who was perfect in every way, mind and body and soul.

Jessica let the book fall to the floor. She could not stop the tears coming. The thought of Lucas making love to another woman was shattering. She entered a world of excruciating pain. The night air was deep in dust and grit. She wanted to feel his hard body against her but it could not happen. She had to isolate herself from the situation Lucas had created.

⋆ ⋆ ⋆

'Guess what, everyone? We are going on a secret drive today, a mystery tour,' she announced at breakfast. It was the announcement of the day. 'All of us. Lady Grace as well if she wants to come.'

'A secret drive, how lovely!' said Lily, munching her way through a bowl of muesli with nuts and sliced banana. 'Where are we going?'

'It wouldn't be a secret if Jessica told you, would it?' said Lucas, sauntering into the kitchen. Jessica wondered if his hair ever saw a brush or a comb. But he had showered and the dark hair was glistening wet. He smelled of a sharp aftershave. He had also changed his clothes, was wearing ancient blue jeans and a white T-shirt. What did it matter? He'd be in greens in the theatre. 'What about school? Is it half-term already?'

'It's an inset day,' said Jessica. 'I'm not entirely sure what that means but the teachers do some sort of bonding and training exercises and the children have the day off. So we are going to do some bonding and training.'

'Sounds fun. The bonding bit. Perhaps I should suggest an inset day at the hospital. It might go down really well with the younger members of staff.' Lucas was already on his phone, asking the switchboard to put him through to Intensive Care. He was enquiring about yesterday's patients and seemed satisfied with the information. 'I'll be in later this morning.'

'Can Floppy Ears come on this secret drive?' asked Lily, wide-eyed with excitement.

'Is he feeling better?'

'Yes, Daddy made him better.'

'He can come,' said Jessica. 'But only if he behaves. No shouting, noisy squealing, or hopping about. One noisy hopping commotion from him in the car and he'll be out of the window, feet first.'

Lily looked horror-stricken. 'You wouldn't really throw Floppy Ears out of the window, would you, Willdo?'

Jessica saw that she had alarmed the little girl. 'It was only a joke, sweetheart. You'll put a seat belt on him, won't you?' she reassured her. 'Of course I wouldn't throw him out of the window. I'd put him in the boot to cool off.'

Lady Grace resisted the idea of a secret drive. She had on her stubborn face.

'I have no intention of going on a secret drive,' she said. 'I'm not a child and anyway I know every road around Upton Hall. There's nowhere that I don't know.'

'Want a bet? I bet you three games of cards that you don't know this secret place that I am taking you to. If I win, you can pay for tea out at a café.'

'Tea at a café!' Lily shrieked. 'Cakes?'

Lady Grace liked betting when she was confident she would win. 'That's a bet. And you will lose. We shall set a time limit. Midday. If I don't know where we are going by midday, you win. If I do, I win.'

'Sounds fair,' agreed Jessica. 'I'll get everything ready. No one needs to rush or panic. Take your time. It's not very far.'

She gave Mrs Harris the rest of the day off. 'Don't worry about making any lunch, I'm not sure of our plans,' said Jessica. 'Just leave something cold in the refrigerator and I'll serve it when we get back.'

'I'll make a sherry trifle before I go and some coleslaw, a rice salad, and a cheese and onion quiche.' Mrs Harris was determined to do her bit.

'That sounds quite a lunch. So kind. Thank you.'

It was a bit of a panic but only for Jessica. She had to pack everything they would need without anyone noticing what she was doing. It was more difficult in Lady Grace's bedroom as Jessica did not want to be caught snooping. But she found what she wanted, hidden in a box, on the top of a wardrobe.

Daniel was his usual uncommunicative self, but he was waiting outside, wearing his cowboy hat, so the idea of a secret drive had appealed to him even if he said nothing. Jessica winked at him. 'Help me put these bags in the boot, please, Daniel. They are all part of the secret.'

He nodded, but still said nothing. He was strong, at almost eight, and heaved the bags in. He showed no curiosity.

Lucas had already left so there was only Mrs Harris to wave them off. She stood on the porch steps, a forlorn figure in her flowered overall. She privately thought that they would be back in half an hour, with Lady Grace demanding a dry sherry or her first gin and tonic.

Jessica knew that her driving was under scrutiny. She was ultra careful with the automatic gears. Lady Grace was a backseat driver, especially when sitting in the front and criticized every move that Jessica made. She had dressed smartly in a soft sage-green tweed suit and pearls. Jessica had checked the route beforehand and knew exactly where she was going. It was to a private estate of big houses facing the sea, past Goring, between Ferring and East Preston, where a lot of pop stars and football stars lived in walled seclusion.

Mrs Harris, who was in on the secret, had given her directions. 'They don't have a road in front of the houses,' she said. 'There's a wide stretch of grass and a path and then the sea. No traffic at all, so quiet. I've walked it many times. So the only access is from the back road. That's why all these stars go to live there. I believe one of the Beatles, or was it the Rolling Stones, lived there once.'

'I know where we are,' said Lady Grace triumphantly, peering out of a window. 'This is the Kings Mead Estate, very exclusive. Not a secret drive any more. You owe me three games of cards.'

'Yes, you are right there but that's only half the answer. You don't know exactly where we are going.'

The backs of the big houses were not so imposing. The usual range of garages and dustbins and car ports as anywhere else. The house she was looking for had a wide curving in and out drive. It was a classic white house, in a sprawling hacienda style, very Spanish with lots of balconies and shutters and iron grille work, dozens of terracotta pots spilling with late summer flowers.

Jessica drove in and parked near the back entrance or was it the front? She had managed to get here safely without an outbreak of fighting in the car.

'Is this the secret?' Lily asked dubiously. 'It doesn't look like a secret place. It's only a big house.'

'Not yet,' said Jessica. 'We are not there yet. The house has a secret. A very special secret.'

The back door opened and a Filipino maid in uniform stood there smiling. 'Miss Harlow?'

'Yes, Miss Harlow and extended family,' said Jessica, smiling back.

'We are expecting you. Please to come this way.'

'And I'm Lady Grace Coleman,' said her ladyship, not wanting to be left out of any introductions.

'Welcome, Lady Grace,' said the maid. 'This way, please.'

Jessica heaved the bags out of the boot.

Without being asked Daniel took two of the smaller bags. He kept up with the party going indoors.

They followed the maid through high, spacious white rooms and along wide white plastered corridors. Everything seemed to be white with minimal furniture, a few sofas and tables and drapes. They went down some steps and the maid opened a double door. Lady Grace held onto the handrail.

'There is no one using it today,' she said. 'You will not be disturbed. Please ring the bell when you wish to leave.'

A wave of warm heat washed over everyone. In front of them was a beautiful sight. A sheet of tranquil aquamarine blue water, perfectly still, not a ripple in it, set in white marble tiles. Round the edges were lounge chairs, deep with blue cushions, and at the far end, floor to ceiling windows that looked out onto the sparkling blue of the distant sea.

'Good heavens,' said Lady Grace, for once lost for words. 'What a place.'

'A pool,' breathed Lily. 'It's an indoor pool.'

'Pool,' said Daniel.

'And it's ours for the morning,' said Jessica. 'You can swim or not swim, Lady Grace. I'm going swimming and Daniel and Lily are going to have swimming lessons with me. But it would be wonderful for your hip. Even walking in the shallow end of a pool is an outstanding exercise. It places so little stress on your knee and the water is buoyant.'

'But I don't have a swimming costume,' she said, the slightest tremble in her voice. 'I'll just watch.'

'There is everything you need in this bag,' said Jessica. 'Those look like changing rooms over there. No steps to go down, only a very shallow ramp and rail.'

'I don't have a swimming costume,' repeated Lily, near to tears.

'Guess what's in this bag for you both.' Jessica waved an M & S bag from Brighton. 'Brand new swimsuits.'

'But Floppy Ears . . . ?'

'Floppy Ears doesn't want to get wet. He's going to sit this one out and watch.' Typically awkward rabbit.

Jessica had never worn her swimsuit before. It was a relic of the humiliation. Fraser had planned a romantic weekend in the Balearic Islands, somewhere warm and sunny, he said. She had begun putting together holiday clothes, endless lunchtime shopping. But the romantic weekend had never happened and the swimsuit had never been worn. She tore off the price label and wriggled into it. The

166

sleek blue and pink striped one-piece swimsuit still fitted even though she had lost weight.

Lily's swimsuit was bright pink and frilly, covered in polka dots. She loved it instantly. Jessica had played safe with Daniel and bought him plain navy trunks. He went straight into the water, splashing, disturbing the glassy surface with ripples of movement. Daniel could swim of sorts. Lucas had taken him twice last summer to the public pool in Littlehampton during the holidays, but it was so crowded and noisy. Daniel had hated it. Lucas had not tried again.

But this was different. There was no one here, no one to splash him or get in the way. Daniel struck out with confidence, remembering all that Lucas had taught him. He could see the end of the pool by the sun streaked window and it was not far away. It looked like a heaven beyond him.

Jessica put blow-up arm bands on Lily and guided her in, holding onto the side rail. 'You are going to learn to kick your legs first,' she said.

Lily decided that splashing Jessica was far more fun so no one actually saw Lady Grace emerge from a changing room. She was in a plain black swimming costume with wide shoulder straps and some sort of club shield in the centre. On her head she had a flowered swimming cap, very popular in the Seventies.

Jessica guided Lady Grace down the ramp into the shallow end. 'This is a bit warmer than the sea,' she said grudgingly. Jessica didn't know if this was a complaint or a compliment. She had no difficulty in getting Lady Grace to walk backwards and sideways, several times.

'You can do any kind of movement that feels comfortable,' said Jessica. 'The water is buoyant so less weight is placed on the hip and the knee. It will strengthen your muscles and make you feel more secure. Hold onto the rail. Or swim a few strokes, if you want to.'

'I can swim,' said Lady Grace with a sniff.

'I know you can,' said Jessica. The proof was there, embroidered on the front of the black swimming costume, the Brighton Swimming Club shield.

It was many years since those swimming days, but after a few hesitant starts, Lady Grace was breast-stroking the length, slow and stately. It was not possible to see her face but Jessica had a feeling that her usual expression of irritation had relaxed. No one could be annoyed in this peaceful water.

It was a beautiful pool. It must have cost thousands of pounds and yet it was hardly used. The house belonged to one of the girl singers in a pop group. They toured the world with sell-out concerts. She was very rarely at home. Then the house and pool would be humming with all night parties and beach barbecues.

Lily had no fear of the water and was splashing about with her arm bands. Jessica swam a few lengths alongside Daniel, slowly and easily. He was obviously in training to swim the Channel.

'All right?' she asked.

He nodded. But she could see from his face that he was enjoying it. This was another of his freedoms. Where he could be himself and no one would bother him. The water was endless and he could go on forever and ever.

No one noticed the maid coming in and placing a tray on one of the glass-topped tables. The sun glinted on the chrome fittings of a tall coffee pot. She smiled at Jessica and indicated the tray.

'Coffee and cold drinks,' she said. 'Bathrobes for your use over here. Please to enjoy.'

There was a row of bathrobes on the wall. Everything had been thought of. Lady Grace climbed out a little unsteadily, glad to put on a bathrobe and rest on one of the blue loungers. She was tired. She hadn't swum for years.

'Thank you,' said Jessica.

Lily, who would never say no to a drink and a biscuit, scrambled out. Daniel ploughed on, determined to beat some personal world record.

Jessica poured out the coffee, glad of a cup herself. Breakfast seemed a long time ago. It was excellent coffee. She had been worried in case this expedition was a failure. She might have fallen flat on her face. But it had been a wonderful morning despite the shaky start.

'So who won the bet?' asked Lady Grace. 'I knew where we were.'

'But you didn't know the secret,' said Jessica. 'Suppose we call it a tie? We could still play cards this afternoon.'

Lady Grace waved her hand round the pool and its surroundings. 'So, how did you arrange all this, young lady? You don't have a magic wand.'

They heard a discreet cough behind them. 'No, she doesn't have a magic wand, but she has a way with words and an inventive mind,' said a man's grave voice. He stopped suddenly in the doorway. 'Good heavens, if it isn't Grace Coleman. It is, isn't it? Grace Coleman, after all these years, well I never. What a surprise.'

Lady Grace had taken off the flowered cap and her grey hair was all mussed up but it was too late to do anything about it. The elderly gentleman walking carefully towards them was not looking at her hair. His face was one big beam.

'Well, I never thought to see you again. You just disappeared into thin air. We wrote and phoned but you never answered. We all missed you down at the club. You were one of our best lady swimmers.'

'Arthur Hopkins,' she said weakly, drawing the bathrobe closely around her body. 'After all these years. What a surprise.'

He sat down and Jessica saw there was an extra cup. She poured him some coffee. He ladled in sugar and milk, hardly taking his eyes off Grace.

'I'm not going to count the years,' he chuckled. 'I stopped counting long ago. It's only numbers after all. But we had some good times, didn't we? My goodness, that seawater was cold, but we didn't care, did we? The youngsters these days, they've got no stamina.'

'Some still swim in the sea,' said Lady Grace, always ready to argue.

'But they wear wet suits and goggles!'

'No stamina.'

Arthur Hopkins turned to Jessica. 'Grace Coleman was one of our best lady swimmers. Always the first in and the last out. Never mind the weather, even in winter. Championship material. Then she stopped coming, disappeared, not a word to anyone to say why.'

Lady Grace looked embarrassed and Jessica decided to come to her rescue. It was time to change the subject. She smiled at Arthur Hopkins and held out a warm but damp hand.

'I'm Jessica Harlow and I want to thank you and your granddaughter for letting us use this lovely pool. It's going to make such a difference even if we can only use it for a few weeks.'

'My dear young lady, you can use it as often as you like when Roxy is away. Roxy is my granddaughter. She sings with some pop group.'

'Miss Harlow is my nurse/companion,' Lady Grace said quickly, making sure he knew Jessica's status.

'What a nurse/companion! I wish I had such a pretty one. We're more than happy to see the pool used and to have your company, especially if it means that Grace comes along.' He chuckled again. 'We can talk over old times. This is Roxy's house, of course, and I'm her permanent house-sitter. It's a bit lonely at times. I'd like a bit of company.' He put down his coffee and clapped his hands. 'I could look out some old cine films, see if the projector is still working.'

'I think it's time for another lesson, Lily, and then we must go. Let's see if you can remember how to do the doggie paddle,' said Jessica, tactfully leaving the two old friends together.

'Woof, woof,' said Lily, grinning, waving her arms about. 'I'm a doggie paddling.'

'What a bonnie lass,' said Arthur, pouring out more coffee for Lady Grace. 'I'm so glad to see you, Grace. We've a lot of catching up to do.'

⋆　⋆　⋆

It was difficult to drag everyone away. Lily didn't want to come out of the water. Daniel also kept on swimming, pretending not to hear. Grace was deep in reminiscences about old friends with Arthur and the colour had returned to her face. But Jessica was determined that they should not outstay their welcome.

At last everyone was in the car, Lady Grace more composed now that she was neat and tidy in her suit and pearls and her hair combed up. The children were dressed but damp. Arthur and the maid stood waving them out of the drive, making sure that no cars were coming and the way was clear.

'Come again soon,' called Arthur. 'Any

173

time. Look forward to seeing you.'

Lady Grace waved from the window like the Queen.

Now that Jessica knew the way, it seemed no time at all before they were on the road to Upton Hall. It had been a morning without thinking of Lucas and her mind had cleared. She couldn't live without him. But she couldn't live with him either. It would be an agony to be his wife in name only, while he took his pleasure elsewhere. It was like a door slamming in her face. It was as if he had told her that he did not find her attractive enough to bed, only to wed. She would have to start the process of getting over him.

She had got over Fraser, hadn't she? She could do it again. It would be a big loss at first, but then the sense of loss would get smaller and smaller.

'So how come this pool event happened, young lady,' began Lady Grace in her most dictatorial tone. 'We are allowed to swim in a famous pop singer's pool? Have you sold your soul to the devil?'

Lily's ears perked up. She always listened to everything.

'No, nothing so drastic. I value my soul more than that. I put a quarter-page advertisement in the local newspaper. I phoned it over and let them design the display. It came out the next day, looked really nice, with dolphins leaping about all round the edge.'

'And what did this advertisement say?' Lady Grace asked grimly.

'Lady and two small children desperately need regular swimming for medical reasons. Public pools unsuitable. Please can anyone help?'

'That's quite appalling. A vulgar newspaper advertisement. Most improper,' Lady Grace snapped. 'You should have asked my permission first. Our address, our phone number in a newspaper. This is really unforgivable. You have overstepped the mark this time, Jess.'

Jessica nearly stepped on the brake. Hard. She was astounded. They had all had a wonderful morning and she was being reprimanded, told off as if she had committed a crime. She could not believe her ears. It took all her self-control to keep her voice level and continue driving. She did not want Lily and Daniel to be alarmed.

'If you have any complaint to make, Lady Grace, I suggest you make it to your son,' said Jessica. 'And you will no doubt want to rest all this afternoon after such a strenuous and upsetting morning, instead of playing cards with me.'

Lady Grace snorted, not answering.

Jessica was so angry she could barely speak to Lady Grace. She gave the children their late lunch in the kitchen, and let Lady Grace eat by herself in the dining room. There was no way she was going to join her and have her head bitten off again.

'Mrs Harris has left us a lovely lunch. I'm sure you are really hungry,' said Jessica, laying the kitchen table. But she couldn't eat. Her appetite had fled. She rinsed out the swimsuits and hung them in the garden to dry. She took the children for a walk in the afternoon and then let them watch some television. It was a treat. Television was not allowed on school days. Daniel didn't watch anything. He didn't connect with television. He was busy drawing in his exercise book.

Lady Grace was still not speaking to her when Jessica took in her tea tray. She simply nodded her thanks, barely looking up from her book.

There was time for reading and writing with Daniel while Lily played with Floppy Ears. She was teaching him to swim in the air. Jessica's anger cooled and left her feeling sorry for the disgruntled woman. Nothing pleased Lady Grace. Lucas could sack her if he liked. She'd get some temporary job somewhere, washing up in a bar, but she would be sorry to leave the two children. Even Daniel was showing a fraction of movement towards her now, some fragile awareness that hadn't been there before.

She heard the Porsche turning into the drive. Her ear was tuned to the sound of his car now and she could recognize it from other cars. Animals could do that. They recognized a car sound. Knew when their owner was returning home.

But Lucas didn't own her. She went to meet him, driven by a basic and primitive force. But she made sure it didn't show. She didn't care what happened to her now.

'Hi,' he said, his coat flung over his shoulder. 'I see you've all been swimming today. I counted the swimsuits. Great idea. Excellent exercise.' His eyes were riveted on her, daring her to give a plausible explanation.

She read war declared on his handsome face. She turned away in bafflement. How could he have changed so suddenly? He looked as if he despised her.

'I suppose Lady Grace has spoken to you on the phone?'

'She has indeed. She wasted no time. She has told me all about the newspaper advertisement. Your public advertisement from Upton Hall for all the world to read. Not exactly to my mother's liking. Did it not occur to you to ask someone first? Perhaps even me?'

He was staring over her shoulder into the garden, not looking at her at all. Jessica felt the first taste of ash and fear.

She took a deep, steadying breath. 'Was that so bad? There's this beautiful indoor pool and we can use it, any time. Your mother needs to swim, as well as Lily and Daniel. It will improve their health. Daniel loved the quietness and the space. Your mother will get the vital exercise that she needs.'

'Well done, Jessica,' he said, coldly. 'You have got what you wanted. Very nicely done. Am I supposed to pay you a bonus? How would you like it? Cash or a cheque?'

'Got what I wanted?' Jessica faltered. 'I don't understand. What have I got that I ever wanted?'

He turned away and marched indoors. Jessica followed him, bewildered, almost stumbling over the porch step.

'Please, Lucas, don't treat me like this. I don't know what you're talking about. I accept that I should have asked someone about the advertisement, but you were busy at the hospital, never here and I didn't think. It seemed like a good idea at the time. Everyone had a lovely swim.'

'I don't give a damn about the advertisement,' said Lucas, his eyes cold as steel. He touched her jaw with a fingertip. It was not a gentle touch. 'I'm far more concerned about the way you have betrayed me and my family.'

'Betrayed? You're talking in riddles.'

'You're a scheming little hussy and I confess, I was completely taken in.'

Jessica's composure collapsed around her feet. She was devastated. She felt crushed into defeat. She shook her head.

'I don't . . . understand, Lucas. This is all wrong. What are you talking about?'

'Your doctor lover-boy turned up at the hospital today. What's his name? Fraser Burton? Very good-looking, blond chap. Apparently you are engaged, have been for several years, and he is about to claim his bride. He seemed very eager. And, no doubt, you are too.'

Lucas stood back at a distance, his mouth set into a hard line.

Jessica staggered, dumbfounded. She couldn't even feel her own feet. They had gone to sleep. She didn't own any, feet or legs, She leaned her weight against the door, unable to stand without support. Fraser. That damned man. Surely Fraser hadn't come into her life again, to destroy all she had fought for in these last years?

'Fraser? Oh God, not Fraser. It's not true,' she whispered. 'Whatever he said, it's not

179

true. I've never been engaged to him.'

'He certainly talked as if you were. He said he had been looking for you after some unfortunate misunderstanding.' Lucas was standing, legs astride, tapping his side with impatience. He looked at her coldly.

'The man is a cheat and a liar. You have got to believe me. He'll say anything about anyone, whatever suits him.' She felt her world spiralling away into an abyss.

'He seemed pretty pleased to know that you were here. He's coming to see you. I'll make sure I'm not around to spoil the lovers' reunion.' He turned his back on her as if she did not exist.

Jessica felt her heart thudding fiercely. She heard the pattering of small feet. It was Lily carrying Floppy Ears by his ears.

'Floppy Ears has got earache,' she said. 'From swimming.'

'Oh dear,' said Lucas. 'Do you want me to have a look at him?'

Lily looked at Jessica and then back at her father. She was an angelic pickle, all sunny smiles and mischief.

'Willdo has sold her soul to the Devil,' she said innocently.

'So I gather. And the Devil has come to collect.'

9

It was a thunderous grey sky, leaves skittering in a mischievous wind, long dark branches swaying in time to incantations. The atmosphere was close and humid, warning the world that the skies were about to explode.

Jessica wondered if she could cope with a storm on top of everything else that had happened this evening. She wanted to run away and hide from everyone. The thought of Fraser back in her life, disrupting her peace of mind, causing trouble with his demands and selfishness was too much. It was enough to send her packing and buying a one way ticket to Aberdeen.

Lily was tugging at her T-shirt. 'You haven't lost your sole, have you, Willdo? I can see both of them on your feet.'

'No, of course not. Your daddy was joking,' said Jessica, swinging the little girl up in her arms. She felt quite a bit lighter than the first time Jessica had tried this manoeuvre. 'I don't think you need a bath tonight,' she went on. 'All that swimming, then a shower. You'll turn into a fish with any more water and we don't want that, do we? How about two stories instead of one?'

'One for me and one for Floppy Ears.'

That rabbit was turning into a tyrant.

Lucas had disappeared into the library downstairs and she had heard the sound of a bottle being opened and the television being switched on. He was going to drown his sorrows. So what? Why should she care if he believed anything that Fraser told him?

Daniel was in his bedroom, reorganizing his rows of shells. They were now in a different rigid line which had a new meaning to him. Jessica had never quite worked out if it was by size, colouring, contours, texture or shape. He knew exactly what he was doing even if no one else did. She felt a split second of softness for him.

'Did you hear what I said about baths tonight, Daniel?' she called out.

He nodded, not looking up.

Somewhere in the distance there was a clap of thunder. The storm was a long way off but it was approaching, like some monster.

'What's that noise?' Lily asked.

'It's the clouds bumping into each other.'

'Does it hurt?'

'I don't suppose so. Clouds are full of rain so it's only water.'

By the time both children were tucked up

and stories exhausted, the rain was beginning to hammer the windows. Lightning flashed across the sky in jagged peaks, followed by the rolling crashes of thunder. Daniel, with his intolerance to loud noise, hated the thunder and put his hands over his ears. But as long as the children were dry and warm and Jessica was with them, they were not frightened.

'Only silly old clouds bumping into each other,' said Lily, yawning, her eyes drooping. She was asleep in moments.

Daniel had elected to go to bed, to put the pillow over his ears. All that swimming had tired him out. Jessica put on one of his CDs of soft sounds, bird song or waves. They always lulled him to sleep.

'You must have done at least twenty lengths today,' said Jessica.

'Twenty,' he mumbled.

'Pretty good. Would you like to go again?'

The pillow nodded.

'No noise, no crowds, no bright lights. It was perfect for us all, wasn't it? That's what you like, isn't it, Daniel? It was a beautiful pool and so near the sea. Almost like swimming in the sea. Goodnight, then. Sleep tight.'

He nodded again, more sleepily. In moments he was asleep. He looked so like his father. It was like seeing Lucas as a child.

At least she had done something right today, even if everything else had gone wrong. Surely Fraser didn't think he could come marching back into her life as if nothing had happened? That humiliation had not been in her imagination and she still remembered the red dress to prove it.

She took some hot milk and two digestive biscuits up to Lady Grace. Her ladyship was as usual, sitting up in bed, reading, wrapped in a lace bedjacket. She actually looked a little more human than usual, her hair braided into two pigtails like a schoolgirl. It was normally rigidly stuffed inside a hairnet. Relic of the Sixties.

'I hope you are not feeling too tired after your swim,' said Jessica, putting the tray on the bedside table.

'I actually feel very well,' said Lady Grace. 'It was a nice surprise, thank you,' she added, as graciously as her name. 'Even if I strongly disapprove of the method.'

'How else would it have happened? I could hardly go round knocking on people's doors, asking if they had an unused pool.'

'Quite. Quite. However, don't do it again, without my permission.'

'It's not likely to happen. I shall probably be leaving soon. Not sure when, probably tomorrow. I think Lucas has changed his mind about employing me. He is going to sack me.'

Lady Grace's hand stopped halfway to her cup of hot milk. 'Oh no, definitely not. He can't do that. I won't allow it. I like arguing with you and having you here. You give me as good as you get. It's more stimulating than all those silly little ninnies we've had in the house these last years. And you're not scared of me.'

'No, I'm not scared of you, Lady Grace.'

'Everyone has always been scared of me. Can't understand it, really.'

Jessica paused, drawing the curtains. It was the first time that Lady Grace had spoken to her in a normal, pleasant way. A bit late for civility now. Jessica smiled as she drew the curtains together against the storm lashing outside. A zigzag of blinding light split the sky, lighting up the forked branches of trees. In a flash it was gone and in a few moments there came the rumble of thunder, louder and louder. The storm seemed to be right overhead.

'Are you all right with storms?' Jessica asked. 'Would you like some music on? We could find some late night music on Radio 2.'

'There was a terrible storm the night that Sir Bernard, my husband, died,' said Lady

Grace, her face changing again, after a moment of silence. 'It was one of the worst storms of the year. He collapsed at the hospital, you know. Quite suddenly. They couldn't save him. He was always working too hard and took no notice of anything I said. I told him to slow down. The storm gave me the most terrible migraine. They brought him home to Upton Hall and I couldn't even look at him. My head was splitting in half. I was in bed with an ice pack on my head. Mrs Harris saw to him. She was wonderful, looking after us. I don't know what I would have done without her.'

Jessica listened to the other half of the story. There were always two halves of any story. If only Lucas would listen to the other half of her story. Fraser was a liar and a cheat. He had lied to her. Now he was lying to Lucas.

'How sad and what a shock for you that your husband should die so suddenly. I'm really sorry. It must have been a dreadful time,' said Jessica. 'But now that you have met one of your old swimming club friends and gone swimming, and your hip is getting better, perhaps lots of things will improve and good things will start happening.'

'Arthur has already asked me if I'd like a game of bridge sometime. Nice old chap.

186

Would you be able to drive me over? You don't play bridge, do you?'

'Never got the hang of the bidding.'

'It does take a lot of concentration. I could teach you.'

It was the first time that Jessica had detected a chink in Lady Grace's iron-clad armour. She smiled again. 'I'd like that, thank you. But if I'm getting the sack . . . '

'What nonsense. Of course you are not getting the sack. I won't allow it. Lucas is overtired. He doesn't know what he's saying.'

Jessica went downstairs with a lighter step. Lady Grace was actually on her side. It was amazing. But it didn't change the situation. Lucas would get rid of her because she was not available as wife material. Fraser had said she was spoken for. She was no longer in the meat market. She had been surgically removed.

Jessica had not eaten. Nor had Lucas. She put a variety of cheeses and biscuits, celery, olives and chutney, on a tray and carried it through to the library. Lucas was sprawled in an armchair, eyes closed, the television twitching with goodies and baddies chasing each other, but no one was watching. She turned it off. He didn't move. Dead to the world.

The storm was still clashing with the

universe outside, rain pouring down the windows, lightning and thunder in dangerous pursuit. Thunder still made her jump. She knew it was coming but never expected it.

No one had drawn the curtains and she stood watching the turmoil in the garden. Lady Grace's roses were being flattened. Leaves were torn from trees and scattered to the four winds. Branches were strewn over the drive. She hoped Lucas had put his posh car away. The Austin was safely in a garage.

Fraser would not come out to Upton Hall in this weather. Thank goodness for a small mercy. He only liked driving when conditions were good. Once he had made her drive home from a dinner party when it was snowing heavily. He'd pretended he'd had too much to drink but Jessica knew that he hadn't. It had been a nightmare journey, snow clogging the wipers, and one she would never wish to repeat.

'The Porsche is OK,' said a languorous voice from the armchair. Lucas was reading her thoughts again. 'I put it away in the stables. My first thought.'

'Good, I was wondering if it was still outside. It's a dreadful storm. I've brought you some cheese for supper,' said Jessica. 'I don't suppose you have eaten.'

'Is this the Last Supper before I am

crucified?' he asked, eyes still closed.

'Don't be silly,' said Jessica. 'I'm not a vindictive person. But I wish you'd have let me explain before you jumped to conclusions.'

She sat down opposite Lucas, not looking at him. She could not bear to see that accusing look on his face again. There were biscuits to butter and top with cheese, as if he were another helpless child. She put chutney on the mild cheese, nothing on the strong Stilton. There were sticks to spear the olives and celery.

'When do you want me to leave?' she asked. 'I can pack quite quickly. There won't be any trains at this time of night, but I could leave first thing tomorrow morning, catch the first train. I won't be any trouble. I'll order a taxi.'

Lucas leaned forward and took her hands, removed the butter knife and laid it down. He looked down at her, his eyes smiling with some secret memory.

'I don't want you to leave, Jessica. I don't want you to go. How are you ever going to forgive me? How am I ever going to explain my stupidity? I've done you a great injustice and you have behaved with the utmost dignity and carried on with your work. Anyone else would have flounced out in a rage and sued me in court.'

Jessica felt the warmth of his hands. She did not understand what was going on. This was another nightmare like stepping into Alice in Wonderland, she was shooting down chutes, changing size. Now she was very small, very small indeed.

Lucas was actually smiling, an apologetic smile of sorts, as if he had forgotten how to do it naturally.

'I don't understand,' she said. 'Fraser told you a pack of lies today and you believed him. You were furious. You didn't give me a chance to explain. Now you are saying something totally different.'

'I was mad with rage. I was consumed with jealousy. This man said you were engaged to him, promised long ago. How could I know what was true? He sounded so plausible. You had worked in the same hospital. You refused my offer of marriage. Perhaps it was because you were already engaged to him. How could I know what was the truth?'

'Do you really want to know what happened with Fraser and me? I'll tell you all about it. It's something I've been trying to forget and since I have been here at Upton Hall, I have managed to forget because I have been happy.'

'You've been happy at Upton Hall?'

'Really happy. Even your mother and I

have agreed to disagree. I love Lily and Daniel, they are super children.' Jessica nearly said and I love you, but she held back. His name might be stitched to her heart but he need never know.

'Tell me about this Fraser Burton person.' Lucas took a cheese-topped biscuit and crunched on it. 'This is good. There was only days' old shepherds pie in the canteen today.' He was not drinking malt whiskey but another bottle of New Zealand white from the vineyard called Oyster Bay. There was only one wine glass beside him. He held it to Jessica's lips and she took a sip. It slipped down like silky nectar. 'Tell me, Willdo, tell me all your secrets, please. I want to know everything. Don't leave out a word.'

Jessica did not know where to start. She had tried so hard to forget.

'It was when I started my nursing training. I was very young and inexperienced. I'd never had a proper home or family since my parents died, shunted around between relatives who didn't really want me. So I became a student nurse who hadn't been anywhere or done anything, or lived in London, let alone have a serious boyfriend. My future career was nursing and I was working hard. It is hard work and I was studious. There's a lot to learn. But I loved it. I knew I had made the right choice. Then Fraser appeared, a young, handsome doctor who had been everywhere, done everything. He was so smooth, so charming. He bowled me over and he liked that. I was a young and adoring slave, ready for the picking.'

'And growing into a very beautiful woman,' said Lucas.

'We went out, on and off, for two years, mostly hospital parties and pubs. Not regular dating. Fraser was always going away to some conference or medical faculty. Sometimes I wouldn't see him for weeks. It was an endless round of engagements. He was important and climbing the medical ladder fast. I was totally out of my mind, bowled over by his attention. Nothing like this had ever happened to me before. I thought I was in heaven and he was the angel Gabriel.'

'So what happened?' Lucas asked, putting the wine glass to her lips again. She took another sip. She began to like New Zealand. 'You must tell me everything, Jessica.'

'We were going to the Balearics for a weekend in the sun. It was the first time that he'd asked me to go away with him. I was ecstatic, innocently thought that this was it; we were finally going to be a romantic item. I bought loads of holiday clothes. There was also a big party in a posh hotel for some top consultant who was retiring. Fraser had invited me to go with him. Wear something special, he said, it's very important. You'll meet lots of people. So I went out and bought this red dress.'

'You would look wonderful in red.'

Jessica paused. It was still so painful even with Lucas feeding her wine and listening to every word. She remembered every moment of getting ready for this important party. This was Alice land again. The Red Queen was about to arrive.

'It was a lovely soft silk dress that cost far more than I could afford on a nurse's salary. I went to the party on my own as Fraser, for some reason, couldn't pick me up. I went by taxi to the big hotel. There were so many people wandering about, I was completely lost. The reception was being held in the ballroom. I remember the chandeliers, all sparkling lights, the mirrored walls. Waiters wandering around with trays of champagne and wine. Then I saw Fraser and went over to him. He was standing with a woman, a sleek brunette who was also wearing a red dress. She was lovely. But her dress was couture. Mine was best Monsoon.'

'What happened?'

'I went over to Fraser, pleased and relieved to see him. There were a lot of people milling

193

around and I was feeling more than a bit nervous. He brushed away my hand, hardly looking at me and turned to the elegant woman beside him. He drew her closely to his side.

'Let me introduce you to my fiancée, Dr Amanda Morgan', he said flamboyantly. Then he turned to her and kissed this woman in front of everyone. In front of me. Can you imagine how I felt? 'And this is Jessica Harlow', he went on, laughing, 'one of the student nurses who thinks the sun shines out of my arse. She never leaves me alone. Follows me around like a pet puppy'.'

'There was a stunned silence and then Dr Amanda Morgan, the sleek, elegant brunette, for no good reason, pretended to trip and her drink, whatever it was, went over my dress. 'Down, doggy, down', she said, in a spiteful voice and turned away, laughing. As she turned away, her bag, a beaded evening bag, caught in the folds of my beautiful dress and tore the silk. The dress was ruined. The evening was ruined. I was shattered. She was his fiancée.'

'What did you do?' Lucas was quite still, listening.

'I hardly remember. I believe I ran down the stairs, out onto the street, a bit like Cinderella at midnight. No coach waiting. It was cold and windy. I got home somehow, in another taxi. Cried all the way.'

Lucas caught his breath, ran his hands through his hair and took a deep breath.

'Do you believe me?' she asked.

'Of course I believe you,' said Lucas. 'You've always told me the truth. I know that now.'

'But today, Fraser arrived at your hospital, and said he was looking for me.'

'He wasn't looking for you. He was checking on a private patient, who had been moved to us, and someone in the staff-room happened to tell him about Lady Grace and my children and the wonderful nurse from London, from the same hospital, who was looking after them. When he discovered your name, he sought me out. It was not pleasant, I can tell you. He said you were engaged to him, that you had disappeared without a trace, that he had been looking for you for months, and that he feared for your sanity.'

Jessica shook her head, began to weep. 'All lies. He made it all up. Clever people can be cruel.'

'I know that now. But I didn't then. In minutes he destroyed all my dreams of you becoming my wife. It seemed to make sense of why you were always turning me down. It became obvious. You couldn't marry me if you were already engaged to someone else.'

'I'm not engaged to anyone and certainly not to Fraser. I hate him. It took me months to get over that humiliation in front of everyone. The word raced round the hospital like a flu epidemic. Other nurses used to come up to me on the ward and ask me where was the sun shining from today? It was horrible. It took me ages to get over it. Only work helped. So, how did you find out the truth about Fraser? What made you change your mind?'

Lucas stretched out in the chair, suddenly bone weary. 'My registrar phoned me half an hour ago. He said that he overheard Fraser asking one of the nurses out for a late dinner and saying that he would drive her home. He said that his wife was at their flat in London and she wouldn't mind. They had a very open marriage.'

'His wife? The woman who ruined my dress?'

'I have no idea, Jessica, who she is. It doesn't matter, does it? He is married apparently but it didn't stop him trying to make a dinner date with one of my nurses. She has been warned and has politely declined the offer.'

'A lucky escape.'

Jessica sat back, regaining her composure, a

warmth flowing through her veins. 'I think I'll fetch another glass. Is that all right? I'd like some more of your lovely wine.'

'And I'll open another bottle. You deserve my best wine. Recuperation. You had a rough time with this bastard. I hope he doesn't come to my hospital again or he could find himself cornered in the car park on a dark night. Fortunately his patient is recovering and will be moved back to London tomorrow. We need the bed.'

'Thank you, Lucas. And thank you for believing me. I've never talked about it before. I couldn't. It was too humiliating.'

'Subject closed,' said Lucas, opening another bottle of wine. 'We shall never mention it again. I'm getting better at this opening lark.'

'It's all the practice,' said Jessica, breathing in the perfume of love, almost silent with delight.

'You're leading me down a slippery path,' he grinned. 'And talking about slippery paths. I hear you worked a miracle today. You got Lady Grace into a proper swimming pool. That was amazing.'

'She enjoyed it, eventually. Even if she did not approve of my method of finding someone who would let us use their pool.'

'Typical. She'll always manage to find something wrong. It's her occupation. If a guardian angel came to visit she'd complain about the draught from his wings. And the kids?'

'They loved it, both of them. It was perfect for Daniel, the quietness, the space, no people about. Daniel can already swim a bit, as you know, and Lily took to it straight away, splashing about with arm-bands on. And we can go again, which is wonderful. Lady Grace met an old friend, Arthur Hopkins, from her Brighton swimming club days. It was quite a touching reunion.'

'She used to swim a lot. I believe at one point, years ago, she was considering training to swim across the Channel. She took it very seriously.'

'So what happened to put her off? What made her stop swimming, and so abruptly? There must have been a reason.'

Lucas finished up the last of the cheese and biscuits. He liked Stilton. His appetite had returned. He was glad of her company and Jessica looked so relaxed and comfortable, so at home with him in the library. It was as if they had been together for years. The colour had returned to her fair cheeks as if a great burden had been lifted. Her story was out in the open now.

'No one knows. It happened, whatever it was, when I was a boy, so I never took much notice of what anyone in the family did. Mother was a private person. Father worked the same sort of long hours as I do now. I was always wrapped up in my own pursuits. All I can remember is that one day she came home from Brighton in a terrible state. Wearing clothes on top of her swimming costume, hair still wet, not speaking to anyone. She went straight upstairs to her room and didn't come down till late the next day.'

'And she didn't say anything?'

'She said nothing. She refused point blank to answer any questions. Dad and I gave up in the end.'

'How very strange. Something must have happened.'

'But I did remember something, although at the time it meant nothing to me, as a young boy. As she staggered up the stairs, I could see her ankles. They were torn and bleeding, skin shredded. I thought then that she had fallen on the shingle on Brighton beach, but now I realize that it was something more than a fall and a few scratches. They were quite serious cuts.'

'Jaws? Maybe there was a shark in the English Channel.'

'You may well laugh, but who knows what is on the floor of the sea, anywhere? There was a lot of activity along Brighton beach during the war. And there were fifty bombing raids. She could have stepped on some rotting barbed wire, or got caught up in it and panicked. The tides are high.'

'You may be right. I'm sorry, I shouldn't have laughed. I bet the beach was covered in barbed wire in case there was an invasion.'

'It was worse than that. There were concrete blocks, barbed wire and landmines all along the beach. They were prepared for the worst.'

Jessica finished her glass of wine. She was ready for bed now. It had been an exhausting day, mentally and physically. She wanted to sail in the shallows of ocean sleep.

'Let's hope she can put the bad memories behind her now and enjoy swimming in this very luxurious private pool. Lady Grace did about three lengths today, very slowly, but she got there.'

'Three lengths?' Lucas pretended to look horrified. 'Good heavens. The Grand had better get in a few more crates of champagne. We're going to need them.'

Jessica started clearing the tray to take into the kitchen.

'What do you mean?'

'The Grand Hotel, Brighton. Remember? It was a wager we made. I bet you that you couldn't get Lady Grace to go swimming and you have. So you have won yourself a slap up dinner in the King's Restaurant at the Grand. I'll make sure we get a table with a sea view.'

'Surely that was only a joke?'

Jessica caught sight of the fire in his eyes and she moved away, coming briefly to her senses.

'You should know by now that I never joke about things that are important,' he said. Everything stopped, laughter, movement, even time. They stood, looking at each other, wondering if they dare break the spell.

★　★　★

The spell was broken by the smallest sound by the doorway. The door into the library had opened a few inches and they saw Daniel's face. He did not look fully awake but he had come downstairs in his pyjamas. He was standing in the doorway, stimming, tapping on the door which was his essential coping mechanism. As he moved forward, he continued tapping on his side.

'Hello, Daniel,' said Lucas, immediately aware of the stress signal. 'Is something the matter?'

Jessica put the tray on a side table, and lowered herself down to Daniel's level. She held out her hand but he did not take it, but

201

went on tapping obsessively.

'Are you all right?' she asked.

He nodded, not looking at her.

'Do you want to tell us something?'

He was struggling. He didn't know the right words, couldn't find them, making small movements with his mouth. 'Floppy Ears,' he said at last.

'What's the matter with Floppy Ears? Has Lily lost him?'

'Lily,' he said, with relief.

'It's Lily,' said Lucas immediately. 'Something's wrong with Lily.' He was out of the door and up the stairs in seconds, straight into his daughter's bedroom. She heard him switch on the main light.

'Good boy,' said Jessica. 'You're a very good, clever boy to come and tell us. You did the right thing. Now I must go up to Lily. Stay here until I come back.'

'Lily,' he said again, more urgently. This was unusual for him to say anything twice with expression.

Jessica hurried up the stairs but she could already hear the wheezing. It was really loud. She didn't need to be told. Lily was having an asthma attack. She was fighting for breath through lips that were already tinged with blue.

'Chair,' said Lucas.

Jessica knew immediately why he wanted a

chair. He sat the pale and clammy child on the chair, facing the back, her arms leaning over to help open the airways. Jessica opened a window so that there was some fresh air coming in, at the same time, draping a blanket round Lily so that she would not get cold. The storm was abating, the thunder more distant.

Lily was unaware of who was there or what was happening.

'Nebulizer and oxygen in the top cupboard,' said Lucas. The equipment was there. He was a doctor. He would be prepared for anything happening to Lily at home. Jessica plugged in the compressor to a wall socket, quickly washed and dried her hands, put the mask over Lily's nose and mouth and gave her a few whiffs of the life-saving oxygen. Lucas controlled the metered dosage of the nebulizer.

Lily breathed in the oxygen. The blue tinge went from her lips, her usual healthy pink returning.

'Adrenaline. The smallest dose. There's a hypodermic pack in the box.'

Jessica found the pack and broke the seal.

By now the terrible wheezing was easing and Lily's breathing was becoming more normal. It was a moment of relief. Jessica did not realize how tense she had become till Lucas took her hand and squeezed it gently.

His hand was firm and warm, the skin smooth, the nails clipped as a surgeon's hand would be. It felt reassuring. A man's hand. A hand you could trust.

'Well done,' he said. 'I wish all my nurses moved as fast as you do. Lily is going to be all right now. She'll be back to sleep in no time.'

But Lily had decided to wake up and pleaded for another story before she went back to sleep. And there was no editing out pages. Lily knew her favourite books by heart.

'Have the clouds stopped bumping into each other?' she asked.

Lucas gave his daughter some water to drink. 'No more bumping clouds,' he said. 'Shall I read you a story?'

'This story has got some long words,' said Lily dubiously.

'I can do long words.'

Daniel was back in bed. His bedroom had its usual soft, low lighting. Jessica put on another CD of natural sounds, wind and rain, the sea and bird song. She knew it was soothing and therapeutic. She stroked back his hair, wishing he would respond to her in some way. He kept his eyes firmly shut as if she was not there.

'Goodnight Daniel. Thank you for coming and telling us about Lily. That was the right thing to do. And you did it extremely well.'

10

Jessica was out in the garden, helping Lady Grace dead-head what was left of the roses after the storm. Her garden had been devastated but her ladyship had not been too dismayed. She had tossed away Fred and was using a stick.

'It's nature,' she said. 'But it will grow again. It always does. Next year. I'll show you how to prune next week. There's a skill, you know, with roses. You have to cut in exactly the right place.'

'If I'm still here,' said Jessica. She was not sure. It had been a good evening, talking to Lucas but her heart had steeled itself against more miracles.

'You will continue to be employed here for your contract, Jess. I'll make sure of that. I can see what you have achieved with the children. My son is an idiot if he doesn't see it. And the children need your kind of guidance. Of course, I would have got better on my own, but still you have been a useful and pleasant companion.'

Jessica hid a smile. There was no point in arguing with Lady Grace. She lived in a world that had moved on.

A fresh breeze combed the garden. Lady Grace shivered and patted down her hair.

'I'll go and fetch you a cardigan,' said Jessica. 'Which one would you like?'

'The royal-blue one, please. You'll see it folded on a chair.'

Jessica sped indoors. There was certainly the cool scent of autumn in the air. She knew how hard it would be to go when her contract ended. She found the cardigan and hurried downstairs, out into the garden.

Her feet stopped in their tracks. Lady Grace was talking to a tall, blond-haired man in casual jeans and leather jacket. He was looking at the house, taking in the graceful lines and big windows. Then he caught sight of Jessica, grinned and waved her over.

'Hiya, Jessica babe. Long time no see. You've done well for yourself. Upton Hall, no less, what a grand house, almost a mansion. You'll be setting your sights on the lord of the manor next. Always the one to grab at good opportunities,' he added with a smirk. 'You never miss a chance.'

Jessica's mind slipped down several notches into despair. How could she have ever thought this man was wonderful? It was Fraser Burton. He was a jerk. A nasty, malicious jerk. He had his hand on Lady

Grace's arm, as if helping her, smoothing back his oddly long blond hair with his other hand.

'What are you doing here?' said Jessica coldly.

'Lucas invited me yesterday. He said drop in anytime. So I thought I'd call by and see how you are. After all, we were very close once. And maybe we will be again. You never know. You have grown into a beautiful woman.'

He dropped his hand and started walking towards her, but Jessica side-stepped his path and went to join Lady Grace. She was furious that he had dared to come to Upton Hall, pretending that Lucas had invited him.

'Surely you are married to the delectable brunette, Dr Amanda? I distinctly remember you introducing her to everyone as your fiancée.'

'Well, it's a sort of marriage,' said Fraser with an easy laugh. 'Didn't last long. We are talking about parting, something amicable. And the first thing I shall do is give you a call, my sweet saucy Jessica. We could take up where we left off. I'd really like that.' He turned to Lady Grace. 'Jessica and I were very, very close once, intimately close, if you get what I mean.'

He was still handsome, but he had put on

weight round the middle. Too many parties. The longish hair did not suit him.

'I certainly don't, young man,' said Lady Grace briskly. 'I do not believe for an instance that my son invited you to call here to see Jess. He knows that she has her hands full looking after me and there is no time for visitors.'

'But he said that Jessica would love to see me. That she has been missing me, done nothing but talk about knowing me, and the fun we had together, since she arrived.' Fraser's eyes were feasting on every inch of her slim figure. Jessica wanted to scream, to run away, to hide somewhere that he could never find her.

'We were almost engaged, you see,' he went on, smoothly. 'Although, Jessica is a scheming young hussy and has probably set her sights on richer prey by now. I saw his car at the hospital. That beauty didn't cost peanuts.'

'It is none of your business, young man, how much my son paid for his car. He deserves every penny he earns. I don't believe a word of what you are saying about Jessica, and I suggest you leave. You are beginning to irritate me.' Lady Grace changed which hand she was holding the stick and began walking firmly back to the house.

Jessica closed her eyes for a second, half

expecting something to happen. She did not like the expression she had seen cross Fraser's face. He was not used to being spoken to in that manner. He usually charmed every woman he met, whatever her age. Lady Grace could not be charmed.

'Well, well, fancy that,' he said, a flush rising on his cheeks. 'I'm beginning to irritate you, am I? I could say the same about your ladyship. Where's the famous Upton Hall hospitality? Don't I get a cup of coffee, a glass of Irish whiskey, a twenty-minute romp in a warm bed? I wouldn't say no to your bed, your ladyship, hip replacement or not, though of course a younger, slimmer body would be preferable. One without wrinkles or flabby bits.'

Jessica heard Lady Grace gasp at Fraser's audacity. She turned to confront him, her own sharp tongue ready to flail him for his impudence. At that very same moment, Fraser put out his foot and sent the stick flying.

Jessica ran forward at the speed of light and caught Lady Grace in her arms, seconds before she was about to hit the ground. She staggered for a moment with the weight, but managed to regain her balance. Lady Grace clung to her, her chest heaving, all colour gone from her face. She was fluttering like an injured bird.

'She's had a hip replacement, you fool,' Jessica shouted. 'A fall could have dislocated it. Don't you know anything? Get a chair for her.'

'Get it yourself,' said Fraser, kicking the stick further away. He got out his mobile phone and switched it on. 'Amanda darling? Quick message. Don't wait in for me. I shall be late. I have some unfinished business with an old flame of mine.'

His eyes were blazing. He turned to Jessica. 'Let the old woman go. I want what is rightfully mine and should have been mine, years ago. But you were always such a prude. Such a prissy. Well, I've waited long enough and now I am going to take what belongs to me.'

He moved towards Jessica, obviously about to pin her arms to her sides. Jessica felt control slipping away from her. Fraser was big and he was strong. He was also very angry. The odds were against her being able to fight him off and keep Lady Grace from falling at the same time.

Thank goodness the children were at school, thought Jessica, as her spine went into a spasm with a flash of pain. Her old back injury. Her throat constricted in fear at the sight of the savagery in his face. He grabbed at her shoulder.

Fraser's face was opaque with rage and desire. The weight of Lady Grace was tearing her shoulder ligaments. But Jessica hung onto the older woman.

A figure hurled from the house, a figure in a flowered overall, holding a wooden rolling pin. It was Mrs Harris. She went straight for Fraser and hit him firmly behind the knees, very hard.

He crumpled to the ground, groaning and swearing. He rolled over, clutching his knees in pain.

'I've always wanted to do that,' Mrs Harris said, breathing heavily. 'I saw it on the telly. Some detective programme.'

'Please help Lady Grace indoors,' said Jessica, still holding up Lady Grace. 'Sit her in the kitchen where it is warm and make her some tea. I'll get rid of this nasty piece of work.'

'Will you be all right, miss? Be careful. I'll stay if you like.'

'You look after Lady Grace. I'll be fine now.'

Fraser was clambering up and stumbling towards his car. He was covered in mud from the night's rain. He glared at Jessica as he fumbled for his car keys.

'I'll be back for you,' he said, spitting out mud from his mouth.

'Get out,' said Jessica. 'And don't you ever dare come round this way again. We've got a record of all that, you kicking away Lady Grace's stick and coming for me. You see we have a very elaborate security system here and you were standing right in the lens of one of the CCTV cameras. So it's all recorded. The Medical Council might take a poor view of your behaviour.'

'I don't believe you.'

'What's that camera up there? The one pointing straight at you now.'

He didn't look.

He started the car and drove away, very badly, driving over the grass and dragging a shrub out by its roots. He didn't speak, he didn't look back. He put his foot down on the accelerator and shot down the drive.

She could not believe he had gone.

Jessica was limp with pain and the weight of her disconnected thoughts. What was she going to say to Lady Grace? All the dreadful accusations that Fraser had made about her. She went into the kitchen reluctantly, wiping the perspiration from her face, longing for a drink. She went straight to the tap and poured herself some water.

Lady Grace and Mrs Harris were both sitting at the kitchen table, drinking tea. The brandy bottle was out and Jessica could smell the fumes. Mrs Harris poured her a cup of tea and added a generous dollop of brandy.

'It's only cooking brandy,' she said. 'But you deserve it, my girl. A real young heroine. I saw him kick away Lady Grace's stick. I was at an upstairs window, dusting. It took me a few minutes to get downstairs. Then I saw him attacking you. So I came out.'

'Thank goodness you did,' said Jessica, putting her head in her hands. 'I couldn't have managed much longer on my own.'

'What a dreadful man,' said Lady Grace. 'However did you get involved with such a nasty person?'

'He wasn't always like that,' said Jessica. 'He can be quite charming. I was very young and blind, I suppose. But he was already engaged to this Dr Amanda, even when he was dating me.'

'A two-timer. Seen a lot of that on the telly,' said Mrs Harris, pushing the tea towards Jessica. 'Drink that now. It'll do you good.'

Lady Grace was looking much better. She had recovered her colour and was obviously not in pain. Jessica checked that she was unhurt from the fall. A dislocation would be a terrible set-back.

'He said some terrible things about me,' Jessica began. 'I don't know how to explain.

None of it is true.'

Lady Grace stirred the last of her tea vigorously as if brewing some obnoxious potion. She had that gleam in her eye.

'Load of rubbish,' said Lady Grace, accepting a second cup of laced tea. 'I don't believe a word. It's the ranting of an ambitious and untrustworthy man. He is envious of Lucas, who is his superior in every way, at the hospital and at home. He just takes it out on anyone he thinks is weaker than him.'

'So you don't believe him?'

'Not a word. And he is mad with jealousy. He saw that you were happy here with us at Upton Hall and also, I might say, looking very attractive.' Lady Grace paused as if she had something momentous to say. 'I don't think we should mention this incident to Lucas. He might react very badly. He might go storming off to London to create merry hell in medical circles. Not good for his own career. Not good for his patients and they always come first.'

Jessica nodded, understanding.

'Thank you. I never want to see him again. The man is a menace. He cheated on me some time ago, humiliated me and made a fool of me in public.'

'Hard to do,' said Lady Grace.

'I agree,' said Mrs Harris. 'Doctor Coleman would be furious. He might even call the police, etc. We don't want that, people tramping about the garden, bringing in mud.'

'I told him it was all recorded on CCTV,' said Jessica. 'That his every action was filmed and recorded.'

'Very clever, my dear,' said Lady Grace. 'Perhaps we ought to get them installed. They might be useful. Well now, do you fancy a game of cards? Shall we play for money? Fifty pence?'

'So the odds are going up? We played for twenty pence yesterday.'

'It's all that exercise.'

11

It was a strange end to the day, trying to act normally, to maintain a happy atmosphere for when the children returned from school. Lady Grace was made of sturdy stuff and her only frailty was to have an after-lunch nap.

Jessica went for a run in the gardens. She needed the exercise to relax her muscles. She was still tense after the morning's episode. It took a phone call from Lucas to wash away the last of the nasty taste.

'Supper tonight at the Grand Hotel,' he said. 'I owe you, remember?'

Jessica was unable to believe that she was going to have that promised dinner with Lucas at the Grand Hotel, Brighton. It had been a joke, a wild wager about getting Lady Grace into a swimming pool.

'Champagne, if you get her to do three strokes,' he had said, confident that he would win.

But Lady Grace had managed three lengths. Not Olympic lengths, but private pool lengths. Pop singer lengths when the sexy Roxy was at home. It all counted.

Jessica could feel her heart fluttering at the thought of time alone with Lucas, time to talk, time to know each other. It was what she had always been wanting, longing for. She knew that now. But would he feel the same way?

Jessica combed through her wardrobe earlier that day. There was nothing at all suitable for the Grand Hotel. She had not brought glamorous clothes, only working gear. That ruined red silk dress had gone to a charity shop, unwashed and torn. They had probably put it in the rag bag. Maybe it was even now being trailed round some dusty refugee camp, used as dressing up play clothes for children who had nothing. She rather hoped it was.

She would have to wear clean jeans and a white shirt.

Lucas had said be ready to leave by eight o'clock. It seemed a bit late to eat but then his work was unpredictable. She heard him come in, the front door of Upton Hall slamming. He was racing up the stairs, two at a time, and knocked on her bedroom door. His arm came round the edge of the door but not the rest of him.

His fingers were dangling a glossy white carrier bag with a fancy logo on the front. 'I've bought this for you, in case there was a wardrobe problem. It's probably the wrong size. I was using my surgeon's guesswork measurements. We often have to make guesses in theatre. They are not always reliable.'

'What is it?'

'Something to help you forget that other red dress.'

'A kind thought. Thank you, Lucas,' said Jessica, taking the bag. 'I've got plenty of safety pins.'

'I'm off for a quick shower. See you downstairs in fifteen minutes.'

Jessica opened the bag. It was full of folds of pristine tissue paper. She would wear whatever he had bought, even if it was sack cloth and ashes, a carpet, a nurse's uniform. He would have an unerring feeling for the right clothes for her, she felt sure. Lucas seemed to know what she would like and wouldn't like.

She shook out the tissue paper and the dress fell over her arm in a cloud of diaphanous folds. It was the soft colour of raspberries, chiffon, with a silky petticoat lining. Stitched round the neckline were a hundred tiny roses made of the same material, cleverly folded and bunched, more stitched onto the narrow shoulder straps and edging around the low back. The length was not formal. It flowed down to mid-calf with an uneven hem that would swish around her legs as she walked.

Raspberry chiffon. It was a dream dress, casual, elegant. All memories of the strident red dress were washed away into oblivion.

'It's perfect,' she whispered, holding the dress to her face, breathing in the fragrance of the material.

The dress fitted because it was loose and unsculptured. No safety pins necessary. Jessica had some spiky heeled sandals with light coloured straps and a small handbag as a perfect accessory.

Her hands were shaking as she finished her make-up. She had pinned her hair up in a crazy arrangement with tendrils falling round her face. Nothing in her scant wardrobe was suitable to wear as a coat. She would have to freeze in the car, whatever the weather. No top down tonight, she hoped.

She went out onto the landing. Both young monkeys were still up, aware that something special was going on. Lily's eyes lit up with amazement at Jessica's appearance, the lovely dress, the high heels, the immaculate make-up.

'You look like a princess, Willdo,' she breathed. 'So beautiful. A fairy princess.'

'Maybe I'm going out with a prince,' said Jessica with a wink.

'She does indeed look like a princess, but he's not a real prince,' said Lucas. He was coming up the stairs, and drinking in how lovely she looked. The dress was perfect on her, the folds clinging to her slender figure, her slim ankles in the high heels, strands of tawny hair in disarray. How he longed to let his fingers disarray her hair even more, to crush her to him. Though Jessica smiled at him, she was keeping her usual distance.

'Thank you,' she said. 'The dress is a dream.' She didn't add that the evening was a dream coming true.

'You're going to be stone cold in that slip of a dress,' said Lady Grace, peering from her doorway. Her curiosity had got the better of her. 'Not much of a top; doesn't cover much. Haven't you got a proper coat, girl?'

Jessica shook her head. 'Nothing suitable, more's the pity. An anorak would certainly spoil the look.'

'Ridiculous. Young women don't know how to dress these days.' She went back in her bedroom. 'No sense at all.'

'You look beautiful,' said Lucas, taking her hand. 'Are you ready? Shall we go now? The car is outside.'

Lily was in her pyjamas and confronted her father, arms akimbo, Floppy Ears under threat of being strangled. 'Is this a date?' she asked suspiciously.

'Yes, I suppose you could call it a date,' said Lucas, hiding a wicked grin.

'Are you going to bring Willdo back? You've never brought your other dates back. None of them ever came again.'

Jessica looked at Lucas. What a revelation from his small daughter. He was wearing slim black trousers, an open-necked black silk shirt and white jacket. She had never seen him look so immaculate. Even his unruly hair had seen a comb. He had made an effort, for her sake. All that extra clothes shopping. It must have taken him at least half an hour.

Jessica hugged the little girl. 'Of course I'm coming back, sweetheart,' she said. 'It's Daniel's birthday tomorrow, isn't it? I wouldn't miss that for the world.'

Lady Grace came out of her bedroom. She had a silvery pashmina in her hands. 'You'd better borrow this shawl of mine before you catch your death,' she said, grumpily. 'Mind, I want it back.'

'Thank you, Lady Grace,' said Jessica. 'That's a very kind thought. It's perfect, I'll take great care of it.'

'You can take Floppy Ears with you, if you like,' said Lily, not to be outdone in the sacrifice stakes. 'He could keep you company.'

'That's very kind as well,' said Jessica. 'But

I think it's past his bedtime. We don't want him to be worn out for tomorrow.'

Lily looked relieved and held up her face for a kiss.

'Goodnight, Willdo. Have a lovely date.'

'Goodnight, sweetheart. Goodnight, Daniel.'

'Night,' he said.

★　★　★

The King's restaurant of the Grand Hotel, Brighton, was their destination. Jessica felt like a celebrity with the graceful dress swishing around her, her heels sinking into the deep carpet as they walked through reception. The great green carpeted staircase swept upwards, round and round, to all the floors above.

'One hundred and twenty-three steps apparently,' Lucas whispered, as they were ushered towards the restaurant. 'It also has the first mechanical elevator ever in a hotel. Do you want to try it?'

'No, thank you.'

The restaurant was grand indeed. Slender pillars in red marble held up the ornate ceiling. Tall windows were draped in pale green damask. Chandeliers shed twinkling light in every direction. Beautiful pieces of antique furniture around the room. It was sedate and impressive.

As Lucas promised, they had a table by a

window. There was hardly much of a sea view at night, but the road was lit with strings of lights, luminous waves washed the shore in the distance. They could be in fairyland.

'Does this feel very strange?' Lucas asked. 'We've never done this before. Life has been so busy, there has never been time for the two of us.'

'Very strange,' said Jessica. 'Not real at all. I'm not used to seeing you looking so smart and . . . ' She paused, lost for the word. She didn't know what to say. 'Sophisticated.'

'I know,' he said, as he pulled out the chair for her to sit down, beating the waiter to the duty. 'I'm usually shredded, unkempt, dead tired and useless in the conversation stakes. But tonight is going to be totally different. We are going to have a civilized meal. Put the world to rights.'

The table was laid with a starched white linen cloth, gleaming silverware, glistening glasses, a vase with real red roses. Nothing like meals in the kitchen or supper in the dining room, trays in the library. This wasn't real life but she was prepared to enjoy it for one evening.

'How come you have the evening off?' Jessica asked, as the waiter shook and spread the linen napkin over her lap. As if she couldn't do it herself.

'Lots of arm twisting. I've lost count of how many days I'm owed, holiday time that I haven't taken. It's never possible. There's always someone who needs my assistance.'

'How do you fit in time with Daniel and Lily, when you haven't got anyone to help?'

'I've always spent as much time as possible with both of them. I used to drive back from East Grinstead to spend some afternoon or evening time with them, and then drive back to the hospital when they had gone to sleep. It's been marvellous having you with them this last month, knowing they are happy with you and that I am not needed so much.'

'Are they happy with me?'

'Jessica, I've never seen them so happy. As I am, believe me. I've never been so happy. You have brought joy to my family, and to me.'

A warm feeling swept over Jessica. Lucas meant what he was saying. He was looking at her with intense awareness, as if he never wanted to stop looking. He was devouring her with his eyes. They could have been alone in the big room.

The waiter planted leather-bound, book-size menus in front of them. They would take half an hour to read. Jessica looked at Lucas over the top of her menu, her eyes twinkling.

'Supposing I ordered a tuna and iceberg sandwich?'

'The chef would have a fit. I should have to go into the kitchen to resuscitate. Start reading the small print.'

Jessica ordered a Waldorf salad, which she knew would be delicious, followed by lemon sole cooked in some special way and served with a selection of locally grown tender vegetables. Lucas went for heartier food, a steak. But she knew that the wine he ordered would be perfect. He knew his wines. She wouldn't look at his meal, pretend it wasn't there on his plate.

Their starters were both quickly served and devoured.

The lemon sole was served with style, a portrait on a plate. 'I am emptying the sea,' said Jessica, looking at the poor fish.

'But you couldn't have stopped it happening.'

'They say that even fish feel pain.'

'I read a paper about that, too. The cerebral cortex of their brain actually registers pain.'

'Perhaps I ought to have a cheese sandwich after all.'

Lucas leaned forward and put his hand over hers, his thumb gently rubbing her finger. 'My dearest young woman, you can't put this crazy world to rights with one sandwich.'

A waiter lit a candle on their table and the

soft light was perfect. Lucas's dark features were a series of contours, slanted, long lashed, strong jaw jutting, eyes gleaming. The tension melted between them.

Jessica felt herself trembling. She knew that she would always love him, even if they parted at the end of her contract. It could happen. She would go to Sheffield Hospital, take up her duties, try to forget him. But she would always keep in touch with Lily and Daniel. They were part of her life now. There was no way she could walk away from them, what ever happened.

It was the same with Lucas. The candle-light was perfect for Jessica. She looked so beautiful in the soft raspberry dress, her shoulders bare and enticing, her skin luminous. She had no idea how tempting she looked.

If only he could make her believe that his wife's accident was in the past. That the hurt and pain was all over. His wife had left him for another man and that was more hurtful than the dreadful accident. Lucas longed for Jessica to believe him, to let him love her as he wanted to. It was like a fine flame invading his brain.

Neither could say the right words. Time was suspended in the air. The evening was full of light and laughter. They looked at each other and longed for each other's touch, never saying what they should say. Letting the time tick by with measured strokes.

They chose raspberries and cream. There was no question. It was the only dessert for them both. Lucas despaired of the time passing and he had not even begun to say what he wanted to say. Why were words so difficult? He was like his son, Daniel, unable to find the right words.

'I'm like Daniel sometimes,' he said suddenly. 'I can't find the right words to say, even when I know they are inside me.'

Jessica caught her breath. She wanted the words to come.

A wave of seagulls flew past the window like pale ghosts, wheeling and dealing in the thermal air. The sky was the colour of dark slate, the moon lost behind shifting clouds.

'It happens to all of us,' said Jessica, slowly. 'We are out of touch with words. We are scared of words. It's today's mania for computers and games consoles and texting.'

It was coffee time already before Lucas forced himself to say what he wanted to say. He saw the time and panicked. He forced himself to speak.

'Jessica, we have to get this right between us,' he said. 'We need to get this sorted out. You have been so marvellous with Daniel and

Lily. I could not have wished for someone who has taken more care of them, who understands them so well. And Lady Grace, what can I say? Somehow you know how to deal with her and she likes you. She actually likes you. It's a miracle!'

'She likes arguing with me,' said Jessica. 'It sharpens her mind.'

'At some point, when I was totally stupid and inept, I asked you to marry me. And you said no. Quite rightly, you refused me. I was being a complete idiot and yet if I had said what was really in my heart, your answer might have been quite different.'

Lucas wasn't making any sense, yet she wanted him to go on. She was still mesmerized by the sweetness of his voice. She was recognizing the honesty of every word he said. They were basking in the wonder of being together. She could not bear the thought of losing him. There were no halves, only wholes. She would give him her all, without thought, without reservation.

'I don't know what you mean.'

'When I saw you there, standing in the pouring rain outside Eastly Station, it was as if I had been hit by a thunder bolt. You bowled me over. Your beautiful blue eyes spat fire at me. Yes, that was it. Fire and ice. You were the fire, and yet you were frozen. That was the ice. I hardly knew what I was saying. I knew that you were the only woman in the world for me.'

'I don't think you know what you are saying now,' said Jessica, stirring what was left of raspberry juice into the cream. It was a satisfactory pink. She dare not look at him, in case his eyes contradicted his words.

'What I am trying to say is that I fell in love with you then, that very first moment, and I have loved you ever since. I've been waiting for you to fall in love with me. Is that so impossible? Even though I have made lots of mistakes, and said all the wrong things. I want to know. Could you ever begin to love me?'

Jessica knew she was trembling. She could barely look at Lucas. They were both so careful and guarded. It was like music that never stopped. She couldn't answer his question without giving away all her thoughts and feelings.

'When you asked me to marry you, I knew it was impossible, because I wanted to marry a man who loved me, the real me. You only wanted me for the children's sakes, and for your mother. You even said that you would take your pleasures elsewhere. That's what you said.'

Lucas sighed. 'That was tactless of me and

I don't know what I meant. It was unintentionally cruel. I think I meant that I wouldn't force you into anything you didn't want. Our pleasure together would come later as we grew closer. I knew the moment the words came out, that I had said it the wrong way. The only woman I really want is you. Jessica Harlow, I want you as my wife, my lover, my sweetheart for the rest of my life. I love you and I always have, since that very first moment in the rain.'

The waiter hovered with coffee refills but had the sense to fade back into the shadows. He could feel the surge of emotion eddying round the table, strong enough to blow out the candle. The man and the woman were wrapped in a trance. The coffee could wait.

'You love me?' Jessica whispered, hardly daring to voice the words. 'You really do? You always have?'

'Dear heart, how am I going to make you believe me?' said Lucas, reaching into his pocket. 'I wonder if this will help you.'

He brought out a small dark-navy leather box and pressed open the lid, turning it to face Jessica. 'Jessica Harlow, will you do me the honour of becoming my wife? I will love and honour you, but I can't promise to obey.'

Jessica felt the world spinning round her. Lucas loved her. She saw the warmth in his eyes and the apprehension. He was not sure of her. Yet she loved him and need not hide her love any more.

'And I love you, Lucas,' she breathed. 'I really do and I always will. It happened ages ago. I fell in love with you, not meaning to but it happened. I want to be with you for the rest of my life. I want to share in everything that you do, and the crazy way you live, those dreadful hours you work. I want to wait up till you come home, scrub your weary back. To help make life easier for you, if I can. Yes, I will marry you. I love you so much.'

He was looking at her with such tenderness, her heart went into a spiral. Nothing else in the world mattered at that moment. He touched her chin with a fingertip. His surgeon's fingers were so light, so delicate.

'I can't believe it, you've agreed, at last. My sweet one, my darling. Just you being with me will make life easier,' said Lucas earnestly. 'To know that you are at home, waiting for me, ready to take me into your bed. You will take me into your bed, won't you, Jessica?'

'I think we might need a bigger bed,' Jessica murmured, her coffee growing cold. 'We are both rather tall.'

'It'll be the first purchase for our home together,' Lucas promised. He moved the opened box closer to Jessica. She looked down at it for the first time. 'Do you like it?'

It was a ring, nestling in white satin. The sapphire winked at her from among a circle of diamonds. It was a magnificent ring.

'It's beautiful,' Jessica breathed.

'A beautiful ring for a beautiful woman. Sapphire to match your eyes. Will you wear it for me, Jessica?'

She slipped it on the ring finger of her left hand. It fitted perfectly. Surgeon's eyes or a lucky guess? The diamonds flashed in the light from the chandelier above and the flickering candle flame on their table.

The head waiter nodded across the room. Another waiter disappeared and returned almost immediately with a bottle of Dom Perignon champagne, wrapped in white linen. He took it over to their table and bowed.

'With the compliments of the management,' he said. 'And may we offer our congratulations to you both, with best wishes for your future happiness.'

He opened the champagne and the cork flew across the room with a sharp, dizzy burst of fine spray. He poured the champagne into tall crystal flutes, the tiny bubbles rising to the rims.

'To you, my darling,' said Lucas.

'To us,' said Jessica, smiling.

They were very late driving back to Upton Hall so it was already Daniel's birthday morning. They could not stop laughing or holding hands, touching each other, to make sure that the evening was still real. They did not want it ever to end.

They went reluctantly to their own bedrooms. His goodnight kiss sent her pulses racing. They clung to each other, arms wrapped in a close embrace, their lips warm and seeking. Jessica had never felt this hunger for any man before. It was lust and liking and loving.

'We'll wait,' he said quietly, on the landing. 'We are both too tired and had little sleep last night.'

'We could just sleep,' said Jessica tremulously.

'I could never just sleep with you. The temptation would be beyond my mortal body. I should want you so much. You would have to fight me off. But we will marry, very soon? Do you agree?'

'Very soon,' said Jessica, every nerve in her body clamouring for him. His arms were still round her and she could smell the manliness of his skin.

'We'll make all our plans, when we have

come down to earth.'

'I'll never come down to earth with you. I'll always be in some kind of heaven.'

'Dearest love, sleep now. I'll see you at breakfast. I may shock Mrs Harris when I sweep you into an ardent embrace.' He grinned.

'I think she would enjoy it. Your mother is more of a worry.'

'Leave Lady Grace to me.'

They drew apart, laughing quietly. Jessica went into her bedroom and twirled around the room, the chiffon floating round her like a pink cloud. They were going to be married. He loved her. Her dream was coming true.

★　★　★

Daniel's birthday tea was a picnic in the garden. September had decided on one more spectacularly sunny day. It was warm enough to spread a rug on the lawn and Mrs Harris had gone to town with birthday tea treats and the garden table was laden with goodies. Lady Grace had a garden chair, padded with cushions. Lucas had raced back from the hospital to be there for his son's birthday.

It was difficult to know if Daniel understood that it was his birthday. Birthday, years and age may not have any concept for

234

him. A party was out of the question because he did not have any friends and would hate all the noise and confusion. But he seemed to like having tea in the garden.

Jessica had spent half the morning blowing up balloons and hanging them from the trees. They hung from low branches, swaying and bobbing in the gentle breeze. Daniel loved them because they made no noise. He started to help, putting them in lines, from low shrubs and bushes. The garden began to look full of globes of colour. Although Daniel's face did not change much, his body looked relaxed and carefree. His shirt had come un-tucked and he did not seem to notice.

Lily raced around creating total confusion. That was her contribution.

'When is it my birthday?' she shouted. 'Can I have balloons in the garden and a picnic tea?'

Jessica didn't know. How awful. She didn't know Lily's birthday. Mrs Harris whispered, 'February 21st.'

'It might be snowing,' said Jessica.

'Snowballs and snowmen?'

'Perhaps. A snow tea, everything white.'

Lady Grace came downstairs, wearing the silvery pashmina which Jessica had safely returned. It was her ownership statement. Jessica made her comfortable in a garden chair and brought her a glass of dry sherry.

'You might like something a little stronger than apple juice,' said Jessica.

'Glad to see you have more clothes on this afternoon,' said Lady Grace.

Jessica was in indigo jeans and her flame red shirt. She called it her Brighton outfit. And she had tied her hair back with a matching scarf.

'Last night was special,' she said, but added nothing more. They had not told anyone yet. 'What do you think about another swim soon? Would you like me to ring your friend, Arthur, and find a free afternoon?'

Lady Grace seemed to think about it, gathering her strength, finding it difficult to be unpleasant. 'Yes, I would like that.'

'No barbed wire in their pool,' said Jessica, without thinking.

Lady Grace went white, her hand trembling. Jessica took the sherry glass from her, cursing her own thoughtlessness. 'How did you . . . know?' she whispered.

'I'm sorry. Please don't distress yourself,' said Jessica, going down on her knees and stroking the old, veined hands. 'Lucas told me. He was there when you came back from Brighton on that awful day. He saw all the cuts and tears on your legs. We know that the beach at Brighton was heavily defended during the war, concrete blocks, landmines and barbed wire. There could so easily have been some barbed wire embedded in the sand, unseen, waiting for someone to tread on it, to become entangled.'

Lady Grace was gripping her hand tightly. 'It was barbed wire, Jess.' She choked on the words. 'My feet were caught up. I went down in the water to free myself but I couldn't do it. I ran out of air. I was struggling to come to the surface to breathe. The tide was coming in fast and the longer it took, the deeper it got. I panicked. Sea was washing into my mouth, choking me. I thought I was drowning and I nearly was.'

'You were so brave,' Jessica assured her.

'I took a great, deep breath and went down under the water again. I could hardly see for all the swirling water and sand. The barbed wire was twisted round my legs and my ankles. I had to drag them free or I would drown.'

'But you did,' said Jessica. 'You managed it. You are here now.'

'Someone helped me. I don't know who it was. There was someone dark and slim, swimming, tearing the wire away with their bare hands. Suddenly I was free and I shot to the surface. I was in such a state of shock, I never stopped to thank them or find out who it was. All I could do was somehow stagger home. I don't even know how I managed that.'

'And you never went back?'

'I couldn't face them.'

'So you don't know who saved your life?'

'My one regret is that I never thanked him. It's been a heavy guilt to carry all these years.'

'He must know,' said Jessica. 'He must know, in his heart, that he did a really brave thing and saved your life. He doesn't need your thanks. Because he knows that you are still alive.'

'Maybe he has gone, died, after all these years.'

'He will still know,' said Jessica. 'Thoughts travel. Send him your thoughts. What do we know about how radio and television work? It's all thoughts and words on invisible waves. Air that we can't see.'

The children were racing out into the garden with Lucas. Lily had dressed up for the occasion. She had added a net curtain train and tinsel in her hair. Floppy Ears was also wearing tinsel but not the train. Jessica gave Lady Grace back the sherry glass and stood to greet her family. For they were going to be her family now. Lucas, Lily and Daniel. Even Lady Grace.

Lucas came straight over and kissed her

lightly on her cheek. It was all she needed. No one seemed to notice the gentle embrace.

'Hello, beautiful,' he said.

'Hello, Lucas,' she said, no need for more words.

The September afternoon swam into a sultry softness. Daniel loved his presents. He was in ecstasy with the pads of paper, the pencils, the books that he didn't understand yet. Mrs Harris gave him a big cake made in the shape of an eight. Lady Grace gave him money. He wouldn't know how to spend it.

And Lucas had another present for Daniel. It was a rocking chair. Daniel loved it instantly, climbed into it, rocking himself, a sketch pad on his knee, drawing leaves, the trees, the clouds. He was lost in his own world.

Lucas sat on the rug, eating everything in sight. He'd had no lunch. It had been a heavy morning. He shifted so that he was leaning against Jessica's knees. She had one of the garden chairs. He looked up at her and took her hand.

'I heard about yesterday morning,' he said. 'I want to thank you for saving my mother from falling and getting hurt.'

'How did you find out? We weren't going to tell you.'

'I know, but Mrs Harris told me. She

239

changed her mind. She said the man had to be stopped from returning at some future time. And I was the only person who could do that. She was right. I have made quite sure that he will never bother you again. You can safely forget him now.'

'Thank you,' said Jessica, so tenderly. The afternoon became saturated with warmth and light. 'I'm glad you know. I never want to keep anything from you.'

Lucas tapped his cup for attention. Everyone looked at him.

'I think this is the right time to give you all some very special news,' Lucas said, swallowing his mouthful of cucumber sandwich. 'Last night Jessica did me the great honour of agreeing to become my wife. So we are going to be married. Jessica and me. Isn't that marvellous? Hasn't anyone noticed her ring? It's big enough.'

Jessica almost stopped breathing. Supposing everyone hated the idea? It was all so new. Lucas could change his mind.

But Lily hurled herself at Jessica, a bundle of excitement and joy. 'Are you going to be my new mummy?' she shrieked. 'Can I be a bridesmaid? And you will stay with us forever and forever?'

'Forever and forever,' said Jessica, taking the little girl in her arms. She was warm and cuddly and a little slimmer.

Even Lady Grace looked pleased. She managed a nod of approval. 'You can borrow my wedding veil,' she said grudgingly. 'It's very old, Brussels lace, but mind you, I shall want it back.'

'Of course, you'll have it back. Thank you,' said Jessica. 'I shall be delighted and honoured to wear it.'

Jessica turned to Daniel. He had tumbled out of the rocking chair and was standing near her, awkwardly, sketch pad dangling from his hand. He looked so like his father, it was devastating.

'Would you like me to be your mummy?' she asked softly.

'Mummy,' he said. Then he gave her one of his rare smiles.

12

Jessica had not been so happy for years. She could not remember the last time she had walked on a cloud. Her happiness was catching. Lily raced around the garden pretending to be a butterfly. Daniel drew a complicated picture of the close-up of a rose and gave it to her, without a word.

'Thank you, Daniel,' said Jessica. 'What a lovely present. I shall pin it on my bedroom wall.'

Even Lady Grace showed traces of a smile cracking her face.

'It's all right having you here, you know, permanently. I quite like the idea,' she said. 'But don't think you will be running the household.'

'As if I would,' said Jessica, shuffling the cards for their afternoon game of cards. 'I've more sense.'

Mrs Harris was far more astute. 'So you and Mr Lucas have been talking at last, have you?' she asked. 'Got things sorted out?'

'Just talking,' said Jessica, hiding a smile.

'Come to your senses, have you?'

'I don't know what you mean, Mrs Harris.'

'I wasn't born yesterday,' said Mrs Harris.

Lucas had asked her to wait but only for a short while. There were still a few loose ends to tie up before they could be married. Something to do with his wife's death. It had to be registered. Jessica did not understand. Surely after a road accident, her death would have already been registered?

Work never stopped and Lucas had been called back to the hospital almost immediately after Daniel's birthday. But he went with a lighter step, knowing that Jessica would be waiting for him when he got home, whatever the time.

Jessica realized that she would not be the sole mistress of Upton Hall when she married Lucas. Lady Grace would still want to think that she ran the household. But it had been a long time since her hands were on the reins, and it would be Jessica and Mrs Harris making the decisions. Even if Lady Grace thought she was in charge.

'We'll agree to everything she says and then do it our way,' said Mrs Harris.

'Mrs Harris! That is positively revolutionary. You must have taken part in the Peasants Revolt.'

'I'm not that old,' said Mrs Harris with a grin.

'When Lucas and I get married, we are

going to have a honeymoon, but only a short one, somewhere warm and sunny. He doesn't think the hospital can function without him. We would like you to stay here, please, at Upton Hall, overnight, and we will also arrange for a girl to come up from the village to help you during the day. Would that be all right?'

'Perfect,' said Mrs Harris. 'I thought you would never ask.'

'And when we come back, we want you to have a whole week off as a holiday. I don't think you have ever had a holiday.'

'A holiday?' Mrs Harris looked taken aback. 'No, I've never had any holiday time. But my Bingo friend, May and I would like to go away together. We fancy one of those Shearing's coach tours.'

'As soon as we get our dates, you can book your coach holiday,' said Jessica. 'You are owed a lot of holiday time.'

Jessica made a note. She and Lucas would pay for Mrs Harris's coach tour. The woman was a saint. But it was loving Lucas's father that had turned her into a saint. And it hadn't happened overnight.

★　★　★

A few afternoons later, they were all in the garden, lolling about after tea, enjoying

244

autumnal sunshine. Jessica was reading a new crime thriller, Lady Grace dozing in a cushioned chair, Lily was teaching Floppy Ears to do cartwheels. He was not getting on very well, a bit out of his usual orbit. Daniel was sketching as usual. No one was allowed to see what he was working on.

Jessica heard a car coming along the drive. It was not a car she recognized. Not Lucas's engine. Nor a delivery van. It drew up outside the front entrance, fired the engine again, and then it was switched off.

Jessica wandered round to the front to see who was disturbing their peace. A woman was getting out of a bright red sports car. The red was an over-bright colour against the mellow yellow and browns of the autumnal trees. The woman was slim, wearing a dark emerald green trouser suit, her hair ebony, cut asymmetrical with one side wing longer than the other. Very Posh Spice. Only it wasn't Victoria Beckham, it was Dr Amanda Burton.

The woman turned on her heel, grinding the spike into the gravel. She smiled at Jessica, but it was not really a smile. There was no humour in it.

'So this is where you are hiding out,' said Amanda Burton.

'I'm not hiding out. This is where I work,' said Jessica.

'Call it work, do you? That's a new one.'

Jessica refused to answer. She was remembering the last time they met when this woman deliberately spilt her wine down Jessica's dress and then her beaded bag caught in the frills and ruined it.

'What are you doing here?' Jessica asked. 'What do you want?'

'I was going to ask you the same thing,' said Amanda. 'What are you doing here? Up to some mischief, obviously. But one thing for sure, you are not getting my husband.'

'Your husband?' Jessica almost choked on the word. 'Fraser? I wouldn't touch him with a bargepole, or anything longer or shorter. He's the most repulsive creature I have ever had the misfortune to come across.'

'Come now, that's not what you used to think,' Amanda mocked. 'You used to think that the sun shone out of his arse.'

'I never said that.'

'It's what you thought. You adored the man. You thought he was a very fine catch for a student nurse.'

'I was very young and foolish. I knew nothing about men, especially ones like your husband.'

'Yet you spent the last two nights with him at the Double Cross Inn, outside Brighton. And I've got the receipts in my hand, and a

246

photocopy of the registry book with your signature. You can't deny it. It's here in black and white.'

Jessica was speechless. It was all a total prefabrication. She had been here at Upton Hall, sleeping in the yellow bedroom. She would never go anywhere with the despicable Fraser. Yet, Amanda was waving bits of paper at her, and was now striding towards her.

'Don't think you are going to get away with this, trying to steal my husband. I'll make sure you are never employed anywhere, ever again. And certainly not at Upton Hall, looking after Lucas Coleman's children. You can't be trusted. You've no morals. Does he know where you were these last two nights?'

Lucas had not come home. There had been some awful flat fire and he had to deal with burned children, rebuild their skin, their faces. He had not been home for two nights. But they had spoken briefly, on the phone, reaffirmed their love for each other, knowing they would be together soon.

'You don't scare me,' said Jessica. 'I suggest you leave and go back to whatever miserable life you have with Fraser. I don't want anything to do with him or with you.'

'I've already faxed copies of these documents to Lucas Coleman. I'm sure he'll be interested to know what you do with your spare time when he is not here.'

'The way out is that way,' said Jessica, pointing down the drive. 'And don't come back here again, ever.'

'Don't think you are getting rid of me that easily. I know you are after my husband, but you are not going to get him. I'll fight you every inch of the way and I have a lot of weapons in my arsenal. I'll get you struck off the Nursing Register, so that you will never work again.'

Jessica felt an overwhelming tiredness. Amanda Burton was a vindictive woman and Jessica could not understand why she was acting this way. It was as if the nightmare had returned. Now it was Amanda who wanted to humiliate her for no reason at all.

'Willdo? Willdo? Where are you?'

She heard Lily's voice calling her. Jessica turned away and went through the rose garden. She heard the car engine start up and drive away with a burst of acceleration. It sounded as angry as its driver.

'Floppy Ears can't do cartwheels. His ears get in the way,' said Lily. 'Shall I get some ribbon and tie them up?'

'I don't think that would be very comfortable for him,' said Jessica. 'Would you like to have your ears tied up?'

'No, I wouldn't,' said Lily firmly.

'Why not try hand-stands? Floppy Ears could probably manage a few hand-stands if you help him.'

'Hand-stands! We'll do hand-stands all over the garden.' Lily raced away.

'It makes me quite tired just watching that child,' said Lady Grace, who had woken up. 'What do you feed her on?'

'Not sugar and spice, for sure. She's beginning to lose weight which is a good sign. But I think poor Floppy Ears is due for a relapse. I shall have to go to Brighton pier and win another one.'

Lady Grace's face changed with what occasionally passed for a smile. 'You might not be so lucky a second time.'

'I might come back with a camel. I suppose he'd be called Humpy.'

★　★　★

Daniel had been listening but said nothing. Jessica had lost her place in her book and she had lost interest in the plot. The unexpected visitor had upset her more than she cared to admit. She wanted to see Lucas. She wanted to find out if Amanda had been bluffing.

It was a very tired and grubby Lily who went into the bath that evening. She hardly had the energy to do her brown inhaler. And she was almost asleep before Jessica finished reading a story.

'Floppy Ears v'good at hand-stands,' she said. 'Better'n me.'

Floppy Ears looked exhausted.

Daniel had already put himself to bed. He was old enough to wash himself now. He handed Jessica a sheet of paper from one of his new drawing pads. It was a perfect drawing of a camel.

'Hump,' he said.

⋆ ⋆ ⋆

Jessica waited up for Lucas returning from the hospital. It was almost midnight. Mrs Harris had long gone home, and Lady Grace was tucked up in bed with her hot milk and two digestive biscuits.

Jessica had a shower and changed into a clean track suit, her blue one. She knew Lucas liked the colour. There was a tray of sandwiches for him but he would probably be past eating. Maybe a glass of whisky and then he would be off to his bed, too tired to do more than kiss her goodnight.

She heard his car coming up the drive. He was coming quite slowly as if it was too much of an effort. The car went round the side of Upton Hall to the stable garages. Lucas seemed to be a long time coming into the house and she was beginning to wonder if he had gone straight to bed.

This was so unlike him that Jessica began to fidget around the room, unsettled by his non-appearance. Then Lucas came into the room and she was shocked by his appearance. He looked gaunt and haggard, shadows under his eyes.

She ran over to him and put her arms round him. His head sank onto hers as if he didn't have the strength to hold it up. She felt the weight of him against her and guided him to a big armchair. He fell into it with a groan, his eyes closed.

'You look terrible,' she said. 'What has happened?'

'We lost one of them,' he said. 'One of the children. Five years old, the same age as Lily.'

'Oh, how awful,' said Jessica. 'I'm so sorry. But I'm sure you did everything you could.'

'Of course I did everything I could.' His voice had a sudden sharp edge to it. 'But it wasn't enough.'

There was nothing Jessica could say to ease the guilt. She knew what it felt like, to lose a patient. She always wondered if she could have done more. If she had missed something, not been at a bedside when she was most needed.

She went to the drinks table and poured Lucas a glass of his favourite whisky. There were still some melting ice cubes left at the bottom of the ice bin. Mrs Harris had forgotten to fill it. She took the crystal tumbler over to him, knelt down and put it carefully into his hand.

'Maybe this will help,' she said. 'At least it will help you to sleep.'

He took a few sips and nodded. Then he opened his eyes, their usual brightness dimmed.

'You're looking very . . . ' Lucas seemed to search for a word. 'Very seductive,' he added.

Jessica rocked back on heels. It was such a strange thing for him to say. He had never called her seductive before. She had never thought of herself as seductive. Seductive was someone who wore black fish-net stockings and a plunge bra, not a blue track suit.

'Well, I don't feel it,' she said. 'It's been a busy day.'

'No, I suppose you don't. At least not with me. A worn-out and tired surgeon who is never at home. You should really find someone more lively and stimulating. Someone who will take you out and give you a good time.'

It was the second shock of the day, to hear Lucas speak to her in that way.

'I've never wanted 'a good time', as you put it,' said Jessica. 'I'm very happy here with Lily and Daniel, and the occasional outing to Brighton pier.'

'Oh yes, I'd forgotten. You like Brighton, don't you? Is it one of your regular haunts?'

Jessica got up from her knees. Lucas must have been drinking and that's why he drove so slowly up the drive. If he had lost a patient, one he cared about, then perhaps he'd already had a few whiskies.

'I think you need some sleep, Lucas,' she said, trying to stop her voice from trembling. 'You'll feel a little more like yourself in the morning.'

'Perhaps I will,' he said, getting up clumsily. 'I don't know what to think.'

He went from the room, not stopping to kiss her, the whisky almost spilling in his hand. Jessica did not know whether to go with him or let him find his own way to the stables. It was his house. He must know the way.

'Goodnight, sweetheart,' she said, her voice still trembling. He had not kissed her. She followed him out into the hall. His coat was thrown on a chair. His briefcase thrown on another chair. It had come open. Some papers had fallen to the floor. She bent down to pick them up and froze.

13

Jessica could hardly remember how she got herself to bed. The pretty primrose bedroom seemed a foreign place and there was no comfort in it. She left her track suit on the floor and curled up in bed, the tears welling up in her eyes. Lucas had copies of the hotel receipts and the page of the hotel registry in his briefcase.

And there was her signature on a line, right below Fraser's. Jessica Harlow, her handwriting. And she had no idea how it got there. Amanda Burton had carried out her threat and faxed the incriminating documents to Lucas at the hospital.

No wonder Lucas was distraught. He had lost more than a patient. He thought he had lost her as well. Now she had another mountain to climb, to convince him that it was all some vile vengeance by a woman who would stop at nothing.

She did not fall asleep until the small hours, exhausted by a turmoil of thoughts and silent weeping. She wondered how she would get through the next day.

Lily woke her with her usual bounce and

hug. Floppy Ears had come too. He did not look as if he had had a good night either.

'Willdo, it's morning. Wake up. Today is here. What are we going to do today? Have you got a surprise for us?'

'Yes, I might not get up today,' said Jessica. 'That's my surprise.'

Lily looked aghast. 'Not get up? Willdo, you can't stay in bed all day. Daddy has already got up and gone to work. You must get up. We need you.'

Jessica heaved herself up. 'Lucas has already gone?'

'Yes, I heard his porch go very early.' She pronounced it like it was the front of a house. 'He has very sick children to look after, you know.' Lily looked serious and worldly. 'Daddy is a very clever man.'

'Yes, that's true,' said Jessica. 'He's a wonderful man.'

'Is that why you are marrying him?'

'Yes, because he's wonderful and clever and I love him.'

Lily's face glowed. 'He loves you too,' she said. 'We all love you.'

Jessica swung her legs over the side of the bed, feeling the softness of the carpet beneath her feet. She still had her job to do, whether Lucas threw her over or not.

'Washing first,' she said. 'You, Lily, not

Floppy Ears. He needs another five minutes sleep.'

'Another five minutes',' she agreed, tucking him into Jessica's bed. 'Go back to sleep, Floppy.'

Jessica went into automatic mode. She got the children ready for school, breakfasted and onto the school bus. She ate no breakfast at all. Lady Grace received her usual attention, the exercises, the medication, a discussion of the state of the world.

Mrs Harris was as sharp-eyed as always. 'No breakfast, miss? Off your food, are you? Not pregnant, are you?'

'If only,' said Jessica.

'So what's the matter with you this morning? Not had a row, have you?'

'Not exactly.'

'A misunderstanding?'

'Sort of.'

Mrs Harris poured out a fresh black coffee. Jessica took it gratefully. It might keep her awake. She watched Mrs Harris toasting a slice of granary bread and spreading it with peanut butter.

'Get this down you, miss, before you pass out on us. Your face is as white as a sheet. I don't like the look of it at all. It must have been something pretty awful.'

'You remember Fraser? The unpleasant

fair-haired doctor who came here?'

'Tow-haired lout? The man I whacked with a rolling pin?'

Jessica nodded. 'His wife turned up here yesterday with a pack of lies about me. And she has sent so-called proof of those lies to Lucas.'

Mrs Harris looked up from her pastry-making, her fingers covered in flour. She looked enquiringly at Jessica. 'Proof? What sort of proof?'

'Documents. One with my signature on it. It's not true, of course. I didn't do what she is saying I did.'

Jessica nibbled at the toast, to please Mrs Harris. Mrs Harris continued crumbling the pastry. She was a light-fingered expert.

'I read a lot of books, you know,' Mrs Harris continued. 'Crooks can forge anything these days. They are pretty clever at it, make passports and identification tags. I'll see what I can find out. If the wife is as nasty as the husband, then they deserve each other.'

Jessica found a wan smile. 'Thank you, Mrs Harris. It's Lucas I'm worried about. He seems to believe the implications.'

'He ought to have more sense, not take the word of a pair of scoundrels.'

'He was very tired last night,' Jessica added. 'Too tired to think.'

'All the more reason for him to come home now and sort it out with you. Before it gets worse. And before you pass out for want of any decent nourishment. Look at you, skin and bone.'

'Don't worry about me. I shall certainly have some of that apple pie you are making. Your apple pies are famous.'

Jessica spent the morning walking Lady Grace round the garden. They did a little dead-heading. The flowers were coming to an end. Autumn was on its way, with more rain and cold fingers. Her patient was gradually becoming used to walking with a stick, sometimes quite briskly. She only used Fred upstairs now, preferring to lean on him while she got her bearings first thing in the morning.

'Pity he's not better looking,' she said once. 'I might take a fancy to him.'

Jessica had to laugh. It was the first time Lady Grace had said anything that was almost flippant. She had a smart reply on the tip of her tongue but thought better of it. She still had to tread warily with Lady Grace. No crossing the social boundary without permission.

They had a light lunch together in the dining room but Jessica still could not eat. She was racked with worry about Lucas and wanted desperately to talk to him, to tell him her side of the prefabrication.

Lady Grace said very little during lunch. But while she was stirring cream into her after dinner coffee, she looked at Jessica with a piercing glance.

'I have perfect hearing you know,' she said.

'Lady Grace?'

'I can hear a pin drop. Yesterday afternoon, I heard that woman berating you. Of course, I couldn't hear everything she said, but I got the general gist of it. What was she saying to you?'

Jessica was shaken that Lady Grace might have overheard what Amanda said. 'She was accusing me of trying to steal her husband,' said Jessica, barely able to get the words out. 'She said I had been cheating on Lucas.'

'And who is her husband?'

'Doctor Fraser Burton. The tall, blond man who came here, who kicked your stick away, who tried to grab me. That's him. He's her husband.'

'That piece of garbage? No woman in her right mind would want him, and certainly not you, Jess. What rubbish. What proof has she of this accusation?'

Jessica felt her face colouring. 'She has hotel receipts and proof of my registering at a hotel with him. My signature is on the line.'

Lady Grace snorted. 'And just when was this illicit rendezvous, may I ask?'

'Sometime this week apparently. I don't know. I didn't see the dates.'

'Absolute nonsense. You've been here at Upton Hall for weeks now, every night. I can vouch for that. Who else brings me my milk and digestive biscuits?'

'I could have slipped out after you'd gone to sleep, driven to this inn outside Brighton,' said Jessica, making it worse for herself. 'It's not that far.'

'And been back in time for Lily to jump on you with Floppy Ears, first thing every morning? I told you I have very good hearing. It's not possible. The woman is an outrageous liar. Like her husband.'

'She is lying but Lucas believes what she has put before his eyes. He barely spoke to me last night. Left me without a word. It was awful.'

'My son is a fool. A clever surgeon but a fool when it comes to women. He trusted his wife so I suppose he is worried that it could all happen again.'

Jessica didn't ask although she wanted to know. The conversation had exhausted her. 'Shall we have a game of cards before the children come home from school?'

'Good idea. Whist or bridge?'

'I don't think my brain could cope with bridge today. A game of whist would be best.'

'I shall certainly beat you then.'

* * *

The afternoon raced by till Daniel and Lily arrived home from school, but Jessica barely knew what she was doing or what she was saying. All she could think of was Lucas coming home, of having to talk to him, having to convince him that he had been sent a pack of lies.

'Don't you want any tea?' asked Lily at tea-time. 'Floppy Ears says you are not eating anything.'

'I had a big lunch,' said Jessica, lying. It was the first time she had lied to Lily. It was a horrid moment. But what could she say? Your Daddy thinks I've been cheating on him?

'You can have some of my tea. I'll save you some,' said Lily. 'You'd like that, wouldn't you? Then I wouldn't eat so much.'

'A very good idea,' agreed Jessica. 'I'd like that.'

'And Floppy Ears will save you some of his lettuce.'

'Wonderful,' said Jessica faintly. She didn't fancy twice-chewed lettuce.

Lucas came home early evening. She heard

his Porsche coming up the drive with quite a determined sound. He didn't put the car in the garage but parked it by the front door. He slammed the door and strode into the hall. He went straight into the kitchen and poured himself some coffee from the percolator on the Aga.

He leaned against a wall, sipping the coffee, his eyes sweeping over Jessica coldly. 'So,' he said, 'what have you got to say?'

The kitchen was empty, apart from the two of them. Mrs Harris had gone home. Lady Grace was reading in her sitting room. Both Lily and Daniel were already in bed, drawing and crayoning. It was a treat.

Jessica had been clearing up the tea things and making a salad supper for Lady Grace. She was slicing tomatoes and beetroot before making a light dressing. She remembered the day she had arrived at Upton Hall when Lucas met her at the station in the pouring rain. She had stood up for herself then. She would do it again, even if it meant losing Lucas, the man she loved.

'What have I got to say?' she repeated. 'Good evening, Lucas, would be a polite start. Are you talking to me this evening? Or is this going to be more of the cold shoulder that I endured last night?'

'Don't you deserve the cold shoulder after

the way you've been behaving? You really fooled me. The cool young nurse who is really a rampant sex-pot. Not exactly the right person to be looking after my children, and certainly not the right person I want to marry and to be my wife.'

Jessica started to lay a tray for Lady Grace's supper. She put a lace cloth on the tray and laid it with pretty china, the dressing in a jug, the cottage cheese salad on a plate. She put a fresh wholemeal roll on a side plate with some butter.

'It would be interesting to know why you have changed your opinion of me,' she said. 'I remember a dinner at the Grand Hotel, Brighton, quite recently, when you asked me to marry me, gave me a ring. A beautiful ring. A ring which you see, I am not wearing. I thought it was hardly appropriate after your behaviour last night.'

'My behaviour last night was that of a man who thought he loved you, who thought you loved him. Who believed you when you said this Fraser meant nothing to you, but then I find you have spent two nights with him, this week. In some inn at Brighton, of all places.'

He said it as if Brighton had some special significance. As if she could only go to Brighton in his company.

'Right on our doorstep,' he went on.

'Under my nose. When you knew I was working late, staying overnight at the hospital, because of the burns cases. You took advantage of the fact that I was not here. It's a wonder that Super Stud didn't sleep in the yellow bedroom with you.'

Jessica listened to the tirade, trying to keep her own temper. It wouldn't help if she lost her temper. She put a ripe peach and a little knife on a dish on the tray.

'If you'll excuse me a moment, sir,' she added the 'sir' deliberately. 'I'll give your mother her supper and then we will continue this conversation. If you can call it a conversation. It's more like an indictment, a charge of criminal wrongdoing. I believe it is my turn to say something.'

'I'm not going anywhere,' Lucas said bitterly.

Jessica took the tray in the sitting room, putting it on the sideboard while she arranged a side table closer to Lady Grace. She put the tray carefully on the table, making sure that Lady Grace could reach everything. There were such awful stories of elderly patients in hospital not being able to reach their meals, and starving to death.

'Very nice, thank you,' said Lady Grace, glancing over the tray. 'Would you approve of a glass of sherry before I have my supper? It would be civilized.'

'Of course,' said Jessica. She went to the decanter of sherry and poured out a glass of dry. Lady Grace always used exquisite cut glass glasses. 'Very civilized.'

'Bring over two glasses,' said Lady Grace.

Two glasses? Lady Grace was hitting the bottle this evening but Jessica did as she was asked. She put them on the side table.

'One of them is for you, Jess. Get that sherry down you and you might not look so peaky. Now tell me, how are you getting on with that awkward son of mine?'

'Not very well.'

'He needs some sense knocked into him. Send him into me, here. I'll tell him that you never left Upton Hall for one minute.'

'I want to prove to him that the documentation is false. That none of it is genuine. That I have never cheated on him. That it is all some ghastly scheme cooked up by the Burtons. Some sort of revenge.'

Lady Grace sipped at her sherry. 'I have a plan,' she said in a voice that brooked no rejection. 'I phoned Arthur earlier today and he is coming over for a game of bridge this evening. You were hardly concentrating on that whist this afternoon. We can keep an eye on Daniel and Lily for a couple of hours, though I draw the line at reading them stories.'

'So?' Jessica could not guess what was coming.

'Lucas can drive you over to this hotel, or whatever it is in Brighton, and sort it out, once and for all. Someone must remember whether they saw you. Take the documents, see if they are genuine or not. Mrs Harris told me this afternoon that they can do wonders with photocopying these days. She read it in a book.'

'Well, well,' said Jessica, suddenly feeling a lot better. She was not sure if it was the sherry or Lady Grace's confidence in her. She had an idea.

'You know all those Sunday paper glossy magazines? Have you got any of them around? I need a photograph of someone famous,' she said.

'Take what you want,' said Lady Grace, finishing her sherry. 'You'll go?'

'We'll go,' said Jessica. 'I think it's a brilliant idea.'

'Well, thank goodness for that. You are doing something sensible at last.'

★　★　★

Jessica threw on a fleece. She explained to Lily and Daniel that there would be no story tonight, because she had to go out suddenly

266

with Lucas. She explained that their grand-mother would be in the house with Arthur, her swimming friend, the man they met at Roxy's pool.

'We could ask him when can we come over again?' said Lily, not slow at seeing an opportunity.

'I don't think that is very polite,' said Jessica.

Daniel rummaged through his drawing pad and opened a page. 'Pool,' he said.

It was a drawing of the pool, perfectly in perspective, even to the ripples on the water, and the robes hanging on the wall.

'That's lovely,' said Jessica. 'I think Arthur would like to see that.'

Daniel closed the page, saying nothing more.

Jessica strode into the kitchen, a batch of magazines under her arm. Lucas was eating cheese and biscuits at the kitchen table. He looked up.

Jessica was in fully fledged Boadicea mode, spear at the ready. 'We are going out,' she said. 'Finish what you are eating. Lady Grace says she can look after Daniel and Lily for a couple of hours, and she has a friend arriving to play bridge.'

'I've had no supper,' said Lucas.

'Neither have I. Nor breakfast. Nor lunch. We are among the starving millions.' She picked up her shoulder bag. 'Shall we go in your car or mine?'

'Where are we going?'

'That inn of ill repute. The Double Cross Inn or whatever it's called. You may know where it is, but I certainly don't.'

'My car.'

They never said a word as Lucas drove towards Brighton. Jessica leafed through the magazines. It was not easy. She hated reading in a moving vehicle. It made her feel sick. But she found what she wanted, several of them, which was a big relief.

The Double Cross Inn was on the outskirts of Brighton. It was partly an old pair of farm cottages knocked together, with a modern attachment. A stark building like a Travelodge had been built on at the back. There was plenty of parking space in a tarmac yard.

'Bring back happy memories?' said Lucas sarcastically.

'Never seen it before,' said Jessica.

The bar was ancient, very pleasant, lots of old brasses and farm implements on the walls. It was full of customers, sitting around at booths and odd tables. None of the wooden furniture matched. Jessica went straight up to the bar.

'Can we see the manager please?' she asked.

'I am the manager.'

He was a sturdy man, grey-haired, worn out by years of pulling pints, his skin pitted with acne. 'Can I help you?'

'We'd like to ask you a few questions.'

'I'm a bit busy. But later on, when my help arrives. Do you want a drink?'

'A glass of house red, please,' said Jessica. 'And half a lager.'

She waited while the drinks were pulled. Even the wine was from a box. She paid for them.

'Why is this inn called the Double Cross Inn?' she asked.

'Because highwaymen were hanged here. Two at a time.'

Jessica shuddered. 'Happy times.'

She took the drinks over to Lucas. He was sitting at a rickety table with uneven legs. He looked ill at ease, brow furrowed. 'Why are we here?' he asked, taking the glass without a word. He folded a beer mat in half and put it under the shorter leg.

'Because I am going to prove to you that I have never been here before, with or without a companion.'

'I suppose you've bribed the manager. Slipped him a couple of twenties.'

'It was fifties actually.'

'Makes sense.'

'It makes no sense at all,' said Jessica.

14

It was half an hour before the manager came over to their table. It was an uneasy thirty minutes when they hardly spoke, sipped their drinks, looked everywhere but at each other. The inn was busy and the noise drowned their silence.

Jessica had turned down the corners of the magazine pages she was going to show the manager. She let Lucas open the conversation.

'My name is Lucas Coleman,' he began. 'There has been a slight family disagreement which we are hoping you can resolve.'

Slight family disagreement. Jessica almost choked on his words but managed to contain her irritation.

'Nice to meet you, Mr Coleman. Jeff Draper's the name.'

'Mr Draper, thank you for your time. We have information that this lady,' Lucas went on, hardly looking at Jessica, 'stayed at your inn for two nights this week, probably in the Travelodge. She stayed with Dr Fraser Burton.'

Jeff Draper looked at Jessica. 'I don't rightly know,' he said. 'We get so many people at the lodge, coming and going. You see, it's convenient for Brighton. I can't keep track of them all. I'd better go get the hotel register and we'll have a look.'

The manager returned with a red leather-bound book under his arm, and opened it out on the table. There was hardly room for it on the small table. The page was crammed with dated entries, names, car registration numbers, home addresses, some readable, some unreadable.

'And that's only today,' he said. 'It's been busy.' He flicked a couple of pages back.

'That's yesterday's and the day before . . . hold on, we're missing a page.' He did some quick checking. 'Well I never, there's a page missing.'

Lucas took the sheet out of his brief case. 'Is this the missing page?'

The manager took it from Lucas. Now it was Jeff Draper's turn to look annoyed. It was clearly a page from his register, same lists of information. 'I have to ask you where you got this page, Mr Coleman. I'm sure it is an offence to remove anything from a hotel register.'

'Be assured, I didn't do it. The sheet was faxed to me yesterday, to my . . . office.' Lucas almost said 'surgery'. 'As you will see, Dr Fraser Burton signed in for two nights, there.'

'Room fourteen,' the manager confirmed. 'I remember it now. It was pretty late at night and he seemed in a hurry. They didn't have much luggage, just a bag between them.'

'And who was with him?'

'I believe it was his wife.'

'Did she sign the register?'

'No. We don't usually ask questions of that nature. We assumed it was his wife. I think he signed for her, put ditto marks. Yes, here are the ditto marks under car registration, address, etc.'

'But the name underneath his is my name,' said Jessica. 'Signed in my handwriting.'

The manager look mystified, out of his depth. 'Really, I don't know, miss. I know nothing about this.'

Jessica produced the glossy Sunday supplement magazines. 'Would you kindly identify the woman in this photograph and this one?' She turned a page. 'And again on this page. Do you know who this is?'

'Of course, I do, miss. Everyone knows who that is. That's Posh Spice, the model who's married to David Beckman. Always getting their pictures in the papers, regular like. I think her name is Victoria.'

'Does she look anything like the woman who booked in with Dr Burton? Do you recognize the hair, the black bobbed hair, with one side longer than the other?'

'Now you mention it, miss, that lady did

have funny hair, cut different lengths either side of her face. I thought it was a mistake and she ought to go and have it tidied up. She was quite a bit older than this smart Posh Spice, but the same hair.'

Jessica sank back in the chair, relief washing over her face. 'Thank you,' she said. 'The lady with Dr Burton was his wife, Amanda Burton. It wasn't me at all.'

'Nothing like you, miss, if you don't mind me saying so. And she was in a right temper, demanding this and that and at that time of night. I told her there's a hospitality tray in the room to suit everybody's taste and I could do no more.'

Lucas was looking confused. 'I don't know what to think. But Jessica's signature is on the next line.'

'If you don't mind me saying so, sir, it's quite obvious to me. This page was torn out sometime, probably the next day, because there are more entries underneath. But it's not the same page because it doesn't have a ragged edge. It has a smooth edge. It's a photocopy of my page. If you look at my register, you can see bits that were left behind, as if it was torn out in a hurry.'

'That's what Mrs Harris said,' Jessica said triumphantly. 'She said crooks often photocopied things and you could never tell the difference from the original. Except in this case, there should have been a tiny ragged edge where it was torn out.'

'And where would he get your signature?' Lucas's voice was gruff now.

'From the hospital. It's in all the records. Nurses are always signing for things. He'd have no trouble looking in an old file. You should know that. He got my signature from somewhere, cut it out and put it over the ditto marks on the empty line below his signature, levelled it up, then photocopied it. No one would be able to tell at first glance.'

'And the credit card receipt is correct?'

Jeff Draper looked at it. 'Yes, sir. Room fourteen for two nights. Perfectly correct. I believe they had some extras but they were paid for separately. Now, if you don't mind, I have to get back to the bar. It's getting crowded and my assistant is looking harassed. Big crowd just come in.'

'I wonder if I could have another glass of your house red,' said Jessica, throwing caution to the wind. She felt like celebrating.

'Of course, miss.'

Jeff returned with a brimming glass. He was grinning. 'On the house, miss.' He was not daft. He'd worked it all out. He hoped the nice young lady would be happy now.

Lucas didn't say much on the drive home, but he drove carefully, not taking any chances. It was dark now and the flashing headlights lit up the road ahead, catching the eyes of rabbits sitting on the wayside grass.

'They are all going blind again,' he said.

'How sad. Poor things,' said Jessica.

A fox dashed across the road, his bushy tail streaming fiery red. He leaped into a hedge and was safe, bounding across a low-lying Sussex field.

'It's the badgers I worry about,' said Jessica. 'They are such slow old things. They don't stand a chance.'

'I see a lot of dead badgers,' said Lucas. 'Road-kill. Coming home late.'

Jessica clutched the magazines to her chest. She felt she ought to cut out all the photographs of Victoria Beckham and pin them round her room. Posh Spice had saved her though she would never know about it in her Californian castle.

They came slowly up the drive to Upton Hall. There were lights on as if Lady Grace and Arthur were still playing bridge. Arthur's car was parked neatly to one side.

Jessica got out of the car and went up the steps to the front door. She turned round.

Lucas was immobile at the wheel of his car, gripping the wheel.

'I'll say goodnight, Lucas. I don't think we need say anything more. I'll make sure that Lady Grace gets safely to bed. I'm sure you need a good night's sleep.'

'Jessica,' Lucas began, hesitantly.

'Tomorrow,' said Jessica firmly. He had made her suffer. She was not ready to forgive him.

★   ★   ★

Lady Grace came out into the hall. She looked enquiringly at Jessica, dying to ask but good manners holding her back.

'All sorted, done and dusted,' said Jessica. 'It wasn't me at all staying at the Double Cross Inn. The manager recognized a look-alike photo of Fraser's wife, Amanda Burton. And the hotel register had been skilfully photo-copied with my signature on a line.'

'That's good. Now we can have some peace at last around here. Daniel and Lily are asleep. Bert kindly escorted me up the stairs in case I had trouble, but of course, I didn't. I can manage the stairs quite well now.'

'You're a star,' said Jessica. She was mentally exhausted. She didn't want to talk any more. She wanted to sleep and sleep. But there was the nightly ritual to get through first. She was still employed at Upton Hall, for the time being.

'And did my son apologize to you?'

'No, not exactly. But he did stop biting my head off. I think it will take some time.'

'That damned Coleman pride.'

'He might get round to it,' said Jessica.

'He might be too late,' said Lady Grace shrewdly.

Arthur followed her out into the hall. He was putting his coat on. 'Time to hit the road. It's been a lovely evening, Grace. I'll beat you next time. Just out of practice,' he chuckled.

'Next week?' Grace was not slow.

'And swimming? Would it be convenient for you to bring Lady Grace and the children for a swim soon, Jessica? Roxy is touring somewhere in the world. She won't be home for at least three weeks.'

'We'll fix a date,' Jessica promised. It all depended if she was still at Upton Hall. She wanted to work out her three months contract. Daniel and Lily were almost like her own children. But Lucas might have other ideas. Their marriage was definitely off. She couldn't marry a man who didn't trust her.

Jessica went into the kitchen, leaving Lady Grace to see her guest off the premises. She heard laughter coming from the porch which was a good sign. She heated some milk and laid a tray with two digestive biscuits. Lady Grace was capable of seeing herself to bed these days.

Lady Grace was sitting up in bed, her hair plaited, her face relaxed and composed.

'So we both had a very satisfactory evening,' she said.

'So it seems,' said Jessica, putting the tray on the bedside table. 'Can I fetch you anything else?'

'No, thank you, Jess. Do the usual locking up, please. We don't want any intruders. Arthur suggested starting a bridge club for we old-timers. We've plenty of room here. Once a month, perhaps? What do you think, Jess?'

'What a great idea,' said Jessica. 'Old friends. Couldn't be better.'

'Goodnight, Jess.'

'Goodnight, Lady Grace.'

Jessica closed the door carefully. Daniel and Lily were both sleeping peacefully. Everything in Daniel's room was lined in rows, as visual, different rows to those the night before. Lily had Floppy Ears in bed with her. Even he looked more at ease for once.

She checked her emails. There was an email from Daniel. It said: Don't GO. The 'G' was the right way round for once, but she got the message.

Lucas had not appeared. She waited in the kitchen in case he came looking for a late supper, but there was no sign of him. That damned Coleman pride. What did Lady Grace mean by that? Lucas or her husband?

Jessica opened the door to the refrigerator. She knew she ought to eat. She could not exist on her nerves. It was not sensible, but all she could swallow was some set vanilla yogurt. It slipped down without any effort.

Bridge parties and swimming. They were setting themselves up for fun ahead in the future months when she would not be here. Once Lady Grace was fit enough to drive, they could take themselves over to Roxy's pool. They would not need Jessica any more. She could take up her post in Sheffield and try to forget them all.

But she knew that she would never forget them. She still loved Lucas. And she certainly loved the children. Mrs Harris was a good friend and Lady Grace had earned her affection. It was going to be hard to leave them all.

Jessica went through the usual routine of locking up and setting the alarms. She had cleared her name but the cost had been exorbitant. She had lost Lucas and he was the only man in the world for her.

There were murderous feelings in her heart

that night as she went to bed. The Burtons had ruined her life. If either of them ever showed their faces again at Upton Hall, it would be hard to stop herself taking a kitchen knife to them both. She could not understand why they were both so evil-minded. They had good jobs, excellent salaries, plenty of money to spend. But they didn't have happiness.

Perhaps that was the answer.

15

Lucas was gone again, next morning, before anyone was down for breakfast. Jessica heard the Porsche driving away, the distinctive engine noise waking her up after a restless sleep. She did not know how to put things right between them.

The ball was in his court but perhaps he didn't know how to serve. She smiled to herself at this ridiculous analogy. Her brain was not yet in top gear.

Lily bounced into the bedroom, carrying Floppy Ears by his ears. 'We didn't get a story last night,' she said. 'Grandma can't read.'

'Your grandmother can read but only her kind of books. Your books are rather different. Shorter words and lots of pictures.'

Lily digested this information. 'OK, so when our books don't have pictures any more, then Grandma will be able to read them?'

Jessica laughed. 'You'll have to see. Now what are you hiding behind your back? Is that a book, I espy? Is it a book I will have to read before I get any peace?'

'Yes, yes, yes!'

The door was open so Daniel could also hear the story if he was awake. Jessica made sure she used her nurse's voice that would carry. Sometimes she had to use that voice if A & E was crowded with drunks and drug-addicts, occasionally on a ward if there was unexpected turmoil.

'This afternoon, after school, we'll go down to Worthing and have a picnic on the beach before the cold weather sets in. Would you like that? There won't be many more days of good weather this year. It's your early afternoon, isn't it?'

'A picnic! Lovely, lovely. Without plates? Daniel will come too and we'll find more shells and paddle in the sea.'

'You might find it is too cold.'

'No, no, it won't be too cold.' Lily was pretty sure.

Daniel sent Jessica an email which said simply: *piknik*.

It required mammoth organization if Lady Grace was coming too. She would need a folding chair on the beach. Mrs Harris prepared a picnic basket of goodies, all easy finger food with two thermoses of hot water so that Jessica could make tea. Lady Grace would certainly require freshly made tea. It was always Earl Grey, of course, in the afternoon.

Jessica was determined that life would go on at Upton Hall even if Lucas cut himself off from her. It would break her heart, but then her heart was already broken, so how could it hurt any more? She had a shut-down look, shielding the pain.

Mrs Harris was delighted that her photo-copying theory had been proved right. She was also interested in the highwaymen being hanged at the Double Cross Inn.

'Fancy that. There's so much history everywhere. And we don't know half of it,' she said.

'Does anyone know the history of Upton Hall?'

Mrs Harris shook her head. 'No one has ever had time to research the history of Upton Hall. The house has been here a long time. Look at the stone room, all those huge slabs of slate on the floor and the big timber post holding up the ceiling. That could tell a story or two.'

'Is it part of the original farmhouse, do you think?'

'I won't go in there at night, I tell you.'

It was the first time Mrs Harris had admitted to feeling anything unusual about Upton Hall. Yet the man she loved had been brought home here and she had laid him out. There must have been many deaths in the house and in the grounds over the centuries, but Jessica did not feel anything strange. And she had been up late many times, seeing to Lady Grace or to the children. Or waiting up for Lucas to come home in the small hours.

It was something she could do during her last few weeks at Upton Hall. She could research the history of the house on the Internet, find books in the library and records at the church. It would keep her mind occupied, so that she did not dwell on her unhappiness.

She had often told her patients the same thing, when they lost someone they loved. Keep busy, do something positive. Live each day for the day. Now she was telling herself the same, now that she had lost Lucas.

For Jessica felt sure that she had lost him. There had been no reconciliation, no words of apology from Lucas, not a single act of kindness. Last night had been a relief that she had cleared her name, but he had said nothing, done nothing to help ease the pain that she felt. Damned Coleman pride, Jessica thought. This was something over which she had no say. It was in his genes.

Everything was packed into the car when the children arrived home from school, earlier than usual. Lady Grace was sitting in the front passenger seat, while the children climbed into the back. She had decided that a picnic might be a pleasant change.

'Please wait. I haven't got Floppy Ears,' announced Lily, trying to get out again but Jessica had already put on the child door locks.

'He won't mind about being left at home for once. You know how he hates getting wet,' said Jessica. 'And we haven't really time to go back for him. The days are getting shorter and we want to have as much time as possible on the beach, don't we?'

Lily absorbed this information. 'If the days are getting shorter, where does the rest of the day go?' she asked.

'We get longer, darker evenings,' said Jessica, hoping this would satisfy the little girl's curiosity.

'So the day becomes an evening instead of being a day?' Lily went on relentlessly. She was trying to take this in.

'Why don't we play I Spy before I get a headache,' said Lady Grace quickly. 'Let me see. I spy with my little eye something beginning with T.'

'Tree,' said Daniel.

It was a shock. Daniel had actually contributed a word of his own that was not a parrot word. It was a moment of joy. But Jessica said nothing. She knew Daniel would not like the attention.

'It's your turn now, Daniel. You choose something for us to guess.'

But this was beyond him so Jessica took over his turn. It was simpler.

The game lasted the drive into Worthing but Daniel did not speak again although it was obvious that he often had the answer. Jessica found a place to park along the sea front and fed some money into the meter.

The tide was higher than she had expected, thrashing against the shingle shore, shifting pebbles. No running along on the sand this afternoon. They found a sheltered spot against a groyne, not too far along as Lady Grace found it difficult to walk even with a stick. She took Jessica's arm, hesitating. She was looking at the pounding sea as if she had never seen it before. She had not realized that it was going to be a picnic by the sea.

'Are you sure this is safe for me to walk on?' she said.

'It will help with your balance,' said Jessica, offering her arm. 'Take your time, don't hurry. Feel each step. We've got all day.' She was also carrying a folding beach chair.

'We haven't got all day if the day is becoming the evening,' Lily informed them.

Lady Grace was glad to sit down when they reached the groyne. There was a blustery southerly wind and it sheltered them well. They had a good view of the long pier reaching out to sea on its spindly legs. There were several windsurfers making use of the southerly, their colourful sails like swerving butterflies. Jessica went back for the picnic tea and the folding table which was solely for making this cup of tea. Lady Grace had to have a certain amount of civilization, even for a picnic.

Lily and Daniel were soon down to the water's edge, throwing pebbles into the waves, escaping the wavelets that washed too near their feet. The tide was coming in slowly so they got caught several times with shrieks of laughter.

'The tide's coming in,' said Lady Grace. 'That's the blessing of a shelving beach, you can always see how far it will come in. We're all right here. This chair sounds a bit creaky. Where did you find it?'

'In the stables,' said Jessica. 'I don't think it has been used for years. Mrs Harris gave it a clean up.'

'I used to love the sea,' Lady Grace went on, more to herself. 'When you swim out past the fringe of seaweed, the water is lovely, so cool and deep. Ouch! I think I heard something. I think the canvas is splitting. It's probably rotten.' She got up quickly, holding onto the top of the wooden groyne.

'Hold on, lady. I'll soon sort you out. Got just what you need.'

A lean and sunburnt man in a fawn sunhat and khaki shorts was striding across the shingle with a folded deckchair in his hand. It was the beach deckchair attendant, quick to spot a new customer.

'Your chair's had it,' he said. 'Look, it's splitting along the bottom seam. Another minute and you'd have fallen right through. You'd have got a nasty bump.'

'How convenient that I heard it going and got up when I did,' said Lady Grace in her don't-argue-with-me voice. She didn't care to be sorted out, as he had promised.

'These are really comfortable deckchairs,' he went on. 'Adjustable height, canvas new this season. I'll put it up for you. You can have it half price as it's the end of the day.'

'I think I might go back to the car,' said Lady Grace.

'What and miss this lovely bit of sunshine? The last of the season. It'll be cold and wet next week, mark my words. I'll be packing up my chairs for the winter.'

'That's very kind of you,' said Jessica quickly. 'If you would kindly put it up for Lady Grace. I can never sort these chairs out!' She opened her purse for some money, hoping a pound would be enough.

The man stopped in the middle of sorting out the mechanics of unfolding the deckchair. 'Grace Coleman? Is it Grace Coleman? Well, I never. You won't remember me. I'm Mark Adams, one of the members of the junior cross channel relay team. Don't do it now, of course, long past the age of any junior team. That was years ago.'

Mark Adams settled the chair firmly into the shingle and against the groyne. He held out his hand and Lady Grace let him help her into it. She seemed shaken by his introduction.

'No, I'm afraid I don't remember you,' she said.

'I was one of the noisy youngsters. You told me off a couple of times for not paying attention to the coach.'

'Did I?'

'We were used to it. You took your swimming very seriously. Quite right, too, because you were one of the champions. Of course, it's all changed now. Different committee, different rules. But they still meet early mornings.'

'It's been nice meeting you again,' said Lady Grace, recovering her composure. 'But if you don't mind, we are going to have our tea now.'

'Quite understand,' said Mark Adams. 'Don't worry about returning the chair to the stack. I'll do it for you. Got a couple of lively kids, you have,' he nodded towards Lily and Daniel and to Jessica. 'I like to see kids enjoying themselves.'

He turned to go, then turned back. He was lean and sinewy, arms muscled and burnt brown by the sun. He looked as if he worked hard all summer, running the deckchair business along the beach. 'Ankles got better, did they? All right now?'

Lady Grace looked even more shaken. 'My ankles? What do you mean? What do you know about my ankles?'

'Got torn to ribbons on that barbed wire, didn't they? Nasty business. The council ought to have cleared the beach. I reckon you could have sued them.'

'I — I don't remember. It was a long time ago . . . '

'I thought you were a goner,' said Mark Adams. 'You were going to drown in that deep water. The barbed wire was twisted round your ankles, all rusty and rotten. And your hair had got caught in the wire when you bent down to try to get your feet free.'

'My hair . . . ' said Lady Grace faintly. She had not mentioned her hair to anyone. No one knew that her long dark hair had been caught in the barbed wire. She'd worn it then, as she did now, in an elaborate French pleat, pinned up with combs.

'I had to cut your hair off,' Mark went on. 'It was the only thing to do and there was no time to waste. You were gasping for air. Had to get your head up somehow. Luckily I had a knife on me. I always carry a knife.' He patted his back pocket. It was buttoned down.

'You cut my hair off?'

He grinned. 'Sorry, it was more of a hack off job than a nice trim and style. I was a little out of practice in the hair department. Then I got your feet free of the wire. They were torn and bleeding. Pretty nasty.'

'So it was you who saved me,' said Lady Grace, pausing. 'I never knew. I never even tried to find out. I wanted to forget it all. This is the first time I've been to the sea since that day.'

'Not surprised. It was enough to put anyone off. You nearly drowned.'

'Did your feet get cut as well?'

'Right mess, they were. And they got infected. I wanted to go into the army but they wouldn't take me. All that marching, I expect. Still, I walk miles along the beach every day, no trouble. Well, I'll leave you ladies to your tea. Nice meeting you again, Mrs Coleman.'

He was gone before there was a chance to say any more, probably spotted another customer. He hadn't taken Jessica's pound coin.

'And I still haven't thanked him,' said Lady Grace. She looked desolate. 'What shall I do, Jess? I must thank him somehow. I could hardly give him a tip, could I? It would be most inappropriate.'

'I think he could see that you were really upset, being reminded of the accident again, remembering that awful day. It was enough for him to see that you were well and had recovered.'

'But it's not enough,' said Lady Grace, firmly. 'I must do something.'

'Let's think about it,' said Jessica. 'We may get a bright idea.'

The children came back, sensing teatime, scrambling up the shelving shingle, waving wet shoes in their hands. 'We're all wet,' said Lily happily.

'How fortunate that I brought some dry socks and trainers,' said Jessica, delving into her beach bag.

Tea was a success in every way, despite Lily's preference for eating out of a box to eating off a plate. Lady Grace enjoyed her cup of Earl Grey and even found an appetite for a home-made scone with strawberry jam and cream, She spent a long time just gazing at the sea as the waves pounded the shore, rising slowly higher, creeping up the steep shingle. She was remembering the days when she had been a champion swimmer with a promising future.

'I don't know what I could get that young man, the beach attendant,' she said, as they were on the drive home in the gathering dusk. Daniel had collected seaweed this time, and the inside of the car smelt of the stuff. For once Lady Grace did not complain.

'You could get him a bicycle,' said Lily. 'I saw him walking miles along the beach. And he was limping a bit. I expect his feet hurt with all that walking.'

Lady Grace was about to say that a bicycle would be a ridiculous idea, but stopped herself. It would be a start and she had to start somewhere.

'You might have something there,' she said quietly.

16

Lady Grace retired to her bed earlier than usual. The afternoon had been mentally tiring and the surfeit of fresh sea air had made her sleepy. She did not want any supper but required her usual milk and biscuits later on.

Daniel came into the kitchen and started wandering around, poking into things and opening drawers and cupboards, getting in Jessica's way. Mrs Harris had gone to her Bingo. He was carrying his plastic bag of seaweed.

'Do you want somewhere to keep your seaweed?' Jessica asked.

'Weed,' he said.

'How about a plate or a jug or an old plastic container?'

He shook his head and went to the sink, turning on a tap. He let the water run, tipping his bag of seaweed into the running water, watching the strands curl and swirl into a dark mass. He had collected rather a lot.

Jessica went into the walk-in pantry, to the back where Mrs Harris kept her spare jam jars. She came out with several jam jars perched on her fingers. 'Would these be any good?'

He nodded enthusiastically, arranged the jam jars in rows on the draining board and began to fill each one with water and a few strands of seaweed. Jessica watched him from afar. He didn't like anyone close, leaning over him.

'You've got several different kinds there. Tomorrow we could look them up on the Internet so that we can give them names.'

'Names,' he said, without looking up.

Jessica left him absorbed in his task of tanking up the seaweed. She had Lily to put to bed, read a story, and then hope that Lucas would come home and they could talk at last. Surely that stubborn Coleman pride would have come to its senses by now. She couldn't endure this not-knowing for much longer. She wanted to be with him, to feel his arms around her again.

Lily had worn herself out on the beach so it was a quick bath and an even quicker story. Now that he was eight years old, Daniel stayed up a little later, needed little supervision going to bed. He preferred to wash alone.

Jessica made herself a cup of black coffee and took it into the library, turned on the television and flopped down in front of it. She did not want to watch any mindless programme, but hoped there might be a good drama or documentary. She needed something to take her mind off Lucas and the current predicament.

Perhaps she had made a mistake, searching for the truth. Perhaps he would have preferred to forgive her in a lordly way and make her pay for it in a marriage of misery. But that was surely not his way, not his nature and certainly not hers. His love had seemed so strong and so true. He had meant every word he said and his warm and passionate kisses had come straight from the heart. He had wanted her and the strength of his body close to hers told her how much.

Fire and ice, Lucas had once said to her. Had they had the fire and this was now the ice? Maybe the fire had consumed them for a while and now the ice froze over their love.

Jessica fell asleep in front of the television, her coffee untouched. The sea air had obviously brushed away the cobwebs that had prevented her from sleeping the last few nights. She dreamed she was in a boat, a small boat, but she could not see who was rowing. He had his back to her.

A shrill, strident bell projected itself through the dream. At first she thought it was a bell from a nearby lighthouse in her dream, then she roused herself and realized that it was Lady Grace's bell.

Even the bell sounded annoyed.

She shook herself awake and tried to stop herself from racing up the stairs. This was not the time for a careless accident. She'd seen enough falls downstairs at A & E.

'I'm sorry,' Jessica said. 'Your milk is late, I know. I dozed off.'

'It's very late,' said Lady Grace, who did not admit that she had also dozed off. She looked accusingly at her bedside clock. 'I'm not used to having it so late.'

'I'll fetch it straight away,' said Jessica, turning away before she got the nightly instructions about two biscuits — as if she had the brain of a peanut.

In the kitchen she noticed that Daniel's jars of seaweed were still on the draining board, but he had emptied the sink of water. She must remember to put them in a safe place before Mrs Harris came in. That good lady might empty them down the drain.

Jessica made the drink and carried the tray upstairs to Lady Grace. She put it on the bedside table.

'Thank you, Jess,' said Lady Grace. 'You know how to do this Internet ordering thing, don't you?'

'I can find my way around a bit.'

'Can you find your way around this Argos firm that sells things and order a bicycle, a good one mind you, to be sent to Mark Adams. No mention of my name. I want him to receive it anonymously. Don't you think that's a good idea? To send him an anonymous gift? After all, a bicycle hardly equates to saving a life, does it?'

Lady Grace seemed pleased with the idea and for remembering Argos, the mail order firm. She might get their catalogue and have a look through it.

'I think he'd like that. Surprise presents are always fun. I'll look Argos up on the Internet and see how you order online,' said Jessica.

'It could be addressed to him care of The Pier. I saw some of his deckchairs on the pier. They'd make sure he got it, wouldn't they?'

'I'm sure they know him. Goodnight, Lady Grace.'

'Goodnight, Jess.'

Jessica crossed over the landing and peeped into Lily's room. She was fast asleep, Floppy Ears on the pillow beside her. They both looked as if they had had a good day.

Daniel's bedroom was in the dark which was unusual. He had not switched on his glow lamps or put on a tape of soft sounds. Jessica hesitated in the doorway. She did not want to wake him by putting on the main light. The landing light shone weakly into the room. His shells were rigidly in rows. His drawing books, his shoes, his school uniform folded, everything in its allotted place.

She looked at his bed. The duvet was flat and untouched. There was no dark head on the pillow. The room was empty.

He must be somewhere in the house, curled up on a chair, or drawing on the floor, little monkey. He'd taken advantage of her falling asleep.

Jessica made a quick detour of the house, expecting to find Daniel at every turn. But he was nowhere. She could not find him anywhere. It was getting dark outside. Perhaps he was doing some mysterious errand out in the garden, drawing the moon?

His anorak had gone from the clothes cupboard by the back door. Jessica began to feel worried. Where on earth had the little boy gone? He was tall for his age but he was still only eight years old.

She heard the Porsche coming up the drive and ran outside. Daniel had probably gone to meet his father. That was it. What could be more natural than going down the drive to meet his father?

Jessica went onto the drive and waved at the Porsche. It slowed down. 'Have you got Daniel?' she asked, keeping any worry out of her voice.

'Daniel? No, why should I?'

'I thought perhaps he'd come out to meet you. I thought . . . ' she faltered.

'Don't you know where he is?' Lucas said forcefully.

'No, I don't know where he is. I've lost him. I can't find him.'

'Have you made a thorough search of the house and the stables?'

'I didn't go into the stables,' said Jessica.

'Why not?'

Because she did not want to meet Lucas. He lived in the stables. She could not go in there, in case there were secrets.

Lucas swung the car round towards the stables and stopped outside. He raced into the building. Jessica began searching the gardens. The humidity was closing in on her, dark clouds gathering. The sky was the colour of dark slate. A storm was on its way. She could feel it in the air.

'Daniel, Daniel . . . ' she called repeatedly. But of course he would not answer. He would not say anything. Nor would they be able to hear anything. How could they find an autistic boy in the dark who wouldn't speak?

She heard Lucas returning in his car. He pushed the passenger door open.

'Get in,' he shouted.

She obeyed, afraid not to. She was already very cold, with fear and with worry. But she steeled herself. She got in and strapped on the safety belt.

'I've searched the house,' said Lucas. 'But there's no sign of Daniel. I have told my mother that we are going out and will lock up when we return. I said nothing about the children. Have you any idea where Daniel might have gone?'

Jessica shook her head. 'We went to Worthing today and had a picnic tea on the beach. Lily and Daniel had a great time. Daniel came home with a bag full of bits of seaweed. I left him in the kitchen, filling jam jars with the stuff.'

'What else?'

'I don't know what else,' said Jessica, desperately. 'There isn't anything else. Who knows what goes on in Daniel's mind? He could have decided to do anything, go anywhere. He has no idea of time or distance, let alone telling anyone of his plans. I know it's partly my fault for falling asleep, but I was so tired. I haven't been sleeping well lately . . . '

She let her voice trail off into a landscape of quiet despair. She'd been thinking about Lucas, going over the situation again and again, wondering how she could put things right. Wondering if they would ever regain that heady happiness.

'We'll go look for him. He can't have gone

far. I'll drive slowly, you look on the paths and near hedges. Here's a torch. I'm sure he'll keep to roads, something that he knows about from the school bus and drives with you. He doesn't like anything unknown.'

Jessica nodded. It was already starting to rain, a fine mist clouding the windscreen. Daniel had his anorak on but not much else. She shivered.

'You're cold,' said Lucas. 'There's a fleece on the back seat. Put it on.'

It was the first kind word he had said to her for days. Jessica reached into the back and pulled on his old navy fleece. It smelt of him and she breathed it in as if he was himself wrapping his arms round her. But the moment vanished as they turned out of the drive onto the roadway.

They drove with the passenger window down so that Jessica could flash the torch onto the paths and verges. Tatters of rain were coming down steadily and soon her sleeve and face were pitted with drops.

Finding Daniel became even more remote as the rain thickened and the windscreen wipers struggled to keep the vision clear. Branches swayed overhead, wailing like banshees.

'Daniel, Daniel . . . ' she continued to call. Lucas was watching the other side of the road, driving slowly and steadily. Moths collected in his headlights for their doom. They came to the village of Eastly, wondering which way Daniel might have chosen.

'Which way?' asked Lucas.

'I don't know.'

'Guess. Try to think as Daniel would think. You know him better than anyone else.' His voice was dry and bitter.

'He had a bag of seaweed,' said Jessica. 'But he had brought home an awful lot of seaweed, far more than the few jam jars would hold.'

'So?'

'Perhaps he's returning the seaweed to the sea.'

'You mean, he's walking to Worthing, to put the seaweed back into the sea?' Lucas sounded incredulous.

'I'm only guessing,' she cried. 'He wouldn't like to think of it dying. It would worry him. He wouldn't wait till morning. He would have to do it now.'

Lucas turned onto the main dual-carriage way towards Worthing, his face set grimly. The rain was now torrential, almost blinding him. Jessica was soaked, her hair flattened against her head. The car heater was on but the heat flew straight out of the windows.

Then she saw him. A small figure, plodding

on, head down, barely visible in the downpour. 'There he is,' she cried. 'Over there.'

Lucas spotted him too in his headlights, drew ahead and then slammed on the brakes. Jessica wrenched open the car door and ran towards the boy over the long wet grass. She clasped him into her arms, cradling him, her face against his wet hood.

'Daniel, you're all right! We've found you. Thank goodness. Thank goodness.' Jessica held him close, for the first time ever. He did not stiffen but seemed to lean into her, the fear of the night taking away his usual reserve.

'Get into the car, love. We'll soon have you home, warm and dry,' she said, guiding him towards the car. She somehow steered him onto the front passenger seat and then got herself in as well. Daniel ended up, curled on her lap, her arms still firmly round him. He did not resist.

'Hello, Son,' said Lucas, turning the car slowly at the next intersection. He realized that Jessica could not fasten the seat belt. 'Not a good night for a walk about.'

Jessica felt the boy's weight against her and she could smell the tang of the seaweed. Somewhere, on him, probably inside his anorak was the bag of seaweed.

'Were you walking to Worthing, Daniel?'

she asked. She felt only the merest of nods.

'With your bag of seaweed?'

'Weed,' came his muffled voice.

'Were you going to put it back into the sea?'

'Sea.'

'We'll do it tomorrow,' she assured him. 'The tide would be on its way out by now and we'd never find the sea in the dark. Seaweed is pretty sturdy stuff, you know. It'll survive till tomorrow.'

Daniel was almost asleep by the time they reached Upton Hall. It was the first time he had ever allowed anyone to hold him or touch him. But he had almost fallen asleep in Jessica's arms and, for both of them, it was a milestone.

Lucas carried Daniel indoors, upstairs to the family bathroom. He took off the boy's sodden clothes and put them and the bag of seaweed on the floor. It was only a quick wash in warm water as Daniel was half asleep. In no time he was curled up in bed, warm and dry, part of him knowing how much he was loved.

Jessica was downstairs in the kitchen, making a pot of tea, knowing Lucas needed a hot drink too. She was still in the soaked fleece. Everything was wet. She knew she looked a sight but she didn't care. Daniel was safe and that was all that mattered.

Lucas stood in the doorway holding an armful of wet clothes.

'He's asleep.'

'Good,' said Jessica. 'I'll put the rescued seaweed in a bucket.'

Lucas came over to her, awkwardly. He was as handsome as ever, but there were lines etched on his face, as if he had aged. Rain was spiking his hair and his clothes were wet, but his eyes were smiling with a quiet hope.

'Are you ever going to forgive me, Jessica?' he said. 'I've been such a fool. A complete idiot.'

17

Lucas was standing barely a few inches away from her. A lump formed in her throat. He was looking at her with an odd, searching look. Jessica refused to allow any romantic thoughts to flood her mind. Lucas had to say them. He had to heal all the hurt.

'Jessica,' he said, his voice gravelly and full of anguish. 'We must put this right. I don't want to lose you.'

Jessica was aware that she was very cold. One side of the fleece was soaked through and the rest almost as wet from holding Daniel in the car. But she had to stay and listen to what Lucas had to say.

'You almost have,' she said, trying to stop her teeth from chattering.

He groaned. 'I know. I don't know what devil got into me. I felt I couldn't go through intrigue and deception again, even when you proved to me that it was all lies. I hadn't the sense to trust you.' He bent and touched the lovely line of her mouth. 'Please forgive me. Please take me back into your life.'

'Take you back?' said Jessica. 'After what you've put me through? You expect me to fall into your arms and say everything is all right? Will it happen again? How many times will it happen? I don't want to be constantly living on a knife edge.' Her feelings washed over her body in a wave of pain. She had suffered so much in the last few days.

Her mind was teeming with angry, bitter things to say even though she loved him. No way was he going to walk in and say he was sorry and everything would be back to square one. There was no way she could handle this now. The search for Daniel had drained her. She was exhausted. She was wet and she was cold. This was not the time for soul-searching.

'I've made some tea,' said Jessica, pouring out two mugfuls. 'Perhaps we should put some warmth inside ourselves before we talk any more.'

Lucas took a step back with his mug of tea. 'Always the nurse,' he said with a note of sadness. 'Where's my fiery, passionate woman?'

'Your fiery, passionate woman is soaking wet and close to hypothermia.'

It was the first time he had looked at her physical condition and it shocked him. He gulped down some tea and then put his hands lightly on her shoulders, turning her in the direction of the stairs.

'Bath and bed, in that order,' he said.

The terse words meant more to Jessica

than any flowery declarations. Some sort of communication sprang up between them. She let him propel her out of the kitchen, taking her tea with her, sipping the hot liquid. She wanted to be looked after, to be taken care of as lovers took care of each other, whatever the world presented.

He turned on the landing towards her yellow bedroom. She was too numb to wonder what was going to happen. The swirling feelings inside her were all part of the trauma of the night's events. They had found Daniel. They did not have to worry about him for a while.

Somewhere on the way upstairs, she lost her sodden shoes. The soft carpet was bliss underfoot. Lucas steered her into the primrose bathroom, leaned over and put in the plug and turned on both taps.

'Get undressed,' he said.

But her fingers were to cold to obey. She struggled with zips and buttons and hooks. At some point Lucas took over, his face intently serious. He unzipped the fleece and removed it. Then he helped her out of her clinging wet jeans. He could barely keep his hands from stroking her long brown legs. He caught a glimpse of her white lace briefs and his desire was on fire.

He pulled her T-shirt over her head, his

fingers skimming her skin, and her heart turned over as his touch became a sensitive delight. How could he know what he was doing to her? Stripping her of her clothes as if she was another eight-year-old?

Lucas could not hold back his feelings as she stood before him in lacy bra and pants. His lips parted in anticipation and he drew her to him, taking her mouth into his, drowning his feelings in an intimate imprisonment.

He ran his fingers lightly over her thigh, hip and waist, caressing her skin with a feathery touch, outlining her soft curves. Then he realized she was shivering, from cold or from passion, he did not know.

'Into the bath,' he said.

He helped her step in and lower herself into the warm water. His eyes were clouded with desire. He could not bear to look at her loveliness. A great wave of tenderness overcame him. Jessica was his woman, the only woman in his life and he wanted her for his wife.

He had not put on the light and only light from the bedroom shone into the bathroom. It was a softness that shadowed any flaws. He took the tablet of jasmine soap and rubbed the suds over Jessica's arms and shoulders. Then he found her feet and legs and gently soothed them with massage and kneading, each little toe receiving loving attention.

Jessica began to relax, sliding further into the warm water. His hands were magic. She did not care what he did to her. She did not have the strength to resist him even if she wanted to. She was starved for this kind of attention. Tears stung her eyes.

Then Lucas was unhooking her bra and sliding his hands over her breasts, cupping them with sweet sensations, letting the suds soften his touch. Jessica moaned, stretching her lacerated nerves, almost unable to keep her fragile composure. They were meant to be together. She was being swept into a torrent of wanting.

Jessica lifted up her arms towards him, not saying anything, sending an unspoken message racing out to him.

Lucas slipped out of his clothes, and with infinite care, stepped into the bath. The water almost overlapped the side. He lowered himself down onto her and without a word, his body told her everything she had ever wanted to know. He held his mouth on hers, reluctant to break the spell, wrapping her body closely, hungry for her, their storm of desire gathering.

★ ★ ★

It was long after dawn when they awoke, in her bed, still wrapped around each other. Jessica could not believe that she was seeing Lucas's dark head on the pillow beside her. He was still asleep, long eyelashes fluttering, breathing soft and even. She studied his ruggedly handsome features and stretched her weakened body. She was spent and sated.

'Lily always charges in here, early morning,' she whispered in his ear.

'She knows me,' Lucas said, half asleep. 'I'm her daddy. She's seen me before.'

'But not in my bed.'

'She'll have to get used to it.'

'Will she?'

He turned and gazed at her, turning her face to kiss her tenderly. How easily and snugly their bodies fitted together,

'But I think we'll need a larger bed. How about a king-sized? When shall we go shopping?' Lucas asked with a wicked grin. 'Though there is a certain delightful togetherness about a small bed,' he added, pulling her close.

They had to savour these last few moments of privacy. Jessica could hear Lily padding along the landing, telling Floppy Ears to hop, hop, hop. Lily climbed onto the bed beside Jessica, then she saw Lucas on the other side.

She looked puzzled.

'Daddy? Did Jessica promise to read you a story and then you fell asleep?' she asked.

'Something like that,' he agreed sleepily. 'It was a lovely story.'

'Are you going to tell me the story now?'

'It's got very long words in it,' said Lucas. 'You might not understand them. Floppy Ears would certainly be lost.'

Lily was instantly diverted. 'Floppy Ears has been extremely naughty this morning already. He wouldn't clean his teeth and he wouldn't wash his ears. He's not going to get any breakfast.'

'That rabbit has a hard life,' said Lucas. 'Shall I take him to the hospital with me as a punishment?'

Lily looked aghast. 'Oh no, he has to stay here. He has to keep Grandmother company while I go to school. That's his job.'

'Does your grandmother know this?'

'Yes, I 'plained it to her.'

'And what did she say?'

'She said she would put him in a cupboard and shut the door when he was naughty.'

Jessica took the opportunity to slip out of bed and put on her bathrobe. Lucas caught a tantalizing glimpse of her bare back, the curve of her spine, her hair falling over her shoulders.

'I'll go downstairs and make some tea.

Everyone will be awake by now, all this racket going on.'

'Early morning tea in bed,' teased Lucas. 'I am being spoilt. Shall I get this service every morning?'

'No,' said Jessica. 'You'll be in the cupboard with Floppy Ears.'

They started laughing, their eyes warm with love. They could not take their eyes off each other. Lily joined in the laughter though she was not sure what she was laughing at.

★ ★ ★

Lucas had to go to the hospital. He had a list that morning and Maggie was still a concern. Laughter united them. He could not stop touching Jessica, loving every moment that she smiled at him. It was going to be all right. One day they would talk about it all, but now was not the time.

Jessica's arm encircled his waist as he ate some toast and marmalade standing up. Lucas was going, after the briefest of breakfasts in the kitchen.

'Tomorrow,' he said, 'I am going to take you out, firstly with a call to see young Maggie. When did you last have a day off?'

'I've never had a day off,' said Jessica, enjoying the consternation on his face. 'My employer forgot about days off. He's mean with days off. I've had a few hours off, but you could hardly call them a day.'

'Then I shall have to do something about that before you sue me or report me to some union. Do you belong to a union?'

'Of course I do,' said Jessica.

'Tomorrow I want you to come with me,' said Lucas. 'It's very important. Can you arrange for Mrs Harris to stay the whole day? Lady Grace is so much better. She can cope, can't she?'

'She's got the trusty Fred.'

He was gone before Jessica could even say another word. His kiss was brief but permanent. It would last until he came home in the evening. Jessica knew she would love him for the rest of her life.

The morning rolled into its usual routine. Daniel seemed none the worse for his adventure. He did not share his feelings. He did not mention taking the seaweed back to the sea. But everyone knew that something had changed in the household.

'Nice to see you smiling,' said Lady Grace, over her breakfast tray.

'Has his lordship come to his senses?' said Mrs Harris. 'And about time too, if you ask me. We don't want to lose you, none of us does.'

'It was difficult for him,' said Jessica, not wanting to give away what had happened. 'But I think it's going to be all right now. I hope so. I can't go through any more.'

'We women always manage somehow,' said Mrs Harris, reminding Jessica of how she had managed for years, through love, to keep going.

'I couldn't do it.'

'You would, if you had to. Believe me, you would. Lots of women do.'

Mrs Harris nodded firmly but she could not conceal her delight.

'I wonder if it would it be possible for you to stay all day tomorrow?' Jessica asked. 'Lucas wants to take me somewhere. I don't know where, but he says it's rather important.'

'Of course,' said Mrs Harris. 'About time too. Lady Grace will be all right. She has that friend of hers coming to play bridge. Nice gentleman. Nice manners. I'll do them a bit of supper.'

'Thank you so much,' said Jessica, giving her a quick hug. 'You're a star.'

'More a burnt-out planet at my age,' said Mrs Harris.

★ ★ ★

Lucas was home early for once. The children ran to him, urging him to play cricket, What's the Time, Mr Wolf? and hopscotch. Tea was in the kitchen. It had turned too cold to eat outside. The table was laden with a healthy tea.

Lucas sauntered over to Jessica, his eyes sharp and bright. 'I was expecting to find you all wet,' he said, picking at the hem of her T-shirt. He bent and kissed her gently.

'Not a hope,' said Jessica.

'Later?'

'Don't count on your chances.'

It was an evening of enchantment. Daniel still drawing pictures of trees and rain, getting the nightmare storm out of his mind. He didn't seem to mind that the seaweed was living in a bucket. Jessica promised that they would take it back at the weekend. Lily was reading a story to Floppy Ears, which made a change. She knew the words by heart.

Lucas and Jessica went for a walk, leaving the rose garden and taking a path towards the Downs. He held her hand easily as if they belonged together.

Jessica saw the South Downs as he loved them, sweeping fields dotted with sheep. Hills with sturdy knolls of trees, those left from Henry VIII's deforestation, when trees were cut down to build his ships of war.

Lucas showed her corn circles from the top of the Downs. Where they came from, no one knew, but they were there for all the world to see far below. Great overlapping circles, patterned in the cornfield.

'Aren't they amazing? Even if they are made here, overnight, by some fun group of people after a few bottles of cider, they are still a work of art.'

Jessica had never seen corn circles before, apart from photographs in newspapers, and they were indeed strangely mesmerizing. She clung to Lucas's arm. 'It's lovely to see them, wherever they come from.'

'Is tomorrow still on?' she asked, as they began the walk back to Upton Hall. Mrs Harris had agreed to stay for the day. There was no reason why Jessica could not have the time off.

Lucas nodded. 'We'll go to see Maggie first. She's looking forward to meeting you. I've told her all about you and she's quite excited about having a visitor. Her grandmother has never been able to make the journey. The nurses make a fuss of her, but they don't have a lot of spare time.'

'Poor girl. How sad. I've some of Lily's toys and both children have made cards for her. Daniel wants to give her one of his drawings.'

'Then I'm taking you somewhere else, but I

won't tell you about that until we get there. It's somewhere quite special.'

They reached the gate into the grounds of Upton Hall. They wandered through the rose garden, the night air still heady with the scent of rose.

'Come into my garden,' said Lucas. 'I want my roses to see you.'

18

It was a cloudy morning and although Lucas said they were going somewhere special, Jessica did not think her smart suit was right for the occasion. Instead she put on her indigo jeans and a long-sleeved white sweater. There was a nip in the air.

'No need to dress up when you are going out with me,' said Lucas with a straight face.

'They are my best jeans,' said Jessica.

'I suppose that's something.'

She held out her left hand. The sapphire twinkled on her finger. 'And this is my best ring,' she added.

'Now that's really something,' he said, his eyes raking over her gently. 'I'm so glad you are going to share my life. I need you and I love you.'

'All this love talk before breakfast?' Jessica teased. 'I could get used to it.'

'Let's skip breakfast and do something more interesting,' he suggested.

'Not a good example to the children,' said Jessica.

Lucas almost said *damn the children* but held back. The children were arriving in the kitchen for their breakfast. Lily had her school shirt on inside-out and Daniel's jersey was on back to front.

'So much for letting them dress themselves,' said Jessica, sorting them out.

They all sat down together round the big kitchen table. A real family. Muesli and fruit, scrambled eggs, toast and honey. Mrs Harris was beaming. It felt as if they were her own family. They were her family.

'We're going to see Maggie in hospital this morning,' Jessica told the children. 'I've got your cards and Lily's toys and the lovely drawing from Daniel. Then this evening I will tell you all about it. I'm sure Maggie will be pleased. You see, she hasn't had any visitors.'

'You could take Floppy Ears,' volunteered Lily, making another ultimate sacrifice. 'He could be a visitor for Maggie.'

'How about another time?' said Lucas. 'Floppy Ears might be a bit tongue-tied going to a hospital.'

Lily looked relieved. 'He wouldn't like having his tongue-tied.'

Once the children were on the school bus, Jessica and Lucas could leave. She made sure that Lady Grace was up, doing her exercises, and promising to come downstairs.

'For goodness sake, stop fussing, girl. I can get myself downstairs by now. Go and enjoy your day off. I shall be glad to have a day's peace from your nagging.' Lady Grace was back on form. But there was little edge to her voice.

Jessica could not believe it when they were driving away from Upton Hall in the Porsche. It was too chilly to have the hood down. It reminded her of when Lucas had picked her up from the station, all those weeks ago. When she had felt drawn to him, despite wanting to turn round and catch a train back to London.

'So Maggie first?' said Jessica.

'And I have a few patients to look at before we can have a spot of lunch.'

'So not exactly a whole day off for you?'

'It's the whole afternoon off for me. You'll understand when we get there. Trust me, Jessica. Soon it will all become clear. I'm trusting you, my sweetheart. You will understand everything soon.'

Jessica felt the intensity behind his words. This was no day off for fun and laughter and a boozy pub lunch. It was something more serious.

He drove more moderately. It was not one of his twenty-minute manic speed journeys to the hospital. The random buildings loomed ahead. They were serious hospital buildings, where Lucas worked and put faces back together. He had his own parking space.

Jessica was at home in the hospital environment. It didn't throw her. She recognized the smells, the hygiene, the silence in some areas. Her feet echoed along the corridors even though she was in her flat pumps.

'I'll introduce you to Maggie and then leave you,' said Lucas. 'These are my wards.'

Maggie had a side room. She was in a single bed with tubes attached to nose and mouth, feeding her both nourishment and liquid. Her face was heavily bandaged. The dogs had torn her mouth and arm. But her brown eyes shone brightly at the sight of a visitor.

'Hi, Maggie,' said Lucas. 'Jessica has come to visit you. She's the lovely young woman who looks after my two children. She's come to read you some stories.'

Lucas waved and left them together. Jessica sat beside Maggie. There was not much of Maggie showing, but Jessica found a hand. It was small and soft.

'Hello, Maggie. I'm Jessica. Lucas has told me all about how brave you are and I am so sorry about what happened. But you will get better because Lucas is a wonderful doctor and he will do everything possible for you.'

Maggie had difficulty in talking. Her mouth was stitched up where the dogs had torn it. She would need plastic surgery to give her a normal, pretty mouth again.

''Lo,' she said, her eyes smiling. 'Story?'

She squeezed Jessica's hand. It was a touching moment.

'Lots of stories,' said Jessica. 'I've brought lots of books. I'll choose one, then you choose one. Is that all right?'

Maggie nodded, delighted. She snuggled down in bed, her eyes on Jessica and the open book.

The morning fled. At some point, coffee arrived for Jessica and juice with a straw for Maggie. By then, they were firm friends. Maggie loved the cards from the children and she insisted that Daniel's shell drawing should be pinned on the wall. She was not so sure about Lily's toys. She liked the soft, rag doll with braided yellow hair, a pinafore dress and white socks and shoes.

'Baby,' she said, pushing the other toys away.

Jessica understood. Maggie was quite a grown-up five-year-old. It came from living with a much older person, her grandmother. She didn't have the same five-year-old bounce of Lily or the same tastes. She was much nearer in age to Daniel, especially as she now had difficulty in speaking.

Leaving Maggie was a wrench. Jessica was sorry when Lucas came to take her away. She knew she must not become attached to his patients but it was so difficult when it was a vulnerable child.

'I'll come again,' she promised, as they clung to each other.

'Please, please . . . ' said Maggie.

'I promise,' said Jessica, near to tears herself.

Out in the corridor, Jessica needed a few minutes to compose herself. She had not realized that she would become emotionally involved.

'Not easy, is it?' said Lucas, taking her arm and walking her away. 'How do you think I feel?'

'I don't know how you do it. Maggie is a lovely little girl. I feel so sorry for her. I'll come again, of course, if I can.'

'Maggie will need a few weeks convalescing after the next operation to sort out her mouth so that she can talk and eat unassisted. Her grandmother would not be able to cope with her diet. How do you feel about having Maggie come to stay at Upton Hall, have fun with Daniel and Lily, be a normal child for a few weeks?'

Lucas was looking at her, full of respect, his words a trap. His kiss was only a breath away.

'Of course,' said Jessica. 'Maggie must come to Upton Hall. I will look after her. She will have a lovely time, perhaps regain what it's like being a child.'

Daniel might find it interesting to meet someone else who had trouble talking, and Lily would bounce Maggie back into childhood fun, show her the joy of running about, doing silly things.

Lucas folded Jessica into his arms, the outside world vanishing for the two of them.

'How about that boozy pub lunch?' asked Lucas, at last.

★   ★   ★

The boozy pub lunch was all that Jessica could have asked for. Two glasses of excellent Merlot went down well and rather fast. A jacket potato with grated cheese and a side salad was the perfect lunch. It was all that Jessica wanted. Lucas had a beer and a ploughman's. Sitting opposite Jessica was all he wanted.

The pub was a cosy, Sussex/Surrey pub. Oak beams and rafters, old hunting prints on the walls, a real log fire already burning in the hearth. Jessica was not sure which county they were in but it did not matter. Surely Lucas had no more surprises which could destroy their happiness?

He leaned over the table and clasped her

hands in his. 'We have one more thing to do today,' he said. 'It may be very hard for both of us, but it has to be done. Our future happiness depends on this, and, oh my darling, I do so want us to be happy together.'

'Good heavens,' said Jessica, shaken. 'Where are you taking me? Newgate Prison or Tyburn? People were hanged at both places.'

Lucas let go her hands and sat back in his chair, staring at the ceiling. 'It was easier in those days to get rid of unwanted people.'

She did not understand what he meant. She did not want to know.

They both had black coffees. Lucas because he was driving, Jessica because she wanted to be alert for whatever was ahead. What could be worse than seeing a five-year-old girl with tubes going in everywhere and hardly able to speak?

They drove through the rolling Surrey countryside. It was different to Sussex, more controlled, more sculptured, trees in staged groups as if being used for a television drama set. They turned in at a driveway, heavy iron gates opened for them after Lucas spoke to the man on duty. He was in a green uniform, belted. Surely it wasn't a prison?

Lucas seemed to know the way without any directions. He parked in an area marked for visitors. Ahead of them was a rambling two-storey white building with what looked like a chapel at the far end. Jessica caught the glint of a stained-glass window. There were gardens and flower beds and people strolling about in pairs.

'You have to tell me,' she said. 'It's not fair. Where are we?'

'This is a sanatorium for the permanently disabled,' he said. 'It used to be a convent called Saint Agatha's, I think. There are still nuns. Follow me.'

He did not take her hand this time but seemed wrapped in his own thoughts.

Jessica kept close to him in case he abandoned her, here in the wilds of Surrey, with no idea how to get back to Upton Hall.

The reception area was cool and empty, except for a vase of flowers and a strong smell of polish. No comfortable furniture, no paintings on the walls. Lucas went straight to the desk and signed in. He seemed to know what he was doing.

'This way,' he said, pointing towards the stairs. The oak treads had also been polished. They went along a wide corridor, doors either side with numbers. Again no decoration of any kind, only the occasional vase of flowers on a wall bracket.

He stopped outside room 24. He did not knock but went straight in.

Jessica followed him. It was a simply furnished room, plain white walls with flowered curtains framing a large window that looked out onto the garden. The bed was surrounded by pulleys and hoists which Jessica knew were only used for the severely disabled. A wash-basin was fitted in a corner. There was no television, no armchair, no table or bookcase.

Facing the window and the garden was a wheelchair. Jessica could only see the back of it. It was not a normal wheelchair, but a fully functional hospital chair with every device known to the medical profession.

Lucas went over to the chair. 'Hello, sweetie,' he said, bending low to speak. 'It's Lucas. I've come to see you. And I've brought a visitor, a very special person. This is Jessica.'

Jessica went over to the window, her heart thudding. The woman in the chair had her head held in a padded clamp. Her pale face was a mass of contradictions. Her greying hair had been combed back without any thought to style or appearance. She was wearing a cotton skirt and blouse, her thin legs bare, her feet in slippers. Her hands were immobile in her lap.

'Hello,' said Jessica, hesitating. 'I'm Jessica. How are you?'

It was a stupid thing to say. The woman

could not move. Her back was obviously broken, if not more. She could not hold her head up by herself. Her face had been repaired but was probably only a caricature of her former feminine looks. She smiled at Jessica but gave no sign that she had understood.

Lucas came over, moving in his usual economical and lanky way. He stood close to Jessica, barely daring to touch her in case she flinched. He barely knew what to say. It could only be the truth.

'This is Liz, my wife,' said Lucas. 'She didn't die in the car crash on the M25. But she is here, in a living death.'

'You told me she had died,' said Jessica, barely able to find a voice. 'You said they had both died.'

'It was easier to say that she had died. She has in a way. This is not Liz, my wife, the mother of Lily and Daniel, this is just a shell, a body with no mind. She knows nothing. She remembers nothing. She says nothing.'

'How long?' Jessica choked.

'Since the accident. Liz went through the windscreen, severe spine and head injuries. He was killed outright, steering wheel trauma. No seat belts.'

'Who was he?'

'He was the man she was leaving me for, leaving her two children, leaving her home and her husband. Lily was only a baby, a few months old. He promised her a life without nappies and bottles and disturbed nights. He promised her Monte Carlo, racing at Goodwood and sailing regattas in the South of France. She wanted the high life and money to spend. She wanted fun.'

'How awful,' said Jessica. 'You must have been shattered.'

'I don't know how I felt now,' said Lucas. 'It was as if a great fog descended on me. A bit like London smog. I barely knew what I was doing. Except when I was at the hospital. It was the only time I could think clearly.'

'This isn't much fun for her,' said Jessica, wondering if her plans were collapsing round their feet. She was unable to think how this would affect their plans. Oh dear God, she breathed, her eyes closed, don't let this be the end.

'No fun at all,' he said. He went over to Liz.

'Hello, Liz,' he said. 'This is Lucas. My friend Jessica has come to see you. Isn't it a lovely day? Look at all the flowers in the garden, they are so beautiful.'

Liz smiled as if she understood but it was obvious that she didn't. Her fingers had some movement. They curled and uncurled in her lap.

Jessica realized she was still carrying the bag of Lily's soft toys, the ones that Maggie had not wanted. Sometimes the feel of something different could stimulate an unresponsive mind. She went over to Liz.

'I've brought you some presents,' said Jessica. She prayed that there was something suitable in the bag. Her hand closed round a fluffy yellow duck. He was rather cute. 'Here's a little duck for you. Can you feel his soft feathers?'

She put the duck into the curled fingers and Liz smiled. Then she seemed to smile quite a lot, as if enjoying the sensation. Jessica found a furry kitten and put the toy into the other hand. 'And this is a furry kitten. His name is Sooty. Can you feel his soft fur?'

Liz smiled again, her fingers curling and uncurling round the toys.

'Are you expecting a miracle?' Lucas asked. 'It won't happen, you know. The brain damage is permanent. There is nothing that can be done.'

'I don't know what I'm doing,' said Jessica. 'I feel so helpless.'

'I think we should go,' said Lucas. 'She likes the duck and the kitten so that's good. Let's leave her now. The nuns will be round soon with tea.'

Lucas said goodbye to Liz but she gave no

sign of hearing. He moved her chair, making sure that she had a good view of the garden. If she could see.

They went out into the corridor, Jessica almost slipping on the polished floor. Lucas caught her arm but Jessica shook it off.

'So is this my treat on my day off? Being shown the reason why we can never marry?' She tried to keep the disappointment out of her voice.

Lucas shook his head. 'No,' he said. 'We shall be married, I promise you. But first I have to divorce Liz. I've never made it legal before. It didn't seem necessary. I've always paid for her care and I come to see her when I can. She never gives any sign that she knows me. There's nothing there anymore, only a shell. But she could live for years more.'

'But can you divorce someone with a major head injury, who cannot say yes or no, who cannot agree to anything, who cannot sign papers?'

Lucas looked wearied by it all, the lines on his face etched more deeply. 'I have spoken to my solicitors. I am her legal guardian. I have power of attorney, but she has no assets. Divorcing a permanently disabled person is a relatively streamlined legal procedure, apparently. I have to ask you to wait and be patient, just a little longer. Please, Jessica, I love you so much. We could be so happy together. I want you to be my wife. I want us to be together for always.'

Jessica's feelings were in a turmoil. Time was standing still. She was only now realizing what an enormous burden Lucas had carried for years. His demanding job, an autistic son, a difficult mother, and now she knew there had been Liz as well. She could imagine that her own arrival at Upton Hall had been like a ray of sunshine, Lucas suddenly seeing some light in all the gloom.

And Lucas had fallen in love with her.

As they walked towards his car, Jessica threaded her arm through his. She could share this burden. She was strong enough. Besides, she loved him. And she would stay with him, even if they could not be legally married.

'Would your roses like to see me again this evening?' she asked.

19

There were busy weeks ahead that turned into months. Jessica sent a regretful letter to the hospital in Sheffield saying that she now had other plans and could no longer take up the contract.

Lady Grace saw her consultant and was reassured that both her legs were the same length. Though she was still not sure that she believed him. These consultants could say anything.

The consultant congratulated her on her speedy and successful recovery from the hip replacement operation.

'I keep strictly to everything that you told me to do,' she said, without blinking an eyelid.

'I wish all my patients were like you, Lady Grace,' he said. 'Perhaps you'd like to come and give a talk to some of my pre-op patients sometime. It would give them such encouragement to see how well you have done.'

'Fred and me,' said Lady Grace, hiding a smile. She also had more secret plans for Mark Adams. She had not told a soul, waiting for the right moment. She had bicycles on the brain. That four mile promenade at Worthing was perfect for cycling, especially in the winter when Mark wasn't doing deckchairs.

And she had noticed empty premises on Marine Parade, on the front. Ideal for a bicycle hire business. She fancied being a silent partner in a business venture.

Swimming was now a regular part of the routine and either Jessica or Lady Grace drove over to Roxy's pool. They even met Roxy on one occasion and Lily was fascinated by her wildly bouffant hair, all different streaks of colour. Roxy rarely swam because of her hair. But she was great on paddling about on a lilo.

'She's got rainbow hair,' said Lily. 'Can I have rainbow hair when I'm grown up and singing in a roxy band?'

'Are you going to be a singer?'

'Oh yes,' said Lily with confidence. 'I'm going to be a rocky roxy star and have my own pool. Floppy Ears is going to learn to sing, too. Rabbit songs, of course.'

Daniel was starting to swim quite fast and with surprising stamina. Lucas wondered when it might be possible to take him to a full-sized pool. But not yet, not for a long time. They would take it one step at a time, or rather, one length at a time.

Maggie came to Upton Hall for two weeks

convalescence and stayed for a month. She had scars on her face and arms but they were healing. She would need more surgery on her mouth as she grew older. She knew that Lucas would make her mouth smile again.

Daniel was fascinated that she preferred one-word conversations and they became unexpected friends. They spent a lot of time together. He taught her to draw and she helped him with his alphabet. They made up funny names for the letters that he had invented.

Lily thought it was wonderful to have a non-stop playmate and Maggie soon lost her unhealthy pallor, racing round the garden and teaching Floppy Ears to do acrobatics. His new ambition in life was apparently to be a circus rabbit.

She brought the rag doll with her. The doll now had a name, Raggety Girl. Raggety Girl was soon participating in events, and had her own chair at the kitchen table.

Arthur and Lady Grace expanded their games of bridge into a thriving bridge club. A group of friends met regularly at Upton Hall and Mrs Harris was in her element providing delicious nibbles for the group. She was asked if she would do the refreshments for a couple of village parties.

'Your canapés are absolutely delicious. And

these dips. We should be delighted if you could help us. We'd pay, of course, your usual rate.'

'Certainly,' Mrs Harris said. 'When I come back from my holiday. My friend and I are going on a coach trip to Scotland. We've always wanted to see the Highlands. Beautiful scenery, we're told.'

Jessica continued her research on the history of Upton Hall but she did not have much time or get very far. She did discover that the original farmhouse was built on the foundation of a long-lost Roman villa.

'Plenty of time,' she told herself. 'History won't go away.'

Jessica and Lucas planned their wedding. It would be a simple affair, they decided, with only a few friends. But they found time every day for a few moments together, walking round the garden, now in the autumn decline, the bronze colours replacing the fresh green of summer. The roses were almost over. Sometimes they found a hardy rose bud, determined to bloom at Christmas.

Jessica revelled in his touch and his closeness. Lucas had been a revelation these last weeks. She could not believe the warmth and passion of his love for her. Their time together was as if there was no one else in the world.

'Not long now, my darling,' said Lucas, pulling her close to him. 'We have our whole life ahead together.' He brushed his lips across her mouth. 'Is it time to chose that king-sized?'

'There are companies in the USA selling a super-king-sized. I found them on the Internet.'

'And I thought you were doing research on Upton Hall.'

'Different kind of research.'

★ ★ ★

The simple wedding in the village church with only a few friends grew and grew like Topsy. There were friends from several different hospitals with a group of grateful patients. Friends from the bridge club, friends from swimming. Friends from the village itself and the school.

Lucas grinned at Jessica in church. 'Be brave. We are outnumbered,' he said as the service began.

The family Brussels lace was out, but Jessica wore it as a shawl round her shoulders. It went perfectly with her long cream velvet dress and it kept her warm.

Lady Grace was in her element, the perfect hostess at the reception back at Upton Hall.

Mrs Harris was an honoured guest, in a new hat. Friends threw rose petals instead of confetti. The sun was clouded over, but warm enough for a late stroll in the garden.

Daniel was not sure what was happening but he looked content for once. Lily was a bridesmaid in a rose pink velvet dress with flowers in her hair. Floppy Ears was also a bridesmaid with flowers in his ears.

'I'm going to have trouble with that rabbit,' said Jessica.